RABBIT HOLE

KATE BRODY

SOHO
CRIME

Published by
Soho Press, Inc.
227 W 17th Street
New York, NY 10011

Library of Congress Cataloging-in-Publication Data

Names: Brody, Kate, author.
Title: Rabbit hole / Kate Brody.
Description: New York, NY : Soho Crime, [2024]
Identifiers: LCCN 2022058946

ISBN 978-1-64129-487-4
eISBN 978-1-64129-488-1

Subjects: LCSH: Missing persons—Investigation—Fiction. | Conspiracy
theories—Fiction. | Electronic discussion groups—Fiction.
LCGFT: Detective and mystery fiction. | Novels.
Classification: LCC PS3602.R63573 R33 2024 | DDC 813'.6—dc23/
eng/20230113
LC record available at https://lccn.loc.gov/2022058946

Printed in the United States of America

10 9 8 7 6 5 4 3 2 1

For Chris

RABBIT HOLE

Ten years to the day after my sister's disappearance, my father kills himself. It's a sleepy Friday night like any other when he drives his car through the rotting barn wall of the most beautiful bridge in town and plunges himself into the shallow waters below. The same shallow waters where divers in seal suits panned for Angie's remains when all of our better leads ran cold. He doesn't vanish like she did. He isn't swept away with the current. His car isn't even fully submerged. He lands in the rocks, bumper sticking out from the water like a bad joke.

Mom and I stand at the edge of the road in police overcoats, watching as state authorities dredge the car from the riverbank with their big tow trucks. The local cops tape off the entrance to the bridge, which looks like it was hit with a wrecking ball. The sheriff they sent up from Portland tells us there are only nine covered bridges left in the state. Eight now, if they can't restore this one. It's the first thing he says. Only after Mom apologizes, only after she assures him that her husband must have been trying to veer off the road sooner, must have been trying to miss the bridge entirely and cut across the steep patch of nothing between the start of the bridge and the end of the guardrail, only after she insists that he must have simply been going too fast, turned a second late, wound up on the bridge— only then does the sheriff volunteer that my dad was killed on impact. He didn't drown. Small mercies.

My mom thanks the sheriff, and his face softens when he hears her lovely, musical brogue. She turns it up for the occasion, leaning into each lilting syllable.

Mark loved that bridge, she says.

The man pats her shoulder.

I think: I wish it ever stopped raining long enough for me to light this fucking bridge on fire. I wish I could throw a match and engulf the ancient lumber in flames, but I know that it would only self-extinguish in a leftover pile of muddy snow.

For years later, at night, all I will be able to think about is the butt-end of the car sticking up like that and the feeling that, if he wanted to, he could have unbuckled his seatbelt, opened his door, and walked out. From this day forward, Angie will appear in my dreams soaking wet, lips blue. My dad won't appear in my dreams very much, and I'll miss him.

Mom closes her eyes and tugs nervously at the streak of white in her auburn hair. She insists on identifying his body alone, and I let her. For now, I am glad, but I will be angry later when I can't be sure if the bloated, bruised, waterlogged version in my head is more or less grotesque than the real thing. I will grow jealous of her for getting to see him, for the visual proof that convinces even the most stubborn parts of her brain that he is dead.

It will all come later. Things take time.

Before I get a chance to email my boss and ask for Monday sub coverage, he emails me and copies the entire faculty.

Teddy,

We heard. We are all SO sorry for your loss. Take some time to be with your mother. Hank and Wendy have volunteered to cover your classes in the interim. Please let me know when the wake will be held. The school would love to send a spray to Brown's, and I'm sure members of the community would attend.

Deepest sympathies,
Rick
Principal, Upper School

Other faculty members jump on the thread. Lots of caps lock. Many sad faces.

Teddy, hon! I saw the news. SO SORRY! xoxo Bea

Ted, more bad news for your poor family?! Hang in there, babe. —Wendy

Theodora, I know we don't know each other very well, but

I want you to know that my uncle committed suicide. My prayers are with you and your mother. Let me know if I can help in any way.

Love, Fred (from upstairs)

I send one email to the group before I mute notifications:

My entire St. Aug's family, I so appreciate your well wishes, and I can't thank you enough for stepping up to cover my classes. However, we will not be having any public services, and I plan to return to work on Tuesday. I thank you in advance for your discretion with the students over the next few weeks.

Best, Teddy

Before Angie disappeared, she was very focused on the things she didn't have: a boyfriend, a car, a beach body, good hair, good skin, a tongue piercing, a full sleeve tattoo, a reliable pot dealer, a chance at a half-decent college, a date for senior prom, a sense of direction. I would sit at the end of her bed and paint her toenails a shade of green or red dark enough to look black, and she would list them off.

When she was gone, it felt like we were drowning in her things: Angie's CD collection, Angie's ripped jeans, ripped sweaters, ripped everything. Angie's sketchbooks, Angie's textbooks, Angie's yearbooks, signed with inside jokes that Mom tried to crack like spy code.

I inherited none of it. I couldn't wear her clothes or her earrings or her perfume. I tried once, with the perfume—a saccharine vanilla scent that I had scored rightfully, as a hand-me-down from herself—and it made Mom so upset that she wouldn't speak to me until I showered.

The only thing I got was Angie's dog, an Irish wolfhound—only a puppy then, all legs and wiry, slate-gray fur—that year's birthday present from my dad, purchased without Mom's knowledge, a month before Angie went missing. For Angie to take with her when she moved out and started her classes at the community college. A security system.

Wolf was small then. Now he is large and blind. Ten is old for an Irish wolfhound.

"Come on, Wolf," I say, hauling his gaunt frame into the trunk of my car for another doctor's appointment, only hours after the bridge. "Help me help you, buddy."

"Does he need more pillows?" Mom asks.

I look at Wolfie. He lies on his side, long limbs extended toward the back of the car. He is surrounded by pillows.

"Come on," I say. "The rest are boxed up."

I regret it instantly, bringing up the move, but Mom doesn't notice. She kisses Wolfie's wet nose and shuts the trunk. Since she let her license expire a few years ago, she only leaves the house for doctor's appointments—Wolf's and her own.

Mom hated Wolfie when he first arrived. She had a strict no-animals policy, and his habits of barking when the house creaked in the middle of the night and peeing on her curtains didn't endear him to her. But Angie trained him quickly and well in a few short weeks. He learned commands and he stuck by her side day and night, sleeping on top of her head when he was small.

Sometimes, I think Wolfie understood that she wasn't coming back before the rest of us did. The one person he would let touch him was me. He was bereft.

Only when the cops announced that they were giving up did Mom express an interest in Wolfie. She didn't want to be his primary caregiver. She just wanted to make sure that he was well cared-for since Angie loved him, and he loved Angie, and Angie was gone.

Sometimes, it seems like part of Angie is inside of him. Or he relays messages to her. Or she can hear me when I talk to him. I know it's only magical thinking. I can only really acknowledge that I believe this when I'm drunk. When I'm drunk, it's very easy to mistake Wolfie's calm presence for listening. It's very easy to understand that if I bury my face in the side of his neck and whisper something into the space where his ear falls against the wavy fur, it will travel to Angie like a message into a tin can telephone.

USUALLY, WE TAKE THE long way to the vet, because the roads are smoother, but today we can't because of the road closure. Because of Dad. So we take the short, potholed way, and Wolfie cries the whole time in the back as his bones and tumors bounce around. I think of the bumper sticker on the back of Dad's car. We couldn't see it last night in the dark, but it was there: *In America, we drive on the right side of the road. In Maine we drive on what's LEFT of the roads.* Every divot fills me with more rage, until I'm clutching the wheel so hard my knuckles go white. *This is your fault*, I think. *All your fault.*

"Take it easy," Mom says. "We don't need another accident."

As we're walking into the vet's office on Main, I spot a clear recycling bag near the door. Inside is a striped lump matted through with bits of gravel and crushed seashells—the kind they use to make rustic driveways for the beach houses.

"What the fuck is that?"

Mom bends down and reads. "It's a cat," she says.

"What?"

"Someone hit a cat with their car. Big one."

I bend down: *Please dispose accordingly.*

"Oh, for fuck's sake," I say. Wolfie is blindly sniffing at the bag. He lifts a paw to prod at it. "Wolf, get away from there."

"Looks like a Maine coon. They probably didn't want the turkey vultures coming," Mom says.

"Let's go." I open the door and usher her in before me.

"Tourists," she spits, despite the fact that we both know there won't be any tourists for at least two more months.

Wolfie digs in his heels with what little strength he has and forces me to drag him over the threshold with his leash. He hates the vet.

Jen at the reception desk is reading a Nancy Drew. "Oh my goodness. Wolfie. We didn't think you'd make your appointment today."

"Well, we're here," I say.

"We didn't want to call," Jen continues. "We heard what happened."

"There's a dead cat outside," Mom says.

"What?"

"It's in a bag," I say. "Hit-and-run."

"You hit a cat?"

"Not us," I say. "Someone else."

"They left a note." Mom gets close enough to see what Jen is reading. "Those books are for children."

"I wanted to see if it was appropriate for my daughter before—"

"Mom." I take her elbow. "Sit."

Mom lets me guide her into one of the hard plastic chairs. "Wolfie's having a hard time breathing," she says, to no one in particular.

I smile at Jen, but she's already pushing through the swinging door to retrieve the doctor. Before she disappears, I think I see a flash of something quizzical and accusatory on her face.

Dr. Miller seems equally confused by our presence. She knew my dad from some early visits, and she liked him. He was a nice man, she says. He played with all the dogs in the waiting room.

"Sounds like him," I say.

Wolfie trembles for the full duration of his visit. We weigh him on the floor scale. All three of us dance around the metal rectangle trying to steady him without altering the reading. Seventy-nine pounds. A lot for most dogs, but not much for Wolf.

"What's the situation?" Mom asks.

"The cancer has spread again," the doctor says. She illuminates the X-rays, and even I can tell that Wolfie's organs are marred with tumors. "There is nothing left to do for him."

I expect Mom to ask for a second opinion, to insist that someone must be able to operate. Instead, she says, "Probably better that he enjoys the time he has left."

"I agree," the vet says, with relief. She's used to Mom's internet research on the effectiveness of infrared heat and B16 and doggie yoga and other things that people in Boston or New York might do, but that don't really exist here, where dogs are still treated like animals.

"What can we do to make him comfortable?"

Dr. Miller drones on about organic food and the power of touch, as if we don't already spend all our time and money spoiling Wolfie. It's only after Mom has paid the exorbitant visit fee and we're back in the car that I realize I didn't ask how much time he had left.

"Shit," I say. "That would have been good to know."

Mom disagrees. "They tell you one thing, but you never really know."

The car lurches, and Wolfie yelps. It can't be long.

A MEMORY COMES BACK in bits and pieces as Mom and I fail to fill the silence in the car. I was young—five or six maybe. Mom left us outside Shaw's with some quarters for the ride-on ponies. It was summer, and we were in shorts. The parking lot—practically empty in the off-season—was filled up with out-of-state plates and Hertz rentals. The painted plastic of the horse stayed cool in the shade, and it felt good under the skin of my thighs.

Angie stood behind me, feet resting on the base of the machine. I sat in the saddle with my feet in the stirrups.

"Ya-hoo!" Angie shouted. "Yee-haw."

An expensively dressed woman entering the store shot her a dirty look.

"Well, howdy there, missus," Angie said, and she pretended to tip her cap. The woman shook her head, and Angie whistled after her as the automatic doors shut. I burned with embarrassment.

"Stop, Ange," I said. "You're ruining it."

"Fine," Angie said. She kicked the horse, and the machine stopped moving. "Giddup, loser." She hopped off and wandered toward the parking lot.

"Hey," I said. "I need another quarter."

"Sucks to be you," Angie said. In the first empty parking spot, there was a pile near the white line—something wet and sinister. She squatted in front of the pile, and all I could see was her back.

"Angie!" I hopped off the horse and ran toward her. "What is that?"

I could tell it was meat of some kind—pink and slimy. Rivets of red blood ran through it. Gray fuzz covered the pile—fungus, moss, mold.

"Angie," I repeated. "What is that?"

She extended her hand toward it.

"No," I said. "Don't—"

She touched the pile gently, hooking her pinky finger around something small. She lifted it up. It was a paw. Four tiny, fleshy pads clustered together. Then, suddenly, the mass took shape. I saw the outline of two little heads, the slits of closed eyes.

One skull crushed, the other intact. Both bodies flattened and printed with tire tracks.

"Kittens."

Mom came up behind us, silently, multiple bags in each hand. "Jesus, Mary, and Joseph, Angie," she said. "Put that down."

In the car, Angie was not allowed to touch anything—not her seatbelt, not her face, not me. Mom was mad at her for letting me see.

"Theodora's going to have nightmares now," Mom said. "And I suppose I'll send her to your room, will I?"

"I won't," I said.

"How, though?" Angie said.

"I don't know," Mom said. "Probably their ma left them under a tire, to be in the shade. And the car didn't know they were there, sleeping, so wee."

From my booster seat, I studied Angie the whole way home. She looked down at the hands in her lap, still sticky with blood. Occasionally a tear would fall, and she'd rub it together with the blood on her fingers. I stretched my hand across the middle seat. I didn't know what I expected her to do with it. She looked at me and smiled, leaned her cheek into my palm, and closed her eyes for a moment before sitting back upright.

For the first time now, it occurs to me that the mother cat returned to find her babies ground into the asphalt. I wonder if she ever recovered. I wonder if she nestled herself under a car tire, too.

We return home, and I unbox only my work clothes. I put them back in the closet downstairs, underneath the carved MONEY PIT house sign I rescued from the trash last Christmas. Dad got it for Mom as a gag gift because she was always complaining about the summer people who thought their tacky new developments deserve cutesy names: *The Egg, Bungalow, Hunters' Lodge*. Mom didn't find the sign funny. She pretends not to see it on the rare occasions that she comes down here.

The house is beautiful; the house is a money pit. Historic, charming, damp, it's Mom's most prized possession, and she is a woman who likes possessions. It's painted robin's egg blue with gray shutters that used to be white and a shingled roof that is going bald in more than a few places. The floors are original, wide-plank, and loud. The windows are all different shapes. My favorite—and Angie's—was a bay window off of the kitchen where we could sit and watch Mom and the deer at the same time.

Mom looks at this house and sees it for what it could be. She doesn't see the crumbling chimney or the peeling wallpaper or the cracked kitchen tiles; she doesn't like to talk about the stair we skip over or the way the rug downstairs squishes a bit in the winter because it's so damp; and she won't call anyone to inspect the water heater that's rusting or the furnace that bangs in the night. She sees character. And anything can be character.

My new place is small, but it's clean. That was important. New appliances, new drywall, new fixtures. Mom called it *sterile* when I showed her the online listing. She wouldn't come to the open house to see it in person.

I fold up my boxes and tuck them into the back of the closet. The new apartment will have to sit empty for a bit longer.

The next morning is spent on the logistics of death, and we are exhausted by lunchtime.

"Almost everyone outlives one husband. Some, two," Mom says, after we both collapse on the couch, unwilling to muster the effort required to make a sandwich. "But no one buries three of these bastards. Not unless they're cursed."

"Don't get spooky on me now," I say. I rub her back and her bones quake, sending a tremor through my palm.

"I'm going to have a cry in bed," she says, pushing down on my thigh to stand. "I'll close the door, but you join if you want."

Mom became a widow for the first time when she was still a teenager, before she was even done growing breasts and hips. This fact seems central to my understanding of her. The way I figure it, the melancholy must have soaked into her marrow. Because by the time we met—she and I—years later, it was present in every cell, every wrinkle and crease. Like a fingerprint. Like a perfume I know her by. It feels like home.

Once, at thirteen, after my first little heartbreak, I got the story out of her: how her first husband was so young he could barely grow a mustache, how they made it official at City Hall after the draft notice came in, how he was lost to the jungle, his body blown to a dozen wet chunks that couldn't be recovered for his mother. Mom told me about the officer that greeted her in her dorm room. About her roommate, Caroline, seated on the floor, pale against the pale cinderblocks. Mom sobbed so hard that she retched bright yellow gastric acid. She strained muscles in her low back and clawed at Caroline's bare arms until she drew blood. She wondered why she ever came to this country.

Made my eighth-grade dance angst seem pretty silly.

Mom didn't meet my uncle Oliver until 1985. At thirty-three, she was hung up writing bad protest poems about the Troubles and the war, decades too late. She enrolled in grad school hoping someone might help her find the exact right words, but it turned out everyone else was there to get drunk so that they could get laid.

Mom still dressed like it was the '60s, with her hair plaited down her spine. She volunteered at a women's center, because she liked helping mothers and babies, but she didn't have any babies of her own.

One day at the center, she met a man in local politics. He was older than her. He was there to make promises and take pictures. He had nice things, and he seemed nice, too. He liked Mom. He had a thing for Irish girls.

By 1986, they were engaged, but before they could marry, Oliver found out some bad news. The problems he had swallowing, the way he sated so quickly—he had chalked them up to turning forty, to heartburn, to general wear and tear. But it was stomach cancer.

The first thing that Oliver did was quit politics. The second was marry Mom. (Another courthouse, another slip of paper.) The third thing was get her pregnant.

And so, when Mom's second husband died, he died whole and in her arms. He died with his head resting on the small mound where Angie—technically my half-sister—was forming, claiming he could hear her heartbeat, whispering that he was going to meet her in passing, that he would slip by her in the ether.

Mom tells me that Dad's car was filled with brown paper bags from McDonald's. She'd like some for dinner, if I wouldn't mind picking it up.

There's only one near here, off the highway. It's better if we go together and eat it in the car, I tell her. By the time it gets home, it will be cold and only half as good.

As long as we bring Wolfie, that's fine, she says. We can eat in the car, like Dad used to.

When I roll the window down, a shock of cold air penetrates the car. Mom leans over me to ask the girl in the speaker for a Big MacDonald.

"I can't remember the last time I had a hamburger," she says. "Years."

She orders Wolfie a double hamburger without the bun as a reward for the vet. We drive down to the beach, but without the moon tonight, everything looks black. With the interior lights on, all I can see is our reflections and the heat from our breath fogging up the glass.

"I don't understand this," Mom says, biting into one of the stale, oversalted fries before putting it back in the container. "When you have all these nice chippies around."

Mom doesn't recall Ireland fondly, and she never goes back. She'll tell you that she grew up in a Catholic ghetto. She harps on the black mold and the constant barking of the neighbor's dog and the sound of her cousins polishing their guns in the dark, keeping her awake with the friction of steel wool. But she gravitated here because of the rocky coast and the rain and the greasy smell of the fish shacks. Homesick in her bones.

"So quiet tonight," she says. If she remembers that my lease starts today, she doesn't mention it.

"Always quiet."

I think back on all the secret McDonald's stops that we used to make—me and Dad and Angie. A few times a year. On the way home from somewhere—a field hockey game or a guitar lesson—whenever it was the three of us. He'd buy one hamburger for himself and one for me and Angie to split. We'd all share the same order of fries and throw the garbage in one of the neighbor's bins to keep Mom from finding us out. Angie would pass out Dad's glove-compartment Altoids before we stepped in the house.

I look out the windshield. We should have gone down to the other beach, where at least we could watch the lighthouse circle, and I wouldn't be listening so closely to the sound of my breath, wondering why it's gotten harder to talk to Mom lately, even before all of this.

"What happened with your obituary?" I ask.

"I reread it," Mom says. "Terrible. I can't write anymore."

"What about a poem?"

"No," she says. "I'm done with all that." She picks up one of my last chicken nuggets and puts it back down. She wipes her hands on her slacks. "I wrote a sonnet last year. This one magazine wanted to run it."

"You never told me."

"I pulled it."

"Why?"

"The editor sent me back a note going on about the

symbolism. About how the deciduous leaves represented Angie and I was the oak or something daft. I'm not doing that anymore."

On the drive back home, it occurs to me that Mom's lost someone nearly every kind of way that you can lose someone.

She nods. "That's true."

"What was the worst—Angie? Because she was your kid?"

Mom says nothing.

"It's okay to be angry with him," I say.

"I'm not angry."

"It's normal."

"That's enough," Mom says, leaning her head against the passenger's seat window, fogging up the glass with her breath. "Please. I'm knackered."

I read somewhere that after 9/11, dozens of women widowed by the attacks took up with the responding firemen, many of whom left their own families behind to be with their new lovers. When I read that, I thought—*there are others*. I had never known any others like us, families united in tragedy and then broken by love. It made me want to move to New York, where we'd at least have some anonymity working in our favor.

By 1987, Mom's parents were dead, but her in-laws—Oliver's parents—were alive and local. Her father-in-law was a well-known, well-liked, retired Maine congressman. They had money to spare, and they helped her with the baby—Angie, Angelina, the little angel—born three months after Oliver died.

The most helpful was Oliver's younger brother, Mark. Mark had a wife and a kid, and seeing Mom broke his heart. He had been close to his brother, idolized him, and he wanted to be a part of Angie's life in any way he could. He had sworn to Oliver on his deathbed that he would be there for Mom and Angie, and he intended to keep that promise.

Mark looked so much like Oliver. His hair was a bit darker, he had a bit more meat on his bones, and he had a mischievous glint in his eye that Oliver, the golden boy, never had. Otherwise, they were identical.

Mom liked having him around. Mark came by after work to fix the leaky sink, to build Angie's crib, to take out the garbage twice a week. Mom would make him a plate, and they'd stay up late with a nightcap, talking about Oliver, remembering him, sharing stories.

Somewhere along the way, Mom, with her bluntness and gap-toothed smile and way of closing her eyes when she was listening, started to feel like home to Mark. Somewhere along the way, his wife started to seem like a stranger, like another person who couldn't understand his pain, until, one day, he came home and she had transformed into an impostor completely. His son, spoiled and somber, felt like a changeling. He looked at the boy and thought of little Angie, so innocent and alone, and his patience ran thin. Mark couldn't tolerate his son's temper tantrums or his wife's childish way of screaming back at him.

So, he left. And I was born six months later. To my sister's uncle, to my mother's brother-in-law, and to the man who would drive clear through a covered bridge in some twenty-six years. My dad.

Angie was the only person excited to see me. To the rest of my family—my grandparents and cousins, my aunt and extended relations—I was dead before I was born. We were all dead. My father for his betrayal, my mother for her ingratitude, and Angie because she was stuck with us. They would have liked to keep Angie, but they couldn't.

This is how Mom tells it. But she elides the part where she first slept with Dad. She glosses over the infidelity, the timeline, Dad leaving his family. In her first version, he didn't even have a kid. I found out about my half-brother much later, after someone teased Angie about it at school, and it started a big fight. I told him that I didn't care as long as he didn't love him and he only loved us. "Deal," he told me, and he tucked me in.

I doubt they would come to Dad's funeral even if we were throwing one.

STILL, I FEEL COMPELLED to reach out. Next of kin. Flesh and blood. They should know he's gone, and my mom won't do it.

I haven't spoken to Henry since I sent him a message on LinkedIn a few years back, when the algorithm suggested we connect. Whereas Angie and I lean toward Mom, Henry looks, in his profile picture, like a carbon copy of my dad—slender and wiry with those dark circles.

I can't remember what I wrote him exactly. I was drunk. I know it began with some kind of an apology—*I'm sorry he chose us.* Henry never responded. By the time I checked again, he had deleted his entire profile.

I get a little drunk again before I google him. This time, I see that he and his wife have started their own real estate company. The website features a picture of the two of them standing in front of a beautiful colonial and a bright red SOLD sign. She is pretty, but severe. Angular and polished with blindingly white teeth and slick, platinum hair. He still looks exactly like my dad. That must be hard, I think.

I find her Instagram, linked at the bottom of the page: @hello__helene. I click through pictures of their own house, bright and modern. Farmhouse-inspired. All the pictures take the same color palette—muted pinks and neutrals. They form a rose-colored mosaic. Helene in a floppy hat on Cape Cod. Helene in a down parka holding an infant with soft blond curls. Helene wearing a clay face mask, hair in a towel turban. Henry and Helene have two daughters, but whenever they appear, they are shot from behind, for privacy. I'm desperate to know what their faces look like. If they also have H names. Harriet and Hillary. Hope and Harper. Holly and Hannah. They lie on plush cream-colored carpets and flip through picture books. They decorate a stainless-steel fridge in watercolor paintings. They stack toys neatly in tasteful, neutral baskets.

I enlarge a few photos. Henry is not in any of them, but the traces of him are visible in Helene's immaculate bedroom, the staging site for many of the pictures. Polished work shoes, ties hung on the back of the closet door, a vintage shaving kit on the bathroom counter. Signs of life.

BACK ON THE WEBSITE, I find an email address in the contact section.

Hi. I stop, unsure what to call him. My dad? Your dad? Ours? Mark? Finally just: *He's dead. I'm sure you've heard. The first time I wrote you was to let you know that my sister went missing. This is related to that, in a way. He didn't pick me in the end either.*

I'm not saying it's the same—you and me. I'm just saying that it's similar.

I'm sure you had your beef with him. I don't know how much peace you've made or whatever. I don't think he was an asshole, though I've considered it a lot. I think he was maybe not built for this world. I think he was damaged in a very particular way, and he probably should never have had kids at all. Some people are like that.

I'm sorry for your loss, I write. *My loss. Our loss. Your family seems beautiful, and if it's any consolation at all, I think that somehow, in spite of everything stacked against you, you came out on top. Maybe he did you a favor.*

AS I'M WRITING, I imagine my brother responding to me. I imagine us meeting up for lunch in a diner near his perfect, rectangular house. Tentative at first, but then familiar. Shockingly familiar. I imagine him introducing me to his daughters in a park some months later. Me introducing them to a new puppy, maybe. Me joining their gorgeous, picture-perfect holiday table and watching the girls grow up. One of them behaves exactly like Angie, and her mom is exasperated, but I tell her it's okay, and I offer to take the girl out for a chat, and we become close. I'm her cool auntie, the one she trusts with her secrets and who knows exactly what is on her mind. I imagine all of this bleeding out from this one frank note. Now, we can share a gallows humor. He can finally let me in.

I get a response almost immediately. It astonishes me how fast it comes on the heels of mine. Like he was waiting for me.

Listen, you're an adult now. Stop with the drunken messages at one in the morning. Leave me and my family alone.

When they run Dad's blood after the crash, they find alcohol, lithium, Valium, and Advil.

"Light day," Mom says, which the coroner does not find funny.

Back when they first met, my dad had a drug problem. A wife, a kid, and a drug problem. He used cocaine mostly then, but also some prescription narcotics. He had humiliated his father, the good congressman, on more than one occasion.

Dad cleaned up when Angie and I were kids, putting aside the occasional bad week or month. Angie took over from him when she was in the eighth grade, drinking to the point of passing out on the bus for a school field trip to Augusta. By tenth, she was puking all over our driveway on a semi-regular basis. And by eleventh, racking up a third suspension for smoking pot in the third-floor bathroom.

Dad was the only one who could handle Angie when she was fucked up. He didn't scream like Mom. He had a way of tranquilizing her. Even when she was being vicious. On nights that she snuck into our shared room after one of her outings, I pressed my eyes closed and prayed she wouldn't start in on me. Sometimes it worked, sometimes it didn't. When she did shake me awake so that she could yell at me for some perceived slight, some way that I thought I was better than her or ignored her at school or whatever, I would tune it out and wish for Dad.

And most of the time, he heard me calling for him in my head. Most of the time, he was there within a minute or two to whisk Angie downstairs for a pot of coffee and a serious talk and a lot of crying.

Mom thought he was too soft, too sympathetic. She thought Angie was getting caught on purpose, so that she could get his attention.

After Angie disappeared, Dad returned to form. He started carrying loose pills in his pockets on a regular basis, and he tossed back odd combinations at all hours of the day. From then on, he was never totally sober, and Mom acted like that was normal. Like, of course I should continue to check the car for anything potentially incriminating before I take it out with my driver's permit. Of course I should empty Dad's pockets into his catch-all mug before running the wash. Of course I shouldn't ask him for a ride to a friend's house, even if no one else is home and even if she doesn't drive anymore and I have no other way of getting there and he says he's fine to take me. Like—grow up, Teddy.

When Dad was up, he was manic and jokey, loopy and weird and uncomfortable to be around. When he was down, he was catatonic. Occasionally in my late high school years, headed out to a party or study group, I'd catch a glimpse of him in his favorite chair, well on his way to some far-off place, his eyelashes fluttering, his head falling and jerking back up. Sometimes, when I'd get close enough to check that he was breathing, he'd smile and touch my face, and I'd see that he was just trying to survive. But most of the time, I was pretty mad at him.

WE CREMATE HIM TO get it over with, and, on Monday, while it's raining and everyone is home or at work, we sneak back onto the bridge where he killed himself to scatter his ashes through the hole he left behind.

"Is this the right place?" Mom asks, when we've already thrown half the dust.

"Where else?" I'm holding a fistful of my father in a gloved hand. The ashes are coarse and gray and Mom told me they taste of metal and eggs. She said she felt compelled to consume a small amount. I didn't ask questions.

"I don't know," she says. "You can let that go."

I empty my hand, but some ashes stick to the wet suede. Mom says they are called cremains. They shouldn't make portmanteaus for stuff like this, I think. What they should do is find a way to make this powder smell like the person it came from. Like bar soap and hidden chocolates.

The mortician put the remains in a large square tin and covered them with loose cotton, like a bottle of aspirin. I thought it was a nice touch. It reminded me of the rabbit holes we used to find in the backyard as kids, covered over with the mama's down. Dad would poke at the cottony fluff using a stick so that we could peek at the bunnies, small as hamsters and blind, all curled together for warmth. Dad would hold the barrier back for a moment, warning us not to touch anything and leave a scent behind or the mama rabbit would abandon her babies and they'd starve to death. Then he'd drop it gently. The cotton would fall and the bunnies would disappear, safe, ready for the mama to come home to them.

We finish the work in silence. There is more to spread than I had anticipated. I imagined one elegant, sweeping gesture, but we have to return over and over to the supply until it becomes rote, a chore. Somewhere in the middle it strikes me as funny. I laugh and Mom laughs, too—neither of us acknowledging the joke. And then at the end, it's sad again. At the end when there is only a little powder left in the plastic lining and Mom shakes it feebly over the jagged wooden posts, and I can tell we're both thinking how small it all feels, the end of a person.

"Why do you think he did it?" Mom asks.

"He was depressed," I say. "You know that. He hadn't been himself for a long time."

"I guess not," she says. "Maybe I should have known he might. He had never tried before. I don't think." She pauses. "The date makes sense. The anniversary."

"That's funny," I say. We're out of ashes, so I peel off my soiled gloves and throw them down into the river. "That's the part I understand the least. I can't imagine him wanting to steal Angie's thunder." I shake my head. "That's putting it wrong."

"Let's get into the car," Mom says. "This damp will chill your bones." She stares out over the bridge. She's not looking down into the shallows where his car fell, but out—out toward the place where the river turns black in the shadow of the narrowing trees, where it snakes out of sight. The last part visible to the eye. "This is a beautiful place, isn't it?"

Through my sunglasses, everything is cast in gray. Sky, trees, river like an artery of tar. "Sure," I say, and I turn my parka into an umbrella, holding it above both our heads so that we can run back to the car together. Soon it will be April, and then May, and then summer, and then, for a moment, this place will be briefly beautiful. I can imagine it for her.

"Anyways," she says, when we're ten minutes into the drive home. We haven't spoken since the bridge. "I'm not surprised, with his obsession."

"What obsession?"

"The little I could gather."

"Angie?"

"All his theories."

"He was still doing that private detective stuff?" I say,

feigning incredulity, even though I knew that it was for his sake that we never acknowledged she was dead. At some point we all tacitly agreed to not ask and not tell. We settled on treating him like a mental patient, and he settled on treating us like apostates.

"I guess he finally gave up," Mom says.

The students don't know what to say.

I greet them as they enter the classroom on Tuesday morning. I smile and try to meet their eyes, but they don't look up. I'm trying to let them know that today is going to be normal, that there is nothing to worry about.

"Hi, Wade. Good morning, Laurie."

They grunt their responses.

Iris is last. She drags her backpack behind her down the hall. She knows she's late; she's always late.

"Pick that up," I say, holding the door. "We're holding class for you."

Iris reminds me of Angie. The other teachers hate her. Sometimes I feel like I'm the only one who can see her for what she is—a kid in some kind of pain. I keep telling her she's creative, that she's got potential, but she barely listens.

"Sorry," Iris mutters as she passes me and heads for her usual spot in the back corner.

I'm wearing an outfit that hasn't seen the light of day since I interviewed almost five years ago: navy pencil skirt, white silk blouse, tan heels. When Angie disappeared, I learned that you have to look like you have it together. You lose the luxury of unwashed hair, of wrinkled tops, of makeup-free days. Every yawn, every coffee stain, every whiff of body odor is confirmation for a well-meaner that you should be at home, consoling yourself in reheated lasagna.

"Okay, guys," I start. "I'm sorry I was out yesterday. Can someone remind me where we left off in *Dubliners*?"

"Ms. Angstrom?" Jamie raises his hand.

"Go ahead, Jamie. Can you sum things up for us?"

"Actually." Jamie rummages through his backpack. "We wanted to give you this." He presents me with a card his mom picked out.

The front of the card says "Deepest Sympathies." Inside, all my juniors have signed. The copy reads, "May your loved one rest in Christ." I feel my face flush with embarrassment, but I know that to these young people it must look like grief.

"Thank you, guys," I say, swallowing it down. I place the card on my desk. "Where were we?"

"Ms. Angstrom." This time it's from the doorway. Rick, the principal. "Can I borrow you for a moment?"

"Of course." I turn to the class. "Jamie is going to recap the basic plot of 'The Dead' while I step out."

In the hall, Rick hits me with a hug that nearly knocks us both off balance, pinning my arms to my sides.

"I'm so sorry, Teddy," he says. The skin of his neck smells like baby powder and garlic.

"Thanks, Rick."

He releases the hug, but maintains a grip on my shoulders. "Teddy," he says. "Would you tell me if you needed extra days? You don't have to be here."

"I would. I'm fine."

"You know," he says, "I remember when your sister was in my physics class."

"Your first year."

"That's right," Rick says. "She was brilliant."

"At physics?

"Her grades didn't show it, but she had a lot of potential."

"I think she was failing."

Rick shakes his head. His pep talk is going poorly. He's getting frustrated with me, his actual former A-student. "What I'm trying to say is—I could barely keep coming in here." He looks down and wrings his hands. "One of my own students missing. A nightmare."

"I can't imagine."

"You should take more time, Teddy."

"Rick," I say, putting my hands on his shoulders this time. "I have to get back to class."

The kids are totally silent when I come back in. They were not recapping. They were straining to listen to Rick and me out in the hallway.

I ask them to form a circle with their desks. I claim a student desk for myself and pull it into the circle.

"Okay," I say, when all of the screeching of metal feet has ceased. "Let's talk about the dead."

I smile, and the kids laugh. Kids are better than adults at letting you take the air out of it like that. I recite the end of "The Dead" from memory, and they are very impressed. For once, they have all read, because they wanted to do something nice for me. They have all read, and because they have all read, we have a great discussion. I teach the shit out of Joyce. I teach like my life depends on still being good at one thing.

We talk about the snow, the snow falling over the living and the dead in Ireland. We look outside at the rain, the ceaseless rain of coastal Maine. The rain that falls over me and my mom and my dad, who is now, in fact, nothing but water. The rain that falls over Angie, wherever she is. We talk about paralysis. How easy it is to get stuck. The kids desperately don't want to get stuck. They are so full of vitality and passion. There are moments with this mostly-shit job where you get to experience a heady contact high from watching young people realize that their whole lives are ahead of them.

The thrill does not last. Instead, the bell sounds and for the rest of the day, I comfort a lot of people who are very upset. I say all the right things to make them feel better about the temporary loss of their familiar work environment. I appreciate the honesty from the few who do not attempt to hide their displeasure at having to acknowledge this macabre development. The ones who are just trying to get through a Tuesday forgoddssake.

"I heard," Greg, the head of my department, offers. Monotone, a statement of fact.

"Indeed," I say.

"Killed himself."

I nod.

"What a shameful thing to do," he says. "I'm sorry for your mother."

"I'll tell her you send your best."

ST. AUGUSTINE'S USED TO be a sanitarium run by the church, established by Irish immigrants in the early twentieth century. Back then it was called St. Dymphna's, after the patron saint of lost minds. It only lasted for thirty years before it was closed again in 1939. Lack of funds, poor patient outcomes, waning public support. It stood empty for another thirty before it was renovated into St. A's in the early '70s by a group of Jesuits with a flair for interior design and a sense of the opportunity created by the influx of educated workers flocking toward the state's latest boom industry—telecom.

They never quite got around to parts of the school. The basement is still basically a morgue, and so it's usually quiet, except for during school dances, when it fills up with kids looking for a quiet make-out spot.

I buy two decade-old Milky Ways from the vending machine they keep down here—the one the kids aren't allowed to use—and I eat them in the single stall bathroom that doesn't get cleaned, sitting on the toilet. I watch myself in the mirror on the back of the door. Some days, I am uglier than I remember. The mirror-person is strange and unfamiliar—I expect her not to move when I move, not to suck in her cheeks when I do. I expect that I will blink and things will be reset. Droopy jowls, dark circles, bent nose—the shapes linger and surprise.

But today is not one of those days. I lick the chocolate off my fingers and smooth the kohl under my eyes. My hair is clean and shiny. I'm better-looking than the version in my head today. Some days are like that, too, I think, pulling my phone out of my pocket to take a picture. I wonder if everyone has this problem—the inability to accurately remember their own face. I save the selfie in a folder where I keep possible profile pictures. I got off the dating apps a few weeks ago, but I never stay off for long.

I flush the Milky Way wrappers and head back up to my desk. During my own St. A's student orientation, I asked why they needed to change the name—why couldn't we have kept Dymphna? I was told that the priests wanted to start fresh. I thought then that it was because Dymphna was too badass, too feminist for those stodgy old priests, what with her having been beheaded by her dad at fifteen for refusing his incestuous advances. I think I actually started a rumor to that effect. But later, as a teacher, I learned that the name change was a PR move. The sanitarium had been the subject of a high-profile exposé chronicling its inhumane treatment of patients and disgusting conditions, and Mainers have long memories.

The day goes by slowly, and yet, when the final bell comes, I find myself delaying. I wait as long as I can for an email request, a frantic student, a broken printer—anything to keep me here a bit longer, but things remain quiet. When I finally grab my jacket, I swear I can hear everyone exhale.

"I need you to help me with the bills," Mom says.

"How much more?"

"No," she says. "Not money. Well . . . maybe. But I need you to help do them." She's lying on the floor of the kitchen with Wolfie, her cheek pressed down to the tile. Two commas facing one another, small nothing between them.

I step over my old sick dog and Mom's head to grab a box of cereal off the counter. "I wouldn't lie on the floor like that. I saw ants in here last week."

"Your father did everything online." She strokes the bridge of bone between Wolfie's eyes. She rubs with one finger down to his black nose and back up. His eyes close in relief. "People keep calling."

"How? He just died."

"They were calling before, too," Mom says. "During the day, when you're at work. He always said he'd handle it, but I don't know . . ." She looks up at me. The pitch of her voice, the desperation stops me mid-chew, and I'm left with a mouthful of sharp Crunch Berries. "Please, Teddy. I can't sleep."

"You can come live with me," I say, but the joke lands flat. "Mom, I'm kidding. It will be fine. I'll do it."

She turns back to Wolfie, and I watch them for a while. She's no longer touching him, just staring into the milky expanse of his eyes.

I set down my bowl and get on the floor behind her quietly, carefully curling my body around hers. She is less muscular than I remember, and I can almost feel her bones, swimming in her drapey, expensive fabrics. I think of osteoporosis commercials. I think of how you never realize your parents are young until they're not anymore. Her hair is clipped up on her head, and I unclip it. I sink my face in, and it smells like her. I wrap my arm around her front and sneak a glimpse over her shoulder at Wolfie. He doesn't see me. He's pleading to her from behind the clouds, and I feel like a voyeur.

"I put everything in bags," she says. "I left them in his room."

Lately, we don't leave Wolfie alone. We don't say it, but we both know that it hurts him, all the attention. I hear him whimper when my hands roll over the tumors in his back that press against his spine. He is tired. He wants to sleep alone on the cold floor. He doesn't want to be touched and called and fed. The car, which he used to love, is now torture with all its bumps and stops. But I take him with me to the store, to the park. I can't let him be. Neither of us can. We're worried that if we give him the opportunity, he'll die on us, neatly and silently while no one is looking, not wanting anyone to make a fuss over him, and he's a good dog who doesn't deserve to die alone.

AS I MAKE MY way upstairs, it occurs to me that I'm not sure when the last time was that I walked all the way to the end of the hall, to the room I used to share with Angie.

In the years after Angie disappeared, we left everything untouched—the cliché thing where the dead kid's room becomes a museum. I even moved out, into the basement. The room felt weird without her.

When I went to college, Dad moved his stuff into our old room. He said he needed office space for god only knows what, but then he installed blackout curtains over the windows and took down our bunk beds, erecting a metal platform with a twin mattress in its place. Mom called it his Batcave. She said she didn't like to go in there. I rarely tried. The door was always closed.

"We can't be together on this one," she told me once, on the back porch, as the sun was setting. "He feels he has to go it alone."

I pretended to understand what she was saying so that I could end the conversation.

The room upstairs still bears traces of Angie if you strain to spot them: her CD collection, a few pictures left on the walls, some Sharpie graffiti in the corner that used to be hidden by a poster. Now the defining characteristic of the space is Dad's incredible, shocking mess. The desk surface is piled high with used tissues and the uneaten, organic protein bars that are evidence of Mom's attempts to feed him. Handwritten notes cover everything like a layer of snow. They spill from desk to floor, in different shapes of crinkled, crumpled, and torn. Clothes on the ground are visibly soiled and heaped in the corner, hamperless. The room smells of human filth and decaying food. I burn with shame at the idea of anyone seeing this place. I preemptively form excuses to the most obvious question: *How could you let this happen?*

It takes me a minute to spot the bags Mom was talking about. Five double-knotted plastic shopping bags filled with bills are lined up along the wall by the door.

An IBM laptop sits next to my dad's flip phone in the center of the desk, half buried under all the garbage. The computer is asleep until I tap it. A login screen rejects my best three password guesses.

I steal two black trash bags from the kitchen and get to work clearing the carpet. I fill one bag with pure waste—food wrappers, used napkins, and unidentifiable rot. The other gets filled with mom's smaller shopping bags and everything else, including:

- A pharmacy receipt for antacids and anti-depressants
- An invoice for $90.95 from Data Services, Ltd.
- A birthday card "to a beloved wife." Inside: *Dear Clare.* Nothing else. Unfinished, unsent.
- One day's worth of food journaling: *banana 70 cal, c&c protein 210 cal; pb protein 240 cal; ensure 250 x 2 = 500, total = 1270, tomorrow +++300*
- A note in his writing: *Mickey → boyfriend??*
- A receipt for two pairs of new reading glasses
- A pair of cracked and bent reading glasses
- Another note: *BH: 603-565-7309*
- A single green Post-it: *r/unsolved*

I take a break to call BH from my dad's cell phone.

A man answers. "Hello?"

"Hi," I say. "This is . . . Mark Angstrom's phone."

"Who is this?"

"Who is this?"

"Bill."

"Bill who?"

"Rooney."

I glance down at my dad's note and see that what I thought was an H was a sloppy R. The ink doesn't form a closed loop, but the paper is indented from pressure. "How did you know Mark?" I ask.

"We skipped a step here. Who is this?"

"Mark left a note with your number."

"Okay. And you are?"

"Why would he have done that?"

"You can go ahead and ask him."

"Not really," I say. "Mark's dead."

"Are you serious?"

"Yeah." I feel myself losing my nerve. "I was going through some of his things, and I saw this number, so I figured—"

"Clare?"

"What?"

"Sorry, is this Clare?"

"No," I say. "Her daughter."

"Angie?"

"Teddy."

"Oh, right. Jesus. That makes sense. I don't know why my mind went . . ." Bill lets his voice trail off.

"How do you know them?"

"I used to do your yard," Bill says. "You probably don't remember."

A guy in his late twenties. His face is fuzzy, but I can see Angie clearly—taking a break from her failed efforts at backyard tanning to sneak around the side of the house and bum a smoke from him. Me, left to man the reflectors we made out of cardboard and aluminum foil, ready to flash a signal if Mom popped her head out of the sliding door. Both of us pudgy with puppy fat in the tiny bikinis we bought with our own allowance. It wasn't that Mom didn't approve of two-pieces; it was that she thought they required a certain figure. She didn't want us looking like the fat tourists.

"I remember," I say to Bill. "You drove a white pick-up."

"Can I ask what happened?"

"Suicide."

"How? I'm sorry, I know that's not polite to ask."

"He drove his car off the bridge by our house."

"On purpose?"

"Yes, on purpose."

"Jesus Christ."

"Why did he have your number written down?"

"I don't know," Bill says. "Maybe he needed some work done in the yard or around the house."

"Right. Maybe he wanted to make sure the gutters were cleaned before he offed himself."

Bill misses my sarcasm. "Getting affairs in order, I think they call it." He clears his throat, and I see him shirtless. I hear Angie in my head.

"Hot Landscaping Guy is here," she says, leaping onto my top bunk, where the view of the driveway is better.

I protest: he's not hot; he's just tan and sweaty.

She's such a mess of hormones that she can't tell the difference.

She's back to staring at Bill as he unloads the truck. "He only looks at you," she says.

He does not. He doesn't look at either of us. Also: he's old.

But from that point on, I make a point to wear makeup on days that he comes by. I make a point to look and sound older than my fourteen years. To walk like my hips have already rounded, to sway.

"Hello?" Bill says. "Teddy?"

"I have to go," I say. "Sorry."

"I'm sorry about your dad."

"Yeah, thanks," I say.

As I go to end the call, I see that the tiny gray flip phone screen reads "bill" rather than the number that I manually entered. A saved contact.

"Hello," I say, raising the phone back to my ear, but I only hear the dial tone.

I click through the contact list. There are only three. I'm not in here, nor my mom. Just "bill," "don't answer," and "ginger." I call "don't answer" and "ginger" but both are disconnected numbers. No ring, just an automated message letting me know that I've hit a dead end. The outgoing call log doesn't show anything past the calls I've made today; the incoming log is empty.

I log onto Dad's computer as a guest so that I can google Bill Rooney. It's a common name, and I have to really dig to come up with anything relevant. Finally, I hit on my guy—William F. Rooney Landscaping in Brookdale, one town further inland. His business doesn't have a website, but he is on Yelp with one five-star review from someone named Jeremy P.

Love Bill and his team! Have been using WFR for years. Fair prices, on time, super reliable. Plus Bill plays a mean guitar!!!

I return to my search bar: *Bill+Rooney+guitar+Brookdale*

In the images tab, pictures of a local band come up. I click through to the website hosting them, and it's the homepage for the Shifty, a dive bar that I've been to once or twice with the other teachers for Friday happy hour. The events page informs me that Mondays are trivia, Tuesdays are two-for-one drinks, and Wednesdays are the standing performance date for the Marching Ants, Bill's band. There he is, fuzzy in the back of the frame, hiding behind the lead singer.

Wednesday. Tomorrow.

I write the time on my hand with Dad's pen, and I have to carve it into my skin, the ink is so dry.

"Teddy," Mom calls. "Wolfie needs to go out."

"Coming," I call. I close the computer and glance back at Dad's notes before I fold them in a square. *Mickey → boyfriend???*

The only Mickey I can think of is our neighbor's old dog, a Yorkie that barked incessantly at all hours of the night. He's dead now.

"Teddy!"

"Coming!"

I tuck the square of notes neatly into my pocket. I slip Dad's cell phone in the other one. I leave the bag of trash and the laptop. One thing at a time.

At dinner, Mom and I make a game plan. I'm going to tackle the bills this weekend, when I have the time to sit on automated hold lines for hours. We'll clean out the room over the course of the next month. Hazmat stuff first. Notes and pills and correspondences later.

"I'll stay here while we're getting it all sorted," I say.

Mom nods and pretends to miss the subtext.

"This way I can move my stuff slowly to the new place. I won't have to get it all done at once."

"What?" Mom asks.

"Like this weekend, I'll probably take some of the boxes that I don't need right now. The kitchen stuff you said I could take and things like that."

"You're still going?"

"At the end of April, maybe," I say. "Not right now."

Mom tugs at her hair and stares at the side door. It's so dark outside, we can't see the yard, just the reflection of our own faces. I try to make eye contact with her in the glass, but she looks away.

"I signed a lease," I say. "We discussed this. Remember? You said you understood."

I know that if I stay, I'll never leave. There will never be a good time.

Mom nods. "Right," she says. "Well, good night, then." She kisses me hastily on the top of my head and proceeds upstairs.

After a few minutes of listening to her pace the creaky floors, I grab Dad's computer and a fresh bottle of wine and retreat to the basement, where everything except my bed and a pile of dirty clothes is boxed and bubble wrapped.

I try *r/unsolved* as the computer password, but that doesn't work, so I close the laptop and google it on my phone instead, and I come up with a Reddit page: r/UnsolvedMysteries. It bills itself as a "a subreddit dedicated to the unresolved mysteries of the world." At the top is the board's latest obsession: unsolved triple homicide in Indiana, where a mother, father, and son were all beaten to death in their farmhouse. The mother was pregnant.

I pour myself another glass and download the app for easier viewing. I let it generate a gibberish username and I scroll.

A girl was murdered in Ohio last month, and the police have no suspects in the case. She was found raped and mangled in her bed. Her mother, who discovered the body, is catatonic, institutionalized. When she comes down off the benzos, she tries to kill herself. Every time.

A woman—nineteen, a college student—went missing in California last year. Broad daylight, camera footage of a man picking her up and throwing—literally throwing—her five-foot frame in his trunk. Neither the man nor the car can be identified.

Two girls—friends—ten and eleven years old—were stabbed in the woods, walking home from school in rural Pennsylvania. One died. The other is in intensive care. There are no suspects. It's the third crime of its kind this year. The police don't know what to make of it.

There is a search feature at the top of the page. I know what will happen when I type my sister's name. I brace myself for the onslaught of men trading information, throwing around detective show jargon, laying out their theories, linking to their YouTube channels and podcasts. Pining and fantasizing. Angie was cute in a punky way. I can see that now. All young people are cute. In the months after she disappeared, she attracted attention from a certain type, guys who were sick of all the blond sorority girls gone missing. They talked about her as though, if they helped rescue her, she might even date them.

What I'm not prepared for—what comes up first—are the posts about my dad. Of course, though. Of course, it's news here, on the very site he must have come to for this kind of update.

- **hop_on_Pop:** Angie Angstrom (remember her?)— her uncle/daddy Mark killed himself on the tenth anniversary of her death.
  - **lil-gerbil-baby:** No shit. Have we been at this that long?
    - **Anon34567:** LOL.

One of the users links to a separate subreddit—r/AngieAngstrom. It has only 157 followers, but I still feel a perverse sense of pride, a thought I try to squash as fast as it pops up: *we're famous.*

Pinned at the top is a years-old summary of the case, upvoted thirty-three times.

For those unfamiliar with the case:

Angie Angstrom (18F), a high school senior, disappeared some time between Fri 3.11.05 and Sat 3.12.05. The night she disappeared, she attended a local party at the house of a school mate. She drank with friends and was apparently very intoxicated. Friends at the party saw her arrive alone and leave alone (around midnight). She told some people that she was getting a ride home from her boyfriend, and it was confirmed by the family that Angie had not taken a car out of the house that night, though they didn't know about a boyfriend. The police questioned dozens of partygoers, confirming this version of events. Three were asked to take a polygraph (host, host's boyfriend, and a guest who was sober and remembered talking to Angie). Several people noted that she seemed "off," like she was on drugs.

Her younger sister, Theodora (16F), said that she saw Angie in the early hours of the morning at home. She claimed that Angie was not drunk/drugged. [Note: this information was late to come out—approx. five days into investigation. Police changed their focus at this point from the party to the Angstrom household given change of the last-seen location.]

Morning of 3.12, Angie was not in the house. Her mother, Clare Angstrom (52F) called in missing persons at 7:30 p.m. No evidence of a struggle was found in the house or car. No one from the party had heard from her after she left. Other students say she had a cell phone (burner type/disposable), but she wasn't on her parents' plan, and a cell phone was never discovered.

Angie's erratic uncle/stepfather (51M) quickly became a target for police. Clare vouched for him, but he has a strange history (look him up: Mark Angstrom). Angie's journal entries, which were leaked to the press, painted a picture of domestic turmoil as well.

Her case remains unsolved.

What do you all think?

The top comments are a glut of conspiracy:

- **cornelonthecob09:** The burner phone to me points to a runaway situation. Things were not good at home (per diaries). Angie knew if she left with her car, she'd be found, so she had her boyfriend pick her up from a place other than her house, created a lot of confusion by acting drugged up, pointed police in direction of a murder and blew town. Smart.
  - **quad_cat:** Ever heard of Occam's razor? It's the dad. That guy's a fucking psycho. Who marries their brother's widow?
    - **FFR30000:** Don't forget "leaves his real kid behind."
  - **SVUfan531:** See I think the kids at that party always seemed shady. Something not right there. They lawyered up so fast.
    - **whatever-grl:** What about the sister IDing her at home later that night?
      - **cornelonthecob09:** I don't put much stock in that. So late in the game. She just wanted attention.
- **SVUfan531:** ANOTHER VOTE FOR DAD DID IT.
  - **FFR30000:** Did you guys see that guy on the news? He was in a full-blown sweat all. the. time. guiltyyyyy
    - **whatever-grl:** What's with the burner then?
      - **FFR30000:** Teenage shit?
        - **whatever-grl:** Walter White shit. You know teenagers with burners?

- **medicalemergency:** What burner?
  Everyone on this sub acts like the phone
  is real, but there WAS. NO. PHONE.
- **hop_on_Pop:** At one point, I thought definite
  runaway, but then when she stayed missing . . . the
  dad did it.
  - **homicideunit4:** Why?
    - **hop_on_Pop:** Why not?
      - **homicideunit4:** could be a straight
        kidnapping. Drifter etc.
- **homicideunit4:** I always felt that they never
  explored the boyfriend angle enough. I followed the
  case closely when it was everywhere around here.
  She told everyone she had a boyfriend, the burner
  points to a boyfriend . . . and yet no boyfriend ever
  turned up.
  - **SVUfan531:** Exactly!!! "no boyfriend ever
    turned up"

I change the sorting feature from "Top" to "New" and the posts shuffle into a different order. The two most recent entries are from MICHAELA345 and bear zero votes. Three months ago, this person wished Angie a happy twenty-eighth birthday. Last week, he wrote simply: *RIP MARK ANGSTROM.* No one responded.

I reply. *He was a good dad. Miss you xx*

Fifteen minutes later, when I go back to delete it, my buzz fading fast and embarrassment setting in, realizing that it could fuel speculation that Angie is out there, reading and responding to the Redditors themselves, I see Michael has already replied to my post:

theodora?

The sight of my name on the screen floods my bloodstream with adrenaline. I throw my phone to the foot of my bed instinctively. Without its light, the room goes dark. I don't move. I hold my breath. I blink repeatedly to lose the afterglow of the screen, so that I might regain my ability to see in the dark, but I remain blind. Blind and overwhelmed by the sensation of being watched from a close distance.

At school the next day, I put the students into small groups. They shuffle and cluster to work on discussion questions I bought off of Teachers Pay Teachers first thing this morning, when I couldn't think of a single thing to do in class.

I take a lap and pretend to check on their work, and then I return to reading tabloid gossip on my phone to keep my mind from wandering. I didn't sleep at all last night, and I can't be expected to teach.

"Ms. Angstrom."

I shove my cell under my thigh and look up.

Jamie is only sixteen, but I can tell that he is going to be successful. When I met his dad on Back-to-School night, I saw a large, graying version of Jamie sitting before me. The man longed for my affirmation as much as his son, leaning into every word, calling me Ms. Angstrom—"Yes, Ms. Angstrom, we understand and we're appreciative, Ms. Angstrom." One of those people who vacationed here first, before deciding to make it permanent. It's a type. Perpetual tourists, sitting on a mountain of cash, imagining that they're living the simple life among us. Jamie, for his part, I've always known will make the reverse of his parents' pilgrimage and rebound back to Boston or New York.

Today, though, I look at him and I wonder for the first time if he will grow up to be big and important and large, and if he will one day hurt a woman or many women. I look around and wonder about the lot of them in here—how many, older than I am now, will hit a woman, hurt a woman, hold a woman down? It's not none. Someone has to account for all these stories of men killing wives, girlfriends, friends, girls, strange girls who owe them nothing. I wish I could rule out the soft-speakers, but they're the ones who will sit at their keyboards and perform the role of audience. They're a part of this, too.

"What is it, Jamie?" I feel my phone buzzing through the wool of my skirt.

"Our group has run out of ideas," Jamie says, holding out his paper. His handwriting is a font. He's a stickler for staying on task. The others resent him. "Are we doing this right?"

Around the room, many of his peers are on their phones, texting each other from feet apart. One draws cartoons on the back chalkboard. I've lost control of the class. This is exactly the kind of situation I don't need Rick walking in on. He'll insist I need to take time off.

I stand, and the room looks up. "Let's hear some responses," I say. "Who wants to begin?"

Jamie raises his hand, even though he is still standing right in front of me. No one else volunteers.

"Let's go," I say to the whole class. "Let's hear what you have."

"I can start," Jamie says. "So, I—we—thought that—"

"Jamie," I say. "Did I call on you?"

"I thought because no one else—"

"I'm not blind. I could see your hand was up," I say.

"Well, I—"

"If I wanted to call on you, I would. Sit down, please."

Jamie ruffles his hair. He remains standing. "Listen, Miss A—"

"Ms. Angstrom," I say. "And I asked you to sit down."

The other kids are rapt, watching this all play out. No one is on their phone anymore.

"I'm the only one doing the work," Jamie mutters.

I snatch the paper from his hands and start to read the responses aloud. "'The imagery in the poem recalls the crucifixion,'" I read. "That's what you have? That's what you're so eager to share?"

"We thought that some of the descriptions of the berries made them seem like blood, and there was also some language about thorns that seemed relevant," Jamie says.

I crumple Jamie's paper and walk it to my wastebasket. "Who can share what they have?" I say again. Every hand stays down. A moment later, the bell rings.

"For tomorrow," I say, as the silence breaks and the kids frantically pack their bags so that they can get out into the hallway and gossip about what just happened.

Jamie stops by my desk on his way out of the room. "I'm sorry," he says. "For calling out."

"I suppose I can look forward to an email from your mother later," I say, loud enough for the remaining students to hear. "She's on the Board, right?"

Jamie shakes his head. "It's not like that," he says. "I fight my own battles."

"Big of you," I say.

Jamie looks up at me, like a dog that doesn't understand why it's being hit.

"Go on," I say. "I'm not writing notes."

Jamie and the others leave, and I lock the door behind them. I sprawl out on the tile in the back of the classroom, behind the desks, where no one can see me from the hall.

Here's the story—the one I've told a million times: I was the last person to see Angie before she disappeared.

Early in the morning on a Saturday—around two or three—she crept into my room and lay in bed with me. I was under the blankets, and she didn't get in. She lay on top in a pair of jeans and a sweatshirt. I remember turning toward her to sniff out her Friday night, expecting to pick up notes of cigarettes, rum, and weed—the usual odors. She leaned into me, burying her face in my neck and sniffing me back. Then I thought she was definitely high or drunk, but she smelled like nothing. Or rather, like herself. Her breath was stale, and her hair greasy, but she smelled normal. Earthy and warm.

I fell asleep like that, with Angie in my arms, my mouth and nose nestled into her hair, breathing her in.

When I woke, Angie was gone, but that side of the bed was still warm from her. It was 6 A.M., and I sensed that I had just missed her, that my body had woken up as the result of a change. I tucked my arms back into the covers and fell asleep until almost noon.

Angie wasn't home when I got up. Dad was in the living room watching TV. He warned me about going in the kitchen. "Your mom's having a day," he said. He mouthed Angie's name.

I rubbed the sand from my eyes and pressed on. Mom was

at the table tapping furiously at her crossword puzzle with the back of a pen.

"Morning," I said, but she didn't look up.

She stayed there until early evening, when she got tired of sighing loudly and clicking her pen and started to panic instead. She called girls Angie hadn't spoken to since first grade and checked our bedroom every half an hour—under the bed, in the closet—like Angie was hiding.

I remember thinking Angie was an idiot for pulling a stunt like this. I was pissed at her for ruining another weekend.

"Have you seen her?" Mom asked me, half a dozen times. "Do you know where she might be?"

I didn't, and I left out the part about Angie coming into my bed in the night. I figured it could only get us both into trouble, and I was beginning to wonder if I dreamt it entirely. Why would Angie go out, come back, and go out again?

It wasn't until the cops questioned us for a second time, to have Mom confirm that the last time anyone had seen Angie was after dinner on Friday night, that I finally piped up.

By that point, Angie had been gone for three days, had missed Monday's classes entirely. Dad was not watching TV anymore. He glared beams through my skin as I talked to the police.

"Why didn't you say this before?" Dad asked. I could see him chewing the inside of his mouth, the flesh of his teeth sucked in between his molars.

"I'm sorry," I muttered, staring down at my hands. "I didn't think it mattered. I forgot."

"Which is it—you didn't think it mattered or you forgot?"

"Teddy," the officer interrupted. "This is great information. Thank you for telling us what happened on Saturday morning. What else can you help us with?"

I refused to talk until my dad left the room. It is one of my greatest regrets, that moment.

I didn't look at him. I looked at the officers, knowing that they saw a young girl, tear-stained, unkempt. Knowing I wasn't the only one who registered my dad's seething rage, the way his swollen, arthritic knuckles gripped the countertop, the vein throbbing in his neck. I asked the detectives if I could talk to them, alone.

To his credit, my dad didn't protest. His shoulders slumped down and he left the room quickly. He stopped at my side and put a hand on my head on his way out. I knew it was his way of saying sorry. Maybe he was sorry, or maybe he was desperate for me to talk to the cops—with or without him there. I think at some point, he had gotten it into his head that I knew something damning about Angie. That I didn't even know what I knew, but if he could get me to talk long enough, we'd find her.

I didn't know anything useful. In any case, I watched the cops watch him leave, both of them with the same posture, hands on hips, waiting for him to make a sudden movement. I watched them twitch when he touched me on the way out, and I saw them see a threat in that gesture.

From then on, he was the target of their investigation, of all of their questions.

"Maybe we should get the doctor in here," was the first thing the short one said when my dad left the room. The tall one in charge fetched me a glass of water while his partner ran out. He didn't ask me any questions about Angie, just about school and Wolfie, who was a puppy then, always barking when the rest of us were trying to be quietly sad. Always embarrassing everyone with the loudness of his grief.

The psychologist who came back was a short middle-aged man, ruddy with a thick head of white hair. I remember thinking that he looked like *Diagnosis Murder*-era Dick Van Dyke—that same kind of jovial demeanor, even though you couldn't see a smile. His thick mustache obscured the mouth.

"Angie," he said. He called me only by my sister's name. No one ever corrected him. "Has anyone ever touched you under your clothes? In a way that made you feel uncomfortable or sad?"

I shook my head. I didn't understand the implication at the time—that he was asking about my dad—but this seemed like a grave line of questioning to go down with Angie missing. Had someone taken her, made her do things, raped her?

It was another hour of questioning—the Santa doctor and me talking at the kitchen table while the cops stood by the sink, pretending not to listen—before a note was written up and the subject was dropped.

They never asked me any further questions about Angie, and for years, I felt a great ambivalence about that. I told them about the tattoos and piercings no one else knew about. That it seemed to me then, at sixteen, like she might be obsessed with making holes in her body. But I never told them that Angie smoked pot, that she snuck out all the time—not the once, like Mom was saying.

For years after she'd disappeared, I'd have trouble falling asleep, even after I'd moved down to the basement. I'd imagine that I had withheld some critical evidence, some key to the case. That somewhere, Angie had been waiting in the dark—cold, alone, scared—taking solace only in the fact that I had the information people needed to track her down. Sometimes, I itched to walk down the hall to our old bedroom, where my dad had started sleeping, to wake him up and to tell him everything. To confess.

Other times—most of the time—I felt good about keeping

Angie's meaningless secrets. *Angie*—I would think, back when I still almost-prayed to her—*Ange, I told them next to nothing.* And in my prayers, she would pat my head appreciatively. I imagined her coming back and realizing how seriously I took our confidence. I imagined us growing closer than we'd ever been. Angie taking me seriously. Both of us in our twenties, in our thirties—best friends. Angie realizing that I was the only one who cared about who she was. The two of us living like sisters in a movie, laughing and giggling in the daylight together, crying with each other at night. Our relationship extending beyond those hours when she would drunkenly crawl up next to me in bed. Our relationship defining the rest of our lives. *In a way*, she'd say, curling up on my couch with a cup of tea, her toes nestled under my thighs, our kids running around the living room together, *in a way it's the best thing that ever happened*. She'd mean her disappearance, though maybe we wouldn't call it that. We'd know then, with the clarity of hindsight, what went wrong—maybe she ran away, maybe she was taken, it changed in every version of the fantasy—but it would be something with a beginning and an end. Something that was over.

As the years went by, that became my big wish—for it to be over.

When Mom asks why I'm getting so dressed up, I tell her I have a date. She doesn't object to the timing. She's too worried I'll never find a man.

A few years back, some shrink said that I was stuck, frozen in time at the age I was when Angie disappeared. She claimed that I sabotaged romantic relationships, because I wouldn't allow myself to live my own life. I told her that I just didn't care about having a boyfriend or getting married or whatever, but she said that I did, deep down. She said that it was too painful for me to believe in happy endings, in together forever, in golden anniversaries and dying in each other's arms. I was protecting myself from the possibility of a loss like my mother's.

"Are you married?" I asked her.

"I am," she said.

I checked myself for feelings of envy and found none, but I didn't tell her that. I didn't want her to feel bad. I go on dates for the food and for the sex. I need a steak every so often, and I need skin-to-skin. I like feeling useful to another person—desired, potent, chemical.

Tonight, I leave early to protect my cover story, and I stop for dinner at Fair Game, where the walls are decorated with taxidermic heads. I sit at the bar across from the bust of a white-tailed buck, and I order the venison, rare, with a side of Dijon.

The mustard burns up the sinuses and mixes with the musk of the game. It leaves a sour taste. I love it.

There is a man eyeing me, three stools down. Close to middle age, bloated, and nervous, he keeps puffing up his chest and correcting his posture. He's dressed in an expensive-looking, brand-new white dress shirt. Drinking a martini. No ring. Good head of hair.

"A girl who knows what she wants," this man says, after I order. I smile and nod, but turn back to my drink.

He catches the bartender's attention and orders a rib eye, blue.

"So," he says. "What's your name?"

"Theodora."

"That's an unusual name." I don't respond, but he slides down to me anyway. "What do you do, Theodora?"

Just then, the bartender brings my plate over. I thank him, and ask for another bourbon.

"On me," the man says loudly.

"Thank you," I say. "That's not necessary."

He waves me off. "I insist." His smile is unnaturally white, and he is so close to my face that I can see his gold fillings and smell the olive brine on his breath.

"I'm sorry," I say. "I'm not staying long. I have to make a show."

"What show?" he says. I'm sure he's not from around here. In town for business maybe, touring a factory or finding land to develop. He's too far from the coast to be a tourist. Too dressed up. Too early in the season. Too single.

"A friend is playing at a bar nearby." I smile weakly, and look around. The bartender is far away now, polishing glasses with a cloth napkin. Only three tables are populated. Older couples who barely speak while they eat their roast chicken and pork chops. Jazzy filler music garbles all other sounds into an inchoate rumble.

"What kind of music?" he asks. "What do you like to listen to?"

"I'm leaving very soon," I say. I saw off big hunks of meat and choke them down, half-chewed, to make a point.

"You're not one of those salad girls," the man says. "Don't finish your whole steak before mine comes out, okay?" He rubs his tanned hands together. "I'll be right back. Just have to hit the head."

I wipe the mustard from my face as he walks away. I wrap three fingerling potatoes in a paper napkin and head to my car, munching them on my way out. They can charge me. I'll get my card back tomorrow.

I'm feet away from my car when I hear steps behind me, coming up fast.

"Are you serious? You're going to run away from me like I'm some kind of creep?"

I spin around to see the man halfway between the restaurant and my car. He is sweaty, flustered.

"I have to go," I say. "I'm sorry—"

"I'm a nice guy," he says, emphasizing every word. His voice shakes with barely controlled rage. "You don't have to be a bitch."

I clutch my keys tightly and say nothing. The parking lot is dark and still. He watches me as I unlock my car and walk sideways to the driver's side, keeping him in my line of sight.

"You're too good to even talk to me?" He takes a step toward me, and I back into the ajar door reflexively. I slip inside.

The lock button triggers the rear lights to flash, and the man's face is illuminated in my rearview mirror. He comes close enough to rest his hands on my trunk. I wait for him to move, but he doesn't. I put the car in reverse and let my foot come off the brake. The car lurches back, and the man slams his hands down on the aluminum as he jumps back. I hit the brakes.

"Are you fucking crazy?" He pounds one fist on the back of my car for good measure and retreats back toward the restaurant. I watch him all the way inside.

FIVE MINUTES LATER, IN the parking lot of the Shifty, I think: maybe that was a sign. Maybe it's not the night for this. But the discordant sounds of the bad bar music make their way across the lot and lure me toward the neon sign.

The band is mid-set when I walk in, and the bar is half-full. Seems pretty good for a weeknight. I order a drink and stand in the back, against the wall. Most of the patrons are young, college kids. No former students, thank god.

It takes three tracks before I realize that the group is a Dave Matthews cover band. Then I see it everywhere, the boys in their DMB T-shirts underneath open flannels. Gently rocking in their matching LL Bean boots.

Bill stands at the back of the stage, dressed in a simple black tee and jeans. I recognize him immediately, because he looks exactly the same except for his thick hair, which had been black but is now completely silver. His muscular body and dark scruff read young, making the shock of gray look almost intentional. The other band members sway rigidly, but behind them, Bill dances. He plays guitar with his eyes closed.

The lead singer announces that they'll be breaking for the night. Before they do, he wants to introduce the band one more time. His name is Matt. On drums they have David. Lenny on bass, and Bill on guitar. When Bill steps forward to wave at the crowd, suddenly sheepish, we lock eyes and a chill runs up my spine, but his face betrays no recognition.

It's easy to keep track of Bill in the crowd of identically

dressed twenty-something white dudes with the same goofy, tousled haircut. He looks like their older cousin. The one who used to be a legend, who now is just a townie. The others stand in close circles, touch each other's arms, talk fast and loud. Bill stands slightly behind his group, gripping a beer by the neck. Every once in a while, someone gives him a nudge and he nods in response.

When he catches me staring again, he beelines for me. The other men don't seem to notice, but the girls do. The girls here like him. That much, I've picked up on.

I inspect the ice in my glass until he sidles up.

"Hiya," I say. I tip my drink.

"Hi," he says. Nothing else. He doesn't mirror the gesture.

I feel compelled to fill the silence. "How are you doing?"

"Do I know you?" Bill asks.

My first instinct is to invent a name, but there's no point. "We talked on the phone. I'm Mark's daughter."

He nods slowly. "And what are you doing here?"

Again, I consider lying. "I saw that you were playing," I say instead.

"You're stalking me," Bill says.

It's not a question, but I protest anyway.

Bill studies me so methodically and unabashedly I have to look away. "You look like your sister," he says.

"You look—"

"Old?" Bill smiles. "It's the hair."

"It's the company," I say, to be polite. "We're both old here."

Bill smiles and looks around. "Fair enough."

I circle back to his earlier question. "I needed to get out of the house is all."

Bill nods skeptically in a way that lets me know he knows I'm full of shit, but we can come back to that later. Instead, he asks me what I do, and when I tell him I'm an English teacher, he doesn't feel the need that some have to test me on Vonnegut deep cuts or critique my syllabi. He tells me he doesn't like to read.

"I can't believe kids this young still listen to Dave Matthews Band."

"Everyone likes DMB," he says.

"I hate Dave Matthews Band."

"No, you don't," Bill says. "You're alone in the car and 'Space Between' comes on. You change the station?"

"One hundred percent," I say.

"I'd have to see that."

"I hate to break it to you, but if these girls are telling you they love Dave Matthews, it's only because they have a crush on you."

Bill scans the room. Several girls who are watching him glance away suddenly. When he turns back to me the intensity of his eye contact is so powerful, I feel myself blush.

"I know," he says.

I have to force myself not to look away. I clear my throat. "Must be daddy issues," I say.

For a split second, he looks surprised by the barb. Maybe a little wounded. But he smiles anyway. I open my mouth to insist it was a joke, but no words come out. Bill goes quiet, focusing on the soggy label of his beer bottle. He peels it slowly back from the glass, rolling it onto itself before readhering it with sweat from the bottle and the pads of his fingertips.

"Also," I say, to break the silence. "Your lead singer is named Matt. The drummer is called David."

"Okay?"

"The Marching Ants? You guys should be called Dave and Matthew's Band!"

"David hates when people call him Dave."

I throw my hands up in mock frustration and Bill laughs. He has a deep, mirthful laugh that crinkles the skin around his eyes.

I ask about his life outside of the Shifty, what he does for a living, for fun. I learn that, in addition to the landscaping business and contract work, Bill rents the four slips he built on his dock. He likes going to the shooting range on weekends. I hear myself tell him that it sounds like he's good with his hands. I hear myself tell him that I'd like to learn how to shoot a gun, even though it's a thought that has never occurred to me before.

"You have to know how to protect yourself," Bill says. "All those nuts out there."

"Yes," I say. "There are a lot of nuts out there." Even though I've just met Bill, I consider telling him about the man from Fair Game. I think of the hundreds of Reddit pages filled with vitriol and nasty jokes. All of the men obsessed with Angie, trading her picture back and forth on the internet, relishing in her absence. I think of how young eighteen sounds now, of the eighteen-year-olds I teach who still see their pediatricians in rooms decorated with firetrucks and butterflies. Of the kind of sick obsessive who would mark Angie's birthday and her disappearance after all these years. Of Michael A, who saw me, somehow, through the computer, I'm sure of it. Of the possibility that Angie is still alive, the very thought that I've worked so hard to press down for so many years and which is now trying to force its way back to the surface of my brain as I stand in this sea of angsty post-adolescents. Of Bill's contact, saved in my dad's phone. One of only three numbers.

At some point while I'm zoned out, I miss a question entirely.

"I'm sorry," I say.

"Don't be."

A waitress retrieves our empties and asks if we'd like anything else. I order a beer, and Bill says he'll have the same, plus some fries. He lets out his belt. When he looks up and sees that I watched him do it, he flushes with embarrassment.

"You really don't know why my dad would have had your number?" I ask. "Why he might have been planning to call you? He had you saved in his contacts."

Bill adjusts in his seat. "I'm not sure."

"And you didn't see him recently? Around town or anything?"

"No. Not that I . . ." Bill looks up at a framed picture on the wall behind me and trails off.

"It's weird."

"Yeah, it is."

"It's weird that he'd have you saved in his contacts, like you talked before."

"Did you check his call history?" Bill asks.

"Nothing," I say.

"You know what?" Bill says. "I'm pretty sure he asked for my number." He snaps, like it's all coming to him now. "At Save-A-Lot."

"So you did see him?"

"Yeah," Bill says. "I think maybe he asked for my number."

"So that you guys could catch up, do lunch?"

"No," Bill says. He scrunches up his face, like he's working hard to access a memory. "I think he said he needed some work done."

"Yard work," I say.

He leaves himself wiggle room. "Or something. We only talked for a minute."

"Long enough for you to give him your number."

The waitress comes back, and we both finish our drinks quickly, barely talking. Bill doesn't touch his fries. I feel him closing himself off to me. I feel the silence calcifying into something impenetrable when I want him to keep talking. I know that if I can keep him talking, I can begin to understand.

The buoyant chatter of the college students around us is suffocating. I ask Bill to walk me to my car. Outside, Bill starts coughing. He pulls an inhaler from the pocket of his jeans and puffs it, twice.

"My sister had asthma," I say.

"It's just the cold," he says. "Listen. A couple months ago now—I lost my mother." He stops in his tracks and looks at me. "She was like your dad."

"What do you mean?"

"Kind of a—junkie. Or whatever."

I open my mouth to protest, to find a politically correct way to insist that we Angstroms are too pedigreed, too educated to be *junkies*. That ours is a different thing all together. It's *addiction, okay?* It's a disease. Medical. Literary. Freudian. It's not whatever socioeconomic chemical tragedy happens to people like Bill, who went to public school and make their living riding lawnmowers. "How did . . ."

Bill makes a face of apology. He speaks gently. "Everyone knows."

"Right," I say. The way people look at us in Shaw's, like our mess is contagious. The letter we got last year informing us that neighbors had been complaining to the township about the state of our yard, now that we don't pay anyone to take care of it. The veiled disgust whenever I run into St. A's friends back in town for Thanksgiving or Christmas and they ask me how my parents are doing, so that they can gossip to someone else. The general, pervasive resentment that people like us—normal, respectable people with so much to lose—could let themselves become such filthy, embarrassing, white trash junkies. "I know."

Bill kicks the rubber toes of his boots into the asphalt. "It's the fucking worst."

When he looks up, I see my mom, the same exhaustion, frustration, relief.

"You know, when she was alive," Bill says, "I wrote all these eulogies for her. In my head. I rehearsed it."

I nod. I've done that, too. For Angie. For my dad. Even my mom.

"But then she died for real, and I didn't even have a funeral. I didn't write an obit. I just buried her. To be done with it."

"It's okay," I say. "Us too."

"I know it's not the same," Bill says. "But I think she must have been trying to kill herself. In her own way. Slowly." Bill shakes his head. "She sure as hell wasn't putting any effort into staying alive."

"How did she die?"

"Heart attack," he says. "Massive heart attack. It was her third one." He smiles at me. "At least you have your mom. How is she? Is she still good? I always liked her."

"Yes," I say. Clare is still Clare. Through it all somehow the same.

"You're built like her," Bill says.

"I don't know," I say. "Maybe."

"It's good," Bill says. "You don't have to worry about ending up . . ." He trails off.

I don't want to let him off the hook, but I want to place my hand under his chin and raise his head until his eyes meet mine and tell him not to worry, that you can't believe in all that stuff about apples and trees. Fuck that. That he should know better than anyone how you can make your own life. Not one but two businesses, for Christ's sake. That doesn't just happen. And good for him.

"I'm sorry," I say. "About your mom."

For a second, the whites of his eyes gleam in the moonlight. His silvered hair glows like a halo. "Thanks."

"You remember my sister?"

"Of course," Bill says. "Angie." I wait for him to say something kind, the way that people do. Use one of the same tired euphemisms—*spirited, unique, marched to the beat of her own drum.* He grins out of one side of his mouth. "She was a pain in my ass. Always getting me in trouble."

"Me too," I say.

"Yeah, I remember her talking you into her schemes."

"Like when?" I say.

"You came and asked me for a cigarette that time. You were shaking like a leaf."

"I don't remember that." I take a step closer and see Bill's breath get heavier. It hangs like a cloud between us in the cold air.

"You didn't like breaking the rules."

"That's still true," I say. "More or less. What else do you remember?"

A door slams somewhere in the distance, and I jump instinctively toward him, until our hips are pressed together like paper dolls. With his flesh against mine now, I can feel the small middle-aged paunch of his stomach. I reach up to touch his thick arms.

"Should we go somewhere?" he mutters into my hair.

I nod. We drive down windy roads at twice the limit. I take my own car and the trees blur by like dark shadows. I love driving when I'm a tiny bit loaded, when everything just slides by in a streak of yellow streetlights and white lines. I should definitely turn back. I know that. But the only way out is through, right? The only way to find out more is to keep him talking. I hear Angie's voice in my head telling me that I'm full of shit. That I'm not exactly doing a honeypot, that I just want to bang Hot Landscaping Guy. *Shut the fuck up*, I think. It's not my fault that the only person who actually gets it is mixed up in all of this. Besides, maybe he's telling the truth. I can't hold Dad against him.

The trees get thinner and thinner, ceding to black skies. I crack the window. My forehead is hot, sweaty—the way I get when I'm drinking. The cold air feels like a splash of water. I can smell that the sea is close.

Bill's driveway is marked by a mess of buoys. It is long, and the gravel crunches under my tires. Without the moon, it's pitch black. I have to hew closely to Bill's taillights to see where I'm going. The moment he comes to a stop, two bloodhounds rush up and circle the truck. I slam on the brakes to avoid hitting them.

"Go back in," Bill commands, and they head around the back of the shingled house.

We follow. I can barely see where I'm going. Bill directs me, holding my hand.

"Big step. Watch the ground here. Careful."

Wherever we are, the ocean is loud here. I hear it breaking against big rocks, churning then receding. The sliding door in the back is unlocked, and we make out on the kitchen table in the dark. It's as cold inside as it is out. Drafty. Bill is quiet, only speaking in whispers.

"Is there someone else here?" I ask.

"No."

"Is this weird for you, because you knew me when I was a kid?"

Bill covers my mouth with a calloused hand. I bite it. He pushes his mouth into mine, our teething clashing against one another. I taste salt. The sea in the air. Or blood.

I pull my face away. "Don't lie to me," I manage. "Okay?"

"Okay," Bill says, his eyes trained on my mouth. "But no more talking."

The sex is rough and good. The only kind of rough sex the younger guys on the apps know how to have is porn-choreographed, almost hateful. The only other mode they have involves too much talking or, god forbid, a playlist. Bill holds the back of my neck in his thick hands and keeps my head pointing toward him the whole time. He's hairy, and I can grab a fistful from his chest to pull him in when I need to. He is very focused. His breath smells like hot dogs and whiskey. We're sweaty and full, but that's part of it. It's heavy. It's like we're sucking poison out of each other. Like we're exorcising something. I feel like we both might vomit afterwards, but we don't. It's exhausting and narcotic, and I sleep a dreamless, heavy sleep.

I return to Mom's house in the morning, where she is sitting on the couch and reading the *Portland Press Herald* with Wolf.

She looks up and smiles. "Is that a hickey?"

"God. No." I raise my hand to my neck. "This is why I need my own space."

"Come on," Mom says. "I'm glad you're having fun." She follows me to the kitchen, where I fill her biggest glass with orange juice.

"Don't get excited," I say. "It's nothing permanent. He's too old, and I think he's some kind of a libertarian." I nod to her newspaper. "He had the *BDN* in the driveway this morning."

"Oh, who cares," Mom says, even though, for years, she's railed melodramatically against the "fascists" at the *Bangor Daily*.

"I thought you might. He's big into guns."

She makes a face at my glass of juice. "You're just supposed to have a taste of that stuff. It's pure sugar."

Wolfie hasn't come with her, and I feel his absence. "How is our ol' fella?"

"He hurts today. I crushed up a pill, and I put it in some peanut butter."

"One of your pills or one of his?" She has been known to split a Valium with Wolf.

"One of his."

Mom's counter is covered in envelopes. I sift through them.

Some are square and seem like condolence and Mass cards. Some are clearly junk, fat with coupons that Mom won't throw away for things she doesn't need and shouldn't buy. The rest are more bills.

"I know," she says. "Criminals."

"I'll add it to the pile."

She kisses my forehead and fishes her checkbook from her wallet as I scoop everything into a plastic shopping bag. "Here ya go, then. Naughty girl."

I forget about the bills until I'm at work on Monday, eating lunch with Wendy from my department. She opens a salad made entirely of romaine, hard-boiled eggs, and red wine vinegar. It stinks like feet. She tells me about the macros and the protein. Her garden is thriving. Aphids. Lupines that only come in the odd years. She's expecting a big fiddlehead haul with this warmer weather. She'll have a bag for me next week.

I nod. "Thank you, Wends."

She asks me if I'm doing my annual cabbage soup cleanse with Mom—she might join us—and that's how I remember.

"Shit," I say.

"What?" Wendy is startled. She checks over her shoulder and lowers her voice. "What is it?"

"No, sorry," I say. "I forgot to do something this weekend." I shake it off. "You were saying about the carbs? Continue."

"Hon," Wendy says. "You seem out of it. Are you getting enough sleep?" She wags her finger at me. "Self-care. Put your own oxygen mask on first."

The honest answer is that I'm not getting much sleep, but I don't say that, and Wendy keeps talking. She's a good talker. Doesn't overthink it. Works through her thoughts aloud. I watch her teeth grind the chalky yolks to a paste. It's grotesque, but weirdly comforting. I have been losing a lot of time. I unwrapped my TV and my reading lamp, but I still can't focus to read a book or finish an episode of anything. Infomercials are good. There is one for a nonstick pan that I watch. It comes on from 2 to 3 A.M. It's repetitive and satisfying and watching it approximates sleep. Fried eggs, burnt caramels, melted cheese all slide off the shiny green surface with ease. The hosts burn all their food and scrape it away with one pass of a damp sponge. Pure relief.

Last night, Bill texted me late. He wasn't looking for sex. He just wanted to talk. He said his asthma meds make his heart race and keep him up at night. I made him turn on SlipPan, and we both watched together, apart.

Wendy leaves to teach a class, and I open up my laptop to check my work emails. At the top of my inbox: *michaelagreeley17@bcc.edu.*

Michael A. He found me.

Before I can open the email, one of my juniors, Maurice, comes by my desk to take Wendy's place. He eats his lunch here sometimes. I don't ask why.

"I haven't seen you in a few days," I say, trying to appear normal, trying not to reveal how claustrophobic I suddenly feel.

"Everyone says you're in a mood." He unwraps his cream cheese and jelly sandwich. "Even the lunch ladies said I should give you some space."

"But they let you come up today?" I toy with the idea of kicking him out, telling him I do need space, but I'm not sure I want to be alone. I'm not sure I have the nerve to read the email.

"I said I was going to the bathroom." Maurice pauses. "Jamie Mason is a prick, by the way," he says. "No one really cares that you freaked out on him."

"Can I get a chip?" I ask. I consider asking Maurice to read the email for me. It could be an assignment, maybe, a close reading. Summarize it and give me the bullet points.

"Sure." Maurice shakes a few potato chips onto my desk. Without skipping a beat, he asks, "Did you see the body?"

"No, I didn't," I say. "And you shouldn't ask things like that."

"Sorry," he says flatly.

I push the email out of my head. "Is that dress code, Mo?" I gesture to his unbuttoned flannel. Underneath is a vintage Metallica T-shirt.

"Khakis, button-down," he says. "I'm fine."

"How's it going at home?"

Maurice doesn't like talking about his family. His mother and his sister died in a car accident ten years ago. It's still talked about. A bee flew into their car, and Mo's mom panicked and crashed into a tree. I've only met his father once, when he dropped Maurice off for a field trip. He drives an old red pickup truck, and he doesn't speak more than two words at a time. He remarried a real church lady. She comes to the parent conferences.

"It's fine. Went hunting last weekend."

"Do you hunt? I didn't know that."

I have a hard time imagining Maurice holding a gun, never mind killing anything.

"Sometimes."

"What's that like?"

"How?"

"I don't know." I think about Bill's offer to take me to the gun range. How it wasn't paranoia. He wasn't hysterical. It wasn't a big deal at all. It was just a fact of life, as far as he was concerned: you have to be ready to protect yourself from wackjobs. Replaying it in my mind makes me feel less crazy. "Is it . . . fun?"

"Someone's here for you." Maurice gestures to the door, where I half expect to see Michael A. darkening the door frame. Instead, Rick.

"Ms. Angstrom," he says. "Could we speak for a moment? I don't want to interrupt."

"Of course," I say. Maurice is already packing up his lunch. "Could you head back to the cafeteria?"

Maurice mutters something about no time left in the period, and I know he'll probably finish eating his sandwich in the bathroom. Or he'll throw it away. He's not much of an eater. I've developed a taste for cream cheese and jelly due to the number of aluminum-wrapped sandwiches that I've fished from my bin when I'm feeling anxious and need something to chew on. Not today, though. Today I'm banking 650 calories for a full bottle of wine.

Rick takes Maurice's spot. He starts on about grief again, but I'm not listening. All I can think about is the email from Michael A and what he might want.

Rick has spent so many years perfecting the art of saying nothing that he has a hard time getting to the point. I catch, "But who's to say what is normal after all? I certainly—well I mean my mother is someone who had her fair share of troubles to say the least—but then I'm getting away from myself." He spends some time searching for the next part. "Things happen . . . People are who they . . . Sometimes in life—" I zone back out. I don't know what his obsession is with my family or why he can't let me do my job.

"Well, I'm worried about you, Teddy," he says. "Because of your dad, but also with the ten-year mark." He looks wounded. "I thought you might be needing more support." I realize I spoke aloud. I wonder if I used the word obsession. I need to be getting more sleep.

"It couldn't hurt," Rick says, and he pats my knee.

"I think I need to take the rest of the day off," I say. I hear myself say it aloud this time. It's deliberate. The words feel like stones in my mouth, clumsy and heavy, but they're a choice.

"Sure," Rick says, though he looks flustered. "I'll find some coverage, I guess."

"Cancel my classes. Give them a free."

"We don't typically do that."

"I have to go."

I slip out of my heels and into the flats that I keep under my desk. I grab my bag and turn off the light, leaving Rick in the student help chair, in the dark English department room.

I take the drive home fast, reckless. I can feel myself cutting too close to the shoulder and then too close to the line. I feel drunk, but not in a good way. Overwhelmed, out of control.

When I get home, I sprint downstairs and collapse on my pull-out couch. My body feels swollen, and my eyes are sticky.

"Wolf," I call, but he doesn't come. I hear footsteps above me. "Wolf."

I take out my phone and open the email:

> miss angstrom,
> i know you don't know me exactly but I knew your dad. i think that you replied to my post a few nights ago and ive been trying to get in touch since then to see how youre doing. sorry for your loss,
>
> > mg

Brookdale Community College is the place we all made fun of at St. A's. The St. A's kids still do; I hear them, and I tell them that they sound like entitled brats, but they don't care. They compare themselves to the kids at our one deteriorating public school—the children of fishermen and loggers and cashiers. They say things like: "I'm failing calc. I'm so going to end up at Brookdale next year," when they know full well they have a solid B in calc, legacy at Dartmouth, and a safety acceptance at Colby or Bates under their belts.

Despite living within ten miles of the campus, until today, the only other time that I've stepped foot on Brookdale grounds was ten years ago for the high school graduation that Angie was supposed to attend. The church was being renovated that year, and they held it in Brookdale's auditorium, the only nearby space large enough to hold all the families and graduates. I went with some friends to watch Angie's classmates graduate, even though she wasn't there. Mom and Dad didn't come. They had probably imagined it before, when Angie was small—her one-day adulthood. They had probably pictured themselves paunchy, gray, and content. They had gotten so close.

The vice principal, a terminally stern woman, read Angie's name third in the alphabetical order, and no one clapped. There was a moment of silence as Mrs. Barnes held the diploma awkwardly in the air, and that's when I first realized that Angie might actually be dead. When I watched a stream of happy, healthy eighteen-year-olds bounce across the stage in their piss-yellow polyester robes, and my sister wasn't among them.

After the ceremony, I had to watch Angie's peers pose in front of the Brookdale auditorium and point to the sign like it was a joke prop.

"How convenient for all the burnouts," one preppy douchebag said. "They don't have to go anywhere."

I wanted to punch him in the face and spray blood from his nose all over his stupid Honors Society sash, since Angie was one of those burnouts who had planned on two years at Brookdale, but I didn't. Instead, I went limp in the crowd and let myself be pulled into photographs with my older field hockey teammates, the graduating Yearbook staff, and the rest of the student council. I pretended to kiss seniors for the camera. I put in a full day's work smiling wide and avoiding every impulse to bring Angie's name into the conversation and kill the buzz.

The next year, I chose not to walk in my own graduation ceremony. Mom and Dad didn't coax me, not even a little. I was awarded salutatorian, having given up on fighting Anita Lee for valedictorian, and the school mailed me my plaque over the summer. It's still in the box somewhere.

I'm meeting Michael here, in public, at his work. Couched in the woods, on property too low-lying and too far from the coast to be valuable, the school is a sprawl of brutalist one-story structures with a claustrophobically low ceiling and a paucity of sunlight that makes them all feel subterranean. In the library, leaves push right up against the windows, overgrown and untended. The interior is dated and humid and smells like mud. The carpet's geometric pattern must have been bright and modern in the '90s when it was laid, but now it is faded and dirty. The space, devoid of students, is eerily silent, and the shelves are spread so wide that it feels like a bankrupt department store in its last days of a closing sale. By the wall, someone has arranged two outdoor patio tables and a Keurig machine to create a makeshift café. Right next to it: the reference desk.

"Hi," I say, trying to keep a lid on my nerves. "Teddy Angstrom for Michael Greeley."

The young man across from me could be one of my students—small, pubescent, fragrant. "Can I help you with something?"

"Are you Michael?"

"Michael Greeley?" he says, smirking.

"Yes."

He calls behind him, too loud for the library. "Mickey!"

I panic, think about turning and running, but I don't. I wanted to find Michael, and I found Mickey. The person who wrote to me, the person who has been keeping a torch for my family online, and the person on Dad's list are all the same: *Mickey → boyfriend.*

A young woman comes out of the library office and seems to recognize me immediately. She grins and offers her hand, which I shake. Her right arm is inked from the wrist up, and her nails are painted in silver sparkles that catch the light.

"Teddy," I say. "I was looking for Michael."

"Mickey," she says. "Michaela. You're looking for me."

Mickey's nose is pierced with the kind of delicate septum chain that Angie only decided she wanted after she'd already pierced her nostril with a stud. Her hair is purplish black, and where it meets her pale skin at the hairline, it looks like a wig. The blue veins around her temples seem to emerge like tributaries, pumping squid ink through her veins. White skin, gray eyes, tattoos in muted shades of ash and navy—if you were looking at her on the television, you'd try to adjust the saturation. She's full charcoal drawing until she applies her pink Chapstick in a neat circle. I forget how to speak. Mickey is Angie, in another universe, standing here at Brookdale, two years out of high school with more tattoos and more piercings. Smiling. Happier.

"You look . . ." I say, but it trails off. "You're not the boyfriend."

Mickey laughs. "You look like your sister." I can feel her inspecting my face and body now, and I find myself holding still and sucking in my gut. "I thought maybe you wouldn't for some reason. There aren't many pictures of you on the internet."

I clock Mickey noticing the things about me that are like Angie: the dimple in my chin, square jaw, high forehead, attached earlobes.

"Did it stop raining?" she asks.

"It's pretty nice out."

"Great." Mickey turns. "We can sit at one of the tables."

"Wait," I blurt. "He had a note. With your name on it."

The last bit of sanguinity drains from Mickey's face. Her jaw goes slack, and she manages only a small cough.

I realize my mistake. "Oh god," I say. "A regular note. Not that kind of note. I'm sorry."

"You scared me."

"Just said something about a boyfriend. Angie's boyfriend."

"Ah, right," Mickey says. She vanishes into a back office. She looks nothing like Angie, I decide—totally different bone structure. The only thing they have in common is the way they dress. And thousands of teenagers dress like this.

But then she returns from the office holding a plasticky leather jacket, and I'm struck again by the resemblance. I try to imagine my dad in my place—what it would have meant for him to meet a bona fide Angie stand-in. Like hiring a commercial actor to play your lost loved one. Like investing in holograph technology as a way of forestalling grief. Not quite the real thing, but maybe enough of a fix to get by. Maybe if he mixed it with something to blur the edges, he could go back in time.

"Paulie. I'm taking my break."

Out of the corner of my eye, I see Paul glance at the clock and sigh, but I'm already following Mickey through the doors, to the patio area I passed on my way in, where a single concrete picnic table sits, covered in bird shit.

Mickey plops down at a dirty picnic table, and I join her.

She pulls a vape pen from her back pocket and takes a drag. The end lights up neon blue. "Do you want?"

I decline. I want to touch her face.

"I was so upset to hear what happened to him."

It didn't happen *to* him, I think. It happened *of* him. The difference is important. "Can we get back to that note?"

"Oh, I told him about Angie's boyfriend," Mickey says. Vapor pours over her bottom lip when she talks.

"Angie didn't have a boyfriend." I've said it so many times to so many people that it comes out robotic.

"She did."

"What? Who?"

Mickey squints at me. "I thought you weren't into this stuff."

"How do you mean?"

"Your dad said something. Like you and your mom weren't into the Angie stuff. You'd . . . moved on."

I try to mask the anger that I feel welling up by smiling wider. "How did you know my dad, exactly?"

"He used to do research here," Mickey says. "Analog research—archived newspapers and stuff. Before I turned him on to the world wide web." She smiles. "I'm a little obsessed with your sister."

"How old are you?"

"Nineteen," Mickey says.

"So you were—"

"Fifth grade," she says. "I went to the public school here for a couple years. It was all anyone talked about. How this girl from St. A's vanished after a party, and it could just as easily be any one of us."

I cringe, remembering the way Angie's story was framed as a teachable moment: travel in packs, don't get drunk, call your parents, even if you're worried they'll be mad.

The township even held annual vigils that my family boycotted, pretended weren't happening. Only once did Mom acknowledge the events, curling her lip at the discarded candles that had melted into the brick outside the public library.

"They think they can hold a funeral for *my* daughter," she said.

I badly wanted to go. I wanted their funeral. I knew that I would have been the star of the show, had I been allowed to attend. It didn't sound so bad, a public outpouring of sympathy, some acknowledgment that everything was not okay.

"I didn't know about any of this," I say. "I didn't know Angie had a boyfriend."

"What's your deal?" Mickey asks. "Like, what do you do?"

In all their talking, he never mentioned me, except to say that I didn't care about Angie. I manage to form a weak response—"I am a teacher"—but it sounds like it's coming from outside my body, and I don't hear the follow-up question that comes next.

"Teddy?" Mickey says. She is starting to sound far away. "Are you okay? Should I call someone?"

"I'm fine," I say between shallow breaths. "This happens sometimes."

Mickey cups her hands in front of my face, blocking out the sun. "In through the nose," she says, and I inhale concentrated lavender.

"It will pass," I say.

Mickey shushes me. "Now out through the mouth. Don't talk. Breathe." Mickey moves her hands to place her fingers on my temples. "Close your eyes." She rubs in gentle circles and hums.

I feel my neck relax instantly. My shoulders drop down from my ears. "My sister used to do something just like this," I say. I had forgotten about her breathing tricks whenever I was being too anxious, too wound-up.

I hear people mutter as they walk by. "Dykes," one guy says. "Nice."

"Get fucked," Mickey yells, and I can't help but smile. "There she is. Keep breathing."

"Thank you," I say, squinting my eyes open. I can see only her fingers, long and slick with essential oil. "This is helping, weirdly."

"Not weird," Mickey says. "Lavender relaxes." She lowers her hands slowly, and I resist the urge to pull them back. To tell her that it's not the lavender, that, actually, I kind of hate lavender, maybe it's the heat from her palms. To tell her how when we were young, my mom used to lay her hands on a minor cut or scrape and heal it by touch. How lately, when we hug, it's more like she's taking something from me.

"Can we go somewhere?" Mickey asks. "I think you could use a real cup of coffee."

Mickey doesn't have a car, so we take mine to the diner. Mickey insists on driving. I ate here once with Angie, but I don't mention it. It was after she dropped off her enrollment paperwork, just before she went missing. I can't remember what we talked about then, but I remember we were fighting. She was being a brat about Brookdale, and I was being a smug bitch. Something like that.

Mickey orders a combo plate—stack of pancakes and two fried eggs, over medium. Side of ham, side of potatoes, side of white toast, buttered. Earl Grey.

The waitress sees her vape on the table and warns us about smoking in here.

"Of course," Mickey says.

I only order a coffee, but when Mickey's food arrives, she puts a pancake and a piece of toast on her side plate and passes them to me.

"Have some sugar," she says.

"Thanks."

The pancake is tepid and dense, but the fake syrup hits right. "This is good," I say.

"It wasn't that he didn't talk about you," Mickey says. "It's that talking about you seemed hard for him, because I think he knew he was letting you down. Does that make sense?"

"Not really."

"My mom"—Mickey pauses to chew a mouthful of pancake —"left."

"I'm sorry," I say.

Mickey waves me off. "It was a long time ago. When I was little."

"Jesus."

"I imagine it's kind of similar. The feeling. Like how do you do *that* when you have a kid?"

"It's complicated."

"I bet."

"Did you know him well?" I ask.

Mickey shrugs. "Probably not. He liked to talk about Angie. And he needed help with the computer."

"You know, I lived with him," I say. "Like, still."

"I didn't know that."

"In the basement, but same roof," I say.

Mickey stops eating.

"We didn't talk very much," I say. "Not lately."

"I'm sorry."

"I knew things weren't good. But that had been true for a long time. Did you ever think . . . ?"

Mickey shrugs. "I mean—"

"I should probably feel guilty. But mostly I feel like—what could I have done?"

"Sure."

"I'm sorry. I'm rambling," I say. "Anyway, tell me about this boyfriend."

"Oh, Gary?"

"I guess. Is that the guy?"

"I mean, to the extent that they were . . ." Mickey says. She takes a bite that includes one full egg. "It was one of those kiddie things. Internet long distance."

"Did the police know?"

Mickey looked amused. "I don't think he'd be much use. She was his girlfriend the way people have girlfriends in Canada."

"Are you sure it was Gary?" I ask.

"I think so," Mickey says.

"Not Bill?"

She shakes her head. "No, definitely Gary. He was one of the ones big into the case early on. Online. But that was before Reddit and everything."

I nod. "Right."

"Who's Bill?"

"No one," I say. "It's nothing."

"I can try to track Gary down. If you give me a couple days. I'm good at stuff like that."

"No, thank you."

The waitress drops the check on the table, and Mickey grabs it.

"You don't have to do that," I say.

"You only had coffee." Mickey pays in cash.

"Can I drop you off somewhere anyway?" I ask on the way to the car.

"Sure," Mickey says. "I'm over in the student housing."

I park in front of a squat brown structure a few buildings down from the library. It's starting to rain again. Mickey unbuckles her seatbelt and lunges toward me. I flinch back into my chair.

"It's okay," she says. "Relax." She puts her arms around me, lays her head on my frozen shoulder. The hug is awkward and brief. "I'm so glad I finally got to meet you."

"Nice to meet you, too," I say.

She reaches for the door handle. "I'll let you know what I dig up on Gary."

"No," I say. "Please. I'm sorry if I gave you the wrong impression."

"Are you sure?" Mickey says.

"Yes."

"There's a lot more out there online," Mickey says. "Way more than you probably know."

"I don't need it," I say. "I'm trying to clean up this whole mess, not make it worse."

"What do you mean?" Mickey asks.

I could scream. *A man is dead. Don't you get it? He didn't kill himself for your entertainment. We are real people. It's not a hobby for me. It's my life.*

I swallow it down. "Never mind," I say. "Thank you, but no."

Mickey lets herself out of the car. "Take care, I guess," she says. She holds the door open and stares at me for a moment. "Okay. Bye then!"

As soon as she shuts the door, I pull away checking my mirrors and almost get clipped. The other driver leans on their horn, and I slam the brakes. Before I hit the gas again, I check my rearview, and I see Mickey standing in the doorway of her building, watching me go.

I log back onto Reddit and find the private messages I missed when I was watching SlipPan.

> hi theodora. i think this is you? I knew your dad. Would love to chat. He was a good person.

> hi theodora. still havent heard from u. do you want to talk? let me know soon pls!

Then, she must have emailed me at work.

r/AngieAngstrom is blowing up with renewed interest in my sister's case, because Mickey cross-posted a message on r/UnsolvedMysteries, r/CrimeJunkies, and r/WithoutATrace:

> Update: Angie Angstrom (missing 05) – NEED HELP
> i know this is an old case but i was working it with AA's dad, mark (obit here) who killed himself last week. we found a lot of stuff but never got there. i thought mark might be close but guess not. anyone want to share notes? We can take this over to r/AngieAngstrom, too. Don't want to post everything publically tho for obv reasons.

The comments:

- **brewerswife304:** He's not her dad!
  - **manny_manny:** You know what he meant.
    - **cyberbaby22:** nah BWs right . . . its an important distinction. her uncle.
      - **Milk-n-cookies:** What is this case? I don't remember it.
        - **chuckiemansonsfavoriteson:** dO yOu kNoW hOw 2 GoOgLe??? Godddd people are so lazy.
- **RealMaine404:** You're going to drop that but not reply to anything? For real?
  - **DearErnie:** This x100. Where is OP? Why is MICHAELA345 not responding to any of us? Asks for help then peaces out for two days.
- **CatDad0340:** ME! ME! ME! Pick me!
- **tazMAINEian_devil:** Obsessed with this case back in the day, but I thought they found her body in the backyard?
  - **DearErnie:** taz--you're thinking of <u>this case</u>.
    - **tazMAINEian_devil:** Ahhh so I am. Thx much!
      - **DearErnie:** Np. All that backwoods shit starts to blend together after a while.
- **SXC_33590:** What is it with yall and dead white chicks? I swear.
  - **CharlieUniformNovemberTango:** lol cool the PC popo are here
    - **SXC_33590:** I'm just saying—do you have ANY idea how many Black and brown girls have disappeared in the time since this bitch went missing?
      - **CharlieUniformNovemberTango:** i think ur looking for r/WhoGivesAShit

- **SXC_33590:** [removed]
  - **rareJoeyB:** [removed]
- **paul_ruiz:** She was cute! I wonder what she looks like now if she's still out there.
  - **CharlieUniformNovemberTango:** Wasn't she bulimic? Fat. Those girls can never keep up the discipline out of high school.
    - **HELLenOtroy:** what a gross comment.
      - **CharlieUniformNovemberTango:** Boo hoo.
  - **MrGrandPappy:** she probably looks like this:
    - **0nogrl:** can't see the pic!
      - **MrGrandPappy:** f'ing mods flagged it.
        - **0nogrl:** what was it?
- **MM_meg:** MARK? You were on a first name basis with the murderer? Girlllll
  - **usernametbd:** ikr? like the girl who got engaged to manson in prison. wtf is it about these guys.
    - **woo4u:** Yo Angstrom was psycho. Do you remember him beating up that reporter?
      - **usernametbd:** cocaine is one helluva drug, man.
- **paul_ruiz:** First I'm hearing that he died . . . someone just made a bunch of $$$.
  - **MM_meg:** when both ur hubbies die (& they rich) maybe you the guilty one . . .
    - **HELLenOtroy:** They weren't married.
      - **MM_meg:** w/e
  - **woody-alien:** I bet the money went to the kids. Remember the sister?
    - **paul_ruiz:** She was HOT!

- **woody-alien:** What was her name?
  Sammy? I'm trying to find the old posts.
  - **paul_ruiz:** Teddy.
    - **woody-alien:** sexy name even

I message Mickey back.

Hi. Thanks for meeting with me today. Quick question:
do you know my dad's username? Yours, Teddy.

I wait a few minutes, refreshing over and over again, but no response comes in. I go back to the boards and search my own name on each. Two threads appear, both created by a user called SonofaBertha. The first is called *AA's sister total smokeshow* and the second: *Theodora Angstrom, Y or N??*

I feel the same jolt as last time. The shock of seeing my name on the screen tempts me to look away. But I fight the discomfort and push through, feeling awful about the notion that these posts have been here for years. I'm sure that somehow, in some way, I should have been notified. It's strange that these discussions could exist, published and permanent, and I didn't even know.

Both threads are years old and haven't been touched since I was in high school. In fact, SonofaBertha doesn't seem to use the account anymore, though he posted a lot about teen girls in the news way back when. His interest in me, in Angie's case, was not unique.

Both threads include pictures of me pulled from the internet in 2005. I'm a junior in all of them—lanky, flat-chested, and moonfaced, with long dark hair in a sweeping ponytail. Most are from my sports profiles. In those days, we mostly wore Soffe shorts rolled down past our jutting hip bones with sheer wife beaters on top, grazing our belly buttons, but in a few pictures I'm in my full field hockey uniform. In some of the shots, I'm posed, like for a yearbook photo, and in others, I'm in motion, biting down on a mouthguard. I remember wearing push-ups under my sports bras to try to help my case, but you can't tell from the pictures. I can't look at these and not see a child.

- **fulldenimjacket:** Y. For sure. Would bang.
  - **local_perv:** the green shorts kill me
    - **fulldenimjacket:** More than the skirt/knee socks combo? With the stick? You could make her wear that little get up . . .
      - **local_perv:** nvm you're right. skirt > shorts. all about access.
      - **soccerdaddy666:** Shin guards, not knee socks u fucking idiots.
        - **fulldenimjacket:** even better . . . you could slam her around a little bit
- **100pHufflepuff:** Eh. Pity bang. Not much meat on the bones if ya know what I mean.
  - **MrMainer:** Hard agree
- **totes_r_mcgotes-phd:** who does she look like?
  - **local_perv:** ur sister
    - **totes_r_mcgotes-phd:** lol youre only making it better
  - **MrMainer:** her sister
    - **totes_r_mcgotes-phd:** for real tho . . . thats it! i was like I recognize this girl . . . because im on this damn thread every day looking at Angie pictures lol
- **YNotTho:** u just know this bitch would be a beast in the sack

- ○ **local_perv:** damaged girls always the best in bed
  - · **Clevergirl:** Why is that?
    - · **local_perv:** the psychos have to have something going for them
- · **SonofaBertha:** fellas/fans of TA (love that thats her initials btw): you know what today is?
  - ○ **i_feel_ya:** one year countdown to 18!
    - · **newsat11:** Hell yeah!
      - · **local_perv:** I thought 17 was statutory cut off in ME?
        - · **SonofaBertha:** Is it?? Can any1 confirm?
          - · **909lawdr:** confirmed.
            - · **SonofaBertha:** pop bottles baby!

I start to count the upvotes and downvotes, but I stop myself. The calculus is dizzying—trying to figure out the number of users that posted and voted and viewed this discussion over the years. It's scary to imagine dozens of individual men at discrete computer terminals in different parts of the world taking part in this rabid conversation about my teenaged self while I carried on, oblivious. I wonder what my dad made of it, if he even saw these threads. I try to take solace in knowing that if these men saw me now—puffier, flabbier, older—they would walk right by. They would have no interest. It's cold comfort.

The membership of the group has doubled since last week. I have to scroll through recent posts expressing an interest to dive back into the case before I get back to Mickey's *RIP Mark Angstrom* so that I can delete my embarrassing, drunken reply. Now, I see that several others have posted below me.

- **gretelscandystash:** MichaelA, saw ur post re: investigation. Would love to work w you. PM me.
- **Mich_stategg:** I have so much on this case. Let's talk. PM.

When I get to my reply, I notice that someone has responded to me directly. One hour ago, someone named ForgetItJake posted: my personal email address, cell phone number, street address, and faculty picture. He doxxed me.

My head spins. It seems impossible that I'm back here, back in the middle of Angie's drama ten years later. The worst-case scenarios flash.

I click on his profile, but there is nothing there. No picture, no posts. I google "ForgetItJake" but all that comes up is lists of top ten movie moments. Apparently, "Forget it, Jake" is a quote from *Chinatown*, which I've never seen.

I delete my entry, but it doesn't solve the problem. My post reads [removed], but ForgetItJake's response with all my personal information remains, and it already has four upvotes.

I can't fall asleep, so I text Bill and ask if I can come over.

Yes.

I wake Wolfie up on my way out the door, which I feel bad about. He wants to come, but I can't bring him.

Before Bill and I fuck, while we're dry humping on top of the comforter, I ask Bill to show me his gun.

"Which one?" he says. I can tell he likes this kind of foreplay.

"The closest."

He doesn't even have to stand up. He reaches into the bedside table and produces a handgun. I can't make out the details in the dark, but I can feel the cold metal against my skin as he runs it up my inner thigh. I shudder.

"Can I hold it?"

Bill hesitates for a split second. He empties the cartridge before he hands it to me. "It's empty," he says. "Safety's on."

"What if someone came in the night?" I whisper it into his neck, and I can feel the weight of his pelvis against me, getting desperate, impatient.

"I'd protect you."

The sex is good, like before—physical and sedative—and it's worth the urine puddle that will greet me at home in the morning. I sleep like the dead until four, when I am plagued by lucid dreams that hold me in a purgatory between consciousness and unconsciousness.

Angie is standing in front of me, soaking wet. Angie in a sheer white slip, her nipples peeking through the material, her pubic hair a shadow on the fabric. She's smiling, and it's making me nervous. She wants me to cover for her. She's supposed to be in charge, supposed to be watching me, but she has to go somewhere. She'll be home later. I'll be fine for a few hours, she says.

She pours something dark and thick into a short glass. Drink this, she says. I drink. It tastes like vinegar and coats my mouth like cough syrup. Angie's face morphs into Mickey's and then blurs into a streak of beige and black. I feel heavy, and the last thing I see is a glimpse of a tattoo that my parents don't know about. On Angie's ass: a slender snake, wrapping down her leg with the head pointed toward the knee, soft around the edges through the gauze of her dress.

My tongue is bitter and furry in my mouth. I try to find Wolfie with my palm, but I land on Bill's hairy chest instead. I hold on until I know for certain that I'm awake.

"Wake up," I say. "I need to see your computer."

"What?" Bill says, half asleep. "Now?"

"Yes."

"Why?"

"I just do."

"Is your phone dead?"

"Bill." I push him. His eyes open. "Give me your computer."

"It's the middle of the night, Teddy," he says, sitting up. He turns on the light next to him and puts on a pair of glasses I didn't know he had.

"Why won't you let me see it?"

"What do you need it for?"

"I need to see your browser history."

"No," Bill says.

"What do you mean?"

"I don't like this. It feels like you're ambushing me."

"I'm not," I say. "I don't care what's on there."

"Then why do you need to see it?"

"I want to be comfortable here," I say. "I want to be able to trust you."

Bill walks down the hallway, and I follow him. He retrieves the computer from where it was charging next to the microwave. "Whatever," he says.

"Thank you," I say. I take it to the couch. The coffee grinder roars to life in the other room. "This will only take a minute," I yell. "Password?"

Bill appears in the doorway. "All lowercase: rockyroad21."

I open up the three different browsers that he has installed on his PC. The laptop is old, and the effort taxes the machine. Already, the bottom is heating up and the fans are whirring loudly. The only recently used browser is Chrome. The history hasn't been cleared in weeks. Email. Pornhub. Yahoo News. A quiz that promises to identify your age based on your favorite foods. I go back further. More porn. More email. An online record store. A few Google searches: "how+to+get+rid+of+plantar+warts+without+doctor," "when+is+Easter" and—from the day after we first had sex—"Teddy+Angstrom," "Mark+Angstrom," "Angie+Angstrom." No Reddit.

I close the computer.

Bill is sitting at the kitchen table. "Did you find what you needed?"

"You have plantar warts," I say.

Bill nods. "Want to see them?" He lifts his foot and the sole is covered in tiny pieces of duct tape. Some kind of home remedy. I hadn't noticed.

"You watch a lot of porn."

"Nothing weird," Bill mutters at the ground.

I smile.

"Are you done?" he asks.

"I also need your phone."

Bill hands me his phone without protest, and I open the browser. I type in *r*, then *e*, then *d*, but nothing auto populates. The history hasn't been cleared here either. I scroll through the home screen to look for apps, but Bill only has three aside from the preloaded ones—food delivery, banking, and meditation. He's not Jake. He's not involved in any of that. I feel the relief flood my body.

I look up and Bill puts out his hand.

"You meditate?"

"Can I have that back now?"

I start to hand it over, but change my mind and pull it back. Bill rolls his eyes.

"One more thing," I say. "Last thing."

I go to his phone logs to find our call, the one I made from my dad's cell phone. Everything before this week has been cleared. There is no call history.

"What's this?" I say. I turn the screen to him.

He leans forward. "What am I looking at?"

"Where is your call history?"

Bill shrugs. "I had to delete my voicemails the other day. It said I needed room. So I deleted the logs too."

"No one deletes their call logs," I say.

"I did."

"Why?"

Bill inhales dramatically, like he's trying not to lose it. "Teddy," he says. "If you want to accuse me of something, maybe you should just do it."

I shake my head and hand him back the phone. "Are you lying?" I ask.

"About what?" Bill says. He can see it was the wrong answer. "Teddy, come on—"

I'm already putting on my shoes.

"I meant no, of course. I don't even know what we're talking about anymore."

"I have to head home." I go to give him a weak hug, but he grabs me, squeezes my whole body hard. "You have to let go," I say, even though I feel my muscles giving in. "Bill, let go."

Bill releases me, and I grab my bag without making eye contact.

"Text me when you're home," I hear him call, but I'm already too far gone to respond.

It takes a few days, but Mickey replies to my message. Late at night. I'm already on the app when the message comes in. Something about knowing that she and I are on Reddit at the same time sends a small shiver up my spine. I pull my comforter a little tighter.

sry for the delay . . . exams. idk your dads un. prob randomly generated if i had to guess. i dont think he posted. just lurked.

I have a dozen follow-up questions: What did you two talk about? Did he read about himself? How did it feel? Did he tell you? Why did you do this to him? Did you know he was a sensitive person? Did you wonder whether or not he could take it? Do you wonder now if you are responsible?

Instead I type: *I'm not sure it's "lurking" when you are the subject of discussion . . .*

I delete it. I send back: *Thanks!*

I wait, hoping that she might write back, might notice that we're both up at the same time, reading the same things. But she doesn't. Instead, I circle through my subs in an order that is becoming something of a routine: r/Unsolved, r/WithoutATrace, r/MaineCrime, r/CrimeJunkies, and finally r/AngieAngstrom. I sort everything by *new*. I read everything. Multiple times a day.

The biggest event on r/Unsolved today is also a national news story: Holden McGill was identified as the killer of

Natalie Morris, whose burned body was found in the woods of Alabama in 1986. Something about the way they solved it, using questionably obtained DNA evidence, is causing a stir. Lots of debate. It's drowning out almost everything else. Almost. There is another story, less exciting, less gruesome: Marlee Fry was found.

Marlee was a high school junior when she went missing four years ago in Sacramento. The blond and beautiful cheerleader type that makes the news and stays there, she was similar to Angie in one regard: circumstances. Marlee went out to a party and she never came back.

I remember seeing her face for months, learning all about her life in California. I remember Mom being very invested in the case, clucking every time they showed her mother and stepdad crying on the TV, begging for answers.

Just yesterday, Marlee was found at a pet store in Kansas City. Someone from her high school who had moved to the area for college recognized her, despite the hair dye and the glasses and the nametag that read *Jenny*. Marlee had been living with her stepdad's estranged daughter and the daughter's family.

At first, the response on the thread had been overwhelmingly negative: *her poor mother; what a sociopath; add this to the list of reasons why I'm never having kids.*

Then, just yesterday, it came out that the stepdad, now dead of a heart attack, had abused Marlee and his older daughter before her. That Marlee told her mom, and her mom did nothing. Called Marlee a liar, called her a slut. That Marlee had found the man's daughter, who hadn't spoken with him in a decade, who didn't know her father remarried. That the daughter had believed her immediately, helped her plan her escape, allowed her to live rent-free in her home for years, allowed her to be Auntie Jenny to her kids, never even told her own husband Marlee's real name.

Now *Thelma & Louise* gifs abound on the thread. So do the refrains of "allegedly" from the stepdad's anonymous defenders, who feel that it is a little too convenient for someone to have been raped by a man who died of a heart attack before he could refute the claims. What's that about anyway?

I think about sending Mickey a link to the thread: *Did you see they found the Fry girl?* But I don't. Not yet, anyway. Instead, I study pictures of Marlee—then and now. She looks different, even aside from the hair and pet store uniform. Her face thinned out, her acne disappeared. She grew up. It's funny how you can look at a younger picture of someone and recognize the themness immediately, but it's not always so easy to imagine someone young older.

I close my computer for the night. Maybe I wouldn't even recognize Angie now. Maybe she has a few crow's feet and she let her hair go back to red, and she took the nose ring out, and she gained thirty pounds. Maybe I'd walk right by her on the street, looking for girls like Mickey.

I discover, in my digging, that Dad gave up around Christmas. The bills have been past due for months. The cable company gives me a hard time about clearing the balance, because my name is not on the account. Mom's name is not even on the account. They finally let up when I explain that the account holder can't come to the phone because he launched himself to the bottom of a river. I use my own savings to take care of the remainder.

Mom helps me comb through the bank statements. There is a monthly withdrawal that neither of us can figure out. It goes back as far as all the statements we have, which is the last year or so. Two thousand dollars. Every month, like clockwork, my check would hit their account for $1,800, and then two days later, my dad would withdraw $2,000 in cash. Mom is convinced it's sewed into the curtains.

"When people get batty, they do things like that," she insists. "I saw it with an aunt of mine back home."

"She sewed money into the curtains?"

"Cash in the curtains, mattresses, taped under cupboards," Mom says. "We'll find it."

"Maybe."

"It's funny, that paranoia about money. Sure sign of a sick brain."

"Hilarious."

"It'll turn up," Mom says. She pats me on the back and dismisses herself back to reading in the other room.

Next on the docket is a bill that is nothing more than a piece of yellow legal paper in a blue envelope. Handwritten. It's for ten hours of psychic counseling by phone. There is a name at the bottom that I'm sure can't be real: Celeste Starling.

I call an 802 number scrawled beneath, and a woman picks up.

"I'm looking for Celeste," I say.

"This is she."

"Great. I'm looking at a bill that my mother received for over a thousand dollars, and I'm going to need you to clear this up for me."

"What's your mother's name, sweetie?"

"Actually, you billed my father. His name was—"

"Oh, Mark," she says. "I've been wondering if I'd hear from you."

"I assume you saw the news?" I say. I don't want her thinking she tricked me into believing that she intuited the name.

"Yes, I did. Oh, Teddy, I'm sorry for your loss. Your dad was a wonderful man. So sweet."

"Yes, well. Thank you," I say. "He told you my name?"

"Of course. We spent many hours talking."

"Yeah, well, that brings me back to my reason for calling, which is this bill for ten hours of 'psychic counseling.'"

"Sure."

"What is that, exactly?" I say. "Other than expensive."

"I'm happy to explain, but if the cost is an issue . . ." She makes a sympathetic noise. "I don't want to put you or your mom out. I sent that bill before . . . you know, obviously."

"Okay," I say. "So I can chuck this?"

"I'll leave that up you, hon. Pay whatever you feel is right."

"And what is psychic counseling?"

"It can be many things. In your father's case, he was mostly interested in using my gifts to get in touch with your sister's spirit. With Angela."

I grit my teeth. "Angelina," I say. "Not Angela."

"It's a long process, and I'd be oversimplifying it if I tried to explain, but basically I commune with her spirit to help determine her location. I use many different methods. I have charts and maps specifically for this purpose. It's my specialty."

"What is?"

"Missing persons."

"Charts and maps," I say, incredulous.

"Mmhmm. Some I made myself, and they work with magnetism and energy that's tied to my particular aura, and then some are just good old-fashioned maps. And some not so old-fashioned ones. Google Maps is a big part of it!" She laughs, and I feel the blood pounding behind my eyes.

"How long was this going on?"

"Oh, I've worked with your father on and off for a few years. The work is better and more accurate with additional information so when he got new leads, that's usually when we'd try to—for lack of a better word—speak with Angela again."

"Angie."

"We were finally getting somewhere, I thought. I'm not sure if you are interested, but I'd be happy to continue our work—"

"Oh, I bet you would," I say.

"I would," Celeste says, so earnestly that I wish I could reach through the phone and throttle her. "You know she's not dead, Teddy. Well, she's not buried, at least. I don't believe she's dead. Though she was in a body of water at one point."

"You should be ashamed of yourself," I say. "Taking advantage of people like this."

I surprise myself with how much I sound like Mom.

"Teddy," she says. "It's not like that. I know that it's hard to let yourself believe." She sighs. "Here, can we try something?"

"What?"

"Can you give me a couple minutes of your time? I won't charge you anything. You seem like you need some help."

I'm angry, but curious. "Fine," I say.

"You've taken a new interest in your sister's case," Celeste says. I can't tell if it's a statement or a question, so I don't respond. She takes my silence for an affirmation and hums accordingly. "It's causing you some distress."

"Wow," I say. "You could tell that my sister's disappearance and my father's death are causing me distress. That's incredible."

"Not them," Celeste says. "There's someone else." She pauses and waits for me to speak; my silence forces her to continue: "I see a young woman. Angelina, perhaps. She has dark hair, tattoos."

"Okay," I say. This is all in the missing persons description.

"She's smoking a cigarette."

"Sure."

"She is trying to indicate something. She loves you, but something is wrong. There's something not right in it."

"What?"

"I see danger," Celeste says. Her voice is starting to waver. "I'm sorry, I can't proceed." She clears her throat, and when she speaks again, it's not dreamy at all. She sounds fearful, stern. "I think you should keep your distance from all this," Celeste says.

"Are you serious?"

"Yes," Celeste says. "I'm sorry."

"After all that," I say. "After you gave my dad false hope. For years." Celeste is calmly protesting on the other line, but all I can think of is his office, clotted with insane notebooks and papers. His flip phone plugged into the wall, old rotary on the floor by the desk. He must have sat on the ground and called Celeste late at night, when he knew Mom would be asleep and the line would be clear. He must have sent her Angie's photo, Angie's things, to touch and read and use as fodder.

"It killed him," I say. "You did." It's a whisper, but it shuts her up. I hear the line go dead.

All totaled, I receive texts from four strange numbers thanks to ForgetItJake's doxxing. They come in over the course of four days, and each one takes me hours to work up the nerve to open, but in the end, they're not that bad. Standard internet fare:

1. XXX-XXX-4565: two dick pics sent at two am on consecutive nights, featuring a purplish erection being choked by a gnarled hand with hairy knuckles, accompanied by a message: *coming to rape and kill you bitch*
2. XXX-XXX-4241: *Hi baby girl*
3. XXX-XXX-1384: a link to a pornographic website
4. XXX-XXX-8871: *i know who killed your sister*

I manage to block the first three numbers, though I suspect that the third number and the first might be the same person. Same area code. I text the fourth one. I can't help myself. I know he doesn't have any information, but I have to be sure. He sends me a gif of Grimace from McDonald's jerking off. I block him, too.

I click on the username: *ForgetItJake*. Nothing comes up— just the response to my post.

I email Mickey: *Hi Michaela, it's Teddy Angstrom again. I was hoping you could help with a quick question about something.*

I sign off with my cell phone number, and within a minute the phone rings. "Hi, Teddy," Mickey says, monotone. She sounds ill. "What do you need?"

"So, there's this guy—ForgetItJake."

Mickey makes a sound of affirmation.

"Do you know him?" I ask.

"I saw he doxxed you."

"Yeah," I say. I guess I shouldn't be surprised that she knows what's been going on. "I got a bunch of dick pics."

"We looked at Jake for a while. Weird posts."

"When I tried to look for his history, there was nothing."

"He deletes." I wait for her to explain further, but again there is only silence.

"Did you track down Gary?" I ask.

"You said not to."

"Do you think he could be this Jake guy? The same person?"

"No," Mickey says. "Probably not. All I have for Gary is an AIM username. I'm not sure it's still operational."

I remember Angie on AIM all the time in our shared bedroom. There was a computer on the desk that's not there anymore—a translucent orange Mac that was shaped like an anvil. It was supposed to be both of ours, for homework, but really it was hers. She stayed up all night talking to god only knows who. On AIM. On MySpace. Angie was very online at a time when that made you a certain type of weirdo. From my bed, I could see her lit up in the blue glow of the screen. I could hear only the tapping of her hunt-and-peck and the occasional under-the-breath giggle. She would never tell me what she was talking about. She wouldn't even add me as a friend. She didn't want me to see her profile. Now, I'm wondering if that's because she had something written in there. His initials and hers. A telling song lyric. Something.

"I saw you were looking for help with Angie's case. On Reddit." There is a long pause. "Can you not do that?"

Mickey mumbles something unintelligible.

I hate the idea of her trading on her relationship with my dad, feeding the wackjobs' demand for our personal information and keeping them going. "I will answer any questions you have."

"Really?" Mickey perks up. "I could look into Jake for you. Help you get his post down."

"Sure, that would be great."

"Could we meet up this weekend?"

"Okay," I say, trying to hide the reluctance in my voice. "I guess this weekend is fine."

"The library or your house? My roommate is always here."

"Not the library," I say. Too public. I think about my mom. How upset she would be by the prospect of us digging up all of this information on Angie. "My house is no good either. My roommate . . ."

"Your mom?"

"You know what—let's meet at my apartment. I have this new place. I was supposed to move in a few weeks ago. It's just sitting there. I'll text you the address."

"I'll see you soon," Mickey says.

I remember Angie's old screenname, because she and Mom fought about it: BigRed22. Mom thought she was trying to sound sexy and older. Angie argued that it was just her birthday tacked onto the end of a reference to her hair color. She had created the account before she started dyeing it black and blue.

When I ask Bill if he has an AIM screenname, he thinks I'm joking.

Does this mean we're on speaking terms? he texts.

Bill and I have both forgotten our old credentials, so we have to create new ones. He texts me his: WilliamFRooney75. I plug my first name into an online screenname generator and it suggests: FarTed, DeathbedTed, TeddySteady, and TedHead. So I go with TedHead. I have to add an underscore though, because TedHead is already taken.

Ted_Head: Hi
WilliamFRooney75: there she is
WilliamFRooney75: is ted head the best you could do?
Ted_Head: Listen, be glad it wasn't Farted.
WilliamFRooney75: lol why would it be farted???
Ted_Head: I feel like I'm in high school, staying up late talking to boys.

WilliamFRooney75: boys, huh? names pls
Ted_Head: Oh, stop that.

For a split second, I consider explaining about ForgetItJake, about all of the Reddit stuff, but it passes. I say nothing.

WilliamFRooney75: im messing w/ u ;)
Ted_Head: How old were you when AIM was big anyway? Like 30?
WilliamFRooney75: late 20s or so
Ted_Head: Who did you talk to?
Your buddy is typing. Your buddy has stopped typing.
Ted_Head: Girls?
Your buddy is typing. Your buddy has stopped typing.
Ted_Head: ???
WilliamFRooney75: i was into chat rooms for a bit
Ted_Head: Dirty chat rooms?
WilliamFRooney75: regular old chat rooms
Ted_Head: What did you talk about?
WilliamFRooney75: idk normal stuff. baseball. the dead. construction.
Ted_Head: Sounds boring.
WilliamFRooney75: it was nice.
WilliamFRooney75: so is talking to you like this
WilliamFRooney75: i have a hard time saying what i want to say on the phone
Ted_Head: like?
WilliamFRooney75: like im sorry
Ted_Head: For what?
WilliamFRooney75: for deleting the logs

I start typing, but then I stop.

WilliamFRooney75: your dad called me
WilliamFRooney75: a bunch
WilliamFRooney75: left some voicemails

I can feel my heart beating in my ears. A line from a book pops into my head, but I can't remember the title. One of the pulpy detective novels I read over summer breaks. It was something like: *When someone is confessing, the best thing you can say is nothing. Let them fill the silence.* I stare at the screen until I can make out the outline of each pixelated box. It takes all the restraint I have not to respond. Finally: *Your buddy is typing.*

WilliamFRooney75: i never called him back
Ted_Head: Why? What did he want?
WilliamFRooney75: drugs
WilliamFRooney75: i think

I stare at the chat waiting for another message to pop up, aware that he is doing the same on his end, staring into the empty text box on his screen. The silence in my room feels heavy.

Ted_Head: Why would he call you?
WilliamFRooney75: idk
WilliamFRooney75: he might have been trying to track
    down my mom
Ted_Head: Did they know each other?
WilliamFRooney75: its a small world at the bottom.
Ted_Head: Why didn't you tell me?
Ted_Head: Why did you delete the logs?
WilliamFRooney75: I did it after you called and said he
    died

WilliamFRooney75: i panicked . . . it didn't seem smart
  to have them on my phone

I feel embarrassed for thinking that my dad had Bill's number
for any other reason. Of course it was for drugs. What else did
he care about as much? Not Angie. Not quite.

I try to put myself in Bill's shoes. My mother dies. A man,
a friend of hers, calls me after she's dead looking for a fix. I'm
sure I don't answer that call. I'm probably angry about it, the
callousness, the impropriety. Then the man's daughter calls
me—he's dead. This was a man in whom the cops had taken a
keen interest in the past. A publicly keen interest. I guess I delete
the calls. I guess I try to decontaminate myself.

When I was at his house, I poked around Bill's medicine
cabinet. It's filled with things like vinegar and fish oil. Honey,
petroleum jelly, Epsom salts. A neti pot. Aside from his albuterol,
he doesn't believe in pharmaceuticals. He uses tape to treat his
warts. I can picture him dumping her stash into the toilet. It
would have been the first thing he did. He would have wanted
to be rid of it.

Bill messages me again. He changes the subject. He asks how
I'm holding up. How's Mom?

She's hanging in there, I say. I don't mean to tell him about her
money troubles—about the library girl and the psychic and the
ludicrous mess of Dad's investigation. Still, in the quiet and the dark,
the words pour out. It's not like texting; I can't multitask. My
entire focus is on the screen in front of me, the conversation that
is zipping up and down wires so fast it feels seamless. I remember
the days when I would toggle between multiple conversations,
rectangular boxes piling on top of one another on the screen.
Whatever happened to those people? All that intimacy, vanished.
No trace. No letters left behind. Now, my Friends list has one

name: WilliamFRooney75. And I find myself typing some things I haven't been able to say to anyone else, like how I didn't know my dad by the end, and how I never stopped hoping we'd find Angie. More specifically—I never stopped hoping we'd find her body.

> WilliamFRooney75: sure, makes sense.
> Ted_Head: I think that's why my mom is so mad at him,
>   you know?
> Ted_Head: People with kids . . . they want to think that
>   if they lost their kid, they'd die.
> Ted_Head: They couldn't go on.
> Ted_Head: But most people can, it turns out
> WilliamFRooney75: What was she supposed to do?
>   She had you
> Ted_Head: No, I know. That's not what I'm saying.
> Ted_Head: I just mean . . . he really couldn't

Bill writes back what everyone thinks when it comes to my dad and Angie: *and she wasn't even his kid*.

Before I log off, I search for my sister's profile. Her screenname yields nothing. I don't know what I was hoping for—one of her away messages maybe. A cryptic song lyric. A glimpse at her meticulously curated profile, all neon lettering on a black background.

I go to MySpace.com, unsure if it even still exists. I search her name on the site, but nothing comes up. I search her screenname. Still nothing. I search "BigRed22@aol.com" and I get something. From *Mixes* → *Classic* → *You* from the homepage, and all of a sudden, Angie's MySpace pops up, a page I forgot I knew. Her profile picture is a shot of her on the day we got Wolfie.

"Sweet boy," I say, reaching over to pat him. He lifts his head and lets it thunk back down.

Angie's page is surprisingly anemic. Her interests are blank, her photos are nonexistent beyond the profile picture. Her Top Friends box on the side of the page has four people, and one of them is "Tom," the founder of MySpace. The other three are blank gray boxes—deleted accounts. The site has her age listed as 28, but her last login was a week before she disappeared. Her about me: "Bitch. Slut. Loser. Whatever."

There are two comments on her MySpace page, and both are from after she died. One is by Shannon, our old neighbor, who moved away when we were little: *Praying for you, Angie!!* The other is by a guy named Gary, whose picture is a cartoon drawing of a mouse in pants, with an erection: *You were always my favorite loser.*

I click through to his profile.

Gary's profile is much more extensive than Mickey's. He obviously used the account well into 2008, which is the date on his last post. There are no pictures of his human form on the site. Rather, he uploaded dozens of cartoon drawings—all lewd but fairly artistic. He took the time to fill out his cultural interests. His favorite bands were Korn, Garbage, and Hole, but his taste in movies was classic meets stoner: *Casablanca*, *Wayne's World*, *The Big Lebowski*, and—*Chinatown*.

There is little useful information about Gary in his profile, and no other way to connect him to Angie. No shared posts or comments mentioning her, no friends in common. His profile has him listed as living in Glendale, hours north of here. His last name is Foff, which doesn't ring any bells for me.

I call Mickey and apologize for the late hour.

"No prob," she says. "I'm up."

"Can I send you something?"

"It's not Foff. It's eff off," Mickey says after she picks through his profile. I feel like an idiot. "The Gary I remember from back then didn't seem like the doxxing type, but then people are strange."

"To still be at it after all this time," I say.

"Well, with the news about your dad," Mickey says. "Maybe he saw her name in the paper again. Renewed interest."

"I guess."

"You go to sleep," Mickey says. "I'll find him."

"Thank you," I say. It's comforting how assertive she is, how take-charge. I know she's younger than me—by a lot—but on the phone she seems older. It's nice to have some help. All of this stuff makes me feel like I'm sixteen again and drowning.

At first, I can barely sleep. This is a proper lead, I think. I wish I had a printer so that I could tack Gary's MySpace page up to my wall. Progress. But then, as I turn it over in my head, it loses coherence. So this kid liked *Chinatown*? It's not exactly an obscure film. I wonder what this looks like from the outside— me and some teenage girl I've invited into my home, poring through old MySpace pages, hanging on movie quotes, making the same mistakes as my dad, seeing signs and symbols all around us, looking for psychics and charlatans and pretend boyfriends named Gary who draw pornographic cartoons.

Just before sleep closes in on my brain, another thought emerges from the blackness of my subconscious, almost like a nightmare. I remember calling Bill's number, the one my dad had scrawled out in his chicken scratch. He answered. He thought my dad was calling, and he answered right away.

He said he never answered.

The days drag in advance of my meeting with Mickey. I check Reddit obsessively, hourly, but there is little movement on the boards. Jake's post with all my personal information was removed, and the renewed interest in my sister has died down.

More notices pour in to Mom's house: domain hosts threatening to release FindAngie.com, Dad's defunct tip website; unpaid vet bills; pharmacies—some more than three towns over—calling to say the card was declined for this month's supply of Lexapro, Wellbutrin, Adderall, Lipitor, lithium, prednisone.

Recent items on my parents' joint credit card statements baffle. Three separate charges for "Cigars" that appear after Dad's suicide. Recurring debits for water bottles that never make their way to the house.

I call Chase and American Express daily to obtain information about a vendor, deny a charge, report fraud, or pay off a debt. I have mastered the art of pretending to be Mom.

She wordlessly hands me more statements with the charges circled in red pen.

"Jesus," I say. "What the fuck is CoedSleepovers?"

"That's not mine," she says. "It's a porno site. I looked it up."

"I know it's not yours." I scan the statement for anything else unusual. "You shouldn't look at this anymore. I'll handle it. Don't open the envelopes."

"I'm shocked he could keep an erection with the number of pills he was taking," she says, tying her hair up in one elegant motion. She wanders into the kitchen to fix me something. "Fair play to him, I suppose."

"Mom," I say. "That's disgusting. I'm sure it's fraud."

Every time I feel I've made some headway, more shit emerges. Today, I tackle the upstairs medicine cabinet and discover—alongside a half-full bottle of lithium pills and his heart medication—stashes of ground powders in various shades of white. Dozens of pills pre-crushed and returned to their respective orange bottles. Unlike the antidepressants and the blood pressure meds, the labels have been peeled off of these bottles, and the gluey paper residue used as a background for handwritten Sharpie labels. *OXY, XANAX, DILAUDID.*

I dump everything down the toilet, including an empty pen casing covered in chalky residue and dried snot, before I remember that we're not supposed to contaminate the water supply like that. Oh well. Isn't a person supposed to get his affairs in order *before* he kills himself? Would it have been so hard to tidy up a little bit? This, my inheritance. I'm beginning to believe that he hated me.

I throw away the empty orange bottles, except for the Oxy, which still has a small amount of crumbly, bitter powder stuck to the bottom. I add tap water and turn it into a shot. It leaves a mild chemical taste in my mouth, but in a matter of minutes, I feel a bit better. I remember getting Vicodin after I got my wisdom teeth out in high school, the sweet floaty dopamine in my blood, the euphoric rush of those first few pills. My mom threw away the rest before we made it home.

"I don't like the look in your eye when you take those," she said. "You can handle the pain. It's not so bad." She put three extra strength Advil in my hand, and I felt my neck get hot with anger.

"Mom," I growled. "Are you kidding me?" I felt sure I would die.

"That's the look," she said, kissing me on the forehead and turning to leave. I threw my Advil at the back of her head, and she stopped, picked them up from the floor, and kept going. I feel bad about that now.

I refill the pill bottle with water and rinse my mouth out. It feels so small in my hand, so insignificant. I run my thumb over the rough residue where the label used to be and smudge the Sharpie ink that had been sitting on top of the glue. There is a part of the laminated label intact, part of it that tore unevenly, leaving behind a triangular patch with three typed letters on it—*RON*.

Dinner goes by in a blur. Mom isn't in the mood for talking, and I am enjoying the effects of red wine with my Oxy residue, so we sit in silence. Neither of us eats very much. Wolf lies across my bare feet, and I knead the thinning fur of his belly with my toes.

"What's going on with your fella?" Mom asks, right as I stand to clear our plates. I'm happy to busy my hands in the sink while I talk and have an excuse not to make limp eye contact with her.

"He's good," I say. I haven't told her that my fella is Bill, who used to mow our lawn. For some reason, it's not the connection to Dad or Angie or even that he's too old. I just don't think she'd approve of his job. She can be snobby, Mom.

"Can I meet him?" she asks.

"You'll meet him soon," I say.

"Maybe you'll invite him for dinner."

"Maybe."

"What does he like to eat?" Mom asks.

"Meat," I say, marveling at how slow my brain is working, how long it takes for the words to bubble up to the surface. "He likes meat."

"Meat," Mom repeats. "I can cook meat."

I rinse the back of the ceramic plate I'm holding. It is a cheap and plain addition to the kitchen from one of Mom's recent, unnecessary shopping sprees. There is a price sticker still on the back: *HomeGoods, $9.95*.

I mindlessly pick at the damp corner of the sticker while she yammers on about something. Pick, pick, pick. It comes up from the plate, and I roll it, slowly, all the way down, until the sticker is off and I'm holding it in my hand like a tiny cigar.

"I'll take that," Mom says. She knows I don't like her buying more and more stuff all the time.

"Thanks," I say, but when she goes to grab it, I don't let go. There is something else.

"Teddy," she says. "Let go."

"Hold on," I say. I close my eyes and roll the sticky tube between my fingers. "It's right there." If I were a little more alert, I'd have it. I know it.

Mom rips it from my hand. "You're being very strange," she says.

There he is—Bill. Sitting across from me at the Shifty, peeling the labels from his beers methodically. Rolling them back until they lay flat in the condensation on the bottle.

I leave the sink running and go back upstairs. I can hear Mom calling me, but I don't respond. The bottles in the garbage are all stripped of their labels. The handwritten replacements are in a blocky caps. I can't discern any handwriting features. I check the others for any left-behind pieces of the original pharmaceutical text but they were done with more care. Only the last one—the Oxy—was done in haste.

Bits of paper still stuck to the glue. The computer-printed *RON* staring back at me.

I START TO REHEARSE what I'll say to Bill, but save it for tomorrow, for morning, when I'm thinking clearly. Before bed, I check my Reddit as a force of habit and find I have a new message—from ForgetItJake. The subject line is: *Hi Teddy*.

The adrenaline is sobering. I have to hold my breath to open the message, not knowing what to expect. Inside is a single link to imgur. I click through, prepared for a pop-up or a virus to overtake my computer, but a picture loads on a black background. It's blurry and narrow—a picture of a picture. Instant film, like Polaroid, but the borders have a pink and yellow floral print, like my old Barbie camera. The left side is cut off and the dimensions are skewed, but there she is, taking up what's left of the frame—Angie.

I don't recognize the house she's in. Everything is yellow-orange—the carpet, the checkered couch, the paneled walls. It doesn't look like any of our friends' houses. It looks older, dingier than anything I can remember from childhood. Angie is wearing the same oversized neon green *St. A's Class of '05* T-shirt that she left the house wearing the night she went missing. Her pants are missing. She wears men's boxer shorts like pajamas. The rose tattoo on her leg—the last one she got before she went missing—is there, bandaged off.

This is it. This is the night. And she is with someone. Someone is cropped out along with the left border.

Then I look at Angie's face, and I have a hard time focusing on Jake. She's half-bent, laughing, knees together like she's trying to keep from peeing. Her hair falling loose from a pony-tail. She looks drunk, young, happy. I can't help but smile. It's like seeing her again for the first time in years.

I place my laptop on the pillow next to me. Wolfie lies on one side, and on the other, Angie. This might be the most joyful picture I've seen of her as a teenager. Our childhood pictures are sweet, but the ones from her teenage years are sullen, resigned, and sarcastic. I can hear that crazy laugh in my head. I remember the way she used to wet herself if she really lost it. How she would literally cross her ankles to hold it in, like a child. I remember how good it felt to be the person who made her laugh that hard. I only achieved it once.

I touch the screen with my index finger and feel the static fuzz of her skin. She's not hiding behind a curtain of flat-ironed hair, she's not caked in makeup. She's not worried about her pale skin or her fat thighs or whatever else. Wherever she is, whomever she's with, she seems free.

I drift off to sleep without meaning to, and I dream of Angie. She's splashing around in an inflatable kiddie pool, laughing with her eyes closed. I'm trying to get her attention. She's too big to be in that pool. I'm trying to tell her that she needs to come back inside, but she's not listening.

I WAKE WHEN THE sun starts streaming through the blinds, and my computer is next to me, still open, but dead. It charges as I shower, and I check my private Reddit messages again before I leave. This time, though, the link is dead. When I follow it, I get an error message—*image not found*.

Panicking, I slowly type "imgur" into my search bar. The saved address repopulates. But again—*image not found*. Gone.

He deleted it. I didn't know he could do that. Angie's face gone. I close my eyes and try to remember perfectly, pixel for pixel, the image. The carpet, the couch, the shirt. But already it's blurrier. Already, I've lost the exact angle of her neck. Was her mouth open or closed? Were her ankles crossed or were her knees pressed together? How will I find him if I can't find that house?

I reload my inbox over and over until I'm late for work. I can't believe I didn't think to download it or take a screenshot. I can't believe I allowed myself to lose more of her in the night.

Once I'm at school, I send a one-line message to ForgetItJake: *Please. Whoever you are. Talk to me.*

I can't stop thinking about the picture, so I check my inbox again. Still no response from Jake. I text Bill and ask if he's home. Can I meet him at his house?

would love it

When I get there, he's on his hands and knees, cleaning the kitchen floor with a ratty scrub brush and mason jar filled with clear fluid.

"It stinks in here," I say. "What is that?"

"It's proprietary," Bill says, smiling. He stands and comes toward me. Kisses me on the cheek. I stiffen my spine to keep from yanking myself backwards. "Vinegar, lemon juice, dish soap, water."

He peels off his rubber gloves and throws them down on top of a wet rag.

"This is why your house always smells like salad dressing," I say.

Bill makes a face. "Does it?"

In truth, his house is immaculate. I assumed he had a woman who came and bleached the tubs or something, because I've never known a man to clean like this.

"Can I get you something?" Bill asks. He gestures for me to sit at the kitchen table.

"Sure," I say. "Water is good."

Bill fills me a glass of water.

"Hey, what was your mom's name, by the way?"

Bill puts the glass in front of me and sits across from me. He is wearing a white T-shirt and jeans and is covered in a thin layer of perspiration. "Oh, yeah. She kept her maiden. Smith."

I take a sip. "No, her first name."

"Shari."

"Sharon?"

"Everyone called her Shari."

I nod. "Hey, do you remember when I first called you?"

Bill shifts in his seat. His face drops. We're back to this. "Yes," he says.

"You answered."

Bill waits like there is more coming. "Right," he says, when it's clear I'm done speaking. "You called. I answered."

"You said you never answered my dad's calls. You said you let them go to voicemail. You never talked to him."

I'm watching Bill closely enough to see his pupils widen, before he looks down to his lap. "Yep," he says. "I hadn't answered before."

"Why that time?"

"I don't know," Bill says. "I guess I just felt like picking up."

I pull the Oxy bottle from my purse and slide it across the table to him. He won't touch it. He looks at it like I've placed a dead rat on his kitchen table.

"Do you know what this is?"

"Oxy," Bill reads.

I turn the bottle sideways in my hand, until the piece of label is facing him. "R-O-N," I say. "My dad's name was Mark. Angstrom-comma-Mark."

Bill looks away, locates Rocky and Red curled up together by the doorway.

"You know what would fit right here?" I continue. "Smith-comma-Sharon. S-H-A . . ." I tap the place where the label used to be.

"R-O-N," Bill finishes.

We sit in silence. I can tell from the clock behind him that three minutes pass. My entire body burns hot, even though the house is cold. Bill turns his head into his shoulder and clears his throat twice.

I'm surprised by my visceral, hostile reaction. By how much I sound like my mother. "Are you crying?"

"No," Bill says.

"Talk," I say. "Don't lie."

"You know everything," Bill says. "What is left to say?"

"He called you for drugs," I say.

"He knew my mom had stuff," Bill says. "He knew she died, and he knew she must have left some stuff behind."

It's not an accusation, but I feel myself preparing a defense for my dad on instinct. For such inexcusably ugly behavior.

"He offered me a grand for everything," Bill continues. "And I needed the money for the funeral . . ." His voice trails off. "I didn't think about it. I just wanted it gone."

I imagine someone calling the house, looking for Dad's stash. Mom answering the phone for some junkie ready to pick through his room like a vulture. A wave of shame.

Bill reaches for my hands. He squeezes them until I look at him.

"Did you crush everything up?" I ask.

"No," he says. "She did."

"Why?"

"When you called and said he died—" He lowers his voice

to a whisper. "I thought it might be my fault. Since I gave him the bottles."

I shake my hands loose. "He would have just gotten it somewhere else," I say. "It doesn't matter."

"I can't imagine how mad you must be," Bill says.

"I needed to know, and now I know." I want to leave. I want to get back to my computer, to finding things out, to fixing them. I don't want any more tears, any more hand-holding, any more of this sick shit.

"Teddy," Bill says. "I'm so sorry."

Stop, I want to shout. *I'm being sad now. You don't get to be sad.*

"It's fine," I say, standing up without looking at his irritating, earnest face. "We don't even know each other. I would have done the same thing, maybe."

I let myself out the back door and into my car. I still have the Oxy bottle, so I chuck it out the window, onto Bill's lawn, and it lands next to the pile of buoys.

It takes me a minute to find Mom when I get home. She's upstairs in Dad's room, lying in his bed with her back to the door, clutching his pillow between her knees and her chest. I know she can hear my footsteps coming down the hallway, but she doesn't turn around. I know she can hear the hinge creak open a few more inches.

I stand there for a moment in the doorway watching the breath move through her body like a shudder. She doesn't make any noise. I could walk over to her and touch her face with the back of my hand, but I don't. It's not me she's missing. Instead, I close the door and walk down the hallway to the stairs. Down the stairs to the door. Out the door and to my car. I'm driving before I realize that I'm going to the beach.

I read somewhere that most people die at twenty-five but are buried at seventy-five. A student essay, I think. One of those bad intro paragraphs where they attribute Maya Angelou quotes to "Anonymous" and attribute anonymous quotes to Ben Franklin.

I remember reading it and thinking, what a stupid thing to say. If you're not dead, you're not dead. I remember thinking, men are so goddamned melodramatic.

I understand what was meant by it, of course. By twenty-five, you've given up all your hopes and dreams, your novel-in-progress, your hot body, your plans to travel to Japan. By twenty-five, you have a steady job and you're right on track for your panic-inducing suburban middle age.

But what is so bad about that? What is so horrible about a warm bed and a softening body and the properly-timed tragedies of living? What could be so bad about giving birth and getting divorced and burying your elderly parents?

That's what you're supposed to get.

Mine is the only car in the parking lot. I pull off my shoes and leave them on the passenger's seat. I walk across the lot and rocks barefoot, moving gingerly, still tender in that off-season way. Needing to rebuild what Dad always called our "summer feet."

The ocean is black and silver and quiet tonight. It shushes against the sand. I think about the Irish selkies from Mom's bedtime stories. As a kid, I thought the stories were sad, scary even. The selkies transformed from seals into beautiful women, mated with fisherman, and then, inevitably, found their pelts and returned to sea. Often, the stories involved doomed human children. Human children that existed to be left behind. The selkies could never stay.

For the last ten years, people have asked me: Do you want kids? Do you think you'll get married? Are you seeing anyone? Is it serious? Did you always want to teach? Do you think you'll teach forever? Are you writing a book on the side? Have you thought about Portland? Or Boston? You could go back to school, you could be principal, you could be a mom, you could do anything, you're so young. So young. So, so young.

All I want is to get through the day. All I want is to take care of my dog and watch *The Bachelor* with Mom and get laid every once in a while. I can't think about when we were four, when we were happy. I can't think about what it felt like to be small enough to be picked up in his arms, to go limp with my small, soft face pressed against his stubbly jaw. I can't think of the smell of him back when he still went to work—shaving cream and shoe polish. Those days on the beach after the tourists had left, when the weather was truly perfect and the water was as warm as it was going to get and the waves were enormous and he let me ride on his back as he ducked them, my arms slung around his neck, my cheeks puffed out with air. The current rushed around us like we were fused together. Like we lived in the sea.

I strip naked. My skin looks gray. The water is bracingly cold, and I run right in. Everything on my body clenches. Now, the thought of slipping on a heavy, wet, oily pelt and sliding into the Atlantic, snug under layers of fat and slicky, downy hair sounds like relief. To have a body thick and powerful that moves through the water like a knife through butter, with no gangly human limbs in the way. I submerge myself and open my eyes and wait for the initial sting to pass. The moonlight comes through like a faint glittering, refracted through the mild waves. My hair floats around my shoulders. The silence. The whoosh of a body alone in the sea. No air, no negative space. Just motion. If I could hold on to it. If I could maintain endless motion through endless black water.

I get out and return my clothes to my body. They turn to a mess of wet cotton and sand. I shiver the whole way home.

There is no accounting for the gulf between who we were and how we ended up. I can't make it make sense. I can't dream, can't plan, can't come up with any vision for the future. I can't consider the alternate universes, the things that could have been. What Angie would look like now, coming up on thirty. Whether she'd have kids. What she'd be doing for work. What it would be like to call her on the phone. What my life might have looked like. What kind of person I'd be.

Instead: What's for dinner? What bills are due? What appointments do we have this week? Everything else hurts too much.

For a second, once, I thought—do I want kids? And almost instantly I tried to scrub the thought from my brain. Why would I create another vulnerable little person I can't protect? Why would I expand my heart in a thousand ways that will only hurt? Kids are an enterprise for the lucky or the insane.

After Wolf dies, after Mom dies, I will become invincible. I almost look forward to feeling that sadness, because that will be the bottom. And then I'll be untouchable.

Whenever I open my laptop, I check my Reddit and Angie's frozen-in-time MySpace page. It's like running my tongue over a mouth sore. I start to worry that Jake will never respond, that Mickey will never find Gary. That that's the end of it. But the morning I'm supposed to see Mickey at my new apartment, I wake up to a text on my dad's phone. The number is not saved as a contact. The area code is unfamiliar.

Hi Mark! So sorry I missed your calls. I know it's probably too late, but I would still be open to talking.

I read it a dozen times before tucking the phone into the pocket of the sweatpants that I slept in. I get in the car without telling Mom where I'm going. Every time I try to talk to her about Dad's one-man cold case investigation, she shuts it down.

"Maybe he loved youse all more, eh?" Mom said the last time I brought it up. "Maybe I should have kept at it. Maybe I should never have stopped looking for your sister and left you to feed yourself then. Is that it?"

"Not the implication," I said. "This doesn't need to be so difficult. I'm just cleaning everything up."

"I'm difficult?" she said. "Him—he goes off a bridge. But I'm difficult."

"Thank you for not driving off a bridge," I said. "Much appreciated."

My new place is the second floor of a multifamily home. It's right on a main street with no sidewalks, and it's dark. But it's cheap and it's newly renovated and it's mine.

My landlady, an elderly woman named Mercedes, lives downstairs, and she answers the door when I ring.

"Hello," I say. "I'm Teddy. I called earlier. I was supposed to get my keys a while back, but my dad died. I'm here now."

"Theodora?" she says. She looks puzzled.

"Yes, but Teddy is fine." I smile as wide as I can. Talk crisply, loudly. Her eyes are cloudy with cataracts, like Wolfie, and it makes me wonder about her hearing.

"But I gave the keys to the other girl."

"What girl?"

"Your sister," she says.

"That's not possible."

"She went upstairs," Mercedes says. She gestures toward the steps behind her. "I'd come with you, but I can't do those anymore."

"Thank you," I say. I think I know what happened.

The upstairs apartment is three rooms—a small, carpeted bedroom, a bathroom, and an open plan kitchen/living area. The first thing I see is Mickey sitting on the floor in the middle of the naked living room. She has spread a beach towel like a picnic blanket beneath her. She has laid out two homemade-looking sandwiches, wrapped in tin foil, and two beers.

"Look at all this," I say.

"I figured we might need provisions," she says. "But I didn't think about toilet paper."

"Shit," I say.

"You better not." Mickey grins.

I wonder if she knows she looks like Angie. She must. She

must have felt my dad staring at her, hungry to preserve her in a big vat of formaldehyde where we could keep her young forever. She must feel me doing it now.

"This is nice," I say. "Thanks for doing this."

"No problem," Mickey says. "I also brought my computer, but I figured we might need to use phones. Unless you have the Wi-Fi set up already."

"I don't."

"Yeah, I figured. Mercedes doesn't seem like the wireless type either."

"I have to show you something." I open up the text for her to read.

"Any ideas?" she asks.

"I was hoping you'd know," I say.

She puts her hand out, and I place the phone in her palm. With a few quick movements, she dials the number. It's on speaker.

"Hello?" A woman answers the phone in a whisper. "Now's not a great time. My kid is here."

"Who is this?" Mickey asks.

"Who is this?"

I can tell the woman is annoyed, feels tricked. The tone of her voice is edgy. I cut in. "This is Mark Angstrom's daughter," I say. "Teddy. Mark has . . . passed away."

"What? When?"

"Pretty recently," I say.

"Oh my god."

"I saw you texted my dad."

"Teddy," the woman says. "It's Ginger. Can I call you back?"

"Sure. Yeah. No problem."

"Okay, two minutes," she says. The line goes dead.

"Who is Ginger?" Mickey asks.

"Ginger is my brother's wife," I say, finally putting it together. "Or ex, actually. First wife. I forgot about her."

The phone vibrates, and Mickey snaps it up. This time, she reads Ginger's text aloud: *Your dad reached out to me about Angelina. Can we get a drink next weekend? I have my daughter right now.*

"Your dad never told me about a Ginger," Mickey says. "News to me."

"It's funny that he reached out to Ginger," I say. "Maybe we think alike. I emailed my brother right after he died."

"How did that go?"

"Not great," I say. I show Mickey the email from him.

"Jesus," she says. "That's a pretty intense response. Why do you think he went on the defensive like that?"

I shrug. "That was my first taste of how much everyone still hates us. Before the doxxing and everything."

I pull up Jake's recent message and pass my phone back to Mickey. "I wanted to show you this, too." *Hi Teddy* and the dead imgur link.

Mickey shakes her head. "What am I looking at?"

"He sent me a picture of Angie."

"Can I see it?"

"It's gone now," I say. "It got deleted."

"Teddy," Mickey says. "You have to save these things. Right away."

"I know, I know. It was her last day. It's the last picture of her."

"What? How do you know?"

"Same outfit. And the tattoo."

"Whoa." Mickey hands my phone back to me. "That's huge."

"I know. It means that if we can figure out who Jake is . . ." I don't finish the thought.

Mickey nods. She knows what I mean.

"It's a lot," I say. "It just feels like a lot is happening. Was it always like this? With my dad?" It feels like maybe we're on to something, but I don't want to be delusional.

"Honestly?" Mickey says. "Not really. The last few months, I got the sense he wasn't really into it anymore. When I first showed him the old posts online—the ex-cops who offered tips and all the theories—he seemed hopeful. But then toward the end, it started to seem like he just wanted to know everything about Angie, like you would if someone was dead. Find all her pictures and posts and blogs and stuff like that. So I helped with that. But this is cool. This is like—we could get to the bottom of things."

"Probably not," I say. "If that was going to happen, it would have happened, don't you think?"

"I don't know," Mickey says. "Cases get solved years later. Happens all the time."

I think about the emails that have started coming from Reddit, now that they know what I like. Almost every day, I receive one with a subject line about a cold case that's been solved, even partially. A suspect IDed or a body discovered.

Mickey is still clicking through my phone, looking at my Reddit. "Like Marlee Fry," she says.

"Yes," I say. It comes out a little too loud, a little too eager. Mickey looks up, surprised. "Just—yes. That's true. I didn't know you knew about her."

"Sure," Mickey says.

"Did you find Gary yet?"

"I'm close," Mickey says. "I have like four emails that I got from different Redditors, and I think he's one of them. I emailed them all, so we'll see."

"Okay."

"I do think he talked to your dad, way back when. When your dad had that website set up."

"That's fine," I say. "I still want to talk to him."

"You got it," Mickey says. She looks around the room. "This place is awesome, by the way." I smile. Only a college kid could think this place, with its stark white walls and dated tile, is awesome. It's motel-esque, depressing. "It's so clean. I'd love to have a place like this."

"Thank you," I say. I take a sip of my beer. I confess that when I first saw Gary's MySpace page, I felt the urge to put what I'd found up on the wall, like in a detective show. "These walls would be perfect for some old-school red yarn, evidence mapping."

Mickey laughs. "I never understood why they do that."

"Maybe if you're a very visual person, it helps you organize your thoughts."

"Maybe." Mickey finishes her beer. "Do you mind—?"

"Not at all. In the fridge." Mickey disappears into the kitchen. "Hey," I call out. "Can I get your read on something?"

"Sure." She comes back in and sits across from me. "What's up?"

I tell Mickey about Bill, about how my dad had his phone number on the same note where I found her name, about the pills and the lying.

"Doesn't sound like he's involved in any of this," Mickey says.

"He's not," I say. "I don't think so anyway. I've checked his phone and his computer."

Mickey nods. "How did you do that?"

"It's not important," I say. "So?"

"So what?"

"Pretty shady, right? That he lied and everything."

Mickey shrugs. "I don't know . . . I get it. From his point of view. Your dad was being kind of ghoulish. And he was trying to make a buck."

"But then he lied to me about it."

"Yeah, but in fairness, you kind of stalked him," Mickey says. "What was he going to do—confess to a crime when you cornered him at his band rehearsal?"

"You don't think he did anything wrong?"

"I didn't say that," Mickey says. "Is this like—girl talk? You like this guy?"

"I don't know," I say. "No."

"Then I'd just forget about it," Mickey says. "It's over."

"You're right," I say. I raise my beer. "Cheers."

"Cheers," Mickey says, copying me. "It's nice to have a partner in crime."

"Crime-solving," I correct. We clink.

At school, I cover the window pane on my classroom door with a piece of construction paper, and I let the kids watch the adaptation of *Never Let Me Go*.

I text Mickey to check in: *Any update on Gary?*

I don't hear back.

When the final bell rings, I'm already in the car, driving toward Bill's house, not really understanding what I'm doing. Part of me expects to find him exactly where I left him, at his kitchen table, hunched over, looking small and feeble. Instead, he's in the front yard, bundling branches with twine. He looks surprised to see me.

"Hi," I say.

"Hi."

"I don't want to talk about it anymore," I say.

"Okay," Bill says. "What do you want to do?"

I tell him that I'm taking him up on his offer. I want to go to the shooting range.

He finishes tying off the bundle he was working on, and I see his triceps flex as he pulls the string tight. He stands up and brushes his hands off on his jeans. "Let me get my keys."

We don't talk until halfway there, when Bill jokes that he doesn't know whether to be turned on or frightened that I'm suddenly so into the idea.

"You don't need to be frightened," I say. "I have to change. Don't look."

As I shimmy out of my work blouse, I explain the Reddit thing to Bill. The why of this adventure.

"What do you mean, doxxed?"

"Like he posted my information online. My address and my phone number and stuff."

Bill sucks his lips into his mouth.

"You look angry." I slip into one of the extra T-shirts he keeps in the back.

He shakes his head almost imperceptibly.

"Are you mad that I thought it was you?"

"No," Bill says. "I'm mad that someone did that to you. With all you've been through. It's not fair."

"Yeah," I say, realizing how much I've been wanting, waiting for someone to acknowledge the unfairness. "It was scary."

"No shit." Bill grips the steering wheel so tightly, it looks like he might rip it off. "You have to be careful. Sickos."

When the song ends, I reach over to put my hand on his thigh. When I slide up toward his crotch, I discover that he's partially erect.

"You had your top off before," Bill says.

"I was changing," I say. "And you weren't supposed be looking. Eyes on the road."

"Yes, ma'am." His jaw falls and his lips part open as I continue to rub him over his jeans.

"Pull over," I say.

He obeys, making the next left down a leafy residential street and finding parking against the curb between two shingled houses. I unzip his pants.

"Here? What if someone is home?"

"No one's home." I don't stop what I'm doing. "Lights are off, no cars in the driveway. They're still at work."

I suck his dick for a minute to get him hard. He smells sour, like sweat, and I can taste it in my mouth.

"Meet me in the back," I say, and I climb over the console in the back seat. By the time he zips himself up, exits the car, and reenters in the back, I already have my pants off.

The sex is quick and cramped, but it's good to get it out of my system. I lie on the seat cushions, and Bill holds my hips in his hands the entire time, pulling me into him. I feel small and inanimate, like a doll. It's very satisfying. I cushion my head with my arms, and I let my breasts bounce around in my shirt with every thrust. I go almost completely limp and let him manhandle me until he comes with a loud grunt. He pushes himself so deeply into me that he crumples me against the far door.

"Sorry," he says, grabbing one of the dogs' bandanas from the floor and using it to mop the semen between my legs.

I sit up and pat him on the head. "Let's go shoot some guns."

Later that night, I watch reality TV in a pleasant haze. I replay the first kickback in my mind—my back pressed up against Bill's body like a brick wall, the force and sound of the gun pushing me into him. For a minute, I felt nauseated, but then—perfectly sharp. The rush of adrenaline, the quickening heart rate, the sweaty palms. The almost post-coital comedown of the drive home. More alive than I've felt in months. Maybe years.

I open my laptop and type the first few characters of r/AngieAngstrom on autopilot. It loads before I even realize what I'm doing. Still nothing. No Jake and no Angie.

Mickey messages me on AIM while I'm waiting for Bill to sign on. I had to convince her to download it, after all her fretting about viruses. She had never used it before, but now for every one line of text Bill and I send each other, Mickey and I send each other twenty. She admits that it's kind of fun, in a retro way.

MICHAELAAA96: send ur boss an email
Ted_Head: ???
MICHAELAAA96: call in sick
MICHAELAAA96: i found him
Ted_Head: Gary??
MICHAELAAA96: yup
MICHAELAAA96: hes off wednesdays
MICHAELAAA96: we can go see him
Ted_Head: Wow
Ted_Head: Did you talk to him?
MICHAELAAA96: no
MICHAELAAA96: called his work
Ted_Head: You think this is a good idea?
MICHAELAAA96: u asked me to do this
MICHAELAAA96: do u not want to? bc i dontt care
Ted_Head: No. I do.

Ted_Head: Is it far?

MICHAELAAA96: ill txt u

MICHAELAAA96: let's leave early

Mickey meets me at my apartment. I'm still in a towel, drying my hair, when she knocks, half an hour ahead of schedule.

"I wasn't expecting you until—"

"Sorry," she says. "My ride had to go to work. I can just hang."

I notice the manila envelope in her hand. "What's all that?"

Mickey smiles. "A surprise. Go get dressed. You'll see."

"Suspicious," I say. "Help yourself to whatever's in the kitchen. There's not much."

When I come back out, Mickey is standing in the middle of my living room, admiring her handiwork. My walls are no longer blank. She has posted, with thumbtacks, printed pages of Gary's MySpace page and driving directions from here to his house, where we're going today.

"What's this?" I try not to react poorly to the holes in my brand-new drywall. I tell myself I can patch over them pretty easily. She was trying to do something nice.

"Your wall!"

Mickey hands me a plastic bag. Inside is the manila envelope and a ball of red yarn, still in the packaging from the knitting supply store.

I think about the work it must have taken. The treacherous bike route from the dorm to the craft store downtown. The money.

"Thank you," I say. "I did always want my own paranoid yarn wall."

"And now you can have one."

"Shall we?"

Mickey holds up another bag, this one filled with Cheez-Its and Gummy Bears.

WE ARRIVE AT NOON after spending the better part of the morning in the car. My stomach is in knots from nerves and the junk food.

Gary answers his door wearing plaid pajama bottoms and nothing else. He's a rangy thirty—5'10"and maybe 125 pounds. His collarbone juts out from his chest like a handle.

"Gary?"

"Yeah."

"I'm Mickey. This is Teddy."

Gary nods. "Do I know you?"

"We wanted to talk to you about her sister if you have a minute. Angie."

"I'm not sure you have the right place," Gary says.

"Angie Angstrom."

Gary's face changes. He studies Mickey. "Wow. Okay. Come in."

His apartment is small, dark, and cluttered. Weed and rolling papers lie out in plain sight. He has a black and white movie playing on the TV, volume muted.

"Do you guys want anything?" He shakes a bag of Cheetos into a bowl on the coffee table and edges it toward Mickey and me. Mickey takes a handful.

"So," he says to Mickey. "What about your sister? I haven't heard that name in a while."

"She's Angie's sister," Mickey says, pointing her thumb at me. "Teddy."

I wave.

"Sorry," Gary says. "It's just—" He looks back to Mickey and then to me. "I guess I kind of see it now."

"Half-sister," I say. "Technically."

"So you were in college when she went missing?"

"I'm younger. I'm the younger one."

Gary nods. "Right, right. Sorry, it's hard to imagine Angie being older than you. Not that you look—in my head she's a kid. In my head I'm still a kid." He laughs. "But obviously—" He gestures to himself.

"And how old were you when she . . ."

"Same age. High school," Gary says. "We did camp together."

It takes me a minute to figure out what he's talking about. "Art camp?" The only camp Angie ever went to, a drawing and painting camp that took place for a week at some small college a couple hours away. I forget what town it was in; I remember going with Mom to drop Angie off and pick her up. She was pissed to have to go, but Mom said that she couldn't spend all summer sitting on her arse.

Gary tugs at the waistband of his pants, and for a moment, I think he's going to expose himself. Instead, he reveals a cluster of tattoos on his hip to match the ones sprawling across his chest and shoulders. I have to lean toward his creeping pubic hair to see Angie's initials.

"I designed it myself," he says. "After she disappeared. It's embarrassing now. She was my 'girlfriend' and all, but honestly, I didn't know her that well. We just dragged it out after camp, because neither of us had a lot of options."

"It's okay," I say. "You weren't the only one." All the girls I went to school with who made a scene in the halls, crying every day, seeing the counselors for grief therapy, claiming to have been close with Angie. Everyone wanted a piece of her after she was gone.

"You could always pretend it's for AA," Mickey says.

Gary laughs. "I don't think I could," he says. He looks at me. "What ever happened? Did they ever figure it out?"

I shake my head.

Mickey speaks. "Do you know anything about what might have happened to her? Where she went or who she was with?"

"No," Gary says. "I would have told the cops. Like ten years ago. I thought they might come to me, but then no one did. I put everything I knew about her on the website her folks set up, but I couldn't think of anything worth calling in to the officials. I hadn't seen her in months, and we pretty much only talked online. I actually think we were breaking up."

"Why?" Mickey asks.

"She was ignoring me a lot," Gary says. "Online. And we used to do these meetups, once a month. Meet in the middle at a park, get stoned, make out in the car. Swing on the swings. That kind of thing. But she cancelled the last few. She said she had school projects or something, but I don't know. I figured she might be with somebody else. At our last meetup, before Christmas, she had a pack of cigarettes in her car. She said she bought them, but I could tell they weren't hers. I think she felt bad for me."

When Gary falls silent, Mickey speaks up. "Can I use your bathroom?"

"Down the hall," Gary says.

"Thanks."

He watches her walk away before turning back to me. "It's not a lot, I know. It was a feeling more than anything else. Oh, and one time she drunk dialed me, and there was some man in the background. He sounded older, and she wouldn't say who she was with."

"This is helpful. If there was another—"

"Oh!" Gary interrupts me. "Sorry. Parliaments. The cigarettes. I remember, because I thought they were for British people for some reason. I pictured some fancy James Bond type. Meanwhile, I used to get those flavored cigars they sell at the gas station." He smiles. "Angie liked the girlie shit. Virginia Slims or whatever."

After a couple minutes, Mickey rejoins us.

"Are you Jake?" she asks, out of nowhere.

"I'm Gary," he says loudly, like maybe she's slow. "Gary Michaels."

"But you're a fan of *Chinatown*?" she asks.

"The movie?" Gary asks. He smiles sheepishly. "I might be too stoned. How is that related?"

"Are you on Reddit?"

"Not really," Gary says. He looks so genuinely confused that I almost feel bad for him. "Sometimes people send me things . . . videos or whatever."

"Are you ForgetItJake?" I ask. "We just need to know."

"Am I what?" Gary asks.

"No Reddit in his browser history," Mickey says. "Laptop was open."

"Did you—" Gary starts.

"It's not him," I say to Mickey. "I know." *Chinatown* is only a coincidence. He's so dumb and earnest. I address Gary, who looks like he's still piecing things together and deciding whether to be scared or angry about the violation of his privacy. I reach out to touch his hand, to reassure him. "I'm sorry she—"

Gary laughs it off. "There were no hard feelings, even then."

"I didn't know any of it," I say. "But you seem nice. I'm glad she had a nice boyfriend."

Gary stands and I stand, too, but my foot catches the leg of the coffee table, and I trip right into him. He's thin but strong, and I let him catch me.

"Hey," he says. "Hey, hey. You're okay." He's pushing me upright, but I don't want to leave yet.

"I wanted it to be you," I say.

"Everyone trips on that thing."

Gary smells like cheap shower gel and cheap cigarettes, and I would pay him to let me take a nap in his bed right now.

Mickey comes up beside me. "Lean on me," she says. "Let's go." We make our way back to Gary's front doorstep and toward the car.

After a few days, Mom makes me come upstairs and watch the late-night shows with her. She says I'm spending too much time holed up on the computer. Working too hard. She pulls out whatever week-old Chardonnay she has absorbing fridge smells, and I bring out the brownies Bill and I made together. He wanted me to pass them along to her, to send his regards, but I have been hoarding them in my stash.

Mom doesn't really believe in eating after eight o'clock, but she says she'll make an exception for something I made.

"Since when do you know how to cook?" Mom asks as she takes a bite.

"They're okay?"

"Delicious," she says. "But so rich."

She pushes the plate away, so I take what's left of hers—which is most—and polish it off.

"I have no idea how you do it. I wouldn't be able to fall asleep."

We didn't know the first guest earlier tonight—some young pop star with cotton candy hair. I'm sure if I threw the name out at school, the kids would whip out their phones and play me something. Now, the second guest ambles out—the latest iteration of the Kennedy family, running for Congress, or currently in Congress, or campaigning for Congress, always campaigning. He looks like a Kennedy—square jaw, angular features, Boston accent.

"Does the name Jake ring any bells for you?"

Mom ignores me, which I take as a no.

"Or Gary?"

"In another life, I could have been Jackie O," she says.

"Not sure how you figure that." I have another one of Bill's brownies. They are delicious—buttery with swirls of toffee.

"Different circumstances."

"It's not like she got off scot-free, you know."

"Oh, please. Her second husband—that boat guy—"

"Onassis," I say. "That's what the O's for."

"He didn't die. He was rich."

"They're all rich," I say. "But they're miserable. A lot of tragedy in that family. Maybe more than us."

"Well, what do I know," Mom says. "The money's gotta help."

I have a hard time responding to that one. Around here, Angstrom is the small-town, Bush-league version of Kennedy or Hearst. If someone far enough outside our circle hears my last name, they make the same assumptions. It's always hard to explain that all that has nothing to do with me. That I came too late, as the sun was already setting. That I was born to the wrong one in the last line of succession, that I'm the grandson Jean Paul Getty wouldn't pay the ransom money for.

"Speaking of," Mom says, like she can read my mind. "I have a new stack for you." She walks to the kitchen barefoot, her footsteps so silent that she startles me when she reappears in my peripheral vision.

"Here you go."

"Thanks," I say. "I'll deal with these as soon as I can." I flip through the stack quickly to see if I recognize any of the return addresses—junk, junk, bank, bank, electric company. Then I stop in my tracks. That swirly handwriting, the blue envelope, the Vermont return address. Celeste Starling, Inner Eye LLC.

"This bitch," I say.

"What was that?"

I don't answer her; I tear open the envelope expecting to see another bill for my dad's psychic counseling sessions—the ones Celeste said I didn't need to pay for—but instead I see Mom's name at the top. She is billed for one hour at the introductory rate and another package of five hours (expiration next year).

"Mom," I say. "Have you spoken to a woman named Celeste Starling?"

"Do you know her?" Mom says. "She mentioned that she knew you, but I wasn't sure if that meant she had met you, or that she could—I don't know what they call it—*sense* you."

"Mom, come on! This woman is a hack. Jesus, we can't afford this."

"I know that she's probably a con artist, love," Mom says. "I know that. But she spent a lot of time talking with your dad."

"Oh, big deal."

"A lot more time at the end," she continues, "than I did." She picks up her brownie, sniffs it, and puts it back down. "I want to know what was going through his mind."

If Angie were here, I think, her eyes would roll back in her head and she'd groan. She had no patience for Mom's victimhood complex, as she called it.

"You're going to need to cut back," I say. "Once I get organized, you and I will need to sit down with all the statements, and we'll figure out a budget."

"What are you talking about?" Mom says.

"You're no idiot," I say. "You're a smart woman. Do you think you can live this lifestyle for another thirty years?"

"What lifestyle? I don't do anything."

This time I roll my eyes.

"Don't get bold with me, girl."

"It's my money," I say. "It's my money that you've been spending. You and Dad. And no one ever acknowledges it."

"You're in my house," Mom says. "Does that count for nothing? You eat my food."

"How is it your food? Explain it to me."

"You are acting like an ingrate," Mom says.

"I'm moving out," I say. "And you are going to have to find a job. Wrap your head around those two facts."

Mom looks like she's been slapped. "Where would you have me work?"

I shrug. "You'll think of something. Maybe you'll marry rich again."

Mom buries her head in her arm and makes soft sobbing sounds. "It never ends. The humiliation never ends."

I stand. "Jesus Christ. There's nothing humiliating about work."

I can't listen to her cry now, so I gather my things and leave. I'll sleep on the floor of my apartment on Mickey's picnic blanket. In the car, I'm still mad, but not at her anymore. At Angie. This should be Angie's job, to be the bad cop. If Angie were here, this would be her job. And we could talk together about what to do about Mom. We could talk about Mom moving in with one of us, maybe, or about one of us moving in with her. Neither of us would be living at home. We could figure it out, and make jokes about the stuff that hurt to talk about. But Angie's not here, and Dad's not here, and I'm all alone to clean up this mess. It was never supposed to be me.

In person, Ginger Angstrom is a rough thirty-four. Her thinning hair is the color of pennies and the texture of straw, and she has it tied up in a meager ponytail on her head. Lines are setting around her mouth and forehead from want of fat and too much time in the tanning beds. She looks like she is being slowly desiccated. Nothing like her profile picture, a tightly cropped shot from her wedding to my half-brother, a decade ago.

I ask about her daughter to get her talking.

"Bella? She's fine. Ruined my marriage, but she's fine."

"Oh," Mickey says. "I'm sorry to hear—"

"Not her fault, of course," Ginger says. "Just the straw that broke the camel's back."

She explains that Henry has primary custody of Bella, plus another daughter, a little one, with his new wife. I don't mention that I've seen them in the pictures on Helene's Instagram.

"And what's her name?" I ask, for our notes.

"I call her Whore," Ginger says. "God, it's fucking cold. I thought it was supposed to be spring." She searches through her bag, and Mickey shoots me a crazy look, teeth bared, like *we're really in for it with this one.* "Uncivilized to make people sit out here."

"We can go back in," I say, but Ginger ignores me. She lights up a cigarette.

"Can I bum one?" Mickey asks. It's the right move. Ginger has been eyeing Mickey suspiciously, unsure what her role is in all of this, but she is happy to share her table with a fellow smoker.

She frowns when I decline to join. "You know all that shit about secondhand is bogus. Made up by the government."

"Why would the government do that?"

"I'll send you the links. It'll blow your mind."

"Thanks." I have a notebook out, trying to write discreetly. Ginger seems cagey, and she keeps looking over her shoulder, even though no one else is on the sidewalk.

"What did my dad contact you about initially?"

She looks puzzled. "He didn't. He was trying to reach Henry. I only heard about it through Bella. Bella was very curious about your dad." Ginger points the lit end of her cigarette at me and shakes it as she speaks, so that ashes crumble over what's left of the croissant I ordered. "Mine is dead, so yours was her only granddad. Oh god—I wonder if she knows he's gone. I bet that bastard left it for me to tell her."

I look down at a crack in the concrete and watch ants stream toward a fat crumb. The idea that my brother wouldn't even tell his own daughter that her grandfather died . . . Was Mark that bad a man? So historically terrible that he should be relegated to the category of *good riddance*?

"Continue," Mickey says, softly, and I'm grateful that she's here.

"What do you want to know? Bella told me that Mark had been calling Henry for weeks. That she knows, because he calls on Henry's cell and the house phone. He calls once a week during dinner, and instead of answering it in that stuck up way they taught her, Bella is supposed to let it ring when she sees the number." Ginger takes a long drag. "Poor baby."

"Why was he calling Henry?" Mickey asks.

Ginger nods approvingly and wags her cig at Mickey. "Yeah, so I'm like—I need to figure out what this is about."

"Did you?"

"I was with Henry in high school, so I knew your dad wasn't the greatest guy or whatever. I know all the stories; I'll just leave it at that." Ginger raises an eyebrow at me like she's discovered my stash of nudie magazines. "But most of it was because he *wasn't* around, not because he was calling the house all the time. I think we got a check from him when Bella was born, but I hadn't heard a peep since then."

Again, I feel my face burning in shame.

"So I ask Bella why he's calling and she doesn't know, but she does tell me—kinda tail-between-her-legs, 'Ma, he also sent a letter and I took it.'" Ginger is smiling now, pride lighting up her sunken eyes. "You know she's such a good girl, she felt bad. But I said, 'honey, if that witch is going to make you get her mail like you're her little slave, you should absolutely hold on to any letters you want.'"

Mickey nods. "Good for her," she says.

Ginger stops to take a sip of her coffee. "This isn't even fucking warm." She pours it into the bush beside her and keeps talking. She uses the empty cup as an ashtray. "A week later, she brought me the letter." Ginger's face turns. "She said she couldn't understand it. So I opened it, and honestly I could barely understand it too. It was gibberish."

"Oh no," Mickey says. "Do you still have it?"

"No. She was so upset, we threw it away. I think Bella thought it was going to be about her. She got it into her head that he wanted to see her or something. But it was all about Angie, as usual."

"Right," Mickey says.

"Same thing after Angie went missing. That was back when Henry and I were first married, right out of college, and your dad—he hadn't come to the wedding or sent a gift or anything—all of a sudden, he was calling and calling. It always drove Henry a little crazy how much he cared about her."

"I understand that," I say.

Ginger wheels her head around to glare at me. "Do you?" she asks. Her voice is cutting.

"I'm sorry," I say.

Ginger goes back to her story. "So, anyway, fast forward to this stuff with Bella. I just called him. Your dad. And I was like, listen, how can I help you? Because this is not fair to my daughter."

"Brass tacks," Mickey says.

"Exactly," Ginger says. She smooths back her fried hair. "Anyway, he tells me that he has reason to believe that Henry lied about his communication with Angie or something. Like before she disappeared. Whenever that was—a decade ago."

"Did you know about this?" Mickey asks.

"No! They're both crazy, so I don't even know who to believe."

"What do you mean?"

"This is all ancient history, but—I thought Henry was cheating on me back then. I don't know who he was talking to. He was on the computer all the time. On his cell phone all the time. That's right when I stopped with the pill, because I thought maybe if we had a baby, that we'd be our own family and that would help the whole situation, but then that didn't exactly work out, did it?"

"Are you saying that Henry knew something about Angie he didn't share?"

"I don't know," Ginger says. "At this point, what difference does it make? But yeah, your dad thought so."

I shake my head. "Insane," I say. "Makes no sense." I look at Mickey to see if any of this rings a bell, but I can tell she's as lost as I am. "Where did he get this theory?"

Ginger shrugs. "I have no idea," she says. "I told him—girls run away all the time. Or get trafficked. I watched this documentary the other day. Sickening."

"So, had you talked to my dad recently?"

"Not recently," Ginger says. She ashes her cigarette onto the ground. "He was a little scary on the phone and I wasn't sure if—if maybe he wasn't all there."

"He had a different number saved for you."

"I shut off my landline last month," Ginger says. "Waste of money. Though I wish I wasn't so reliant on this fucking thing." She holds her cell phone up. "They can track you wherever you are."

Mickey and I race back to my apartment when we finish with coffee. We barely speak in the car. I know that her brain is working the same way mine is, trying to make sense of it all, trying to reconcile Gary's story with Ginger's story.

"Let's say your dad was on to something," Mickey says, finally. When I don't answer, she proceeds tentatively. "Could your brother be Jake?"

"Why? Why would he be involved in any of it?"

"I don't know," Mickey says. We sit in silence for a minute. "Because he's angry."

"It's been a long time," I say. "Twenty-five years."

Back in the apartment, Mickey opens her computer. We both know what we're doing without speaking.

Ginger is very active online. She posts a lot of pictures of her daughter, Bella, my niece, who is in the fourth grade now. I've never met her, but she looks sweet with her too-big front teeth and shaggy bangs.

My brother, on the other hand, has no online presence, aside from the website he shares with his wife. No old blog posts, no anemic Facebook page, nothing.

We cycle through the same search results a few times before Mickey slams her computer shut. "No one is this unplugged," she says.

"Ginger said he was on the computer a lot."

"Well, not anymore," she says. "Drop me off for class?"

"Sure."

On the drive back to Mom's, I picture Henry. I don't know him at all, but he is my brother. He could be quiet and serious, like my dad. He could be intense and unpredictable, like Angie. All I know is that he never wanted to meet me. If anyone ruined his life, it wasn't Angie. It was me.

Wolfie doesn't even wake up, some guard dog he is. I find everything in the morning, on my way to work. My car is parked outside in front of the house, and the first thing I see is a smear of red on the curb. Blood. No—too red. Paint.

I walk around to the passenger's side, and there it is: BITCH. The paint is dry now, but it ran when it was applied. The letters appear to drip, like something from a horror movie opening sequence.

My first feeling is of embarrassment. I wonder how many of my neighbors saw the carnage before I did. I wonder how many of them paced by on their early morning dog walks and thought—this family can't keep out of trouble. No one called.

It's less difficult to believe that someone came here and did this than that I slept through it. That I didn't have any intuitive sense that something was wrong in the two hours I've been awake so far. That I have no instincts to protect me.

I touch the B. It's glossy and thick, not misty like most of the tags I see around school. Someone must have held the can really close to the metal, taking his time, a deliberately tight grip.

I touch the window. There is a hairline crack. When I pull my finger away, I have a wound as thin as a papercut. I suck the finger and taste pennies.

I call in sick, and drive straight to the apartment, taking the back roads so that I pass fewer cars. My heart surges to see

Mickey already outside when I pull up. I didn't know how to deal with this on my own.

"Thank you for coming," I say. "Roommate give you a ride?"

She nods. "And don't worry. The old lady isn't in."

We assess the damage. Mickey turns pale and quiet, which makes me think it's serious.

"Do you think it's Jake?" I ask.

"Could be anyone who saw your information."

"I didn't tell my mom."

Mickey traces the letters without speaking.

"Should I call the police?"

We both let that suggestion hang in the air for a moment. What would we say? How would we explain?

Mickey takes a step back from the car. She speaks decisively. "Okay. I know someone who can help."

"What?"

"Give me the keys. I'll be back."

"I'm not going to sit on the floor here for two hours."

"It's not a good idea for you to come."

"Okay," I say. "You can drop me off on your way."

WHEN I GET TO the range, I recognize the woman at the front. She's petite, mid-forties, with graying black hair that she's cut into a spiky pixie. She doesn't ask about Bill, and for that I'm glad.

Before I even have the chance to talk, she volunteers, "So you need to rent a gun?"

"Yeah," I say. "Can I rent two?"

"Let's do them one at a time," she says, her voice monotone and disinterested.

The first gun I rent is a handgun, bigger than the one that Bill lent me when we went. The woman doesn't try to move me to a smaller gun, one of the ones on the far left that are clearly made for women's handbags. She certainly doesn't suggest one of the pink models.

"You need help with loading that or are you okay?"

I look down at it. It's all hard metal, cold and heavy in my palm, and I can feel the grated etching making imprints on my skin already. Bill's hands are calloused and rough. Mine aren't used to the grip.

"You've got it," she decides. "You've practiced before."

I appreciate her confidence.

I don't know what the rooms are called where we shoot, but I have taken to thinking of them as cubicles in my head. Perhaps it's because I've never worked in a cubicle, but I always liked the idea. A small room set off from the rest of the world where you could work alone. A tidy area decorated or undecorated as you wish, quiet and peaceful with no one to bother you.

The cubicle that I'm sent to is number seven. It's freshly swept and there is no one shooting on either side of me. The range is quiet at this hour. I feel briefly self-conscious about being the only one making noise, but then I decide that the woman is not listening anyway.

I miss my target—a large deer head, antlers and all, printed on a piece of thick white paper. In fact, I miss the paper entirely on the first five shots, but I'm getting used to the gun. Its kickback is stronger than that of the one I used with Bill. The barrel smokes with each shot, and the air in my cubicle grows thick with the smell of gunpowder. The fuzz of the muffs tickles my ears, and a dull ringing tapers off as I empty the chamber of the ammunition I paid for and begin to hit the antlers, the thick neck, the matte black eyes.

I go back out front to see the woman.

"I want to try something bigger," I say. I'm talking too

loudly, still slightly deaf. My voice sounds strange inside my head.

"Okay." She turns to her collection of pistols.

"No," I say, laying down the handgun I had been using. "Much bigger."

"Like what?"

"A shotgun. Or a rifle, maybe."

"Which is it?"

"Rifle."

The woman fetches me a rifle. It's smaller than some others I've seen, but it's heavy, and when it's in my hands, I realize that I have no idea how I'm supposed to hold it.

"You need ammo, too?"

"Yes, please."

I sign all the forms for my new rental, and I go back to my cubicle. It takes me almost fifteen minutes to figure out how to load the gun. Fifteen minutes that I'm paying for as part of this new hour. When it's loaded, I lift the gun and hold it straight out. The barrel is heavy and unbalanced, and I have a hard time keeping it aimed at the target. I tuck the back end under my armpit and squeeze it there, stabilizing the weight between my bicep and my ribcage.

I fire and the rifle jerks up, startling me. A dull pain shoots through my side. I don't even know where the bullet went, but I hear the shell casing tinkle to the ground at my feet. My ribs feel instantly bruised, and my hands are shaking. I put the gun down and rub my hands, shake my arms out, stretch my neck. Again.

I lift the gun, this time balancing the back end on the top of my shoulder. I have to lift the front higher this way, and I strain to see the target through the viewfinder. Keep your eyes open, I tell myself, you can't close your eyes and shoot a gun. I try to channel Bill.

I shoot, and the ringing is even louder now, closer to my ears. This weapon makes a much bigger hole in the paper. I get the sense that with this one, you just need to get close.

"How much?" I ask at the front.

"I told you. It's five for the hour on top of the regular rate." The woman looks behind me, up at the clock on the wall. "You still have twenty minutes."

"No, I mean, how much is the first one, to buy?"

"I'm not a gun dealer, honey," she says. She picks at her nails, turns back to her magazine. "I can't sell it to you."

I realize I'm panting, holding the oxygen for too long between breaths. "Okay," I say. "I'll pay for everything else then. I don't need the rest of my time."

She examines me. Looks at my hair, tied back in its neat pony-tail; the goggles pushed up on my head, flattening my bangs back; the row of zits on my forehead where my bangs leave their trail of grease, impossible to zap away with acids, creams, or masks; my T-shirt, inherited from my dad, oversized and worn from too many washes; the leftover mascara under my glasses.

"You're looking for a gun, huh?"

"Yes," I say. "Something small. For self-defense."

The woman nods thoughtfully. Her eyeglasses are anchored to her head with a bedazzled chain, and the jewels hanging by the sides of her face slap against her skin with the movement. She doesn't ask any more questions. Maybe she thinks I'm going to kill my boyfriend, whom she has met, and she doesn't care. She assumes I have my reasons.

She taps the glass countertop, and I lay the rifle down. "You can get something like this at Walmart," she says. "That's cheapest. Or one of the sporting goods stores. They should have a good selection, too."

"And—"

"Oh, right. I would say a couple hundred. Depends on the model. If you're okay with nothing too fancy, you should be able to get one for, like, two hundred."

I pay cash to close my tab, which is scrawled out on a menu receipt like a restaurant bill. The total with tax is circled at the bottom. I sit on a curb in the parking lot and wait for Mickey the way Angie and I used to wait for a ride after ballet.

When she finally arrives, I can see that the spray paint is gone. From far away, the car looks completely normal. Up close, it's too matte, but good enough. I could kiss her on the mouth.

"Sorry about the clear coat. He tried a few other things first," Mickey says. She looks back at the range. "I'd want to go some time."

I reach out to touch the car and fresh wax comes off on my fingers. "This is so much better. Thank you."

"He said next time try nail polish remover."

"Next time," I say. "Let's hope not. Hey, any chance you want to crash with me at the apartment tonight? I feel like it's better if I'm not at my mom's house and my car's not there, but I don't want to be alone either."

"Yeah, sure," Mickey says. "I guess that's fine."

"You can say no."

"No, no. It's fine."

We swing by the outdoor store and get two blow-up mattresses and two sleeping bags. It runs me a fortune, but it's better than stopping home. Mickey throws a pack of trail mix and two sports drinks in the cart.

"That stuff's on me," she says.

I write into school, and I explain that there has been an emergency. I won't be in tomorrow either. Rick doesn't ask questions, but I can tell from his less-than-chipper response that he's growing weary.

I text Mom to tell her that I'm not coming home. She needs to let Wolfie out. She asks me where I'm staying, and I lie and say Bill's.

When everything is all set up on the floor, it feels pretty cozy. Mickey pulls a flask of vodka from her backpack and we mix it in with the sports drinks. It's sweet and warm and makes me gag with every sip, but we pound it back.

Mickey laughs at me. "I can tell you're not trailer trash like me."

We spend the night hunched together over a single cell phone—Mickey's first, then mine, then Mickey's—watching funny dog videos and stalking my half-brother.

Mickey's fingers hover over the search bar. "What's your man's name?" she asks.

"Bill," I say.

"Bill what?"

My tongue gets stuck in my throat. I don't want her to look him up. "Bill Rooney."

Mickey types it in. "There are a lot of Bill Rooneys," she says. "Is this him?" She turns her phone to show me a very old man at the beach with no shirt on.

"You found him," I say.

"Hot," Mickey says.

"I'm tired," I say. "I'm going to go to sleep."

"Okay," Mickey says. "Good night." She turns down the brightness of her phone, and I zip myself almost entirely inside my bag. As I'm drifting off to sleep I hear humming.

"Hey," I say. "Angie used to sing that song." But no one can hear me. And everything goes black. And Angie slips out of my grip again.

Mickey and I turn the Wall into a cathartic ritual. All the bullshit that comes my way goes up on the Wall. Celeste's invoices—Wall. Mysterious bills—Wall. Particularly vitriolic Reddit comments—printer, then Wall. We even add things to the Wall that aren't new. Mickey contributes the most relevant parts of Angie's police report, the things my dad kept coming back to again and again. I put up the results of Jake's doxxing—the threats and even the dick pics—upon which Mickey Sharpies dozens of question marks. We connect everything to everything else at random, making a tangled web of red string. Mickey has taken to affecting an old-timey, 1940s movie detective accent as we go.

"Well now, Pepper," she says (she changes the nickname each time). "What do we have here?"

"Well, Sarge," I say. "This here is an email from my brother, telling me to fuck off for life."

"Very interesting. Could be a clue!"

It makes us both feel better to treat it all like a joke. Mickey, like it's a game, a fun and naughty hobby. Me, like it's a game, pretend, not real, not my life.

Along with her contributions to the décor, Mickey has been filling the built-in shelves in the new apartment with old

CDs—poppy, angsty girl music from before her time: Fiona Apple, Aimee Mann, Alanis Morissette, certain Sheryl Crow albums. For some reason, I was expecting something harder, like Angie's preferred metal and grunge. She has an old boombox set up in the corner next to the small portable DVD player she brought in.

"I have to watch these for school," she says, when she sees me inspecting the stack of movies.

We eat dinner on our air mattresses, with *Casablanca* playing on the tiny screen. My fridge is broken, so we order Chinese and leave nothing in the cartons.

"Tomorrow I have to check in on Wolfie," I say. "And I told Bill I'd spend the night there."

Mickey doesn't acknowledge that she's heard me.

"The day after, too. I have to be home."

Mickey twirls some lo mein around a fork.

"He keeps asking to meet my mom. We're doing dinner."

"Teddy," Mickey says, pausing the movie. "I really do have to write a paper on this. Can we talk after?"

Mickey likes spending the night here, because her roommate "is a slut and pretty dirty." Her name is Ashley, and she never washes her clothes. Apparently, she bought two hampers so that she could rotate them in and out of her closet. When she fills one up, it goes into the closet. When she fills the second one, she switches them, taking the old hamper out and pretending as though all of the clothes were magically cleaned.

Mickey tells me she's on the dance team. "Sweats like a pig."

Almost every night, Ashley has a guy in the dorm room. Mickey says it would be better if Ashley sexiled her, because at least she could sleep in peace on the common room couch, but that's not what happens. Usually Mickey is already home, and

Ashley doesn't care whether Mickey's there or not. She'll do it right next to her.

"Our beds are so close, we could hold hands," Mickey said, when she was telling me. "It's awkward to leave once they've started. I pretend to be asleep."

Meanwhile, here in my apartment, our beds are so close, they touch to form one big air mattress. We've unzipped our sleeping bags to make one the bottom layer and one the blanket. It makes it easier to get out and move around in the night.

"That was great," Mickey says when the movie is over. "I can't believe it took me so long to see it."

"Oh," I say. "I stopped paying attention. Was it good?"

"Teddy," Mickey says. "What's going on?"

"I feel like we're missing something," I say. "I feel like we're missing something critical."

"What if we didn't learn anything useful?" Mickey says. "What if everything stayed the same?"

"What do you mean? Are you asking if I'll kill myself?"

Mickey does not return my smile.

"What will *you* do?" I say. "What else do you have going on? You were hanging out with my dad before. Now you're hanging out with me."

Mickey nods. "That's true enough."

"Maybe you're the one we should be worried about. At least she was my sister."

Mickey looks at me for a long time. "It was right after my mom left that Angie went missing," she says. "And no one cared that my mom left, but everyone cared about your sister."

"I'm sorry," I say.

"I found her online," Mickey says. "My mom. She didn't want to be found."

"That's awful," I say.

"It's okay," Mickey says. "I'm past it."

I get up to turn off the lamp, and Mickey closes the DVD player.

I wonder what my dad meant to her. I wonder about the way that my pain gets to win. Because I have a legitimate claim. I wonder if she's been thinking about her mom. If she finds that it all compounds.

I squeeze Mickey's hand hard. She holds firm. I can tell she understands.

There is a game I play with Bill. While he's inside me, I wrap my legs around his back and pull him in deep. I lock my ankles so that he can't pump his hips, can't move. We stop in our tracks.

I don't do it every time. It's important that he can never be sure if it will happen.

Bill gets frustrated by the halt in momentum, but he likes being frustrated. It builds the anticipation. After all, he could throw my legs off if he wanted to. He could overpower me. But he doesn't. One moment, he's close to coming, the next we're perfectly still, frozen together like two Greek lovers etched in marble.

While Bill's inside me, stuck until I give the go-ahead, I ask him questions. That's the game. I make him tell me secrets. He's so flustered and desperate, he doesn't even think; he comes right out with the information. I could ask him for his social security number and credit card number and he would give it to me if it meant he could scratch that itch again.

Tonight, we are fucking hard when I stop him. I cross my ankles behind his tailbone and I dig my nails into his shoulder blades, pulling him into me. He has one arm on the bed propping himself up and the other under my back, holding me off the mattress and keeping me close. When I stop him, his kickstand arm begins to tremble. He is balancing both his weight and mine on the one hand.

"Wait," I say. Our breath is commingling in the narrow space between us. I can feel his stubble in my neck, rubbing the skin raw.

"Teddy," he whines. "Come on."

"Who was the first girl you ever fucked?" I ask.

"Mary Ann Hennike," he says, breathy and fast.

"How?" I ask. "Did you fuck her in your car? Did you fuck her on prom night?" Almost all of the information I glean this way can be repurposed.

"I can't remember," Bill says. "Not a car. I didn't do prom."

"Why didn't you go to prom?"

He begins to resist, grinding himself into me ever so slightly.

I catch him. "Not yet." I adjust my feet, lock him back in. "Tell me why."

"No one wanted to go with me," he says, and he collapses into me a bit more, lowers his head so that his nose is in my armpit.

I run my hands through his hair and tug at the roots. I put my feet back on the mattress. "I would have gone with you," I whisper.

"Did you lose your virginity on prom night?" Bill asks, playing the game. He pulls his head back up and stares at me. In the faint light of the alarm clock, we lock eyes. His are dark puddles with a sheen of red LED.

"I did," I say. It's not true, but it doesn't matter.

Bill lets out a guttural sound. He's moving inside me again— slowly at first.

"I would have fucked you," he says.

"Show me."

When the sex is done, the bed is damp with sweat. I dab at the sticky spot between my legs with the top sheet.

"That was fun," Bill says. He's already drifting off to sleep.

He sleeps on his back, and usually I curl up on my side in the crook of his left arm.

"Is that true, what you said?" I ask.

"What?" He doesn't open his eyes to respond. His voice is trailing, tired. "That no one would go out with me?"

"Yeah."

"Yeah, that's true." He scoops me up in his arms.

It helps me to understand Bill and the mannerisms that have thus far been a mystery to me. Things I've attributed to the age difference. Now, they make sense. He's a guy who no one but me wanted to date.

"Hey," I say.

Bill opens one eye. "Yes?"

"I have to chaperone one of the kids' dances weekend after next."

"That's fine. I have stuff to do around here."

"No," I say. "Would you come with me? Will you be my date to the dance?"

It seemed terribly clever in my head, but now that I've said it, I feel dumb. Even the fact that we're two grown adults getting off thinking about fucking one another at prom. It feels almost perverted, given my position at work, but then most bedroom stuff can't be spoken of in daylight hours without a degree of shame.

Bill smiles a lopsided grin, but he seems to roll his eyes a bit. I try to tell myself it's exhaustion.

"I'd love to," he says.

When I return from the drug store the next day, it's raining, and Mickey is standing under the portico at my mom's house, next to the front door.

"What are you doing here?"

"I have something to show you. I was in the area." She taps the glass panel on the side of the door. Wolfie is lying there with his nose fogging the window. "He's been keeping me company. I didn't want to knock."

I unlock the door and push Wolfie's large, bony body with my foot. He slides across the linoleum tiles until I can open the door all the way. "He'll do that." I remove my shoes and my coat.

"Mom," I call. I gesture for Mickey to follow. "Get in. It's pouring."

She looks even younger in this state, without makeup. Her stringy hair hangs in clumps, sticks to her cheeks. Her face looks pink and swollen.

My mom calls back from the kitchen. She sounds far away. "Did you get my stuff?"

"Listen," I say to Mickey. "Bill is coming over tonight."

Mickey smiles in a way that tells me that's at least partly why she's here.

"Really, Mick? Why?"

"I'm freezing," she says. "Can I shower?"

"Downstairs," I say. "There are towels in the cabinet above the toilet."

"Great," she says. "Thanks, T."

No one but Angie has ever called me T.

"What?" she says.

"Nothing. Go," I say.

I watch Mickey disappear down the basement stairs. There is a knock at the door.

"Come in," I yell.

Another knock.

"Come in!"

I have to slide Wolfie aside once more to open the door.

"I tried, but it wouldn't open." Bill hands me a bottle of wine.

"It's the dog." Wolfie is trying to stand and greet Bill, but he can't get purchase on the floor. His back paws keep pedaling, kicking his thumping tail. He tries to turn onto his side for a belly rub, but only manages a couple degrees. The knots on his ribs stop him.

Bill gets down on the floor. Puts his face against Wolf's. The silver in Wolfie's beard bleeds into the silver of Bill's sideburns. I feel a surge of gentleness. "Poor guy." Bill rubs his side, and I know that he's counting the tumors as his palm crests each one. The tumor and the space where the muscle has wasted from the bone. Every time I pet him, I think I count more than the last time. The vet has warned me that sooner or later, Wolfie will starve himself to death. It's a pack animal thing. If he could slink off into the woods and save us all this agony, he would.

Bill stands and puts a hand on the small of my back. It makes me shudder.

"You okay?" he asks. "You seem harried."

"I'm fine." I give him a kiss. "We have one more tonight."

"What does that mean?"

"A friend," I say. "Sort of." I take his hand and bring him to the kitchen. "Come on. I'll explain."

I hand Mom the bottle of wine.

"Mom, Bill. Bill, this is my mother, Clare."

They shake hands and exchange pleasantries. I can tell that she is eyeing him, trying to figure out his age. Bill can tell, too. He tousles his hair the way he does when he's feeling self-conscious about it.

"You look so familiar," Mom says.

I expect Bill to shoot me a look or remind her that he used to work here, but he doesn't. He smiles sheepishly and says, "One of those faces."

Mom hands us some brown cocktails that she had prepared. The ice is melted, and the glasses are sweating. They're still very strong. We toast to Bill being here.

"We have a bit of a full house tonight," I say. "I have a young lady who dropped in this evening. She's working with me on a research project."

"What kind of project?" Mom says.

"It's a genealogy thing."

"Where is she?" Bill says.

"She's downstairs, getting washed."

"She's here now?" Mom says.

"Yes," I say. "Just now."

"She's showering here?" Bill asks.

"She was soaking wet, so I offered." I realize as I'm talking that I have no idea how Mickey got here. There was no car in the driveway when I pulled up. She must have gotten a ride or walked.

"Let me go check on her," I say, downing the rest of my drink. "You guys can get to know each other."

Mom smiles. "The more the merrier. It's so nice to have company."

I keep offering to get her another dog before Wolfie and I fully move out. Something small—a King Charles cavalier or a cocker spaniel—with big round eyes that could stare at her all day. But she keeps refusing.

"I don't need more dogs," she says, whenever I bring it up.

I hear her and Bill laugh in unison when I reach the bottom of the stairs, and I'm grateful for how charming he can be when he wants to be. I've been anxious at the prospect of seeing them in the same room, but now I can see that they make sense—Bill taking care of her like some men do with old ladies, making sure she has what she needs, acting the part of the gentleman. It's not something she's used to, but maybe it's something she could enjoy.

Mickey is wearing a bra and my sweatpants, which are rolled a few times at the waist and cuffed at the ankles. "Do you have a T-shirt?" she asks.

I step in and shut the door behind me. "Yeah," I say. "Bottom drawer."

Mickey throws on the first shirt she sees, and it hangs from her shoulders. She wraps her hair into a bun on the top of her head, tucking the end into the loop, securing it without a tie. Women with such tricks have always made me feel inadequate. I don't have any tricks. My mom has dozens of tiny feminine movements that allow her to glide through the world like a nymph, but she didn't teach me a single one.

"It smells great," Mickey says. "What are you cooking?"

"My mom is making a stir-fry," I say.

"Yum."

"Don't get excited. She's a bad cook. She won't use any oil or salt."

Mickey laughs.

"Bill is here," I say.

Mickey tucks the front of her T-shirt into her sweatpants. "I feel bad that I look so sloppy."

"I told them that you're here because of a genealogy thing," I say. "You cannot bring up my sister. Or my dad. Or the apartment. It'll upset her."

Mickey is looking past me to the stairs.

"Hello? Did you hear me?"

"Genealogy. That's fine. I'm good with that."

"No Angie talk."

"Got it," Mickey says. She whips a chapstick out of her bra and swipes it on in a single swoop. She then places her hands lightly at the base of my neck, purses her lips, and leans forward. For a brief and paralyzing moment, I think that she might kiss me, but instead she blows a cool stream of air onto my face. It carries the scent of bubblegum.

"Relax," she says.

She brushes past me and is upstairs before I can even move to follow her. She's in the living room introducing herself to Bill and Mom, and I'm stuck listening from the bottom of the stairs as she invents a backstory for herself (former student, now at the community college) and oversells our relationship (mentor/mentee).

Bill excuses himself and heads toward the kitchen, where I meet him.

"She seems sweet," he says. "Energetic."

"I think so."

He scoops some rice into each of four bowls, tops it with the stir-fried chicken and vegetables.

"Kind of a lame dinner, don't you think?" I say.

"It smells amazing." He hands me two bowls to carry to the

dining room. "When is the last time your mom ate? She looks so thin."

She has always looked like that, I want to say, but I don't. She's looked like that since before I was born, before Angie was born. I've only ever seen her not looking like that in old pictures, from when she was younger than I am now.

For almost forty minutes, everyone makes stilted small talk. Bill peddles his tired conspiracy theories about agrochemicals and big banks. The food feels strange and bland in my mouth. The rice is gummy, and I chew one bite for so long that it turns into a paste between my molars. I give up and attend to my wine instead. When we finish Bill's magnum, I open a bottle from Mom's collection. Mom doesn't say anything, but Bill shoots me a look. I make sure to refill everyone else's glass first.

"Sláinte," Mom says, for the second time.

"Thank you," Mickey says. She takes a sip. "Wow, this one's nice."

Bill furrows his brows. "Don't you have to drive home, hon?"

"That's good looking out," Mom says. She's very taken with Bill. Every time he speaks, she folds her hands in her lap, leans across the table, and listens, rapt, unable to eat or drink while he's talking. "The drinking age in this country is a little silly, but then so is the drinking culture."

"You can crash here," I say. I hear myself, and I sound drunk, slurring together "crash" and "here" so that it sounds like "cashier," but I don't care. "In the basement."

"There ya go," Mickey says, and she raises her glass to me.

"You can have my bed," Mom says. "I've been sleeping with Wolfie on the couch when you're not here anyway." She reaches under the table to pat the dog's head. She's been giving him bits of chicken all night, and I know that they are piling up on the rug somewhere. He can't chew meat anymore, so he rolls it around in his mouth and then abandons it.

"Slumber party," Mickey says. "I'm the only one already in jammies."

"So, Mickey," Mom says. "Tell us more about this project. The genome project."

"It's not that interesting."

"How exactly is Teddy involved?" Bill asks. I put my hand on his thigh, but he nudges me off. His cheeks are splotchy, and his voice has grown gravely. If he doesn't get to bed soon, he'll be in a bad mood, drunk and nasty. I've seen it once before, and I didn't like it.

Mickey doesn't miss a beat. "Teddy has been so helpful in locating records. St. A's has great archives, better than Brookdale's, believe it or not."

"What kind of records?" Mom asks.

"Birth, death, marriage," Mickey says. "The usual. We're trying to trace the town's mobility. Specifically looking at the first families. Mainers stay pretty local, even over centuries, but the last few decades, we've started to see some interesting trends. Changing demographics."

I'm so convinced by her that I briefly forget it's a lie. "Is this what you study?" I ask.

Mom shoots me a puzzled look, but thankfully Bill speaks before Mickey has to answer.

"Makes sense why we'd have people coming in. Fishing, hunting . . . you've got everything."

"People aren't coming," Mickey says. "They're leaving. Permanent residents, anyway. Pushed out by the summer renters. But speaking of hunting—I didn't know you hunted, Teddy."

"I don't."

"Teddy doesn't even believe in guns," Mom says. "My

husband used to hunt very occasionally when she was young, and every time he went out, she wouldn't talk to him for days. Mostly because of *Bambi*, I think."

"What is there not to believe in?" Bill says, looking from me to Mom. He leans back in his chair, puts his hands behind his head. "It seems you both eat meat. Or do you just prefer not to think about where your food comes from?"

"You know what she means," Mickey says to Bill, and I'm so proud of her for standing up for Mom that I could hug her. But then she continues. "I didn't mean to start a whole *politics* thing. I noticed the box, and I assumed."

"What box?" Bill and Mom ask in unison.

"Nothing," I say.

"The gun," Mickey says.

"What?" Bill asks. "You bought your own gun?"

"What's going on now?" Mom says. "What is he talking about?"

"Everyone settle down," I say. My skin feels itchy and hot. Mickey was snooping around under the bed. "Everyone stop talking about me like I'm not here." I take a deep breath. "I bought one teeny-tiny nine-millimeter lady-gun. For protection."

Mom opens her mouth like she's going to respond, but then she purses her lips tightly and crosses her arms over her chest instead.

"Calm down, Mom," I say. "It's for protection. You can't seriously be mad."

"What did you buy?" Bill asks. "I would have gone with you."

Mom stares at him like horns have sprouted from his head.

"Let's change the subject," I say. "Mom, Bill has two of the most beautiful dogs."

Mom pauses, and I can see her thinking. She decides to let it go. She's being magnanimous. "Do you have any pictures?"

Bill takes out his phone and shows her Rocky and Red.

"Lovely," Mom says. "Look at that fine face. Have they met Teddy's Wolf yet?"

"No, I don't know if they'll get a chance."

Mom cocks her head, takes a sip from her glass. "Why's that?"

"I don't think he has much time left, now, does he?" Bill asks. "The cancer."

Mom shrugs. "Who knows how much time. Dogs can go on for a long while sometimes."

"My aunt's dog lived with a tumor on his neck the size of a grapefruit for like, years," Mickey says. She helps herself to more stir-fry from the bowl in the center of the table.

Bill shakes his head. In my brain, I'm begging him not to have this fight with her. I'm shooting daggers at him, but he's not looking at me.

"That's not exactly humane, though," Bill says. "I've had a lot of dogs, too, so trust me—I know how hard it is. But at some point, you've gotta put them out of their misery."

"Yikes," Mickey mutters under her breath. She shovels another mouthful of rice.

Mom's one eye is drooping the way it does when she drinks, and her face slowly turns red from holding her breath. She looks like she's stroking out.

"Mom," I say. "Mom, are you okay?"

"I'm grand."

"Be careful," Mickey says. "Kevorkian over here will 'put you out of your misery.'"

"Excuse me?" Bill says.

"I'm kidding," Mickey piles on. "Unless you have your parents chopped to bits in the yard, that is." She looks to me, smiling with her mouth full of food.

Mom is halfway under the table, petting Wolfie, making sure he didn't hear what the bad man was saying about him. I can barely keep my eyes open to watch the train wreck that is unfolding between Mickey and Bill. I try to respond, but I'm a second too late, and Bill is already talking.

"What are you—twenty years old?" Bill says.

"Nineteen," Mickey says. "I won't ask how old you are, though, don't worry." She smirks at me again, though I wish she wouldn't. It makes me feel complicit.

"She's only taking the piss, Bill," Mom says, trying to mediate.

"No one has any bodies," I say, drunkenly. "Mick, his mom died; it's not funny. Bill, she was kidding. It's okay."

Bill looks to Mom for some sympathy about his mother, but she barely acknowledges the information. Historically, Mom has not been great at condolences when people over the age of sixty are involved. It doesn't register on her scale.

"I'm sorry," Mickey says. "I was trying to lighten the mood—"

"It's fine," Bill mutters.

"—since you were threatening to kill their dog."

"What is your problem?" Bill stands and casts a shadow over Mickey. She takes a sip of her wine and chuckles, a challenge.

"Hey," Mom says, raising her voice. "That's enough."

Bill looks instantly ashamed. He sits back down in his chair, stares at his napkin, unmoving.

Mom turns to Mickey now. "My daughter was eighteen," she says. "About your age."

For a moment, I panic, but Mickey feigns confusion. "You mean Teddy?"

"No," Mom says. "The other one."

Mickey doesn't push. *Thank you*, I try to scream with my eyes. *Thank you, thank you.*

"Everything was delicious, Clare," Mickey says.

"I should go," Bill says. He stands and gathers his plate and utensils, starts reaching for Mom's dishes to put on top of his.

"You're not staying?" I ask.

"I have work early." He falters in his grip of Mom's plate and her utensils clatter to the floor. "Goddamn it."

"Are you okay to drive?" Mom asks.

"I'm fine," Bill says. He flashes a tense grin. "Thank you, Clare." He turns to Mickey. "It was nice to meet you."

"Bill," I say, but he's already turned on his heel and walked into the kitchen.

"He's *langers*," Mom says, under her breath. She looks at me like *shouldn't you follow him*, but I stay where I am. My body is anchored to the chair, my face muscles feel slow. I don't want to fight right now.

Mickey, Mom, and I sit in silence. We wait to hear the clatter of plates in the sink. Bill makes no effort to work quietly. Then, silence. Silence for a long while, and I know that he's waiting for me to come talk to him in private. I don't move. Then, finally—footsteps, the crack of the door hinge, a dull thump as it shuts behind him.

Mickey is the first to move. She gets up to clear the rest of the plates. Mom stays put. I can tell that she's petting Wolfie with her bare foot, because her body is swaying slightly above the table even though she's using all of her concentration not to fall. Her palms are flat on the tabletop and she's staring almost through me, heavy-lidded and sad. I stay in her line of sight as long as I can before I get up, excusing myself and leaving her alone.

"Your mom is awesome," Mickey says, when I enter the kitchen. She's loading the dishwasher and tidying up. "So real. Such a firecracker. Must be fun."

I sit at a counter stool and wonder at Mickey's relative sobriety. I can't muster a response. I rest my elbows on the Formica and cradle my face in my hands. My head feels like concrete. I'm not sure that my neck can hold it up without snapping.

Mickey throws a rag over her shoulder and steps toward me. She places the heels of her hands over my eyes and taps her fingers on my temples. Her hands are cool and damp, and they smell like lemon dish soap.

"Poor Teddy," she says, and suddenly I'm crying very silently, like I used to when I was a kid. Hot, stupid tears are leaking from my eyes, and I don't even know why. "You're not feeling good, huh?"

"I'm sorry," I say. I can hear Mom lecturing us as kids: *Laugh and the world laughs with you; cry and you cry alone.* "Can we talk about your thing tomorrow?"

"Yes, that's fine," Mickey says. "You're too drunk." And somehow, coming from her, it doesn't sound judgmental.

She sidles up to me and puts her arm around my waist, guiding me off the stool. "Let's go," she says, and she leads me downstairs, slowly, to my bedroom.

"Night, T," Mickey says.

"T," I repeat. It's so strange in my mouth. "I'm T." And then the light is sucked from the room.

I wake early, the way I always do after a night of drinking. It's 5 A.M. and the house is still. Mickey's sleeping next to me, on top of my comforter. In the confusion of waking, with her back to me, in this haunted place, my brain takes her for Angie. I reach out to touch her shoulder, and she flops onto her belly, still out.

Mickey's dark hair is tied up in a bun and she's wearing only a tank top and a thong. An enormous bandage covers the lower half of her right calf and wraps all the way down to the bottom of her Achilles tendon. I hadn't noticed before, with her pants on.

In the shower, I can feel myself sweating in the steam, and I can't stop gulping down mouthfuls of hot water. I dress in the dark, feeling around for black stretchy pants and a black cotton tunic.

Upstairs, I stop to pet Wolfie. When I try to move, he puts a paw on my foot.

"Do you need to go out?"

I swear he rolls his eyes at me before collapsing on his side.

"I'm taking that as a no, buddy."

When I get to my desk, I text Mickey a picture of my credit card, front and back. *If you need to get back to campus, do a rideshare. Don't walk. XX.*

I'm the first one in the department, so I'm able to leave the lights off. I lay my face on the rough wooden surface of my desk.

"I'm dying," I say to no one.

"Teddy?"

I start. Rick is standing in front of me.

"Good morning," I say. I sit up quickly and the blood rushes to my head. I have to keep myself from wincing.

Rick sniffs the air twice and makes a face. Despite my shower, I still smell like wine. It's coming out of my pores.

"Dark in here," he says.

"Getting my thoughts in order. Sometimes—"

"I'm sorry to cut you off. But I never got that worksheet."

"Right," I say. "Right, I meant to email you, but my internet was down."

Rick crosses his arms and frowns. I sound like one of the kids. He looks at my desk. A few scattered Post-it notes, loose aspirin that I knocked out of the bottle and meant to put back. I try to cover up the crumbs from the gas station muffin I bought on my way in.

"Anything else?"

"Talk to Marianne about getting on my calendar."

"Sure thing."

On his way out, Rick turns on the light, and I reflexively shield my eyes.

At lunch, I pick up a sandwich in the cafeteria downstairs, and I notice several students watching me. I smile and wave, but they all look down at their plates. Upon my return to my desk, I discover that they have beaten me back to the English department room and are lined up, wanting to contest their most recent essay grades. Jamie leads the charge.

"Gentlemen. Ladies," I say. I slip into my chair and open up my laptop like I don't notice they're waiting.

"The average on this essay was a C minus," Jamie says.

I click through Reddit.

"You shouldn't be comparing grades," I say.

"You didn't even put any notes on mine," Iris says.

I snap my laptop closed. "If you want to talk to me about your papers, you are free to email me and make individual appointments during my office hours."

Jamie rolls his eyes.

"Do you have something more you need to say?" I ask him.

"No," he says. "I'll make an appointment. Assuming you're going to actually honor your office hours this week."

"Great."

The kids march out of the English office, looking dejected.

Greg, my department head, chimes in. "The entitlement."

I pretend I don't hear him. *This is why they all hate you*, I want to say.

Back in the apartment, I apologize to Mickey for things getting out of hand last night, for Bill's mood and my weepiness, for the gun debacle.

"That was not okay that everyone behaved like that. We all drank too much."

Mickey laughs. "That was nothing. Don't think twice." She thrusts her phone into my hands. It's open to Helene's Instagram account. She's bouncing on her toes a little, watching me intently. Waiting for some kind of reaction.

"Yeah," I say. "I've seen it."

Mickey takes her phone back, scrolls down to a specific picture, and clicks on it. When she hands it back, I'm looking at a picture taken last summer, during a pool party. The girls are in the pool, surrounded by other kids who are splashing and playing around.

The comments on the pictures are different than the ones I'm used to seeing:

> *Love love love!*
> *You are a force a nature, lady xx*
> *Big fan!! I'm trying to get my own brand started. FB FB FB FB pls pls pls.*

"I don't get it," I say.

She takes her phone and scrolls to another photo. This one is from a couple months ago—around Christmas time. The older girl and a woman, standing in the snow.

"Do you see it now?"

"The same woman," I say.

Mickey nods.

"Go back."

She flips back to the previous picture.

"Who is she?"

"Took me a while," Mickey says. "But she appears in one other photo, from four years ago. In the comments there, Helene called her Olive, the 'au pair.'"

"Let me see."

Mickey shakes her head. "You can't really see anything in that one. Hoodie up, kid on her shoulders, shot from behind. Same build though. Pretty sure it's the same girl."

"You're thinking it's Angie?"

Mickey shrugs. "You tell me."

"Like Marlee."

Mickey lets me keep her phone. I toggle back and forth between the two most recent posts a dozen times. In both pictures, the au pair's head is down and she is playing with the children. Both shots seem to intentionally obscure her face. In the winter picture, the au pair is bundled up in a coat, a hat, and winter boots. She looks down at the girl, so you can only see the top of her head. No identifying features. In the summer one, she is in the pool with the kids, visible in profile. Her hair is damp, but it sheens red where the sun hits. Her skin is pale. She looks to be about my height, my build. She wears large sunglasses that cover most of the top half of her face and obscure the shape of her nose. She has a lower back tattoo that looks like a blur through the water. She dons silver bangles, the kind Angie used to love.

"Angie hated kids," I say. I don't know if that's true per se, but she definitely didn't like hanging out with me and my friends.

"In plain sight," Mickey says, looking at the pool picture again.

"I'm not sure," I say. I'm worried I'm going to shit my pants, that's how much my stomach hurts.

"It's probably not her," Mickey says.

"It could be anyone."

"I can't believe they call her the 'au pair,'" Mickey says. "So pretentious."

"Why? What should they say?"

"Nanny," Mickey says.

"Two different things," I say. "Au pairs usually just stay for a short time. It's almost like a study abroad."

"Hm," Mickey says. "This girl's been working for them for—well, I don't know."

"Years, though," I say.

"Yeah, years."

"Could Angie have gone to him? Could he be—" Mickey reaches for the right word. "Hiding her?"

"Hiding," I repeat. "Why?"

Mickey shrugs. "No one knew why for Marlee Fry, until they did."

"If it's like that—" I don't finish my sentence. I push away the thoughts about what my dad would have had to do for Angie to take such drastic steps. I push away the voices of the internet commentariat who insist that the fact that she was not his daughter would make him more likely to do terrible things to her. Unspeakable things. "What about Jake or whatever?" I say.

"I'm not saying we should abandon the Jake angle." Mickey reads my mind again. "My mom left. And it wasn't because any of us did anything to her. She just wanted a fresh start. Maybe Angie wanted to get to know her grandparents, and her nieces. Her other family. Maybe she didn't think it through."

"That doesn't make sense, Mickey. She could just leave if that's what she was after. She wouldn't need to vanish."

Angie and I never discussed my dad's family, but for some reason, I always assumed that her position was that they were rich yuppies. That she felt abandoned by them. That she was loyal. But what if it was us she was mad at? What if she resented being trapped in the wreckage of Mom's affair, being collateral damage, being lumped in with me, the product of complete shamelessness? What if she figured out that it was always unnatural, unfair, untenable—the bastard above the orphan? What if the way she tells it, we're the villains? What if she's alive? What if she doesn't miss me at all? What if seeing my face again is the moment she's feared?

"So," Mickey says, when the silence gets too loud. "Let's go see."

"I don't know."

"Maybe it's not that. But you said it yourself—Henry was very aggressive with you. Your dad thought something was going on with him. Ginger thinks something was going on with him, too. Maybe he's the one doxxing you. Who knows."

"Why would he—"

"Why not?" Mickey says.

"Okay," I say, thinking of my little nieces, picturing them looking like me and Angie back when we were small. "We can go. Just to look."

Mickey and I leave at 7 A.M. on Saturday and drive two hours to Helene's open house. We can't find my brother's address, so the only thing to do is con our way in.

The neighborhood is beautiful—verdant and picket and brochure-perfect, especially as the sun comes up over thick oak trees and brick chimneys.

I lean my head against the steering wheel in my parked car and close my eyes.

"You're awfully precious about your sleep," Mickey says. "For someone who goes to bed so early."

"You'll see when you get older."

"You're not that old."

"Two rough mornings in a row."

A gray SUV pulls up behind us, and Helene steps out of the car. From her trunk, she retrieves an open house sign that gets planted in the lawn and a bouquet of balloons that she ties to the mailbox. In person, she is much plainer than her profile. Her hair is tied back in a tight bun, and she wears jeans and a white blouse. The only makeup is a swipe of red lipstick.

"She's pretty," Mickey says.

"I guess."

"A couple more minutes, then we can go in," Mickey says. "A little before the start is fine."

I look up at the two-story white colonial with black shutters. It looks like a house in a children's book. Short hedges rise to the windowsills. The lawn slopes up to the front door, with brick stairs leading down to the street, flowerbeds lined up along the sides of the path. There's no sidewalk, because, I assume, the kids play in the street. Basketball hoops and hockey nets litter neighborhood driveways. Bikes are strewn carelessly on front lawns. There is a lot of trust here.

Mickey and I make our way toward the front door. She has promised to do most of the talking. All I have to say is that I'm looking into housing for my mother, who is recently widowed and could use a fresh start. True enough.

"Hello!" Helene says, throwing open the front door seconds after we ring. "Welcome. Come in. The early bird gets the worm."

"Sorry," I say. "We saw the balloons."

"Don't be, don't be." Helene gestures to a plastic bin by the door. "Would you mind removing your shoes?"

Mickey unlaces her Chucks and puts them in the bin. I take off my boots, and become immediately self-conscious about the foot smell and my loss in height. Helene gets to keep her pristine nude pumps, it seems.

"Let me show you around," Helene says. "Who is the broker and who is the buyer?"

"I'm looking for my mom," I say. "She's getting up there in years, and she needs a new house."

Mickey holds her hand out to Helene. "I'm her sister."

"Of course," Helene says. "I see it now." Mickey catches my eye, and we both smile. "I'm Helene. From the sign."

"I'm Cleo and this is Marigold," Mickey says.

"What unique names!"

Helene leads us around the kitchen, opening all the cabinets as she goes and waxing on about the energy-efficient appliances.

The tile is dated, and the wood is stained that orangey color I hate, but Helene is charming and very convincing. With her help, I find myself believing my own bullshit, thinking about how Mickey and I could make this place beautiful for Mom. The projects we could do together. A clean fit: three rooms, one for each of us.

As we follow Helene around, I can't escape the growing sensation that something is wrong. If I'm meant to believe that my brother is hiding something, that he was involved somehow in Angie's disappearance, then I have to believe he is harboring a lot of anger. That he looks at us and feels resentful, jealous, and bitter. Do bitter people marry beautiful, successful women? Do they churn out cherubic daughters and keep cozy but modern colonial homes? It doesn't make sense to me.

The doorbell rings and Helene excuses herself to answer it. "Why don't I let you show yourselves around," she says.

We wander into the living room first.

"I never understand this," Mickey says. "Wall-to-wall white carpet in the same room as the fireplace."

We head back toward the foyer so that we can make our way upstairs. Helene is still at the front door, talking to someone in low, hushed tones.

"It's a Saturday," she says.

The response is muted by the door.

Helene speaks through grated teeth. "Why can't she go to your open house with you?"

When she hears our footsteps, she whirls around and smiles wide. "All good so far?"

"We love it," I say. "Might be perfect for Mom."

The front door opens wider, so that we can see who is standing on the stoop. A girl of about ten and her father. Bella and Henry.

Henry doesn't look at us, but my stomach flips when I see his face. It's like seeing my father's ghost. The little girl watches me, logs my reaction, and shoots me a puzzled look. I try to force a smile.

"She'll just read," Henry says to Helene, getting her attention again. "Put her on the patio or something."

"Fine," Helene says. "Whatever."

Bella nudges her way inside and takes her shoes off without being told. She heads straight for the kitchen with a book tucked under her arm. As Helene shuts the door, Henry looks up behind her. He and I make the briefest of eye contact, and the door closes.

Mickey pulls me upstairs.

"Wow," Mickey says. "That was him."

"I know," I say. I inspect the medicine cabinet in the guest bathroom. "How long do we need to stay?"

"You're doing great," Mickey says. "He didn't see you." She pats me on the shoulder and glides back into the hallway. I follow her silently through each of the upstairs bedrooms. I barely notice what they look like, but Mickey opens closet doors and checks all the light switches. She murmurs sounds of affirmation as she goes.

I follow her downstairs to the kitchen, where Helene is sitting at the table with Bella. Bella is absorbed in her book, and Helene is texting. She pops up when she sees us, and her furrowed brows relax.

"What do we think?" she asks.

"It's so nice," Mickey says. "A lot of character. But doesn't feel like a fixer either."

Helene nods aggressively. "Exactly. They've really put the money into keeping this place up. Not in a flippy way either. Quality materials."

Mickey cocks her head to the ground and looks up at Helene from beneath her eyelashes. "You know," she says. "I'm a big fan of yours."

"Really?" Helene says. "Thank you so much."

"I'm trying to start my own blog. It's going to be about powerful career women. Work/life balance. Interviews, how-to, things like that. For girls of my generation."

"Love that," Helene says. "It's so important to have role models."

"I was wondering if I could interview you at home some time," Mickey says. "For the launch."

"Oh, it's not launched yet?"

"No," Mickey says. "We've been working out the backend and the sponsorship. I want it to be really high-end from the jump. The first few weeks are so critical, don't you think?"

"Sure," Helene says. "I'd love to."

"Hopefully it would drive some new followers your way, too," Mickey says. "Younger traffic."

Helene flinches a tiny bit, and I can almost track where she's had Botox. Not twenty-two anymore. "Let me get you my card," Helene says. "You can email me to set something up. Also if you have any more questions about the house, I'm happy to represent your side of the transaction as well, and we might be able to shave something off the fee." She leads Mickey out to the foyer where her cards are arranged on a console table.

I'm left alone in the kitchen with Bella.

"What are you reading?" I ask the girl.

She holds up the book so I can see the cover. *The Swiss Family Robinson.*

"One of my favorites," I say.

Bella doesn't respond. I hear Mickey making small talk with Helene in the other room.

"Hey," I whisper.

Bella looks up at me, then around to see where her stepmom is.

"No," I say, sitting down next to her. "Don't be worried."

"I'm not," she says.

"I know your mom."

"She's not my mom," Bella says.

"No, not her. Your mom. Ginger."

Bella's eyes narrow. "Who are you?"

"Listen," I say. "My dad, he was your grandpa."

"I don't understand," Bella says.

"It's okay," I say. "Don't be upset. You should just know— you were really helpful."

"What?"

"With the letter."

"I don't know what you're talking about," Bella says, loudly. She looks desperately to the door. "I didn't do anything."

"It's okay," I say. "I'm leaving. You can go back to your book."

I try to reach out to touch her on the shoulder, but she pulls away from me. I wave instead.

"It was nice to meet you," I say.

I meet Mickey in the hallway, where Helene is greeting new visitors to the open house.

"Ready?" Mickey says.

We race down the brick steps so fast I'm sure I'm going to take a tumble and crack my skull open. When we reach the car, it's like we need the oxygen inside to survive.

"We're set," Mickey says. "We're going to her house next week for tea, and I'm supposed to interview her about how she built her brand or some shit."

"I think I fucked up," I say. Mickey waits. "I talked to the kid."

"Teddy," Mickey groans. She leans her head against the steering wheel. "Okay, walk me through it."

As we make our way back to the highway, I recount the conversation with Bella.

"That's not so bad," Mickey says, when I finish. "She seems like she hates her stepmom, and if she tells her dad it would probably cause problems with him and her mom."

"I put her in a bad spot," I say.

"It's fine," Mickey says.

"We have to stop off somewhere," I say.

Mickey pulls into the first restaurant we pass. The lot is empty and the sign is faded and the exterior is made of thick wooden siding without windows.

"This place?" Mickey says.

I rush out of the car and into the restaurant. A sign says "seat yourself," and I throw my coat in an empty booth to make it clear that I'll make a purchase. Then I rush to the bathroom. My stomach is churning, and I barely make it to the toilet on time.

This morning, I was in the car driving fast on the highway, no cars in sight, sun coming up over the trees. Mickey was dozing next to me, and the air was cold like ice water in my throat. I felt alive. I gave myself five miles of believing I would find Angie. Not just allowing for the possibility but believing that we would definitely find her. I wasn't worried how to tell her about Dad dying, and I wasn't mad at her. I let myself imagine what would happen if it all went our way for once.

It was a wonderful five miles.

Then, I hit 115,034 on the odometer, and I shoved the thought from my brain.

My abs clench involuntarily and a cramp forms under my ribs. There is no question in my mind that my body is purging something. I pull the menstrual waste bin closer with my foot in case I also need to vomit, which seems possible.

One more wave. One more seizing of all my muscles, a shudder and release. It passes like a sudden rain. I feel filthy, but lighter.

I wash up and go back to the table.

"That took forever," Mickey says. "What should we get?"

"Ginger ale," I say.

"Yuck."

"You can't get any food," I say. "I'll barf if I smell your food."

"Then let's go," Mickey whispers. She takes my clammy hand on the table and scooches out of her bench. She holds my hand past the hostess stand, where an older woman does not seem pleased by the display. She holds my hand all the way back to the car, where she pours me into the passenger seat.

"Drive slowly, please."

"You got it."

Despite all the braking and frenetic lane switching, I fall asleep with my head pressed to the cold glass, and when I wake up, we're back home.

The next time I see Bill, it's at my apartment. He's here to introduce the dogs and see my place. He lets Rocky and Red sniff Wolfie's butt, and he apologizes for being rude to the girl.

"Mickey?" I ask.

"Yeah," he says. "Her."

"It's fine." I laugh. "I don't think anything you say could ever really bother her."

Bill makes a face. "What does that mean?"

"Nothing."

"What's the real story there?"

"Let's walk." I consider sticking to the genealogy thing, but figure what the hell. "She knew my dad," I say. "She's into Angie's case."

Bill frowns again. He pulls the dogs closer to the shoulder. We move slowly with Wolfie in tow. Even on a good day, like today, he barely ambles along. Cars make room for us as they pass. One guy leans out the window and barks. The traffic is starting to pick up. Soon it will be hard to get out of the driveway.

"You're still doing that?" Bill says. "The online stuff?"

"No." He hasn't forgotten me checking his phone and computer. Or the fight that came after. "Don't worry," I say. "Mickey took your side when I told her what happened, by the way. Before the dinner."

Bill rubs his head and sighs loudly.

"What?"

"Didn't some guy post all of your personal information online? Isn't that what you told me?"

"Yes," I say. "And Mickey is the one helping me find him."

"Teddy." Bill raises his voice. "Why would you want to find that man?"

"Not find him," I say. "But know who he is. He might be my brother."

"What?"

"My half-brother. From my dad's first marriage."

Bill yanks Rocky away from a patch of poison ivy. "Why would your half-brother be docking you?"

"Doxxing."

"Doxxing. Fine. Why would your half-brother be doxxing you?"

"I don't know. I barely know him," I say. "We've never met in person. But have you heard of Marlee Fry?"

"Sounds vaguely familiar."

"She disappeared a few years back. Sacramento. Then she turned up recently with her adult stepsister, living in a different state. Their stepdad had abused them both."

"Jesus. Why do you read about this stuff?"

"Well, Mickey found some pictures. My brother has a nanny for his kids. Looks like Angie. Could be a similar situation."

"Was Angie abused?"

"I don't know."

Bill gets agitated. "What does that mean?"

"How am I supposed to know?"

"Are we talking about your dad here?" Bill asks, exasperated. "This all makes no sense. First your brother, who you don't actually know, is antagonizing you online, and then he's hiding from you because he's been harboring your sister for a decade in—where?"

"Boston area."

"Boston. You think Angie ran away, all the way to . . . Boston."

"You're being a dick."

"You sound insane."

"If someone had said that Marlee Fry ran away to Kansas City—"

"Who the fuck is Marlee Fry? Stop talking to me about Marlee Fry."

"Let's turn back," I say. "Wolfie's losing steam. I don't want to have to pick him up."

We walk in silence back to my apartment, where I unlock the door and carry Wolfie up the stairs. Bill follows me, with Rocky and Red pulling up the rear.

Inside, I pour three bowls of water for the dogs. Wolfie collapses by the door, too tired to even rehydrate. Bill's dogs splash around noisily, drinking everything I give them and demanding refills.

By the time I return to the living room, Bill has done the tidying that I meant to do before he got here. He has pushed the air mattresses to the corner and folded the blankets, stacked them next to the pillows. He is standing in front of the Wall.

"Charming," Bill says, pointing to one of the dicks.

"It's a joke," I say. "Like in the movies."

Bill nods, keeps examining the documents. He tugs at a piece of yarn and it snaps back into place.

"We call it the 'Wall of Insanity.'"

"Apt."

Bill and I order pizza and we eat on the floor, cross-legged, balancing paper plates on our laps. I pick at the cheese on a single slice, pretending not to be hungry, stubbornly refusing to enjoy it.

Bill doesn't notice. He asks when I'm going to order furniture.

"I have some stuff going on right now," I say.

"I can see that."

"My dad did just die."

Bill was never going to stay the night, but I thought we might at least have sex. Now, that's off the table, and this whole thing is feeling increasingly pointless.

I scroll through Reddit on my phone while he cleans up—collecting my garbage and his, putting the leftover slices into Ziploc bags in the fridge, and sweeping the floor of the living room.

"Okay," he says. "We're going to take off." He slaps his thigh, and the dogs stand at attention.

I stand, too, and offer him a half-hearted hug. "Thanks for coming by."

Bill squeezes me back hard. "Teddy," he says, into my ear. His breath is hot and itchy. "I know grief is weird. But this is a lot. Are you okay?"

"I'm fine," I say. "Thank you."

"All right," Bill says. He rubs my back for another minute, and I don't move a muscle. It's claustrophobic. It's suffocating. He releases me. "Bye," he says.

"Bye."

When he's shut the door, I take out the leftover slices and eat them all. When they're gone, I feel full and victorious, and I lie back down on my air mattress, open Reddit, and, as the kids say, inject that shit directly into my veins.

What I learn about Mickey once my TV is set up is that she likes to watch shows that teach you something. That includes true crime, naturally, but also travel programs, documentaries, craft shows, and cooking competitions. I let her choose when we're folding my laundry, since she's excellent at it. She used to work in retail, and she can get my shirts folded so perfectly, the corners make right angles.

"Not another *Chopped*," I say, coming in during the entree round. "Please."

"Look at that basket," Mickey says. "Buffalo sauce, marshmallows, pig ears, peanuts, and cactus."

"Disgusting."

"I think you have to go barbecue, right?"

I motion for her to lift her legs so that I can sneak under them. The new couch is tiny and it sucks you in like quicksand. We have to pull each other from its grips.

"What are we doing for dinner?" I ask. "What do you feel like?"

Mickey pauses the show. "Let's do a *Chopped*."

In the kitchen, Mickey prepares a work station—cutting board, mixing bowls, chef's knife. I choose my mystery ingredients from what we have on hand. There isn't much in the new fridge. I hand her: low fat Greek yogurt, ground chicken, a can of diced tomatoes, and coconut water. I pour myself a glass of white wine.

Mickey assesses the lot. "This is only four."

I pour her a glass, too. "Here's the fifth."

Sitting at the counter, I watch as she gets to work. She grabs an onion and parsley from the fridge.

"So," she says, though I've said nothing. "I'm thinking with this basket—"

"There's no basket."

"I have to go curry. Like a Thai chicken curry kind of thing. Right?"

"I like Thai."

"Are you timing me?"

I top off my wine as Mickey heats a pat of butter in a pan with some olive oil. She softens some red onions and garlic in the pan, then vinegar and coconut water.

"What about the yogurt?" I ask.

"I have to add that last," she says. "Or it will separate and get weird."

"How do you know this?" I ask.

"I pick things up," Mickey says.

"You know a lot."

"I like knowing that I can survive with what I've got on hand." Mickey stirs her curry. "I like knowing that I can make something tasty out of, like, three cans, you know?"

"I guess," I say. "I'm not big on cooking."

"I feel like—when you're kind of poor, people expect you to be trash. To eat like trash, to have no taste or culture or whatever. So it's like a way to—get around that."

"Sure."

"Nothing on *Chopped* is super fancy, usually. Some stuff is weird. But a lot of it is pretty low-end."

We eat together at the island counter, and I can't get over how young she looks tonight. Sometimes, I forget that she's right there with the kids I teach. Barely a year older than my seniors. I understand how Dad could have felt that this was his do-over. That if he could help this girl, at this moment in her life, he might get a taste of what it would mean to carry Angie to the safety of her twenties. When I look at Mickey, I see all the things that she might do one day, the way that all similarly young people contain infinite possibilities, only visible to those older than them, for whom those doors have already closed. I never saw Angie that way, but of course she had it too—all those different, potential lives locked away inside her. I see them now.

"You don't talk much about how you grew up. What about your dad?"

"He's dead," Mickey says, without looking up.

"Were you guys poor?"

"I'm still poor."

"Well," I say. "You go to school. You live in the dorms. Seems like you're doing okay."

"I'm good at finding money," Mickey says.

"Yeah," I say. "I remember that. I had jobs at the ice cream shop, the Little Gym, and the regular gym all in one summer once. Plus my usual babysitting gigs."

"I can't picture you babysitting."

"I babysat a lot," I say.

Every time we're alone, it feels like there is something she wants to say to me that she's working toward. I pour her another glass of wine.

"Do you love Bill?" she asks, while we're eating.

"Wow. What a question."

"You don't have to answer. If it's too personal."

"No," I say. "It's okay."

"He loves you," Mickey says.

"I know," I say.

"You don't love him?"

"It's not even that. Okay, it's like how—in high school and college—I had this group of friends, and every once in a while, someone would start going on about how we were going to be in each other's weddings and know each other's kids and we were basically sisters and blah blah blah."

"So?"

"So, it makes me feel like I'm living on a different fucking planet. It's why I stopped seeing them after college. I couldn't take it."

"You feel that way about Bill?"

I shrug.

"I have the opposite problem," Mickey says. "I always have."

"How so?"

"I thought this girl Janey was my best friend in seventh grade. I told everyone she was my best friend—my dad, my aunt. And then I didn't even get invited to her birthday party."

"Oh no."

"It wasn't a mean girl thing. She told me about it in advance, that her mom was taking her to Boston for the weekend with her three besties. She offered to bring me back a souvenir."

"Brutal."

"It is what it is. People mean a lot to me. More than I mean to them, sometimes."

I pour the rest of the bottle for myself and drink it while I think. "Let's watch a movie," I say. "If you're done."

One of the cable stations is halfway through *You've Got Mail*, so we let it run. On screen, Meg Ryan is stood up on her blind date with Tom Hanks, though she doesn't know it's him yet. The melancholy music swells. It's all very dramatic. And I think—*you don't know this man, you stupid, stupid woman. You chatted with someone on the internet because you're lonely.*

"Nowadays," I say to Mickey, "this would not be a rom-com. This would be a horror movie. A thriller. About catfishing. Cyber stalkers."

"So cynical," Mickey says, as she pulls a throw blanket over my lap and takes the glass from my hand to set it on the end table.

Helene answers the door with a platinum-haired toddler strapped to her chest, sleeping.

"Come in," she says. "Sorry about the mess."

The house is immaculate, decorated entirely in shades of white, with fresh flowers in vases on every surface. There are no toys or crayons or stains in sight.

"Is your husband here?" I ask.

Helene cocks her head. "Were you hoping to speak with Henry, too? He doesn't usually do these sorts of things."

"No," Mickey interjects. "She's just being curious."

"What about Bella?"

"Bella is upstairs," Helene says. "I'm sorry. Do you know—"

"The other day . . ." I say.

Helene slaps her forehead. "Right," she says. "I totally forgot. She was there, at the open." Helene gestures to the round table in the kitchen and we sit down. She fetches a tray holding several pre-poured glasses of water with lemon. "I hope she wasn't bothering you."

"Not at all," I say.

Mickey takes out her phone and props it up against some books. "Do you mind if I film?" she asks.

"It's not a vlog, is it?" Helene asks. She looks slightly pan-icked. "I couldn't find you online. I meant to ask your handle."

"Not a vlog," Mickey says. "Just easier to transcribe."

Helene laughs. "Okay, good. Because I have some pictures I can send you where I look less sloppy."

Mickey asks Helene some basic questions about her brand—number of followers, years publishing, etc. I tune out and stare at the bare feet dangling around her belly button. My nieces. The only ones I'll ever have.

The baby starts to squirm and whine, and Helene shushes her gently, bounces the carrier up and down. The baby still squirms.

"I can take her," I say. "If she wants to go down, I can watch her."

"That would be great," Helene says. "She'll stay close, but she's in that stage where she is more confident in her walking than she should be, so you have to be on her all the time. Hard to do while you're doing something like this."

The clips to the carrier come off, and the baby is loose in Helene's arms. She places her down on the white tile, and the baby holds on to the edge of her mother's chair.

"What's her name?" I ask.

"Noelle," Helene says. "She calls herself No-No."

"Hi, No-No," I say. I slide onto the ground where I can hold on to her tiny elbows to spot her movements. She doesn't seem to mind my being close. I touch the short, light curls on her head, and they are impossibly fine.

"I have some more in-depth questions," Mickey says. "If that's okay."

"Okay," Helene says.

"Your husband's family has been subject to a lot of scrutiny in the past," Mickey says.

Helene nods. "Sure," she says. "It comes with the territory, to some degree. His grandfather being who he was."

"Right," Mickey says.

"They were lovely people," Helene says. "Very down-to-earth."

"I'm thinking more about Henry's dad," Mickey says, "who died only recently. And his sister, Angie, whose case was—"

"His cousin," Helene corrects.

"Sorry?"

"People are always doing that. She was not his sister. She was his cousin. No common parentage."

"Well, same father, biological or not."

"You know what," Helene says. "I think I'm not going to do this. I don't like where this is going."

"I'm sorry if I—"

"I change my mind," Helene says, her voice tight and anxious. "You should go. I don't give you permission to publish any of this interview."

"Well," Mickey says. "That's not really how it works."

"Mickey," I mutter. Why be stubborn? It's not a real blog. There's nothing to publish.

"I thought your name was Cleo," Helene says.

"Nickname," Mickey says.

Helene snatches Noelle away from me. "You both need to go. Now. I'll call the police."

I hear footsteps behind me and turn to see Bella, standing in the doorway.

"What are you doing here?" Bella asks.

"Bella, go back upstairs," Helene says. She clutches Noelle close to her. "Close your door and call Daddy."

Bella turns around and runs up the stairs before I have a chance to speak. Mickey makes a quick dart for the fridge in the chaos and takes down a child's photo collage. Helene lets out a high-pitched scream in response, and the baby starts crying. Mickey grabs my arm. "Go," she says.

I drive as Mickey pores over the collage in the passenger's seat. I'm still shaking when we get back onto the highway.

"What did you take?" I ask.

Mickey points to three pictures. I have to glance as I drive, so I can't inspect any one photo too closely. Two are low-resolution pictures, taken on a cell phone, in selfie mode. They are of Bella, Noelle, the third girl, and a woman with bright red hair. In one, her face is mostly obscured by the kids. In the other she is wearing those big dark sunglasses again and turned to the side, with Noelle strapped to her chest. The third photo is a Polaroid from a birthday party. There are a dozen people lined up behind Bella as she poses with her cake. One of them is the woman. It's poorly lit and fuzzy, but the hair gives her away.

"Is it her?" I ask.

Mickey holds the collage closer to her face. "It's not that they don't take photos with the nanny, it's that they don't post them."

"Is it her, Mickey?"

"Helene posts everything. But she doesn't post this person. The photographs they take of this person stay inside the house."

"It's not her," I say. "I don't think it's her."

"Probably not."

I look down to see that I'm going ninety. I take a deep breath and try to calm down. "That was bad," I say. "That was so bad."

"Wasn't great."

"She acted weird though, right? When you asked about Angie?"

Mickey nods. "Sure did."

"I don't know," I say. "Let me think about it."

The day of the dance, I stay at work with three hours to kill. The students have to leave the building and come back later; they can't hang around. Some of the other teachers who are chaperoning suggest drinks in the faculty lounge.

I volunteer Bill to pick up booze and bring it back to us at school, and he obliges. When he shows up, he's wearing a suit that is slightly tight and slightly short, and his hair and beard are groomed.

"You look nice," I say, taking the plastic bag from his hand. He got vodka like I asked, but the one that comes in a plastic container. I should have been more specific.

Bill grabs my wrist. "I'm overdressed."

It's true; he is. The rest of us are in our work clothes—pencil skirts and sensible flats, slacks and sweaters. Nothing fancy.

"No one can tell. You look like you're coming from work."

"Teddy," he says. "I didn't know—"

"Let's not," I say. "I don't want to think about it."

"I feel like I should explain."

From the couch, Steven calls out. "Hey, lovebirds! Enough with the chatting. Do we have some booze or what?"

Steven is the youngest member of the faculty at twenty-three. He went to high school here, too, and the students love him. The boys think he's cool because he was one of them and he curses in class and wears tight button-downs without a tie or an undershirt. The girls want to fuck him. I heard two of them say as much in the bathroom when they didn't know I was in a stall.

Bill waves to the other chaperones—a motley crew of ten or so teachers from all different departments. We're all under thirty-five, which makes him the oldest person here. The administration pays a stipend of fifty dollars to chaperone the dances, but you have to be here until eleven, so none of the older teachers ever volunteer. They have their own kids to get home to, and it doesn't pay to hire a sitter. It works out to far less than the minimum wage if you count the waiting time and the cost of alcohol.

"Is this your first dance, Bill?" Wendy asks.

I sit next to her and Bill is next to me, so she talks to him over my lap. She keeps kicking my ankle with her boot, which I think means *well done with him* or *he's cute* or something, but I can't be sure.

"First dance," Bill says.

Steven hands him a cup of vodka with ice. He has the same drink for himself. "They suck," he says. "Good luck to you."

Bill hands me his drink, and stands. "Wendy, what can I get you?"

"Such a gentleman." She looks at Steven. "Unlike some people."

"You're not crippled," Steven says. "Bill is our guest."

I can tell Bill is very uncomfortable by the attention, so I stand to help him make drinks. I offer Wendy my vodka, but she says it's too strong, so I keep it.

"Mostly water for me."

We don't have any mixers, and the taste of the cheap vodka is acerbic, but I chug it down and refill while I'm up. "These things are torturous," I say to Bill. "But I'll get you a stipend."

Bill frowns. "They're going to think I need the money." He pats his forehead, which is sweating. "Embarrassing."

"It's fine," I say. "Relax."

I pour us a couple shots, which we take discreetly, in succession, before rejoining the group with our drinks. We have an hour until the kids arrive.

The students always show up at this thing three sheets to the wind, and I look the other way. For fifty dollars, I will make sure that no one dies or does any hard drugs in the bathroom. It's not enough money for me to deal with parent phone calls over trivialities like light drinking or over-the-clothes groping.

Bill and I are stationed at the front door for the first part of the night. We're meant to check student IDs to make sure the kids' dates are other high school students and not twentysomething dealers.

Bill and I are tipsy. He strokes my thigh under the ticket table, and I occasionally return the favor, letting my hand drift up to the crotch of his pants when the line gets thin. It's like nothing ever happened.

Rick stops by our table on his way home for the night. The one nice thing about Rick is that he understands how unwelcome his presence is, socially. He never joins our happy hours, and he even leaves the kids alone to have their fun without the principal present.

I introduce him to Bill, and they shake hands.

"Watch out for this one," Rick says. "She had a bit of a naughty streak in high school when it came to school dances."

I laugh, nervously, unsure what he's talking about.

"Oh yeah?" Bill says.

"Got caught making trouble in the bathroom once or twice, as I recall." Rick winks at Bill.

"What?" I say. "What are you talking about?"

Rick pats the table. "Okay. Get home safe, you kids."

"I think you're thinking of my sister," I say, but I'm too late. There are kids in front of me looking impatient, waiting for me to stamp them through, and Rick is already slinking out the side door.

"That was weird," Bill says. "What a creep."

At nine o'clock, we all rotate positions, and Bill and I are reassigned to the dance floor in the auditorium. It's dark, save for the light from the kids' cell phones. I'm feeling unsteady on my feet, and I have to yell into Bill's ear so he can hear me over the music.

"Let's take a lap." I point him in one direction. I'm taking the opposite route.

"What should I be doing?"

"Three things," I say. I count them off on my fingers. "One: If you see anything more than kissing, break it up. Two: Confiscate any water bottles. They're filled with vodka. Three: If you see any kids looking shady, give them the Eye." I demonstrate the Eye.

Bill laughs at me. "Okay," he says. "I can do that."

"You're intimidating."

"Old," he corrects.

I take off in the opposite direction of him, weaving through sweaty, smelly teenage bodies. The male to female ratio is askew, and for every couple making out on the dance floor, there are four boys standing around, watching enviously. Few students are properly dancing.

"Hey, Ms. A," I hear, but I can't identify the greeter in the crowd. Most of my students ignore me at these things.

I stand on my tiptoes to spot Bill, towering over some students ten yards away. He isn't moving, but standing and staring at a group of boys who keep looking back and forth between each other nervously.

"Bill," I call, but he can't hear me. I push in his direction until I crash directly into his sturdy chest.

"Ms. Angstrom." He smiles and lowers his mouth to my ear. His breath is warm on my skin and his lips graze my earlobes, tickling. I shudder involuntarily. "That eye move of yours." He pulls back and stares me down, demonstrating.

"That's it," I say. "You got it."

"It doesn't work."

I follow his gaze to the group of students he had been stalking out. One of them smokes a vape pen, its butt end lit up in neon blue. Another has a crushed water bottle sticking out of his back pocket.

I walk over and tap the young man on the shoulder. "Marcos," I say. "This is mine now, okay?" I take the water bottle. I put my other palm out to receive the vape pen from his friend, whom I don't recognize. "Thank you."

I walk away, and I know they are watching, wondering if I am going to report them to the principal, who will call their parents in for a meeting, follow up with the Dean tomorrow, etc. It's a lot of paperwork.

Instead, I grab Bill's elbow, and lead him behind the auditorium stage.

"Are they okay out there?" Bill asks.

"They're fine for a few minutes."

I take a swig from the confiscated water bottle and taste warm gin. I can feel the bass from the DJ's speakers even more powerfully now. We're standing behind the woofer. Passing the bottle to Bill, I take a hit of the vape pen, expecting nicotine, but getting pot instead. Good pot.

"Whoa," I say. Bill is staring at me, not drinking from the bottle.

"I don't want mono," he says.

"You're going to get whatever I have, buddy." I take the bottle back and drain it, and then I pull him into my face and kiss him.

I take another hit from the vape pen, drawing deep and holding it. I throw it back toward the curtain. It hits with a thud and rolls to the ground somewhere. They'll find it tomorrow during play rehearsal, and it will be a minor scandal for a few days.

"Let's get back out there." I take Bill's hand in mine and lead him back to the dance floor.

"Should we make another round?" Bill asks.

We are standing in a sea of children. The air is wet and thick and smells like cheap cologne and hormones. Bill is taller than the next tallest person by a head. A gaggle of girls walks by in crop tops and yoga pants. No doubt, they showed up in different outfits and stripped down in the bathroom, when their parents were out of sight. They form a chain with their hands and nearly Red Rover us as they pass. To the young, we're invisible.

I feel young again in the middle of them. The promise of these kinds of nights when you're a teenager. The possibility of something great and terrifying happening. The secrets and the risk. I wonder if it's how Angie felt leaving the house for the last time. Like she was going to a party that would change everything.

The DJ comes on the mic to announce the next song. I assume it will be more of the same—vaguely electronic music with female vocals. Instead, he plays "Don't Stop Believin'," and the kids go nuts. They're all singing at the top of their lungs.

"Wow," Bill says. "Who knew?" He laughs and looks at me. Puts out his hand.

He pulls me into him. We dance, and I close my eyes. My head is buzzing from the weed and the alcohol. The whole room is spinning and I'm spinning with it. I'm floating pleasantly in this damp auditorium. I sling my arms around Bill's neck. For now, he isn't a middle-aged lawnmower who until recently lived with his mother. For now, I'm not the object of everyone's pity and gossip surrounding my family. We don't have to worry about where my dad fits into it at all. We're a boy and a girl at a dance. I kiss his face hard, and he kisses me back. His hands move down my spine to my hips and he pulls me close. I feel an erection forming and pushing against my belly button. We rock and sway rhythmically and I let myself go heavy. Let Bill hold and drag me. We're fused.

There is a hand on my shoulder, and it's not Bill. I turn around to see Steven, smirking at me. Wendy behind him, not smiling at all. There are students in a circle around us, staring and whispering. I'm not sure how long we've been at this, but the song playing now is one I don't recognize. I can't seem to account for the time.

"Sorry to break up the fun," Steven says. "But we need you to start clearing out the cafeteria."

"We're wrapping up," Wendy says in a small voice.

"What time is it?"

"It's almost ten-thirty," she says, looking down.

I wipe my face and smooth my hair. Bill stays close to me, and we head toward the cafeteria.

Wendy rushes to my side before I can get far. "Hold on," she says. She adjusts my blouse, pulling it up to cover my bra, and she tugs my skirt down around my hips. I'm too scared to look up and make eye contact with any of my students. I tell myself that they've already gotten back to their own tiny dramas. That no one cares about whatever I'm doing.

My face is on fire. My head is pounding.

"I need water," Bill says.

We skip the cafeteria, and head up to the faculty lounge without speaking. I get Bill a water.

"You should get going," I say. "I have to finish up here."

"Okay," he says. "Are you sure?"

"Yup. Thank you."

On my way out, I run into Janice, the librarian whom everyone avoids. She is lonely and sweet, but she'll trap you for ages if you so much as make eye contact. She works all the school functions, because she has nowhere else to be. The kids all hate her because she's too strict. Recently, the administration took her detention privileges away because she was abusing them. Her favorite topic of conversation is how out of control the students are this year. Every year.

"Have a good night, Theodora," Janice says. She collects her coat from the faculty lockers.

"Thanks, you too," I say, trying my best to find my keys so that I can hurry out.

"You know," Janice says, and I die a little inside. I'm so tired. "I've been meaning to tell you—"

I gesture for her to go on without looking up from my key hunt.

"It's rotten what those kids did. I'm really sorry."

"Excuse—how do you mean?"

"I heard them—the boys—saying how they painted your car. Terrible. I hope you reported them to the police."

"The boys," I say. "How did you . . ."

"Oh, I'm invisible," Janice says. "And now that I can't give detention, no one even lowers their voice. It's a free-for-all in there." She clucks and shakes her head. "I thought that Jamie was supposed to be a good one, but this whole cohort—they're out of control."

I feel like the wind is knocked out of me. It takes me a second to inhale, to remind myself to keep breathing. "They are," I say.

"Two years ago for me," Janice says, failing to register my shock. She is bundled to go and throws her purse handle over one shoulder. "Not that bad, obviously. Not my car. But the disrespect."

I nod. I remember what she's talking about, on April Fool's Day, when the kids posted pretend flyers around school advertising a freakshow attraction: *The Incredible Cat-Lady!* In the center of each flyer was a photoshopped picture of a cat with Janice's head. A speech bubble came out of her mouth: "Have I ever told you about my niece? She studies computer programming . . ."

At the time, I thought it was mean-spirited, but a bit deserved. What did anyone expect working in a high school? If you fuck with the kids, they'll get you back the only way teenagers know how.

In a few short months, I've gone from Steven to Janice. Worse, because I thought it was Jake that defaced my car. I thought some invisible boogeyman was stalking me, but it was one of my own. One of the sweet, round faces that used to follow me through the halls from class to class and count the days until graduation to hear me say *congratulations and please, no more Ms. Angstrom, I'm Teddy now*.

When I collect my fifty dollars from the assistant principal, she tells me to get some rest. "You look tired, honey," she says. Her half-smirk, half-frown tells me that she's already heard about Bill and me on the dancefloor. I don't ask her for Bill's stipend.

The faculty parking lot is quiet, even though the student parking lot is buzzing with informal tailgates—dates trying to milk every last minute before curfew. Moms in minivans and midsize SUVs form a pick-up line at the curb for sweaty underclassmen, who wish they could be sitting in the back of a senior's truck in the lot. One day.

I watch them mill about in their familiar patterns. I'm too drunk to drive, but no one seems to care.

In my glove compartment, I have an emergency kit that Mom got after Dad's "accident." It is designed to help me escape from drowning in my car, even though that isn't what happened to him.

From the kit, I remove the dual seat belt cutter/window hammer tool and turn it over in my hand. It is top-heavy, shaped like a wrench with a little pointy metal stud on the end. That is the part that breaks glass. Standing on the passenger's side of the car, I'm invisible to everyone in the big lot. All the staff have left except the ones who have to stay until the bitter end. The small lot is empty. The coast is clear.

I hit the window of my passenger's seat hard. I expect very little, but the window shatters with one strike. Glass floods into my car, creating a glimmering puddle of shards in the moon-light. Mom would be pleased to know that her kit works.

The sound of breaking glass was loud, but no one seems to have noticed it over the competing radios and car engines. I chuck Mom's gift into the sewer grate and head back inside.

"You're back," the assistant principal says when she sees me. Her smile quickly curdles into something else. "Oh my. You're bleeding. Are you okay?"

She touches her head, then her forearm, so I check those areas on myself and sure enough find blood.

"Someone smashed my car window," I say. I start crying, which isn't a challenge. When I'm this drunk, I'm always close to tears.

"I'll call the police. Sit down."

"I tried to fix it," I say. "But I only made it worse."

The AP hands me Kleenex after Kleenex. She seems irritated that I won't go to the bathroom and clean out my wounds.

I tell her and the police officers the same thing. I don't know who did it. I have no idea. Though some of the kids have been bragging about an earlier vandalism to my car. And they were here tonight—Jamie and his friends. But that's all from Janice. Take it with a grain of salt.

The AP looks alarmed. Janice is annoying, but she's credible. Uprightly Christian, she does not lie. She barely takes a joke.

The officers look at my car and take pictures.

The assistant principal tells me that she'll take care of everything. "I'm calling parents now," she says. "I'm so sorry about this, Theodora. I wish you'd felt you could have told us about the spray paint."

I shrug. "I didn't want to get anyone in trouble," I mutter. "Paint is one thing. But this—I could have really gotten hurt."

She nods gravely.

I strain every muscle in my body to stay awake the whole way back to the apartment, where Mickey is asleep. I clean myself off in the kitchen sink, finish a bottle of wine while standing directly in front of the fridge, and pass out next to her, hoping to black out as much of the evening as possible.

On the phone, Mom is panicked, angry.

"There's a sheriff here," she says. "They're looking for you."

"I'm coming," I say. "Don't worry."

She's sitting at the kitchen table with the uniformed sheriff when I walk in, and I feel like I'm in trouble. They are both drinking tea and not talking.

The man stands. His portly belly hangs over his belt, tightly cradled by his gray shirt. "Are you Theodora Angstrom?"

"Yes, I am," I say.

"I have to serve you with this document, ma'am. It's a formal notice that a restraining order has been filed against you."

Mom gasps audibly. My face burns.

"Thank you," I say. "Understood."

"There are some numbers in there. Some information in case you want to contest it. I was just telling your mother—people can make all kinds of claims. Doesn't make them true. But you have to go with the system."

"Thank you," I say. "I appreciate that."

"Usually I'm giving these out to men," he says. "Big guys who beat their wives. Ex-boyfriends who can't let go. And you seem like a nice young lady. I'm sure you'll get it sorted out."

Mom continues fretting her hands and whimpering as I escort the officer to the door. When I come back, she's perfectly still. Almost spooky.

"Open it," she says.

I do as she says. I spot my brother's name at the top as the plaintiff. The document is filled with lots of tiny font. Several phone numbers. A court date. A notice of temporary restraint until the hearing—no contact, court ordered.

"What does it say?"

I fold it back up. "Nothing," I say. "It's fine."

"Is it from Bill?"

"What?" I say. "No. Of course not."

"Then who?"

I stare back at her, mute.

"Who, Teddy?"

I shake my head.

"Give it to me," she says. She stands and moves toward me. "Give it to me. Now."

"No," I say. I clutch the document to my chest.

Mom comes within inches of my face. She puts her hands over my hands, but she doesn't wrestle it from me. She leaves them there until I yield, until she can slip the order from my fingers with ease.

I watch her open it and see her face morph from confusion to horror.

"What did you do?" she says.

"Nothing," I say. "I didn't do anything."

"This says you are harassing him. Antagonizing his daughter."

"I have to go," I say. Mom stands dumbfounded as I leave without the document. I ignore Wolfie's thumping tail as I pass, withholding eye contact from him. In my head, I apologize. I can't slow down. He would understand.

I take another rideshare back to the apartment, and I text Bill to tell him I can't make it tonight. I have to deal with an emergency with Mickey.

Good luck, he says. I see him typing more, but nothing else arrives.

I get into the real bed in my room—the one I haven't slept in yet—and pull a blanket over my head and fill the cavern with my hot, disgusting breath and try not to picture my niece, try not to imagine what they said about me to her.

An hour later, when I've fallen asleep, I feel a hand on my shoulder.

"Teddy," Mickey says. She pulls the blanket back from my head. She laughs. "What are you doing?"

"It's so bad," I say, remembering the letter and feeling instantly hungover.

"What is?"

"My brother," I say. "He served me with a restraining order."

"What? Are you serious?"

"Today, at my mom's house. It was awful."

Mickey looks away, bites her lip like she does when she's thinking about something. When she turns back, she's smiling.

"Ted," she says. "You know what this means, right?"

"I don't know," I say. "I guess I'll have to go to court. I'm not sure."

"No," Mickey says. "Listen. He's a realtor, right? They do a lot of contracts. Know a lot of lawyers. I'm sure he pulled strings to get that. We didn't do anything to justify it—legally."

"Really?"

"Yeah. You have to, like, hit someone or threaten them in some way. We did neither."

"That's true."

"He's scared, Teddy. He wants to keep you from getting close again. He's scared because he's hiding something."

"No. No, Mickey. We can't—"

"We have to. We won't violate the order. I'll do it. Let me see it."

I shake my head. "I left it at my mom's house."

"Why?"

"Mickey," I say. "The car. It was some kids."

Mickey stares back at me. "So what? That doesn't change anything. Jake is still real, right? You were doxxed by someone. Someone who didn't want you poking around at Angie stuff. And now you have your brother running scared. Is that a coincidence?"

"You're not listening. Mickey, they're all over Reddit, these boys. It's where they live. I knew this too, they used to show me things from Reddit. They're fucking with me. They figured out I was on there somehow, and they're fucking with my head. Trying to make me insane. The car is part of it. It is related."

I pull the blanket back over my head. Within a few seconds, Mickey has wriggled her way under. I shut my eyes tightly.

"Do you want me to tell you about my day?" Mickey asks.

I nod.

"Let's see," she says and she sweeps a piece of hair away from my mouth and behind my ear. "Where to begin . . ."

When I go back in my new rental car, I tell Mom what happened. Some of it, anyway. I tell her that I wanted to meet my niece, wanted to see if she looked like Angie or Dad. I tell her that Ginger reached out to me, so I thought my contact would be welcome, but maybe I stepped into the middle of their custody dispute by accident.

I tell her that it's nothing, the restraining order. That I'll get it sorted out. I don't tell her that Mickey was with me, at Henry's house. I do mention Mickey in the context of Angie, in the sense that she's helping me remember more about her. Lately, I have a hard time not bringing her up—Mickey, that is. I know that Mom knows that Mickey isn't who we said she was originally. She won't ask what our relationship is.

"When we were talking, I realized that there are all these stories that you don't even know," I say. "I thought maybe we could talk about Angie more, me and you."

"Okay."

So I tell Mom, for the first time, the real story of how I lost my front tooth. How Angie lifted me on her shoulders and ran in circles around the support beams in the basement. How I laughed and laughed, loving the dizzy feeling of whipping around on her shoulders, how I grabbed on to her forehead for stability, then lowered my hands, inadvertently covered her eyes, and caused us both to fall onto the cement floor below.

"There was a lot of blood," Mom says, quietly, remembering. "Why didn't you tell me then? You didn't want to get her in trouble?"

"Are you kidding?" I laugh. "No, she wouldn't let me. She said she'd knock my other tooth out, too."

Mom pushes her chair back from the kitchen table. She goes to the sink and starts loudly cleaning some dishes.

"What?"

"I don't want to do this if you're going to try to make her look bad," Mom says and she leaves the room.

Twenty minutes later, Mom comes back with the restraining order. She hands it to me.

"Thanks."

Mom sits across from me. She tells me that she's thought about it, and she wants to try again. "It's not one specific memory," she says. "It's a thing that happened sometimes."

"Okay," I say. "There are no rules."

"When Angie was a baby, sometimes I would take a bath after she went to sleep."

"Sure," I say.

"And I'd take the monitor into the bathroom with me, and I'd watch the wee lights move with the sound of her breathing." Mom pauses. "And the thing I remembered is that my bathwater was never clean. Because in that apartment, when it was just the two of us, there was only the one bedroom and the one bathroom. And Angie was a messy eater. All babies are, but she—she would carry big fistfuls of spaghetti marinara from the high chair to the bathtub, and I couldn't pry it out of her hands, she was so strong. And so there would always be something left in the tub."

"What do you mean?"

"I have these images—being in the bathtub and the surface of the water shining with olive oil. Or a line around the tub like mildew—but it's dissolved Cheerios. A rogue noodle in my hair while I shampoo. That kind of thing. I was always bathing in her dirty water."

I keep waiting for the end of the story, because I thought Angie had to look good. Mom is done talking though.

"Disgusting," I say.

"Oh, it didn't bother me. It was proof she was real and that I hadn't made her up," Mom says.

I just nod. It sounds gross to me.

"I told you it's not a good story. I thought of it, because I was bleaching the tub in my room the other day, and I thought— why should I do this? This tub is already clean, and I never take a bath in it anyway."

"Maybe you should."

Mom sighs like I've entirely missed the point. "You'd understand if you had kids."

"I don't like it when you do that," I say. "When you act like I barely knew her."

"I'm not acting like you barely knew her."

"She was my best friend," I say.

Mom makes a sound like a snort. Very unlike her. But before I can form a retort, she produces a small photograph from the back of her jeans pocket. In it, Mom is eight months pregnant with Angie, round as a globe. Beaming. In spite of her recent loss. In spite of everything.

"This made me think of it," she says.

I take the photograph in my hands. It's worn down in the corners from years of touching. I've never seen it before. She must keep it close, in a nightstand or a jewelry box. It's a beautiful picture.

It reminds me of the picture I lost. The one of Angie drunk and laughing. "How many of these do you have?"

"What?"

"Pictures I've never seen."

Mom laughs. "What, am I required to inventory all my belongings with you now?"

"Don't worry," I say, handing it back to her. "Most parents' favorite kid is their oldest. I don't take it personally."

Mom snatches the photo out of my hands and presses it flat against a coffee table book in front of her. She speaks slowly, deliberately. "Your sister constantly—*constantly*—accused us of loving you more. Because you were our kid." Mom gestures upstairs even though Dad isn't here.

"If only she could see how little anyone gave a shit after she left," I say. I make my most annoying smirk.

Mom's nostrils flare, before she exhales and pastes a big fake smile across her face. "You know what," she says, standing. "I'm not going to do this teenage stuff with you." She pats me on the head. "You can do that with your little friend. I'm going to bed."

"That's good. Let's never talk about anything."

"God willing," I hear her mutter from halfway up the stairs.

I pick up the picture that she left on the table and trace the outline of Mom's swollen belly. She couldn't have known then what she was carrying inside her. A timebomb. A death.

I think back to those fights. The ones where Angie snapped at Dad that he wasn't her father. Where she accused the three of us of being in conspiracy together. It was usually after she had gotten in trouble for something or other. I felt so smug then. Watching her spiral out of control, screaming and crying and smashing things, half in the bag, dressed like a freak, and thinking: of course they like me more. Look at yourself.

The kids at school are driving me crazy. When we were young, Mom used to say, "My nerves are frayed," at the end of a long day, and I finally feel like I know what she meant. I can picture my nerves, long silver wires looped around and tangled up in my brain, and someone is rubbing the blade of a knife against them, peeling back the rubber insulation, slowly wearing down the metal part, shredding the filaments so that they break like taut strands of hair until the signal is only conducted through one tiny connection, one narrow thread that looks like it could snap at any moment.

I know it's not the students' fault. It's not even the whispering about what happened to Jamie. The rumors that I'm crazy. Those died down quickly. Maurice tells me that everyone knows the spray paint was Jamie and his crew (he's sorry he couldn't tell me sooner; he's not a narc), but the consensus is that I probably broke the window myself. On account of how crazy I am. I offer a mirthless, hollow laugh. I broke my own window? That's something. Maurice changes the subject.

My tolerance for the usual bullshit is diminished. Of course, my students are not responsible for managing my emotions; they are just kids. Of course. I know this rationally. And yet every day, I find myself thinking back to how things were when I was about their age, when my Angie went missing and I didn't have the option of bad behavior, and I feel it's unfair that they get to live such unfettered lives. How many times can I be expected to smile and return to my routine? Why just me?

This morning, as I'm counting down the minutes in my freshmen homeroom and the students are shouting about some new game, I find myself dying to bring up that my sister is gone, that my dad is gone. I don't even need an opening; I could just blurt it out. Fuck *inappropriate*. What if they were abandoned like I was? Over and over again, abandoned without warning. Could they get back to normal?

I would like some acknowledgment that I have suffered, that I have borne these insults and injuries one after the next, and I'm still here working for their idiot parents, who pay my measly salary. That's all.

The shouting and the throwing things and the way they are blatantly breaking Responsible Tech Use policy right in front of my face—it's the last bit of indignity that I can take.

"Phones away, guys," I say. I will make them sit quietly for the rest of homeroom, so that they know I am still in charge. Their silence will have to pass for respect.

One or two of them put their phones away. I can hear Thomas shouting above everyone. He's one of those kids who has no indoor voice, as they say in the lower grades.

"Oh man," he says. "Ethan sucks. Is everyone seeing this? How bad Ethan sucks? What are you doing, man? Get him. Right there. Oh my god!"

I look up. He's tall for his age—five eight or so—and chubby, and he's towering over Ethan. One of the smaller boys, Ethan looks permanently sick, even when he's well. He's too blond, with nearly translucent eyebrows and eyelashes. If it weren't for the freckles covering his arms and the dark brown of his eyes, I'd have wondered if he was albino.

"Thomas," I say. "Sit down. Guys, phones away. I'm writing up RTUs."

Thomas takes one step back toward his desk, but as Ethan puts his phone down, Thomas steps forward again and picks it up as I lower my eyes to my laptop.

"Thomas!" A hush falls over the room. I've never been a yeller, and when I raise my voice, it tends to come out with an edge. The wires inside of my brain are overheating, melting their encasements, sending the wrong signals at the wrong times. If someone put a hand to my head, it would be warm, like my old laptop before a crash.

I step out from in front of my desk and toward Thomas. In heels, I'm taller than he is. As I approach him, he leans backwards, and I realize that I'm scaring him. My brain is shouting at me—stop, this is not okay, cool down. But something in my veins feels a rush from the eyes on me, the way the room is waiting for what I'm going to do next. I see Thomas's face, and I want to slap him.

I'm inches away from him now, my fingers balled in front of my chest.

"Do you ever shut the hell up?" I hear myself say. It's a normal volume. I'm not yelling. And yet the words seem to come from outside of my body.

"You can't talk to me like that," Thomas says. "I'm going to tell my mom."

"Your mom," I say, not sure where I'm going with the sentence as I'm speaking it, "feels the exact same way. I guarantee you."

The fear on Thomas's face—the fear he is trying to mask with courage—drops. In its place, something else. Horror, curiosity, and pity. It's the way you look at someone when you realize they're totally insane. I don't think I've been on this side of it before.

The bell rings, and Thomas exits the room with the other kids.

I go straight to the faculty kitchen, and I lay my head on the cold Formica of the countertop. I try to cool my frayed nerves, and I wait for Rick to find me.

"I've never heard of that," Bill says. "Bereavement leave. Did you make that up?"

"No," I say. "It's a thing."

I can tell by his tone that he thinks it sounds soft. New age feel-good nonsense. What happened to putting your head down and working? I almost pick a fight, but I decide not to.

"Are you staying over tonight?" he asks.

"As long as I won't get in your way in the morning."

"Nope," Bill says. He refills the dogs' bowls and dumps out the remainder of the wine—which he knows will piss me off. "Will Mickey be able to get by without you?"

I don't respond.

Bill keeps scrubbing his cast iron with a wad of steel wool. "I have to go look at a property at ten," he says.

"An estimate?"

"They want a gazebo."

"Why?"

"I need to reseason this," he says.

"Maybe a backyard wedding," I say. "No one builds a gazebo for no reason."

I sip my wine. It tastes, typically, like vinegar, even though I've explained that a nicer bottle might help with the flush and the occasional hives that Bill gets. He insists he doesn't have allergies. That most allergies are made up.

"A full week paid," I say. "Vacation."

"Mmhmm."

"At least I got something good out of this, right?"

"What will you do?"

"I have some stuff to catch up on," I say.

"Your online conspiracies?"

"Grading," I say. "Mostly."

I know he doesn't believe me. He doesn't believe me about the car either. That it just broke down.

"They didn't give you a loaner?" he had asked.

"No," I had said. "Weird, right? Such a rip-off."

Bill had touched the Hertz sticker on the front windshield and nodded. "Weird."

We left it at that.

The sex is drudgery for both of us tonight. Sometimes I think Bill is repulsed by me, and sometimes that makes me want him more, makes me want to make him want me. Not tonight. Tonight it makes me defiant. Makes me want to be repulsive and annoying in all the specific ways. I loudly fake moans, performing my part well enough that it's almost believable. Poorly enough that I know he'll know I'm faking it, but have no way of asking. I throw my hips out of sync with his thrusts until he gets frustrated and holds me down. Then I lie there, limp and silent, until he finishes, so that he feels gross about the whole thing. I watch the loathing spread across his face in the seconds after orgasm, the way he can't get off me quickly enough. I feel smugly satisfied in the dark.

"Today was not our best day," he says, after a few moments of silence.

I play dumb. "What do you mean?"

He kisses me on the forehead, rolls me onto my side away from him so that he can wrap himself around me. I want to hold on to my rage, but it's hard. I love being held like this.

"What's going on with you?" he whispers into my ear. "Talk to me."

"About what?"

"How about Angie?"

"She was funny," I say.

Bill makes a noise of affirmation. I keep going.

"Sardonic, clever." I blow my nose in the top sheet he hands me. "But also—goofy, sometimes. She'd dance like a crazy person in the car whenever we stopped at a red light. No matter what music was playing. It could be some slow, sad song—the emo stuff she made me listen to—and still she'd start thrashing around, beating wildly on the ceiling, the steering wheel, the driver's side window." I pause, but Bill says nothing. "It doesn't sound funny," I say. "But she was so moody. It was the last thing you expected."

"I get that." He puts a hand on my shoulder, traces the roundness as he kisses my skin.

"Lately, I feel like I didn't know her very well." I turn my body around and look Bill in the eye and he becomes my mirror in the dark. His eyes turn down and his mouth forms a frown.

"You can never really know anyone," Bill says.

"Is that a jab at Mickey?"

"No. It's just true."

I work the sheet in my hand—folding and unfolding my little wet section—until I'm ready to talk.

"She was unhappy," I say. "It's so clear now, looking back. I've lost so many memories, you know? But the ones I have— she's miserable."

"Why do you say she was unhappy?"

"Because she was." I say. "She didn't feel like one of us. Or one of anything."

"It's hard being that age."

"It is. It's already hard."

"Teddy," Bill says. "Can I ask you a tough question?"

I swallow, hard. "Okay."

"Do you think she's still out there?"

Pressure builds behind my sinuses. The space between my eyebrows is tingling pins and needles.

"She would want you to live your life, don't you think? To take care of your mom and live your life and be happy."

"She would be devastated about what happened to my dad," I say. "Devastated. Especially if—"

"So, don't be another person who throws their life away here, okay? Come on, Teddy. You've got to stop this craziness with that girl."

I turn away again and dangle my arm off the side of the bed until I feel a rough, warm tongue start to lap at my palm. I look down to see Rocky, halfway buried in pillows on the floor.

"Thank you, buddy," I say, and I pet him on the head.

Bill strokes the side of my face. He stops and lays his hand there, heavy and sweaty on my face. "Put an end to this," he says. "You're going to be fine," he says. "You will."

In minutes, I can feel his breathing slow, becoming steady and dull on the back of my neck. He's asleep, and I'll be awake for hours—hot and claustrophobic under his hairy arms, my thighs sticking together with sweat and come and itching in places I can't reach.

Jake is back. Whoever he is. He pops up on all the boards I follow at once. A single line post: *I was with Angie Angstrom on the night she died.*

Everyone freaks out.

- **brewerswife304:** WTF!!!
- **tazMAINEian_devil:** Partygoer? Can this be an AMA pleaseeee pretty please
  - **MM_meg:** omfg id shit -- AMA/angieparty yaaasss
    - **brewerswife304:** ikr? i have sooo many questions
- **paul_ruiz:** Post history is pretty thin. Can you verify?
  - **bbymonkee:** how do you expect this dude to verify he was at a party a decade ago?
    - **paul_ruiz:** Yearbook picture, license . . . something to put him in the right geo zone/age demo to be there.
      - **bbymonkee:** oh shit lol thats actually smart
    - **anonna:** MySpace pics? Come on . . . people had digital cameras. I'm also shocked there are NO pictures from that night.
- **local_perv:** LOL sure you were dude. Sure.

- ○ **YNotTho:** cant believe everyone's freaking out like this. dude has no post history. trolling.
- **throwaway99934353:** Troll.
- **rosymerrybaby:** TROLL
- **GG1984:** . . . and? give us something.

Obnoxious, I think. So I post myself, under the same username where Jake has been DMing me: *Jamie. It's over. This is getting pathetic. Don't make me put in another call to Mommy.*

A few comments filter in under mine over the next few hours. I leave the window open while I watch TV.

- **paul_ruiz:** Am I forgetting something? Was there a Jamie?
- **MM_meg:** Oh shit! Watch out, Jamie!!
- **TATERtat:** ???
- **GG1984:** Is Jamie the boyfriend?
- **CharlieUniformNovemberTango:** "call mommy" . . . *shudder* wtf is this

I'm feeling pretty self-satisfied when a private message comes in. It's Jake. And it's long.

How's this, Teddy?

It was a couple months before she went missing. Angie called the main office of the school from the girls' bathroom on the flip phone she used to buy weed (did you ever tell the cops about that phone btw?). She pretended to be your mom, accent and all—family emergency, the girls need to come home right away. I guess with your family, that was easy enough to believe.

Angie was called out of class as soon as she returned from the bathroom. She waited for you at your locker. She let you pack up your books believing something was wrong. She said she didn't know what the call was about, but you were freaking out. You were always so worried about your parents.

The two of you were in the car, pulling out of the school, before she turned the music on. Whatever moody punk band she had on rotation that week. She relaxed in her seat, smiled at you, and asked you where the two of you should spend the day.

You laughed hysterical, nervous laughter. You thought something had happened to your dad. Angie felt bad.

"The beach," you said. "Let's go to the beach."

You drove two hours with Angie to the nearest beach, a rocky, cloudy, depressing bit of coast. It was too cold to swim, and you hadn't packed anything, so you could only huddle together with your feet in the sand, trying to keep each other warm long enough to listen to the waves for a few more crashes.

On the way home, you got sandwiches, and Angie ate hers with one hand while she drove. You worried about her crashing, but you also worried about the fact that you were going to be at least 90 minutes late coming home. Would your mom call the school? Would you get in trouble? But when you got in, your mom wasn't home, and your dad was on the phone—consulting on a local campaign happening somewhere else in the state.

You and Angie rinsed the sand from your feet together in the bathtub, and she asked you if you had fun. "Yes," you said. "That was the best day."

I read the message through three or four times. Some of the details aren't quite right. We drove to a lake that we had gone to as kids—not the ocean. We stopped off for sandwiches—we didn't eat them in the car—and I cried because I was so anxious about being home late and blowing our cover. Angie got annoyed and threw her turkey club in the garbage. I never knew anything about a cell phone. It was a big deal that we were going to get cell phones that summer after she vanished. Angie was mad because I was still in high school and I was getting one, too, and technically the phone was her graduation present, but Dad reminded her about Wolfie, and she stopped complaining.

Most of the post is right, though. Most of it is how things happened.

Angie? I type into the reply box. I let my cursor blink for a moment before highlighting and deleting.

I should be perplexed that Jake is real, that he's not one of my disgruntled students fucking with me, but I'm exhilarated. I barely sleep.

First thing in the morning, I text Mickey: *Jake not one of my kids. Sending you a DM from him.*

Mickey responds: *!!!!!*

I call Ginger to clear the air, and she answers right away.

"You should not be calling here," she says.

"Ginger," I say. "It's Teddy Angstrom."

"I know," she says. I can tell she is making an effort to keep her voice down. "You have a restraining order."

"Oh, don't worry about that," I say. "We don't think it's legit. He's just throwing his weight around. Trying to scare me. I need to ask you about the kids' nanny."

I hear Ginger breathing into the receiver.

"Hello? Ginger?"

"I'm going to have to call the police," she says.

"Wait, hold on," I say. "Why? Ginger, you know this is all crazy."

"It is crazy," she says, "that I have to sleep in my daughter's bed when she's here, because she's worried you're going to come through her window and kidnap her."

I laugh involuntarily.

"It's not funny!" she says.

"No," I say. "I know. I'm sorry. It's just so ridiculous. I would never. You know that."

"I don't know you."

"No, Ginger, listen," I say. "Helene is telling her that I scared her. Helene is trying to poison her against me."

"I have to go," Ginger says. "Please don't call here again."

I call Mickey right away, because I need to feel human again. I don't tell her about Ginger.

"When did you want to go back?" I ask. "I'm off this week now."

"Tomorrow?" Mickey says. "I have class in the afternoon, but we could go early."

"Great," I say.

We start our stakeout early, before the neighborhood is awake. Parked on the curb opposite my brother's house, right where the school bus is scheduled to stop, we're deep into our coffee and donuts by the time the early-morning power walkers and newspaper delivery boys emerge.

"There she is," Mickey says as a two-car garage door creaks open, revealing a gray SUV—the same one from the open house. It is the only vehicle besides a couple of pink bikes. I slouch down in the passenger seat as Helene walks down the driveway in her yoga gear to retrieve the paper.

"Perfect," Mickey says. "The other car's already gone. He must get up early."

"What if she doesn't leave?"

"She will," Mickey says. "She has an open house. It's listed online."

Sure enough, half an hour later, Helene hauls her signage into the trunk of the car and pulls out. We duck down in our seats as she drives past us.

Mickey checks the clock. "Soon."

Sure enough, with five minutes to spare before the bus is meant to arrive, Bella bounds out the front door first, backpack slung over one shoulder. She runs down the damp, sloped lawn with abandon. I'm amazed she doesn't fall. She doesn't look like the same girl I talked to the other day. She catches the light, she bounces.

The nanny comes behind her, with the baby in tow. She carries a lunchbox in one hand. She calls out to Bella, but Bella is too focused on something she found in the grass. I hear the bus. It is only a couple houses away.

The nanny gets closer to the street, but I still can't make out her face. She wears a Sox cap and black hipster frames. Her hair is tied into a loose chignon at the nape of her neck. Her bulky jacket hides her figure, and yellow rain boots come up below her knee, even though it's not raining anymore.

"Angie didn't wear glasses."

"She could wear them now," Mickey says.

I watch the woman walk toward the street, balancing the baby on her hip, and I feel a terrible sinking feeling. Is it the height? The weight? The shape of her neck? The way she holds her body lopsided to keep the baby up? Is she too old? Too young? All those little movements that make up a kind of fingerprint are off.

"It's not her," I say.

Mickey cracks the door open and is out so fast I barely have time to grasp at the space where she no longer is.

"Stop," I whisper.

Mickey nearly slams the door on my fingers. She approaches the nanny who is not Angie, who clutches the baby tightly to her chest. From where I am, almost everything gets consumed by the wind, but I catch words and phrases—"not appropriate," and "please"—but it's clear that the nanny has an accent.

Bella curls herself into a ball in the grass and rocks back and forth, cradling her head in her knees.

I get out of the car.

The baby squirms in the nanny's arms, and the nanny grips her tighter. The child starts to cry. The nanny looks like she might cry as well. She's very young. I can see now she's much younger than I am.

Mickey crouches down and speaks directly to Bella. "No, it's okay. You're not in trouble. We just want to know what your grandpa said to you. We just want to know about the letter."

I step on a twig, and Bella looks up. She sees me and lets out an audible gasp.

At the same moment, the front door flies open. I look up to see my dad, incandescent, tearing down the front steps. No, not my dad. My brother.

A woman with a walking stick, who had been approaching us with sharp, military steps, stops in front of the house next door. She takes out her cell phone.

Henry scoops Bella into his arms and runs her back up the hill with astonishing athleticism.

"Go," Mickey says to me.

We make it across the street to the car, but before we can pull out, the bus stops beside us, and we're trapped. The bus lines up alongside us, and there's no room to pull out.

"Fuck," Mickey says. She leans on the horn.

"Stop it," I say, pulling her hands off the column.

The moment the bus starts to move, Henry emerges from behind the bus, crazed and wild. He slams his body against the front of the car. He pounds on Mickey's window, but she doesn't open it. He sprints around to my side. We're both frozen.

"Roll it down," he yells at me. "Roll it down."

I roll it down.

"What's wrong with you?" he says. "Why can't you leave us alone?"

I shake my head and look down at my hands.

"Look at me," he says. "Answer me. What do you want?"

I look up. His build is slighter than my father's. He wears

quirky Lennon-style glasses and keeps his facial hair neatly trimmed. His eyes are red, and his lips are parched. He is struggling to catch his breath.

"Ginger—My dad—" I stutter. "He thought—he thought that—I thought—your nanny—"

"I deal with this once with him and now I have to go through it again with you?"

"I wanted to make sure—my sister—"

"The whole world doesn't revolve around you and your sister! What do I have to do to convince you people to leave us alone?" He turns to Mickey. "And who the fuck are you?"

"I'm sorry," I say. "I'm so sorry. I should never have approached your daughter."

"She can't sleep."

"My dad—"

"He was my dad, too," Henry corrects me. He rubs his head several times. He takes a deep breath. "Leave," Henry says. "Please leave. You are in violation of your restraining order."

"Okay. I'm sorry."

The first half of the drive home is silent, and all I can think about is the little girl on the front lawn holding her head between her knees, the look of utter terror when she saw me, the desperation in my brother's eyes when he was at my window. It was never him. It was never her.

"We ruined his life," I say. "And now we're doing it again."

"He'll be fine," Mickey says. "You saw his house, his wife. He has a nice life."

"I told you to stop," I say. "When you opened the door."

"I didn't hear you," Mickey says. "Are you mad?"

I don't respond. I drive exactly the limit.

"I'm sorry," Mickey continues. "But you agreed something was weird. Why would they have hidden her?"

I think about Helene's public profile. All the pictures of the baby in different outfits, wearing those floral baby headbands. The nanny must have been just off to the side in some of them. She dressed the baby while Helene crafted the letterboard message.

"She doesn't want people to know she has a nanny," I say.

"Yeah, why?" Mickey says. "Weird."

"It's not weird," I say. "It doesn't fit with her whole . . . brand."

Mickey chortles. "I'm not sure Helene is high-profile enough to have a *brand*."

"What does it matter," I say. "It's not her. It's not Angie."

I don't answer Mickey's calls for a few days. I stay at Mom's house. I barely leave the couch, and she doesn't ask why. Wolfie keeps me company. I watch soaps and eat whatever I can find. At one point, I find myself eating stale breadcrumbs out of the cylinder with a spoon. Mom refuses to feed me.

I keep my phone off entirely, except for a few minutes before bed each night, when I turn it on to check if I've gotten any more hateful messages from my brother or his wife or his ex-wife or their lawyer. I don't check Reddit. I try to not even think about Jake's last message. He's not Bill, not Gary, not Henry, and not one of my students. I try to make peace with the idea that I'll never know who he is. Up until a couple months ago, I lived in ignorance of all of this. Up until then, I never thought of myself as the kind of person who could give a small child nightmares. I'd like to go back to that time.

Texts pour in from Bill and Mickey. They are both concerned, for different reasons.

Bill wants to know why I've vanished. If I'm okay. I stop just short of telling him it was all a big mistake. That I have to pretend we never met in the bar that night. Instead, I tell him I need some space. He says he doesn't understand, but he's here. *Whenever you're ready.*

Mickey, on the other hand, won't take the hint:

im sorry!!
rly sorry
sorrryyyy
teddy this isnt cool, answer ur phone wtf
teddy im sorry, can we pls talk?
ok now im worried. u ok?
im going to have to call ur mom if u don't respond
teddy??
r u ok? just y/n pls
hiii i know u wont respond to this but i have an idea . . .
  call me
pls call when u can, xxoo
teddy u ok?? worried . . .

Wolfie stays by my side the entire time. He thinks I'm ill. He thinks I'm like him, dying of something. I pet his rump with my foot and vow to take him back to the apartment with me, whenever I go back. I'm done leaving him behind in this house. I apologize for ever doing it. We will make it work, I tell him. The stairs, no yard. I will figure it out. If I have to carry him up and down every day, then that is what we will do. It will be our house—just ours—me and Wolfie. I don't think about the cancer. In my fantasies, we go on like that forever, me carrying him up and down the steps. Him groaning and pissing himself all the time. It's better than the alternative.

I chase a handful of cacao nibs with cold milk. It all turns to wax in my mouth, but I swallow it anyway. I chew up some more nibs and spit them back into my palm in a shiny clump. I feed it to Wolfie.

On my last day home, I find Mom in her living room, and announce my new plan. "I go back to work tomorrow," I say. "And I'm turning over a new leaf."

Mom looks pleased. "That's wonderful, Teddy."

"I think maybe it's not too late for me to start over."

"Of course it's not."

"And I'll help you figure out the money stuff," I say. "But then I want to get rid of all of Dad's things. Because they don't make any sense. And they're making me crazy."

"Sure," Mom says.

I nod, speech delivered. I sit next to her on the couch and let her pet my hair for a while. I leave out the part, for now, where I tell her that I think it's time for us to move somewhere else. The new apartment isn't far enough after all. Somewhere with more sunshine, where no one knows us. I can teach anywhere. She can come with me. We can sell the house, take the cash, rent somewhere cheap. Cut back on expenses.

Once Wolfie's gone, we'll talk about it. What choice will she have? If I go, she goes. I'm all she has left.

Bill calls me during my first day back at work and asks me to come by his house on my way home. He sounds grave.

"What's wrong?"

"It's better if I show you."

We go back and forth a few times. "Bill," I say, finally. "I'm exhausted. Can you please tell me?"

"It's about Mickey," he says, and I groan.

Every time I bring her up, he responds the same: first, to tell me that there is something not right about her, that something he can't put his finger on rubs him wrong; second, to ask me, with a pained look, what on earth she is doing with a key to my apartment.

"This Stabler and Benson routine you've got going," he said the one and only night he stayed at my place, back before everything went sideways with Henry. "It's not funny anymore." He gestured to the Wall of Insanity.

"You know I hate that show. Anyone who likes to watch girls get raped week after week after week is a pervert," I said.

"I like that show," Bill said. "This is perverted."

"She's helping me," I said.

"How is that?" Bill asked. "How is she helping you?"

I couldn't explain. He wouldn't have understood.

Bill clears his throat into the phone, the way he does when he's stalling for time.

"Out with it," I say. I consider telling him that it doesn't matter, that I'm past all that. It ended poorly, like he said it would, and I've turned a new leaf. But I don't want to give him the satisfaction.

"I think Mickey does porn," he says.

"Now you think she's a porn star? Bill. Please."

"Not porn like movies. Webcam girl, whatever it's called."

I think about it for a second before responding. It makes sense right away. In my gut, I feel it to be true. There is no point issuing denials. Her comfort with nudity, the way she takes forever in the shower because she shaves her entire body bare, the internet income that's been alluded to. It adds up.

"So what," I say.

"Excuse me?"

"What do you want me to say, Bill? Do you need me to express some Puritanical outrage?"

"I guess I was at least expecting—" Bill stammers, searching for words. "Some curiosity."

"Okay, fine. How did you find it?"

"That's what you want to know?"

"You must have been pretty intent on seeing her naked."

"What's your problem, Teddy?" He huffs into the phone. "She lied to you."

"No, she didn't."

"By omission."

"I have to get back to work now."

"She's doing the videos in your apartment." He catches me off guard. I let the line go silent long enough for Bill to wonder aloud if we've lost the connection.

"I'll figure it out."

"What does that mean?"

"Is that all?"

Bill makes a noise of disbelief—half grunt, half sarcastic laugh. "Yeah, Ted. That's all."

I hang up without a goodbye, and I open my laptop. I realize that I shouldn't be doing this on my work computer, never mind in school, but I don't think I can wait until I get home.

I search "Mickey Greeley" with every keyword I can think of: *webcam, tits, nudity, porn, masturbation, chat, sexy, teen, video, vid, fuck, blowjob, anal, hardcore, fetish, feet, food, BDSM, gag, torture, leather, cum, lesbian.* Nothing.

Giving up, I text Bill: *send me the link.*

I get a web address on my phone, and my stomach drops. I knew it would be the site from my dad's credit card statements, somehow. That I'd never be able to outrun all his bullshit. I thought I could turn back the clock to a few months ago, but I can't. I can't unknow any of what I know now.

I copy it over letter by letter into my browser. CoedSleepover.com followed by a series of random letters and numbers that are programmed to conjure Mickey specifically.

A name pops up under a crisp, clear image—Indigo Moon. Indigo Moon with the same tattoos I've come to know so well. A dark thought flits across my mind: if Mickey were to die in a violent manner, and the police needed someone to identify remains, I could do it. Me and, I guess, her subscribers.

I mute the sound on my computer. The school library is quiet, and I'm seated in the back, with my screen facing a stack of books. A green circle tells me that Indigo is online. Home alone at my apartment and ready to "chat now." I enter a username made of random characters, and a pop-up fills my screen. When Mickey's face appears, I instinctively cover my camera with my thumb, even though it's not turned on.

There are five others in the room with me. Below Mickey's image is a running chat log where they encourage her to do various things. As of yet, she seems unconvinced. She has on an unremarkable bra and panties set and is sitting cross-legged on my guest bed next to a pile of pretzels that she's snacking on.

To the side of the box, a button flashes encouraging me to BUY VIRTUAL COINS. I enter my credit card information and use the chat feature to "tip" Mickey the equivalent of ten dollars.

I pull a pair of tangled headphones from my pocket.

"What would you like me to do?" she asks, gazing into the camera.

Three of the other viewers beat me to the punch, suggesting everything from "take off bra" to "2 dildos." Mickey continues to stare into the lens, and it feels like she's making eye contact with me.

I want you to stop, I write. But I don't send it.

"I have some ideas," Mickey says, when a few seconds elapse without my suggestion, and I close the window.

I have a hard time focusing for the rest of the day. I sleepwalk through my lessons and almost miss a class entirely when a passing bell escapes my notice. I find old Reddit posts about what a scumbag my dad was, and I consider commenting on them in full agreement. Imagine how the boards would light up with that information—*I thought he was just a loony, but Mark Angstrom has been watching underaged girls via webcam for years. He especially has a thing for chicks who look like his dead daughter. What a fucking freak.*

I could be the hero of Reddit, for a day or two. I could give the parasites something big. A piece of my real, actual, shitty life that would keep them entertained for the length of an episode of *Intervention*. I could invite them to restate their most insidious incest theories—the ones that begin with my dad molesting my sister and end with him burying her body somewhere in the woods. Maybe that would lure Jake back out of the shadows.

Mickey gives me a hug when I walk into my own apartment. It's clear that she's been living here all week while I've been at Mom's.

I let her cook me dinner and apologize for the debacle at my brother's house. She was wrong, and I was right—we should have never gone back.

"I've been thinking a lot about that message that Jake sent you," she says.

"Please," I say. "Not now. Not tonight."

Mickey nods. "No problem."

After dinner, she paints her nails on the edge of the bathtub.

"Is your roommate worried?" I ask, taking a seat on the covered toilet. "Does she wonder where you are?"

"No," Mickey says. "Want me to do yours when I'm done?"

"Sure."

Mickey finishes up her own toenails with a clear topcoat and waves them dry. She scootches onto the floor and starts to take off my shoes and socks.

"I never paint my toenails," I say. "And they're probably a bit long."

Mickey grabs an emery board from her kit and starts to file. She's laser-focused, not talking, committing all her attention to my dry and rough foot in her soft hands.

"You don't have to—"

"What?"

"You don't have to do all that."

"I do," she says. "This is necessary."

I looked it up before I left school—my dad's subscription to CoedSleepover tracks back about eighteen months. He must have found her in the library and then followed her online. It can't have been a coincidence. He must have liked that she looked like Angie.

Did she know about it? Did she tell him where to find her? Were they fucking?

I'm beginning to sympathize with the detectives that stalked him for a year. I try to look at the situation objectively: he left his wife and kids, he slept with his brother's widow, he was a drug addict, he engaged in something adjacent to child porn, he killed himself, leaving all this shit for me. If he was someone else's dad, I think I'd say without hesitation that he was a bad man.

You shouldn't be able to love bad people. You shouldn't be able to miss them.

Mickey is in a pair of oversized basketball shorts that I recognize as mine, inherited from a short-lived college boyfriend. Their drawstring has long since vanished, and she has knotted them at the waist with a hair tie to keep them from falling down. Her right leg is tucked under her butt in a way that looks painful, and I wonder if she's losing sensation on the hard ground.

"What is that on your leg?" I gesture to the shadowy underside of her calf.

"Have you not seen it? I guess this one is new-ish."

"You've had it bandaged."

"Yeah, it's all healed now."

Mickey picks at a yellow callus on the side of my big toe as if the foot were her own. I'm shocked as much by her comfort as my own. I try to imagine relaxing while Bill touches my feet, and I can't.

"What is it?"

Mickey twists her leg so that I can see it. It's a serpent wrapped around a rose, all black. It reminds me of the last tattoo that Angie got, the one I told the cops about. The one on the back of her thigh, toward the inside. The snake looked like it was slithering out of her butt. The rose looked like a mistake, overly red. Like blood. I told Angie it looked like she had her period, and she punched me in the stomach.

"My sister had something similar."

"I know," Mickey says. "That's where I got the idea."

"How do you know?"

"I read the police transcripts, your interview with them. I hope that's not weird. I got this before I came to stay with you."

"I guess not."

"I have a lot of tattoos. It's really not a big deal."

"Sure," I say. I try to match her tone. "Plus, hers was on her thigh, and it wasn't really the same . . . shape."

"What?"

"It was on her thigh, like sort of in the middle. Yours is better. Hers looked terrible in color."

Mickey stops filing my toenails and presses her lips tight. She shakes her head almost imperceptibly.

"Are you okay?"

"I thought it was lower leg."

"No," I say. "It was her thigh for sure. Easier to hide from my parents."

She goes back to filing. "That's fucking annoying," she says, halfway under her breath.

I'm not sure what to say. I want to ask her why she's here, what she's doing with me.

Maybe my dad's death fucked her up. Whatever it was they were doing together. Maybe even Mickey couldn't tell who was taking advantage of whom by the end of it. Her friend, her abuser. Maybe it was heavy. Maybe the intimacy of sharing this space with me, of listening to stories about my sister—all the while concealing this secret—maybe it was too much to resist. Maybe she wanted to find a way to help me understand, but she kept getting in her own way.

"Tell me about your family," I say. "You grew up with your aunt, right?"

Mickey keeps filing. "Why?"

"I'm trying to make conversation."

She pulls at a hangnail, and I start to bleed.

"That hurt," I say.

"What do you want to know?"

I want to know how her family could have allowed this. I

want to know why she's even on those sites, why that seemed like an option for her. I want to tell her that she could do anything she wants if she gives up this stupid shit.

Mickey picks furiously at my wide cuticles, pushing them back into thick white lines and peeling them off. Every time she does it, I brace myself for her to rip the skin.

"There's not much to say about Franny," Mickey says. "She's pretty normal, for us." She pushes herself off the ground and perches on the edge of my hamper. Her freshly shaven calves glisten with my moisturizer.

"When is your housing up? Must be soon, right? Where do you go home to? For summer break."

Mickey lets her head drop back, rolls her neck left and right. I stare at the underside of her chin. She folds herself back down onto the floor.

"Can you do me a favor, Teddy? I'll tell you whatever you need to know if you insist. But I feel like—I've painted enough of a picture of my home life, no? It wasn't great."

"No problem," I say, even though I feel like I know nothing about her home life. Even though she's told me jack shit.

"I'm fine," Mickey says. "I'm a big girl."

"Of course," I say. I smile and nod, but I feel nauseated, aware that my dad has somehow posthumously made me party to his own crimes against children, aware that I am now in the company of whatever bad men hurt my sister.

I bring home lice from the kids at school. I don't know how it happened.

"High schoolers?" Mom says when I call her.

"Yeah."

"I've never heard of it."

It drives me crazy when she does this. I know she's only being incredulous, but it feels like she's doubting my version of reality.

"What do I do?" I ask.

"Come here. I remember what to do."

This is what I wanted. Something about having an infestation of my body makes me regress. "Thank you."

I check Mickey's hair with the flashlight on my phone. They're there. Fewer than on my own scalp, eggs mostly, but they're there.

"I'm sorry," I say. I want to die, but Mickey shrugs.

"It's lice. It's not cancer."

"Have you had them before?"

"Yeah, three times."

"Jesus," I say. "The once was enough for me."

"Twice, now."

We change into bathing suits, throwing our infected clothes directly into the overfull washing machine. The number of loads we will need to do seems overwhelming—sheets, duvets, towels, the slip on the couch, everything in the hamper, everything on the floor, everything.

We wear garbage bags like muumuus for the drive to Mom's house. Mom looks surprised to see Mickey, but she doesn't say anything. We march straight up to her bedroom, as directed, and throw our hairbrushes and clips into a plastic bag she left on the bed. I tie it off and put it in the wastebin. I worry we are raining down lice into the fibers of the carpet and onto Wolfie's back with every jostling movement. We whip our filthy, crawling hair into tight ballerina buns and step into the master bath with our knees pulled up to our chests, our toes touching. Gooseflesh forms on our skin from the moment of contact with the cold ceramic.

Mom enters, carrying a grocery store bag filled with mayonnaise and plastic wrap.

"Making sandwiches?" Mickey asks.

"Mom," I say. "Come on. What is this?" I rifle through the bag and I find one small commercial lice kit, Nix brand.

"Don't worry. We'll do the chemical one. I knew you'd love that. But then we'll finish the job right. I know what I'm doing," she says. She gets to work unboxing the commercial kit and addresses Mickey as she does it. "She forgets sometimes where I grew up. I had lice a dozen times or more."

"That's supposed to be inspiring," I say, and they both ignore me.

The chemical cream goes into our hair first, and we let it sit for the ten minutes prescribed on the box. It smells like something I used as a kid to try to perm my hair at home. When I rinse it out, my hair's texture reminds me of that misadventure as well—coarse, tangled, fried.

"Okay, now for the mayo," Mom says. She scoops it out in big, jiggling chunks with a cupped hand.

"I hate mayo," I say.

"Do me first," Mickey says.

Mom plops the mayo in a loud splat on Mickey's head. Some of it falls and drips down into her bikini top. She tries to fish it out and she ends up smearing the greasy goo on her décolleté.

"Oh god," I say. "It's like those commercials where a girl in a bikini is dripping hamburger juice on herself."

Mickey laughs and then she closes her eyes and cranes her neck back like she's at the salon. At first I think she's doing a bit, but she's not. She stays like that, eyes closed, body relaxed. Mom hums softly and it echoes off the tiles a bit. She's kneeling on the edge of the tub, humming and working Mickey's hair in her hands.

"Should I start on myself?" I ask, to remind them that I'm here.

"I'll get you next," Mom says.

"Is this taking you back?" I ask. "Is this how we did it the first time? I can't remember."

"No, no," Mom says. "That first time was so awful, sweet Jesus. I had you and Angie out on the porch—it was September and hot—and I sprayed you down with the hose and I threw your clothes directly away and I shampooed you out there and tried to pick them all out by hand. I wore . . ." She chuckles. "A big garbage bag with a hole for the head. And I tied my hair up in a shopping bag."

"But you had it as a kid," Mickey says.

"Yeah," Mom says. "I think that's why though, you know?"

"Wow," I say. "I can't believe you picked them all out."

"Well," Mom says. "Not really. I didn't do a good job, seeing as they came back again."

"They did? I don't remember that."

"They came back in force. And poor Angie—she knew how

worried it made me, so she cut all her hair off in the school bathroom. She could be a bold girl, that one."

"I definitely don't remember that."

"You were so wee. You were barely four years old," Mom says. "She said she didn't want the hair if it was going to be so much trouble, if she was going to sit outside again with the two of us crying—me and you, Thea."

"She was bald?" I say.

"Oh my god," Mickey says. "That's too funny."

"It drove me crazy," Mom says. "She looked ill. I could barely stand to look at her until it grew back out. They let us do her picture day in spring that year."

"How have I never heard this?" I ask.

"It's not a nice story," Mom says. "I didn't handle it right. And she caught a lot of flak in school. Even in first grade, you know, kids can be cruel."

As Mom begins wrapping Mickey's hair in a turban of cellophane, I rack my brain to remember a single picture of Angie from first grade. The only one I can think of is the two of us before Angie left on the bus for her first day. Her hair is shoulder length, like mine. It must have predated the lice incident. I close my eyes and try to remember Angie without hair. I can picture her with hats on, with short, Twiggy-style hair, but I can't picture her with a buzz cut. It doesn't exist for me. I wonder for a moment if Mom's making it all up for Mickey's sake.

"Your turn," Mom says. She comes to my side of the tub and starts slicking my hair back with wet, eggy mayonnaise.

"Why did you get Hellmann's?" I ask.

"What?"

I gesture to the jar. "Why not get the store brand?"

Mom shrugs. "I always bought Hellmann's for you girls."

I want to respond, to chastise her for wasting the extra dollar or two dollars or whatever the difference between generic and brand name mayo is—ten cents, a penny maybe. Don't you know how precarious your finances are, I want to say? Don't you understand how little you have to live on? But I don't. Instead, Mickey curls her toes around mine.

"Can I run the bath?" she asks. "You look cold."

"Yeah," I say, and she turns the knob. The water fills in around us with reflective rainbow shapes forming on the surface from the greasy mayo. Mickey lowers her legs to submerge them and they slip below and between mine. We interlace, my stubbly calves rubbing against her smooth ones.

For a moment, I'm four years old again, in the tub with my sister, my mother wrist-deep in my hair, lather up to her elbows. Mom is singing us a song in Gaelic, and Angie's begging her to stop. It's too much noise, the angry, rushing water and my loud splashing and Mom's singing. We ignore Angie, so she screams. She screams that she can't hear the quiet in her head, and she wants to be alone. *Leave me alone.*

Sometimes, I find myself impatient with sex, preferring to masturbate. I lack the graciousness necessary to wait for Bill to figure it out on his own. Like a mother at the end of her rope, watching her toddler try and fail to tie his own shoes for five straight minutes. *Here. I'll do it.*

Tonight, at my apartment, I stop Bill after twenty-three minutes of oral. I've been watching the bright neon numbers on my alarm clock while he's been down there doing whatever it is he's doing. It would be better if I could be on my phone at least, but that offends him.

"Okay," I say. "Come on." I tried to put an end to this ten minutes ago, but he shook my hand off his shoulder and carried on. He's trying to make up for lost time. He's overcompensating because I said I needed space. Bad idea. At this point, I feel nothing except slobbered-on. The image of Wolfie flashes in my mind and I shudder. Bill makes an approving noise. He thinks it was a good shudder.

I start to shimmy up and away from him, but he grabs my hips. I resist him harder and push away from his neck. "Enough," I say. The insides of my thighs are beginning to chafe from beard friction.

"Fine." Bill comes up and flops down next to me, wipes his mouth on his forearm. "What's your issue tonight?"

"You need to stop when I say stop."

"Got it," he says. He turns away from me. I'm supposed

to feel bad. The thing with Bill is he loves to go down on me, but he always acts like he's doing me some great service. Like I should be grateful. And I could take it or leave it.

"I've told you that you need to stay up top," I say. "Less is more." He has a tendency to wander downwards and stick his whole tongue in my vagina, which I hate. It's slimy and squirmy and reminds me of when I was a child and petrified that an eel would get in there in the ocean, because Angie told me that was possible.

"Got it," Bill says.

I reach over to feel his penis. Still hard. I straddle his legs.

"I don't want to have sex if you don't want it," Bill says. "I'm not sure why you called me over here. You're so hard to read lately."

"Poor baby." I smile and slap his face lightly, playfully. "Are we feeling sorry for ourselves?"

He pins my hands down at my sides.

"What do you want from me?"

"I want you to fuck me senseless," I say. I jerk my hands, but he holds them down harder, squeezes my wrists until they hurt. In one swift motion, he flips me onto my back and shoves himself inside of me as he clamps his palm down over my mouth.

I love an angry fuck. I find myself pushing Bill's buttons lately so that he'll slam my face down on the kitchen table and take me roughly from behind or pull the car off to the side of the road and shove my head down on his lap until I drool and gag. It's becoming an unhealthy dynamic, but I can't help it. It's the only way I can stop my brain from rushing with thoughts in the dark.

I hear in his breathing that he's getting close, so I push his hand off of my mouth. "Don't come," I say. "I need to get off tonight." I haven't had an orgasm in three days, because I no longer have any privacy. Lately, Mickey even comes into the bathroom to brush her teeth when I'm in the shower or the tub.

Mickey is in some state of undress almost all of the time, which was true before I found the webcam site, but it reads differently now. She spends much of the day without pants on, and I try to act normal about it. She's almost always in her underwear when I come back to the apartment. She never wears a bra, and most of her shirts are white basics that she picked up at the drug store, so her hard pink nipples peek through the fabric even in dim lighting. After a shower, she spends half an hour mostly naked before she lotions up her entire body. She said she read somewhere that it was better for your skin to air dry. I had to lend her pajamas tonight, when I told her Bill was coming over. He still couldn't look her in the eye.

I find myself thinking about all of this as Bill moves slowly inside me, his wide rough thumb pad pressed firmly against my clit.

Mickey in her cheeky boy shorts and little else, the way her breasts form perfect teardrops, the dimples on her low back, the ridged bony curve of her hips. Mickey listening to us have sex from her air mattress in the living room.

I feel myself getting closer. "Harder," I say, and Bill obliges.

But it's too fast. He can't hold out. He comes guiltily and tries to finish me off, but I push his hands away.

When I look over, he is lying on his back with his eyes closed. His breathing deepens. He's so relaxed, so vulnerable. I could murder him no problem. Get a knife from the kitchen, come around to his side of the bed, and cut his throat.

I wonder if everyone has thoughts like this.

"Do you think Mickey has a good body?"

"Don't play games, Teddy."

"I'm not."

"I don't even understand why she's still around."

I could tell him about Jake's latest message. It would feel good to watch him get all hot and bothered, station himself in the window with one of his guns. I'd probably sleep better than I have in a long time. But I can't get into all that now.

"You can go back to sleep," I say.

"Mickey looks like a child," Bill says. "She's all skin and bones." He puts a hand on the fleshy part of my thigh. "You have a great body."

"We look alike," I say. "So if you like how I look, you must like how she looks."

"What?"

"She looks exactly like my sister. Who looks like me. So she looks like me."

"Are we talking about the same person? Mickey does not look like Angie. And she definitely doesn't look like you."

"Yes, she does."

"Okay, Teddy. Whatever you say. Maybe I'll dye my hair black and we can all be sisters."

I hear Bill turn his back to me, and in a few minutes, he's snoring again. I try to finish myself off. All I can imagine is Bill fucking Mickey. Bill looking old in contrast to her youth. Mickey's smooth, tattooed skin, all contrast—pale flesh and black ink—tearing into his muscular, hairy body with some violence, rocking her pelvis against him, putting him in his place, not letting him throw her around like a rag doll, making him beg for her.

I come so quickly it's almost frustrating, so I log into Reddit on my phone to check what Jake's been up to. Old habits. Still nothing, though. I fall asleep rereading his messages, all screenshotted in my photos, and when I wake up, my hand is still wedged between my legs.

Later in the week, I cancel plans with Bill, claiming illness, and instead Mickey and I watch *Chinatown*. Finally. We play it in my bedroom, where we can cozy up with Wolfie on the bed, and we call it research. This is how desperate things are getting. Our pizza box rests on a pile of maps, Reddit print outs, Facebook pages, etc. There's so much stuff that we don't even bother to put it all up on the Wall anymore. Only the really important leads.

Every morning, I log into Reddit to find that Jake has not sent me any new messages. Every morning, I stand in front of the Wall with my coffee, and I wait for my epiphany about Angie. In the movies, detectives catch things when they least expect it.

Mickey tells me that she has an idea, and I'm not going to like it. I tell her I'll try anything. At this point, I feel like I need to figure it all out. It will be the only thing to justify any of this suffering.

"I wonder if we can go away for the weekend. Get a change of scenery."

I try to find reasons not to go, but there aren't any, really. "Where were you thinking?"

"Burlington," she says.

"That's far. What's in Burlington?"

Mickey looks at me, and smiles, and I remember the blue envelope. Celeste.

"No," I say. "Why?"

"Come on," Mickey says. "It's a cute town. Half an hour with Celeste and then we can explore. You're the one who keeps talking about getting out of here, finding a new spot. They have a university, a lake. It's a nice place. You and your mom would like it."

"We can go to Burlington, but no Celeste."

"I know you want to be done," Mickey says. "And maybe she's a fraud, but maybe she gives you a little closure." She waits for me to respond. "It would be my treat."

I don't know why I'm surprised by Mickey's acceptance of this hokum. She reads me my horoscope every day and keeps a blue-green rock in her pocket when she's on her period, to help ease cramps. She keeps adding sage to my grocery lists so that she can burn it, to get rid of the bad vibes in my apartment.

"What if it's not bullshit?"

"What if she can talk to the dead? Are you kidding me?"

Mickey looks at me. "Why not?"

"Mickey, please. It's ridiculous."

She shrugs. "Okay. We don't have to go."

"I'll go," I say. "But I'm not talking."

"I can't believe you've never seen this," Mickey says. "It's a classic."

I've learned that Mickey is a film buff. She says if she goes to a four-year college, she might minor in Cinema Studies. She says she watched a lot of TCM with her dad growing up, but that's all she'll say about her parents.

"Wasn't your sister into movies?" Mickey asks.

"Yeah, but more like rom-coms. *How to Lose a Guy in Ten Days*, that kind of thing."

Mickey makes a face.

"What?"

"Nothing. Surprising to me," she says.

I drift off during the movie, but Mickey pokes me in the ribs toward the end so I don't miss the big moment. When Jack Nicholson's partner tells him, "Forget it, Jake. It's Chinatown," we both hoot and high-five, as if to say, *hey, that's our guy!*

Once the movie ends, Mickey falls asleep where she is, with Wolfie laying his head on her lap. I don't have the heart to wake either of them. I stare at Mickey's face. Her piercings, the lock of dark hair that is caught in her mouth. In the dark, she could be my sister.

On the drive to Vermont, Mickey eats jelly beans out of her pocket. I listen to her teeth noisily stick and unstick. She comments on every cow we pass along the way. She doesn't offer me any of her candy.

"I made you a fake Facebook," I say, when we're halfway there.

"What?"

"You can delete it after. It's some real stuff, some bullshit."

"Why?" Mickey asks.

"We'll know if she's giving us a fake reading if she uses any of the fake info. We'll know she googled you," I say. "They call it a 'hot reading.'"

"Whatever."

I'm not sure why it's so personal with Celeste. More than the other vultures. More than the private investigators and the tabloid reporters and the religious mom groups. More than the girls who went on TV and claimed to know Angie and the neighbors who tried to adopt her dog for the story. More than the IRS agents who audited my parents that first year for continuing to claim two dependents. More than the message board freaks who think we belong to them.

I guess I still don't like to think of my dad as a fool, as someone to be scammed and laughed at, as the kind of weak-willed man who would invest in witchcraft. I'm still looking for reasons to believe that he was the man I thought I knew.

And I hate the tiny part of myself that's still holding out hope that Celeste is the real deal. I hate the piece of me that can't face reality. It makes me wonder if the only thing that's keeping me from the same kind of madness is ignorance. Maybe if I finally faced reality, erased all hope, accepted things for the way they are, I'd lose my mind. Maybe that's what happened to him. He set a deadline: ten years. Ten years he'd let himself believe in magic, and then it was time to decide whether or not life was worth living on these terms. And he decided that it was not. And maybe I'm worried that I'd decide the same thing. That there is not enough here for me.

"I can pay you back for my half of the hotel," Mickey says, but I know she doesn't mean it. She may make money online, but she's exceedingly frugal. If ever I want to throw food away—leftovers or pizza scraps—she objects, claiming that the food is perfectly good. She also picks the empty makeup containers out of my bathroom garbage. I saw her doing it once after I showered. I came back into the bathroom to look for my glasses, and I saw her crouched on the ground trying to scrape clean my foundation pot with a Q-tip. When she heard me, she startled, dropping it on the floor and shattering the glass.

I tell her not to worry about it.

Three rest stops and two hundred miles later, we make it to Celeste's office, which is off a quaint main street. We go straight there, before the hotel, to a little room above a shoe store. At the top of the narrow staircase, we are greeted by an orange tabby who makes a threatening noise before slinking away. Celeste emerges from the exact spot, the cat herself. She's wearing black slacks and a cream-colored sweater. Her auburn hair is clipped in a pile atop her head. She has reading glasses tucked into her collar. She looks normal, pretty.

"Hello, dears," she says.

"Nice to meet you," Mickey says, extending a hand, but Celeste embraces her in a hug instead.

I watch their exchange, trying to figure out what kind of reading is happening here. Is Celeste trying to smell something on her? A dog or garlic, to predict a love of animals or cooking? Is she trying to feel how thin Mickey is, to predict an eating disorder or a problem of scarcity?

When they pull away, she lunges at me, but I dodge her. She doesn't know who I am yet. We made the appointment in Mickey's name and said she'd be bringing a friend.

"Not a hugger," I say. "Thanks." I extend my hand and resolve to speak no more.

Celeste's office is underwhelming. I was expecting velvet and tassels, maybe mood lighting. Instead, it looks like an office, with a desk in the center and two chairs where Mickey and I sit. Celeste plops down across from us.

For the first few minutes, Celeste asks some questions and jots down Mickey's answers on a sheet of paper in front of her.

"What is your full name?"

"Michaela Robin Greeley."

"How old are you?"

"Nineteen."

"What do you do for work?"

"Student."

"What's your sun sign?"

"Leo."

Celeste makes a knowing sound. She stops jotting for a moment. "You have a very interesting aura," she says.

"Oh?"

"It's quite brilliant," she says. "Somewhere between violet and blue."

I look at Mickey in the light from Celeste's desk lamp. I close my eyes. Blue-black floaters appear. The glossy sheen of her cheap home dye kit.

Celeste gets to the most relevant question last. "Why are you here?"

"I'm trying to connect with someone—Jake. I need to know where he is."

This was not the plan. I kick Mickey hard under the desk, and she pulls her legs away. I watch Celeste for a reaction to the name Jake—a flutter of her eyelids or a quickening of her breath, but I see nothing.

"Well," Celeste says. "That's not how this works. The power works through me. I can't direct it like that."

I feel my shoulders collapse.

"Let's talk about you."

"Okay," Mickey says.

"And let's talk about what you want." Celeste puts her hands, palms up, on the desk. "Those two components will help you think more clearly about your future."

Mickey puts her hand on top of Celeste's.

"Sweetie," Celeste says. She's talking to me. "You take one of mine and one of your friend's." I concede, and we form a small circle.

Celeste has us both close our eyes. She rattles off some theories about Mickey. She had problems in high school, she is a bit of an outsider, et cetera.

Celeste continues: Mickey has secrets. She sometimes feels as though she's living a lie.

I squeeze Mickey's palm to indicate: what a crock. Instead of reciprocating with a squeeze back, Mickey's clammy hand goes limp in mine. I open my eyes to get a look at her. Her mouth is open and she's breathing heavily.

I stare at her extra hard and try to communicate with her telepathically. *Come on, Mickey. You're too smart to be buying this.*

Then, as if cued, Celeste starts rattling off some facts that she gleaned from Mickey's Facebook. Some are true—where Mickey went to school, her exact birthday. Some are fake. Mickey doesn't have a dog, for instance, but Celeste keeps referring to the golden retriever whose pictures I swiped from Google Images. Celeste is getting a vision of a large dog. Running. A field. Did he like peanut butter?

Finally, I get the kick under the desk I was waiting for. I open my eye to find Mickey's one eye also half-open.

"Hold on," Celeste says. "There's a presence."

For a minute or two, Celeste keeps her eyes closed and her brows furrowed in concentration. She swivels her head from one corner of the room to another at one point, like she heard someone call her name. She makes small sounds.

"I'm getting a woman. An older relative, maybe," Celeste says. "Not much older. I saw an A. Maybe an aunt? Unless your mom's name began with A?"

Time stops. My veins fill with ice water.

"Must be my aunt," Mickey says. "I guess."

"She wants to know how you're doing."

Mickey squeezes my hand tightly now, too tightly. Her fingernails dig into my skin.

"She wants to tell you that she's sorry she couldn't do more for you."

I hear Mickey swallow loudly and take a sharp intake of breath. When I open my eyes, I see that her face is pale. Her chin rests on her chest.

In a small voice, she manages, "It's okay."

"Can I tell her that you forgive her?"

Mickey nods.

"She wants to know if you're safe now."

Mickey nods again.

"Okay, good." Celeste's eyes open now. Her eyebrows pull together in a semblance of concern. "Mickey," she says. "I'm very sorry."

Mickey lifts her head. "It's fine," she tries to say, but it gets caught halfway in her throat.

I kick Mickey under the desk, but she doesn't kick back. This entire ordeal has gotten away from us.

"I'm sorry," Celeste says. "That's all I have for now." She looks to me. "We can try your friend for a few minutes and then maybe come back to it."

I release both hands. "No," I say. "We're leaving." I take Mickey by the elbow and hoist her out of her chair. "Let's go, Mickey."

"Teddy," Mickey says. "Come on."

"Teddy," Celeste says, realization dawning. "Beautiful."

I scowl back.

"You knew her dad," Mickey says, stating the obvious.

"A." Celeste snaps her fingers. "Of course. I'm feeling Angela with us now," she says.

"Angie," I say. "Jesus Christ."

"I'm sorry," Celeste says. She recoils from me and knocks a few pens off her desk.

"Do you know about Jake?" I ask. "Was that you?"

"Ah, Jake." Celeste clears her throat and stands tall, with her hands on her hips. She looks around the room, like she's tracking a fly with her eyes. "Yes, a man is here, too. I can feel him."

"Teddy," Mickey says. "It's not her." She touches my shoulder.

"Hold on," Celeste says. "I think I'm getting something. He loves you."

"Please," Mickey says, gently. "Please stop."

We're halfway down the stairs when Celeste calls out to us. "Wait," she says. "You didn't pay."

Mickey starts to root around in her purse, but I clamp my hand over it.

"We're not going to."

"I'll pay," Mickey says, shaking me off.

"Fine," I say, leaving. "It's your funeral."

When Mickey meets me on the sidewalk a minute later, I don't look at her.

"I need a hit of that vape thing," I say.

"I forgot it," she says. She retrieves two real cigarettes from her bag and puts both in her mouth, lighting them at once before handing one to me. We walk to the nearby hotel in silence, smoking and coughing and moving slowly.

When we get to the lobby, I head for the bar, a small dingy room with worn leather furniture that smells like dirty carpet.

Once we have our whiskies, I ask about the reading.

Mickey doesn't respond for a while. She downs the rest of her drink. "It wasn't fake."

"It clearly was."

"I don't want to fight with you. Let's get another drink."

"On me, I assume."

"Yeah," she says. "On you. Because you're rich. And you made a fool of yourself."

"Oh wow," I say. "Neither of those things are true. But I guess I have to get the drinks anyway in case he fucking cards you." I whisper the last part before I stand and head to the bar.

When I return to our seats, there are two men—one on either side of Mickey—perched on the arms of her chair.

"Teddy," the tall one says when I walk up. "We were learning about you."

The muscles in my shoulders tense with annoyance. These two are wearing the remains of business suits—they've taken the jackets off and stuffed their ties in the pockets. The short one has a red face and an indent on his finger that suggests he usually wears a ring. The tall one is beginning to bald, hair thinning above his temples. His forehead is shiny and bulges with symmetrical veins.

I hand Mickey her drink. Her skin looks clear and bright. She laughs readily at their dumb jokes and has rolled her shoulders forward in a way that emphasizes her collarbone and her breasts. The men touch her when they talk.

"What's the relationship here?" the tall one asks, pointing at me.

"We're sisters," Mickey says.

"No," I say. "Not sisters."

Mickey smiles at the man and he mirrors her. "Okay, more like step-sisters," she says.

"Ah," the short one says. "Got it."

"We're totally unrelated," I say.

"I'm close with her sister," Mickey says. "Basically family."

The men have lost interest. We're not blood, which ruins a particular fantasy. Beyond that—who cares.

For over an hour we sit there drinking with them. I barely participate in the conversation, and no one seems to miss my input. I only stay because they keep buying.

"Do you girls want to come up to our suite?" the tall one asks. He lowers his voice and leans in. His breath smells like stale beer. "We have edibles."

"Yeah, let's go," Mickey says. She's drunk and slutty, touching them on the thighs to respond to questions, tossing her greasy hair back and forth and leaving her fingers near her mouth. She has barely acknowledged me, hasn't tried to direct their attention my way even once, except when she prompted me to thank them for the free drinks.

I allow myself to be guided to the room without thinking. The three of them walk in front of me, and I trail behind like Mickey's luggage. It's only after the men venture to the in-room safe briefly together and return with the edibles that I realize something has changed. The short one has lost some kind of rock-paper-scissors and ended up with me. He is no longer hovering near Mickey. They have divided us up, and he takes the couch where I am.

The tall one feeds a chocolate chip cookie to Mickey, who gobbles it up. His free hand is on her flat belly, and I can see his pinky finger creeping down toward the waistband of her pants. Even the short one, stuck with me as he is, can't help but to watch them.

"How old are you guys?" I ask.

Everyone looks up.

"I'm twenty-six," I volunteer. "Almost twenty-seven." The room is spinning a bit. I drank too much, and I'm starting to feel like I might puke if I don't eat something.

The short one looks at his friend and chuckles. "We're a bit older than twenty-seven," he says.

Everyone laughs, including Mickey. "I'm a bit younger," she says.

"Thirty-five? Forty?" I ask.

The short one seems irritated that I have continued this line of questioning.

"Sure. Something like that." He tries to sidle up next to me and put his arm around me, but he smells like B.O. and it's the last straw for my nausea.

"I have to go."

"All right," Mickey says. "Sorry, guys. It's late." She pushes the tall one away from her.

"Stay," he says to her. "You don't have to go."

The short one doesn't even try to convince me to do the same. He scurries to the other couch and boxes Mickey in, one man on each side. "Yeah, you can stay."

Mickey shoots me a look. Pleading. They both have a hand on her, playful, forceful.

"You don't need to go," I say. "I'm tired. You're having fun."

"I shouldn't let you go back by yourself," she says, again trying to stand up, but finding herself physically restrained by the two men. She looks powerless for the first time all night. Things have shifted against her in an instant. All night, she'd been lording her desirability over me. The free drinks, the men, it was all because of her. She wanted me to know it.

I smile at her now. "Not a problem." I have had this power the whole time. I want her to realize that. "I think I can manage the elevator by myself."

She tries once more to stand, but falls down. "Whoa," she says as the tall one helps her back to the couch. "I'm kind of faded."

"That's the good stuff," the short one says.

It's the last thing I hear as the door clicks shut behind me. The Do Not Disturb sign falls to the ground as it slams.

I'll be back in the morning, I think. I'll pick her up from this mess then. She'll learn that she's only invincible online, that things are a little different in real life, when you're dealing with strange old men in the flesh. She'll learn about putting herself in situations like this. What did she think would happen?

But disturbing images of Mickey intrude on my fantasies of vindication. Tomorrow-morning Mickey, disheveled and exhausted-looking, meeting me at the door but not making eye contact.

I make it all the way to the elevator bank before I turn around and run back to the men's hotel room. I knock on the door, but no one answers. I knock louder, start yelling for them to open up.

The short one opens the door, and I half expect him to be undressed. He looks exactly the same. It's only been a few moments.

"Did you forget something?"

"Mickey," I say, pushing past him into the room.

She's still on the couch where she was before. Her shoulders are hunched into her body, but now it doesn't look like a feminine affectation. It's an animal's way of protecting vital organs from predators. Her arms wrap around her middle and her spine is folded.

"Mickey, let's go." I take her hand and pull her up. The tall one doesn't resist, though I half-wish he would. I'm prepared to knee him in the crotch.

Mickey drapes herself around me. I can feel the desperation in the way she clings to me, I think I can feel her pulse racing where our skin meets, but I know that's impossible. And yet, her voice betrays none of that anxiety.

"Thanks for having us," she says breezily.

The tall one throws his head back against the couch cushions in blue-balled frustration. The short one stands by the door where I left him.

Outside the room, Mickey takes my hand and we sprint to the staircase, tripping our way down three flights to our floor.

I open our door, and we push inside, securing the chain lock though no one has our room number.

Without even acknowledging what has happened, Mickey

collapses onto the bed. I do the same. We both start laughing, hysterically, unstoppably. My abs hurt.

"I don't even know what's so funny," Mickey says.

"Me neither," I say. "I must smell terrible. I need a shower." My tongue scrapes against the inside of my mouth like sandpaper as I talk. "And water." The adrenaline is leaving my body, and I'm crashing fast. I don't even have the energy to turn the lights on or move my body under the comforter. My limbs feel leaden.

Mickey is breathing heavily with her eyes closed. It takes all my energy to reach over and feel the artery in her neck. Her eyes open instantly.

"I'm okay," she says, dimly. "I just need some sleep. Thank you for coming back."

In the middle of the night, I am woken by Mickey's snoring. I pee and get some water. It's not enough. My head throbs and my stomach feels sour. The smell of my own breath, still tinged with whiskey, makes me ill. My phone is dead, so I lie awake and stare at the ceiling for an hour. By three, it's clear I'm not falling back asleep. I grab my computer from the floor next to the bed. The battery is low, but my laptop charger is with my phone charger in my bag, all the way across the room.

Ted_Head: Hey.
WilliamFRooney75: ur up late
Ted_Head: I can't sleep
Ted_Head: Miss you
WilliamFRooney75: me too
Ted_Head: ??
Ted_Head: Can't sleep? Or you miss me too?
WilliamFRooney75: both i guess

Ted_Head: Do you want to come over tomorrow?

Ted_Head: After we get home

WilliamFRooney75: i don't know. i don't think so.

WilliamFRooney75: the girl will be there?

Ted_Head: . . . Yeah

Ted_Head: Mickey

Ted_Head: hello?

WilliamFRooney75: have to get up early

WilliamFRooney75: i should hit the hay.

Ted_Head: Fine

Ted_Head: You only liked me when it was easy

Ted_Head: When it was uncomplicated, easy sex

WilliamFRooney75: not going to do this tonight.

WilliamFRooney75: night, teddy

WilliamFRooney75 has logged off.

When the computer battery dies, I take Mickey's phone from the center table and click the home button. It requires a passcode or a fingerprint. I lift it to Mickey's hand, which dangles off the bed. It takes a few tries, but I get it.

The banking app is open. She must have been worried about her money after Celeste. Always worried about money.

I use her thumb to unlock the app, too. She has one checking account, and the balance is overdrawn.

I click through her transactions out of morbid curiosity. Mostly college expenses—books, tuition fees, gas, food. Cigarettes from the rest stop on the way up here, when she started detoxing in the car. She spends little but she makes even less. The amounts that come in from her webcam stuff are so low, I wonder if it she couldn't make more as a barista.

I scroll back a few months, and things get better. Higher balances. More money coming in than going out. $2,000 in

February. $2,000 in January. $2,000 in December. Always around the middle of the month. Always a cash deposit.

I have to go back a year before they disappear, before the same pattern of overdrawing and reconciling comes back.

My money. The paycheck I gave to my parents for rent and expenses. The money my dad was taking out in cash every month. The money Mom was so sure was somewhere in the house, squirreled away for her.

I close out of the banking app and put Mickey's phone back on the bedside table. I stare at the ceiling. Two thousand dollars a month. There is a short list of things that Mickey can provide that cost two thousand dollars a month.

I look over at Mickey. Her arm hangs limp off the bed. Her nails are painted dark—almost black. She has rings on every finger. Dressed up for the trip. Asleep, with her cheek bunched up under her eye, she looks even younger.

I think about my dad. My dad who, before things turned, was fun and mischievous and young at heart. Who cried alongside me when my guinea pig, Martin, died. Who let us dress him up in feather boas. Who conspired in our make-believe. Who bought Angie a dog without telling Mom. Who lied every time he took us to McDonald's. Who was great at keeping secrets. Who slept with his own brother's wife. Who abandoned his son. Who could justify anything in the name of love.

I see him in my mind. A thousand flashes of his sly, crooked smile that speed up and warp like a funhouse mirror. Memories or memories of pictures or something else entirely. The grin morphs from puckish to hungry. His glinting eyes grow black and terrible, like a wolf.

I squeeze my eyes shut to stop the wheel. Focus, focus. Find something solid, something to latch on to. A memory, a real one.

There it is. His hands. Only his hands. His big soft hands, like bear paws. The rough yellow calluses at the base of each finger, from gardening. I pick up one hand with both of mine and it falls back down, limp. He's asleep. I'm lying on top of his massive warm body on the couch. Watching but not watching a black-and-white movie on TCM. Rubbing my hands on the scratchy stubble of his jaw. Trying but not trying to wake him up. Exploring his body like he's a wild animal that I found and tranquilized. Lifting his upper lip to see his teeth, square and orderly in their rows.

"Stop that," he mutters. Only half-asleep then. All my prying and poking.

"Show me the shiny ones."

He opens wide, eyes still closed, and I see the glint of the three gold caps in the back. Beautiful. Special. He closes his mouth and lets his head fall to the side.

I rest my cheek on top of his chest. I ride the rise and fall of his breath. The safety floods my body. Warm and inviting. Narcotic. It lulls me to sleep.

I snap my eyes open. Mickey lies in front of me, small like a child. I reach out to stroke the greasy hair away from her face, but my hand stops just short. My gaze traces the lines of her body, folded into a Z. I move my palm over her side, from her neck to her thigh, keeping an inch away from the skin. Never touching. She shudders.

I can feel him inside me, an echo, a virus—the wolf, twitchy and ravenous.

I shudder, too. How close I came to a monster. How little I understood.

I wake to a text from Bill:

I'm not coming there, but you can come here if you want.
Just you.

We leave the room early. Mickey shoves some Danishes from the continental breakfast in her coat pocket and we check out of the hotel.

It's fifty miles before Mickey breaks the silence. "Are you still mad at me?" she asks, like a child, without a trace of bitterness or anger or embarrassment in her voice.

"What do you mean?"

"You were mad at me," Mickey says. "You were going to leave me there with those guys."

"I wasn't."

"Sorry," she says. "It's not a big deal."

"Those guys could have raped you."

Mickey pokes me. "Don't be dramatic."

"I'm driving."

I turn on the radio, and Mickey curls her legs up on the seat and stares at me. I can feel her continued gaze as I watch the road.

"What?" I say.

"You look pretty today."

I glance over at her. She's hunched, using her hands to tear apart and de-matt her slept-in braid. The impression is simian.

"I shouldn't have left you," I say.

Mickey abruptly shifts her attention to working the channel knob back and forth. "It's fine," she says, clearing her throat. "You came right back."

There is more to say, of course. There is more to know. Eventually we will need to talk about my dad and what he did and where and how many times and if it hurt and how it hurt. But first I need to remove him from my brain, remove him from my heart, make him into a stranger. Erase everything I know so that I can overwrite it. My human brain is not equipped to handle both versions.

Maybe Mickey is better, more evolved. Has a higher tolerance for mess, for gray area, for ambivalence. Maybe if I told her that I know and I still love him, she could forgive me. Maybe that is what she is here to find out.

When we're a few exits from home, Mickey instructs me to turn off the highway "for a surprise."

I groan and begin to object—I hate surprises—but Mickey dials the volume high. She pantomimes confusion. What was that? She can't hear me.

"Fine," I say. "Fine. Turn it down."

But right then a song that we both love comes on, and we turn it even higher instead. We sing the rest of the way, barely talking or looking at each other, instead indulging in some painful earnest harmonies.

"You have a nice voice," Mickey says.

I know it's not true, but I'm embarrassed by how flattering I find the compliment. I confess to Mickey how I thought, as a girl, that I might grow up to be a singer.

Mickey finds another song she likes on the station that only plays '90s hits and she belts it out the window, letting her hand slice through the fast air outside the car. I just listen. The on-the-nose lyrics coupled with the genuine emotion in her voice. I could never even admit that I know the words, though of course I do. I admire it—the lack of pretense, of artifice. The lack of self-consciousness. I wish I could tell her that I admire some things about her, too.

She directs me through a town I've never visited. It's rural, and bleak, and I'm not sure what business we could have this deep in the woods.

"Here," she says. "On the left."

In the middle of nowhere, at the intersection of two roads that are lined with nothing but trees, there is a brown shack with a single neon light in the window—TATTOOS.

I want to ask if this is urgent, if she has to get a tattoo right now, but I am in debt to her, and I know that now, so I say nothing. I pull into the driveway, behind the brown van that's already parked.

"How long do these things usually take?" I ask.

"Come on," Mickey says. She slips out of the car and walks up the four wooden steps to the front door. She's knocking by the time I manage to turn off the engine and follow her.

"Hi, Mick." The man who opens the door is cute and clean-cut, in a button-down shirt and jeans. He looks like someone I would have dated in college—blandly attractive, unoffensive, forgettable. He has no visible tattoos himself.

"Graham, Teddy. Teddy, Graham. Oh hey—" Mickey laughs. "Like the snack." She steps inside. "Graham goes to school with me. Beautiful artist."

"Oh, you," Graham says. He reaches forward to shake my hand, and I notice that he has a diamond stud in each ear. "Nice to meet you, Teddy." He can barely hold my eye contact and looks down at the ground, bashful. Part of me loves him. Loves that Mickey has people like this in her life. Warm people.

"What will it be?" Graham asks.

"Okay, so for me," Mickey says. She scrolls on her phone and shows him a photo. I can't see it.

Graham smiles. "Okay, then. Not your usual vibe."

"For Teddy—"

"What?" I try to snatch her phone away, but she's too fast. "No," I say. I look at Graham. "No. I'm not getting anything. Thank you."

"Teddy," Mickey says. She walks toward me until her chest touches my chest. She puts her head on my shoulder. My arms come up around her instinctively. Past Mickey's head, I can see Graham looking down at the floor to give us a moment.

"Fine," I say. "But small."

Mickey hugs me back, her wiry strong arms pinching. "Yes."

I go first, to get it over with. I'm worried if I have to watch the needle hit Mickey's skin, I'll lose my resolve, so I sit in the chair, close my eyes, and ask Graham to turn up the music. It takes about ten minutes total, and it hurts a lot less than I thought it would. A sting around my ankle, in the place between my Achilles tendon and the bone. Mickey let me choose this spot, which I can hide with a sock or boot.

Graham applies the bandage before I open my eyes. Then it's Mickey's turn. She's a pro, chatting and laughing like nothing is happening, like she isn't sitting topless in this cold room while Graham works from the photo on her phone.

"Don't look!" she says, when she can see me squinting to make out the shape on her ribcage. "It's a surprise."

When it's all done, I pay Graham. It's a hundred dollars for both, since the tattoos were small and Mickey is a friend. Back in the car, I ask Mickey when I can see the tattoos and why she doesn't date Graham, who seems lovely, and if this whole thing was a crazy stupid thing to do.

"First of all, Graham is gay. Second of all," she says. "It's just skin. And you can see them at home, but I'll tell you what they are now if you want."

She pulls up the pictures on her phone to show me.

"Yours," she says, and she shows me three hollow circles pressed together. It takes me a moment to realize that I'm looking at the symbol for Mickey Mouse. "Mine." Hers is a teddy bear—Corduroy, to be exact, in his broken overalls.

I can't speak for a minute or so. I stare ahead at the road.

"Now you'll never get rid of me," I say.

"Ditto."

I drop Mickey at my apartment, and I head to Bill's. When I pull up, the dogs greet me at the car.

"Good boys," I say.

"Rocky, Red," I hear Bill call. Red howls and Rocky echoes him. They run ahead of me, up to the back sliding door, which is cracked open.

"Smells garlicky in here." I hold up the wine I picked up. "Should I open this?"

Bill is over the stove, cooking in a white undershirt. Rabbit and mashed potatoes. He rubs his face with the back of his forearm and gestures to a row of drawers. "Opener is somewhere in there."

When it's time to eat I put on the Four Tops and pour us both some Merlot. "Did you assassinate Peter Cottontail yourself?" I ask as I cut into the meat.

"No," Bill says. "A friend of mine went out last weekend. Had extra." He takes a swill of wine and clears his throat.

"What?"

"Never mind."

"You're in a mood."

"I'm fine."

We don't talk while we eat. All I hear is the sound of my own jaw masticating the overcooked rabbit and the grating of Bill's steak knife on his plate.

"I'm really glad I came all the way out here," I say.

"The sarcasm is immature," he says. "Like your little detective game. And your teenage girlfriend."

"Okay," I say. I throw my napkin down on top of my plate. "I'm going home."

"Wait, Ted." Bill grabs my arm as I pass his seat. "Come on. Slow down."

I can feel a lump forming in my throat, and I swallow it down. "I was looking forward to seeing you, but you're being a dick," I say.

"I don't—" He pulls me onto his lap, and his face is in my hair. "I just don't know how to talk to you lately."

"What do you mean?"

"I'm worried about you."

"Well, don't be." I yank myself away and go back to my chair. I start to eat again, joylessly sawing off pieces of meat and putting them in my mouth. One chew, two, three. I count to ten and swallow. Everything tastes like sawdust-flavored sand.

We finish our meal in silence with Bill staring at me the entire time. Afterwards, I clean the dishes while he takes the dogs out. In bed, we pretend to sleep alongside each other, both understanding that sex is off the table. Bill reaches over to my side of the bed with one besocked foot. I have to pull my ankle and its fresh bandage away.

"Night, Ted," he says. He turns his body toward mine and cups my face in his hand. He kisses my forehead, then my cheeks, the bridge of my nose, my jawline. I hold perfectly still. He kisses everywhere but my mouth. Softly, my hairline, the lobes of my ears, my neck. He shifts his weight on top of me as he moves down toward my clavicle, my sternum.

My body rises toward his and he scoops his arm under the small of my back, so that my hips are elevated. I feel him press into me. In the dark, his face is a silhouette. I can't see his eyes. I reach out with my hand and brush his hair back. I find his eyebrow with my thumb.

Bill kisses me on the mouth slowly, then more urgently. "I love you," he says. "I love you."

"Shh," I say. "No more."

Bill moves my underpants to the side in one motion and is inside of me within seconds.

I wrap my legs around his back. I let him carry on for a while. It's rhythmic and nice.

I feel him getting closer, his arms shaking with focus, and I stop him. He whimpers and buries his face in my hair.

"Teddy," he says. He makes a guttural sound as he finishes.

I have my old car back, new window and everything, so I retrieve Wolfie from Mom's before work. He looks decidedly worse than when I left him. He can barely keep his eyes open, and Mom is eager to see him go with me, back to my apartment for a few days.

"Take him to the vet, Teddy," she says.

"I will. I'll call tomorrow."

But when I come home that afternoon, Wolfie is lying on the bathroom floor, and something is seriously wrong. He is surrounded by towels, my apartment smells like dog shit, and he doesn't so much as raise his head to greet me. I hear him breathing and watch his ribs strain with the labor of each inhale.

"Mickey!"

She comes running from the kitchen with a roll of paper towels in her hand and a bottle of Lysol. "Thank god," she says. "I didn't know what to do. You weren't answering."

"My phone was dead," I say. I get down on the ground with Wolf. His eyelids flutter open for a second. His nose is dry. "What happened?"

"I don't know," Mickey says. "I thought maybe he fell, because when I tried to pick him up to take him out, he made a sound like he was hurt. He couldn't support his weight. He went right back down."

"How long has he been like this?"

"Hours," Mickey says. She's upset. Her face is streaked with liquid eyeliner. Her hands, holding the cleaning supplies, shake. "Should we take him to the vet?"

I imagine loading Wolfie into my trunk, and it seems brutal. The bumps in the road, him jostling around back there, only to arrive at the place he hates most in the world, so that he might die by a long, sterile needle. I can't stomach the betrayal of leaving that office without him.

"No."

"Should I call your mom?"

"Absolutely not." I wriggle one of the towels under his torso. It's damp with urine. "Help me lift him."

"Where?"

"To the bed."

Together, Mickey and I carry Wolfie, the weight of his body hammocked in the towel, his head and tail hanging down on either side. We're careful not to let his skull strike the furniture. We lay him on top of my comforter, and I lie beside him.

"Do you want me to get more towels?" Mickey asks. "He's completely incontinent."

"It's fine."

For hours, I hope that death will meet him quickly here at home and that I won't need to take any action. *Spare me from having to be the one to do it*, I tell him, using my body. I hold his paw in my hand, which he would never let me do ordinarily. I stroke the scratchy pads on the bottom and trace the fur that runs between them. I put my nose against his nose, then in his open mouth to breathe the fishy smell that I know so well. I rest my cheek on his face and close my eyes.

At some point, I fall asleep, and I wake in a panic. The room is dark, and I worry for a moment that I missed it, but no—he's still hanging on, which is even worse. His lungs are rattling now, and I can feel that we are both wet from another accident. At some point, Mickey must have covered us with a blanket.

I gently pry open one of Wolfie's eyes. His cloudy irises dart back and forth, seeing nothing. I try to be delicate in hugging him, but he lets out a whimper, involuntary, pain squeezed from the body. I pull away from his bony frame, and I bury my face in his whiskers.

"I'm going to miss you, bud," I whisper. "I'm really going to miss you." Maybe I imagine it, but I think I feel Wolfie's head move slightly toward mine.

"Okay," I say. "Let's go for a walk."

I carry Wolfie down the stairs by myself. His body is long, but light. I get him set up with his pillows in the back of the car before we pull out of the driveway. The last thing I see as we pull away is Mickey's frame silhouetted against the upstairs window.

The roads are quiet and pitch black. I can only see as far as my headlights, and I try to anticipate potholes from memory, swerving preemptively to dodge them. I hit a few, but Wolfie doesn't make a sound in the back.

When we get to the trail—the one where we used to hike all the time when he was a baby, in the park where the volunteer crews spent weeks sweeping for any sign of Angie—I carry him out and into the woods along with one of his pillows. The only light I have is from my phone, and a rogue tree root nearly takes us both out. When it feels like we've gone far enough and my arms start to fatigue, I lay him down in a bed of rotting leaves, resting his head on a mound of dirt. It's unseasonably chilly.

For a moment, we sit and listen to the nighttime sounds—the crickets and the wind and the rustling of small creatures. I describe to Wolfie what the stars look like. I can't identify the constellations like Angie, I tell him. She used to know all of them. She was very into the zodiac.

I tell Wolfie about Argos. Late in *The Odyssey*, our hero returns home in disguise, after years of torment at sea, to find his loyal dog waiting at the door. Argos was a puppy when Odysseus left, but now he is old, neglected, and flea-ridden, sleeping on a pile of dung. The two make eye contact, and, unlike Odysseus's wife and son, Argos recognizes Odysseus immediately, intimately. He musters a feeble wag of the tail. Unable to betray his cover with a touch or a kind word, Odysseus wipes a single tear from his face and crosses the threshold into the palace. With that, Argos takes his last breath, free to die with the knowledge that, at long last, his best friend has returned.

Year after year, my students fail to recognize the beauty of that kind of love. They get hung up on the fleas and the piles of shit and the improbability of a hound living to twenty years.

"Ten is old for your kind," I remind Wolfie.

He doesn't respond. I feel his chest to see if he's still breathing. He is.

"I'm sorry she never came back to you," I say. "I hope I was a decent substitute."

I wait as long as I can on the ground with him, until my teeth are chattering. He's still hanging on.

"I can't let us both freeze to death," I say. "No more pain. I'm sorry."

I pull the gun out from the back of my jeans, where I stashed it on my way out. I hold it to Wolfie's head, and he doesn't move. He lets me rest the heavy muzzle of the weapon between his eyes, on that hard, flat part that used to be my favorite. I hold it there and listen to the sounds of the forest for another minute. This is a nice place to rest. This is better than whatever happens at the vet's office, I think. This was one of his favorite places.

I'm sure that it's much better to do this sort of thing under the cover of darkness than in the glaring fluorescent lights of an office park. It must be better.

"I love you, Wolf," I say, and then I pull the trigger.

It's impossibly loud in the silence. Even after I know the quiet has returned, I can hear the shot echoing in my head. It seems to have deepened the blackness of the night, and I have to blink several times to be sure my eyes are open. When they readjust, I can only make out Wolfie's general shape, but I'm glad not to be able to see the full extent of the damage. I'm not sure I'd be able to forgive myself for ruining the face of love. I stroke the top of his head, which is still intact, and I resist the urge to move my hand lower, to assess the exploded flesh and feel the shards of bone jutting out from the bridge of his nose.

I realize now—too late—that I forgot a shovel. And I can't take his body back to my car or I'll have to see the hole I made in his head. I start digging with my hands. The earth is hard and wet, and my fingertips ache. Within a few minutes, I've made only enough progress to bury my own foot up to the ankle.

I pet Wolfie. "Hold on," I say.

I need to find a big stick. I need to find something strong and flat for digging. Something oar-shaped. I grab at things with my hands to move through the darkness—things that could be living or poisonous or sharp. I trip several times, once landing on the ground with an ankle so badly twisted that I worry, briefly, that I've broken it. I finally find a stick—inferior, spoon-shaped, good enough. But when I turn to find the hole that I started, to find Wolfie, I can't remember the direction. I point with my phone for light, but the battery is dying, so I put it away. The woods are tricky out here. I remember Mom forbidding us from leaving her side on hikes when we were young. I remember kids getting temporarily lost, starting small panics.

I want to call for Wolfie. I want to whistle and slap my leg and hear him running out from between the trees, barreling toward me. But I stop breathing, and all I hear are insects.

Time slips by as I scramble around, waiting in vain for my eyes to adjust and turn to night vision. I consider the fact that if I stay long enough, the sun will come up, but I don't know when that will be. Minutes? Hours? I pick a direction and walk in as straight a line as I can. The chill is deeper now, and it reaches my bones. My pants are wet from falling, and I consider lying down under a tree and waiting for daybreak. Maybe Mickey will find me.

I walk and walk until I hit a service road, and that service road takes me back to my car, like an invisible guiding hand. I look up the hill, and I know that I'll never find him.

I'm exhausted. I can't scale the hill I just descended. I'll never remember how I wound my way into the trees and where we landed. I'm holding this tiny, useless stick like an idiot. I get in my car and drive home. The clock lets me know that I've been outside for three hours.

I'm sorry, I repeat as the air from the vents blasts my pants dry. I'm sorry, Wolfie.

The drive feels long, and the car feels empty. The emptiness is a pressure crushing my chest cavity. I hate myself for leaving him in the woods by himself. I start to grow paranoid that maybe Angie's body is out there too, among the trees, in a state of decay. I try not to imagine the rodents that might already be feeding on his mangled flesh. That's part of nature, I try to tell myself. It's a nice place to rest, to be laid down. It will give me somewhere to visit, I think, even as I know that I'll never return to that trail. I wonder if I took him far enough into the woods that he won't be found by hikers. Even if he were, though, what would happen? No one calls the police when they find a dead animal in the woods. Animals die. That's life.

Mom. Fuck. What about Mom.

The building is dark when I pull up, but the upstairs light comes on as soon as I shut my car door. Mickey meets me on the stairs. She takes my hands in hers, turns them over. They're covered in blood and dirt.

"What happened?"

"I need to shower."

Mickey follows me up. I peel off my urine- and blood- and mud-stained clothes and take a long, hot shower, letting my mind go completely blank. While I'm in there, she moves everything out of sight. Puts my shirt and pants in the hamper, or god willing, the garbage. When I crawl into bed, I'm clean and the bed is still soiled, but it doesn't matter anymore.

We would never have accused you of liking anything, Angie. What with your sour face and your penchant for rage music that made my brain feel like it was drowning.

But you did have a soft spot for Bruce Springsteen.

Of all Dad's corny music—all the incessant Yes and Billy Joel concert bootlegs that we had to suffer in the car—you could tolerate Springsteen, in some ways, in my mind, the corniest of them all.

Dad would start in on a lyric about working behind an old guitar factory or whatever before the song even started and you'd roll your eyes, but then when the drums picked up, you'd be there in the back humming along. I could hear it in your voice that you wanted to belt it. I'd catch you, shoot you a look, and you'd punch me.

Mom liked Springsteen enough, too. Maybe that's what gave him cachet for you. She was a poet; she knew these things. You always trusted Mom's taste. Even when you didn't see eye to eye, she wasn't embarrassing.

Dad was the embarrassing one. The way he was so desperate to be around us and Mom, that hungry look in his eye when we stepped out of the car in the morning, back when he used to do the school run, like he was worried we were going to leave him alone forever.

He wanted to make you laugh so badly. He wanted to be able

to teach you something. He wanted something you two could share. Springsteen was a start.

Your last birthday, we all woke up to "Thunder Road" at 6 A.M. You came down the stairs last, pissed as hell.

"Are you guys kidding? Can I not sleep in on my freaking birthday?"

Dad was undaunted. He lunged across the living room floor, looked over the banister to you, and struck the air guitar. He put one hand out to you.

You didn't take his hand, and he waited a beat before going back to the air guitar. He made his way across the room while you descended.

And then suddenly, we heard it. A woof.

Dad stopped in his tracks. Feigned confusion. Mom put a hand to her forehead. "Jesus, Mary, and Joseph, pray for us."

Your arms fluttered. Your voice was paralyzed. I started laughing hysterically, uncontrollably, watching you.

"Turn it down!" you hollered.

Mom turned the music down with one hand, while Dad swept her into a dance with the other hand.

Woof. Whimpering. Scratches. Coming from the door. Under the hall table was a big plastic crate, peeking out from the small, dated tablecloth. You and I spotted it at the same time.

You raced over and let him out. Wolfie. He was tall, but he was obviously a puppy. Fifty pounds of legs. Face like a stuffed animal. His grip slipped on the tile floor, and he turned it into a roll. Belly up to you, Angie, you buried your face in him.

Dad turned the music back up and danced with Mom around the living room. I moved between you and them.

"They didn't have anything smaller, huh?" Mom said.

"I needed an Irish one," Dad said. "Love my Irish pups."

"Ach, you."

That was the best day. All day, you kept going over to the stereo and replaying "Thunder Road." It made Dad happy to have done one great thing for you.

Mom threatened us about picking up the shite in the backyard and walking him every day. "I won't be taking care of this wee dog because yer father is a sap and an eejit," she said. Her accent always got extra heavy when she was pretending to be cross.

"Wee?"

"Shut your gob, miss."

That day was crisp and beautiful. We walked as a family, in the middle of the road. The air felt like mint in my lungs. It was the kind of day that would become Wolfie's favorite. The kind that would always have him running himself ragged.

You actually burst into song, hollering at the top of your lungs as we walked the dog, then unnamed, through the neighborhood. You weren't embarrassed or embarrassing. It was like you were in love.

Dad suggested Bruce for the dog.

"Don't push it," you said.

"Wolfie," I said.

"Okay," you said.

It was small to you, probably, but it was big to me. I knew he was your dog, but I got to name him. You trusted me.

That was the last time I saw Dad happy. That was the last time we were all together like that, laughing, having fun. Even then, without knowing that you would soon vanish, that Dad would soon retreat into himself, I knew somehow that I needed to cherish it. That I had to bottle every last part of it and hold it inside my heart. It was that special. You were the sun, and we were desperate to please you, all of us, no one resenting it. And when you left, the sun went out. And, naturally, it got cold.

We are a week away from graduation, from final exams, from the last day of school. One week.

I have my coffee at my desk, read my emails, send an almost perfunctory message to Jake, grade papers. Some days, I threaten Jake, some days, I manage a professional tone, and today, I find myself pleading with him: *I just want to know how you knew my sister. Please stop ignoring my messages. I just want to talk to you.*

My first class is at ten, with the freshmen, and they have an essay due soon, so I let them use the time to work independently. Uneventful. For lunch, I've brought a Ziploc of dry cereal, which I eat with my hands in front of my computer. I watch movie trailers with headphones on. Nothing interesting. I nod off for a split second and manage to spill coffee straight down the V of my cashmere sweater.

I clean up in the bathroom. Somehow, I've gotten lucky— the camisole beneath my sweater got wet, leaving the outer layer spared. I shimmy the white tank down to my feet and stuff it into the trash. While I'm here, I fix my hair and examine my reflection. I've been picking at my skin more than usual, and it shows. Last week, I tore at a small pimple on my face until it ran blood into my mouth thanks to a minor dispute with Mickey over the laundry. The scab is still there, along with some similar spots near the scalp, where I've been tugging at my hair during the school day. Individual strands at first and then a few together. Then small clumps.

I lift my shirt up to reveal my 9mm to the mirror. It reminds me of when I was going through my fitness phase two years ago, and I used to check my abdominal definition in the mirror throughout the day, monitoring any fluctuations in bloat.

The first day that Wolfie was gone, I retrieved the gun from the glove compartment and expected to feel repulsed. Instead, I found the curves of the iron more alluring. The entire first day that Wolfie was gone, I rubbed my hand up and down the barrel. My body slackened and my brain slowed, and I felt relaxed like I'd had a stiff drink. When I put the barrel to my face, I imagined that I could smell Wolfie on the metal.

I intended to put it back in its storage box—the expensive, foam-lined number that I felt was worth the optional add-on—but I haven't been able part with it. For days now, I've kept it snug against me, patting the spot above my hip bone compulsively, checking for its positioning. My skin is starting to chafe and sting, but I don't care. Even at night, I sleep with the gun under my pillow, my hand on the stock, and I wake up having barely changed position. I keep the safety on, of course, but the thought of having an accident in my sleep makes me dizzy.

My junior class is when it all goes sideways.

It's our third day talking about *Frankenstein*, and the students were supposed to read the first hundred pages by now. It's one of my favorites. I start by asking the kids what they've noticed about the text so far. They're in chairs in a semi-circle, and I'm up front at the board, chalk at the ready to record their observations.

"Epistolary," Margaret says.

"Right," I say, logging her note, and including the phrase "frame device" alongside it. "What else? How about thematically?"

A few students comment on science and the danger of

knowledge. Some object and say it's not so much about the danger of scientific knowledge but about the lack of ethics and foresight.

Maurice, my sometime lunch buddy, raises his hand. "Parenting," he says.

"Can you expand on that?"

Maurice cites a quote from the book: "'A new species would bless me as its creator and source; many happy and excellent natures would owe their being to me.'"

"Why did that quote stick out to you?"

"That's a fucked-up reason to have kids," Maurice says.

"Watch it. Come on."

"Sorry."

"Language aside," I say, "you have a point. There is a lot of anxiety about creating life, nurturing life. What it means to be a child, a parent. What the two owe to one another."

"Did she have kids?" Craig asks.

I'm tempted to snap back at him, asking if he would inquire about a male author's parental status, but I don't. Partly because I think it's a fair question, but mostly because I love Mary Shelley and her goth girl ways. I love her factual bio and I love all the myths about her—how she first fucked Percy on Mary Wollstonecraft's grave, how she pressed and preserved his heart between pages of his own poetry. I don't even care if they're true.

"She did have kids," I say. "Only one survived, but he was born later. When she wrote this book, she was barely older than you are now and she had already lost an infant. In her journals, she wrote about a dream she'd had where she tried to revive the baby in front of a fireplace, not unlike the way Victor brings the monster to life from dead parts."

Rhys, my least favorite student, raises his hand, and I feel my scalp start to itch. Sometimes I think that he lives to annoy me.

He loves to have an opinion about everything we study, and he usually chooses the opinion opposite my own. He does copious online research about a book's history, and occasionally he will ask me obscure questions in order to watch me fumble around for an answer I can't remember. Then he swoops in with the information. I would love to fail him, but he is one of the few who reads all the assigned pages, and he's a pretty strong writer. Even if he's a prick.

"Percy Shelley heavily edited the manuscript for the novel," he says.

"Yes, he edited it. He was her husband."

"No, like, he basically shaped the book."

"That's debatable—"

"Despite its clear influence on sci-fi and horror genres, as a novel it's not all that well-written."

"I guess we disagree on that one."

"Is it going on the board? A lot of scholars agree that the prose is amateurish."

I feel a rage bubbling up in my core. "No," I say. "'Amateurish' is not going on the board."

Rhys looks genuinely confused. "Not the story," he says. "But the quality of the writing." He talks slowly as he speaks, enunciating the last few words like I'm some kind of simpleton who can't understand what he's getting at. I'm sure he's one of those kids who insists that his teachers are idiots, and he's smarter than all of them. I'm sure his parents tell him he's right about that.

"Mary Shelley grew up in a time when women were barely educated," I say. "Her mother—incidentally one of the great proto-feminist thinkers—died in childbirth. Her upbringing was lonely, stressful, and sad, and her adulthood was filled with death—her sister, her children, her husband. She channeled some of that early grief into this book—" I brandish it at him. I know I'm projecting. I know that if Shelley hadn't been eighteen and moody and filled with pain and misunderstanding, I wouldn't see so much of Angie in her. Wouldn't feel the need to defend her two-hundred-year-old work, which has stood the test of time just fine on its own. I might even agree with Rhys on the language point. "Which she wrote over the course of one summer while she was basically your age."

"And that's all well and good . . ." he begins.

The very sound of his voice is irritating to me, and I start to have a physical, bodily response. My fists clench, and my face gets hot. People used to describe me as having "the patience of a saint." As in, "you must have the patience of a saint to work with high school kids."

I realize too late that with both my elbows in the air, my fingernails embedded in my scalp, my sweater rides up, way up. At first I breathe easy; the camisole has me covered. But then I remember. The gun is exposed to my class.

Everyone but Rhys notices, and their faces scan with horror. Rhys rambles on about the text while I scramble to pull the fabric down, but it's too late. I turn to the board to hide my face, which is burning red, and I write "amateurish," to buy myself some time.

I can't deny what they've seen with their own eyes, and I can't think of a reasonable alternative to what it could be, so I decide to say nothing. Pretend nothing happened, act as though it's the most natural thing in the world for me to be carrying a gun in their classroom.

For the rest of the lesson, I barely talk. The kids barely talk. Long stretches of silence build to a crescendo, and I feel smothered by the tiny sounds of students shifting in their desk chairs. Twenty minutes pass so slowly that twice I wonder if the clock has stopped, but finally the bell interrupts us. By now they've usually bolted.

They don't move, and that's when I know I'm fucked.

"You're dismissed," I say, for the first time ever.

The kids pack up their bags urgently, without speaking to one another. They each exit the classroom as quickly as they can, no one waiting for a friend, no one hanging back to chat about next period's test. Even Maurice—my Maurice—who usually hangs around to ask me some inane question because of his crush on me, vanishes in the stampede toward the door.

The seniors in my creative writing class are waiting in the hall to come in when the last junior boy exists.

"Hey, Ms. A," Chris says. "Did you see—"

"Guys," I say to the few who are trickling in. "I have to go downstairs. I've had—an emergency."

Chris and Lexia exchange looks, like "it's always something with her," and I ignore them.

"Should we do something?" Emma asks.

"You should do a free write," I say. "No talking and no phones."

I wonder why I didn't dismiss them. They're seniors; they can handle some unstructured time. Now, they will be expecting me back, and I'm fairly certain that I'm not coming back. Before I go downstairs, I stop at my desk and jam my pocketbook with whatever will fit from my drawers—some good pens, a book I haven't finished, a framed photo of Mom, a bar of chocolate.

The first thing Rick says to me when I make it to his office, taking a seat on his beat-up leather couch, is that he thought, looking at me through his glass door, that I was one of the parents.

"Nope, it's me," I say.

He gestures at my bag, but a question gets stuck in his throat. He seems to realize as he's forming it that something is wrong, something more serious than the oddity of seeing me with a handbag in the middle of the day.

"What's going on?" he asks. "Shouldn't you be in class?"

"I have to talk to you about something. I wanted to get ahead of it."

"What does that mean?" He sits down across from me, on the couch's matching sister—a worn armchair that bears the impression of Rick's ass cheeks.

"The kids talk, and I wanted you to hear from me and not one of the parents—"

"Teddy," Rick says. He stands and makes his way over to the door where he gestures for his secretary, Marianne, to join us. "You need to tell me what's going on."

Marianne comes in with a pen and legal pad in hand and stands behind Rick in his chair. It's like they were ready for this.

"Get to the point quickly," he says.

"I was in class, when my sweater rode up—"

"Oh, Jesus," Rick says.

"No, not like that." I don't know what to say, so I simply show him.

Marianne gasps and ducks behind the chair like I'm going to execute her.

"Marianne," I say. "My god." I pull my sweater back down. "It was an accident."

Rick is speechless. Marianne is whimpering behind the chair.

"Marianne!" Rick shouts, when he finally gets his bearings. "Go call the police." She scurries out of the room with her legal pad still tucked under her elbow.

"Lift your shirt," Rick says.

"What?"

"Don't touch the gun. Don't move," he says. "Put your hands on your head."

I put my hands on my head and he approaches me slowly, watching me like an animal. He feels around my waist gingerly until he touches the gun. He lifts my shirt and pulls it out from the holster with two fingers. He must have seen a cop do it like this on a show. He's moving like he's worried about fingerprints and evidence. The feeling of his hand against my skin and the metal dragging slowly upwards makes me shiver.

He yells at me and drops the gun. "I said don't move!" It falls into my lap.

He scoops it out of my lap quickly with two hands and moves it to his desk, where he places it down and steps away from it.

"It's not a bomb," I say. "The safety's on."

"Shut up," Rick says through gritted teeth. "Shut your damn mouth, Teddy. You're not helping your own case here."

"Police are not necessary."

"They are, as a matter of fact." Rick shakes his head back and forth. "You brought a gun into my school." He pauses, remembers the rest. "And my students saw it!"

"I know. It's not good."

"It's a goddamn nightmare."

"I think we should reconsider the police. I don't have all the permits."

"You think I care?" Rick says. "We practice this, Teddy. You're part of the lockdown drills. Come on."

"It was a lapse in judgment."

"Why do you even have a gun? Let's start with why." Rick is agitated, pumping himself up and down on his desk. "Can you tell me why?"

"It doesn't matter," I say. I can't get into it now. With Rick.

"Fine," Rick says. "You know that you're fired, right?"

I nod.

"I tried, Teddy. I tried to give you the benefit of every doubt."

"I understand," I say. If he wants me to grovel, I'm not going to grovel. My immediate feeling is: relief. Then: surprise, at my own reaction. And finally: impatience, while I sit in Rick's office with the school security guard standing by the door, all of us not making a sound as we wait for the police. Just let me go home.

I watch the clock for the moment my senior class comes to a close. I know I'll never teach again. I don't think I'll miss it. Maybe now, I think, I can figure out what I want to do with my life.

When the police arrive, Rick lets them into his office and pulls down all the blinds. It's no use; there is already a small mob gathered outside his door, peering in. The students can tell that something is going on, and I'm at the center of it. I can only imagine the stories they will invent. The speculation that will become record, that eventually Mom will hear at the grocery store from someone whose darling niece attends the school.

The cops talk to me for over an hour. They take my gun, but they don't take the holster, still around my waist. I say all the things I should say. I talk about being a woman, the trauma of my sister's disappearance. I shape some version of the truth into a story about a stalker and a bad ex-boyfriend. I cry and tremble and agree that I need to find a healthier way to cope than by carrying a gun into a crowded school.

"Listen, Miss Angstrom," one of the officers says. He's young—too young to have been on the force when Angie vanished. He doesn't look familiar to me, but we might have gone to school together. "No one thinks you're dangerous."

I sniffle and blot my face on my sleeve.

"But these kids. Their video games. If one of them grabbed this from you . . ."

"I understand," I say.

"We can't be having weaponry inside a place of learning."

The older officer is not as sympathetic. He comes close to calling me a moron at one point, and I have to say that I like him a bit better than the other one.

"What were you thinking?" he asks. "You weren't even being discreet, for chrissakes."

Ultimately, Rick cools down. He buys my weepy woman routine, and he ends up corroborating my story to the police by confirming that I've experienced several recent tragedies and have been acting rather unlike myself. He tells them that my ex is a rather intimidating-looking fellow; he met the man himself at the last dance. A drunk.

"I want you to promise me you're going to talk to someone," Rick says. "Okay? Someone professional."

"Yes," I say.

On the way out, he gives me a big hug. He whispers in my ear that he'll do everything he can to talk to the Board. Make it a summer probation and not a permanent firing.

"Don't put yourself out too much," I say.

"Everyone deserves a second chance," Rick says. He pats me on the back.

On the drive home, I blast "What's Up?" by 4 Non Blondes on repeat, screaming out the top of my lungs like the junior high schooler I once was. The summer air coming through my window compounds the adrenaline in my blood. I have to stop myself from speeding for fear I'll run into the same cops again.

That night, I surprise Mom by picking her up for some McDonald's. I bring Mickey with me, and I don't mention work. Mickey recaps hours of reality TV, and Mom listens patiently, rapt. She holds her milkshake like it's taking all the upper body strength she has to keep it upright, but maybe we're going to be okay.

Bill asks if he can see me. He wants to talk.

"Okay," I say. "Take me to the range."

Bill picks me up, and we listen to his bland country music until we get there. He turns off the car in the lot, but he doesn't get out.

"At the risk of you shooting me," he says. "I need to tell you something."

"Okay," I say.

"I know why your dad called me."

"You told me," I say. "Your mom."

"Not exactly," Bill says. "I think he thought I had been Angie's dealer. I think he was just getting desperate."

"What would make him think you were Angie's dealer?"

"He kind of caught us fooling around at one point," Bill says. "It was like a month before she went missing."

The car feels very small all of a sudden. The air is stale, and I'm nauseated breathing it in. I turn up the air conditioning.

"I'm sorry I didn't tell you," Bill says. "I ran into her at a party and drove her home, and we were in the car in your driveway. We were both kind of wasted."

I'm tempted to physically cover my ears with my hands. "Why are you telling me this?"

"Because I want you to know everything. I want to be able to move past this. I want to give this thing a shot for real, and I want you to move in with me."

"What are you talking about!" I can hear myself screaming, but it's like it's coming from outside my body. I feel disgusting. I pound my fists against the hard plastic of the console until my arms are tired, and then I slump into my chair.

"You ruined it," I say. "It's fucking ruined."

"It was meaningless."

"You were so old!"

"Come on. I was your age."

"She was a teenager."

"It was one time. And it wasn't exactly a high school party," Bill says. "I don't even know how she got there. She was in bad shape."

"Lucky for her that she had you looking out," I say.

"It was dumb! I'm not arguing with you. It was also ten years ago." He sighs. "I knew this would be a fight, but I don't really understand why it's such a big deal."

"It's like you're both laughing at me," I say, and I feel fourteen years old again. I remember the lawn going to shit right around the time Angie disappeared. At the time, it made perfect sense to me that everything should fall apart. Now, I realize. "He fired you," I say.

"Yeah," Bill says. "And then I got questioned by the police when she went missing a month later."

"Why?"

"Because Angie told your dad I got her drunk that night to cover her own ass, and then when she got caught with drugs, like, a week later, she told him they were mine, too. I guess it was like—*why not, he's already fired*." Bill shakes his head.

"You seem angry," I say.

Bill preempts the accusation. "I was in the hospital with my mom the night she disappeared. There were logs and cameras. I was cleared."

"You're disgusting."

"I don't want to keep anything else from you. Everything else you already know. It was a one-time thing, with your dad. I needed money for the funeral, I had my mom's stuff lying around, and honestly, I kind of felt like, well, fuck him."

"Why should I believe that?" I ask. "You were her drug dealer. And his. You're probably responsible for what happened to both of them."

"I wasn't," Bill says. "I really wasn't. Why would I lie about that?"

"You lie about everything."

"I knew Angie's dealer. He was everyone's connection for a while. Lived in that trailer park by the tracks that they tore down."

"Stop talking," I say. "I don't want to hear you talk anymore. Drive me home."

Bill reluctantly puts the key in the ignition and takes me back to Mom's.

"Who was it?" I say, before I get out of the car. "Who was the guy?"

"Rockin' Robin," Bill says. "Very weird guy."

I rack my brain for any Robins. Some Robs, some Bobbys, but no Robins. "Robin who?"

"I don't know," Bill says. "Green. Greenleaf. Something like that."

"Robin Greenleaf?"

I hear Mickey in my head, talking to Celeste:

What is your full name?

Michaela Robin Greeley.

"Greeley," I say.

"Yeah," Bill says. "Yeah, that sounds right. Do you know him?"

I slap Bill when he's not expecting it. It's sloppy and weird. I catch part of his nose and his shoulder. "Are you fucking with me?" I shout. "Are you trying to get her in trouble?"

"Who?" Bill says, lifting his arm to protect his face from further blows. "God almighty, Teddy. I'm fucking driving."

"Mickey."

"I don't know what you're talking about. I said I'm sorry."

"I need you to take me to my apartment," I say, as we pull into Mom's driveway. "Not here."

Bill doesn't ask questions. He reverses out with one fluid motion, and I see Mom watching us through the window. She doesn't wave and I don't either.

I wait until we are at my apartment: "Mickey's last name is Greeley." I open the door. "Michaela Robin Greeley."

Bill stammers something incoherent.

"I know," I say. "You told me so."

"Teddy," Bill says. "Wait. You need to come back to my house. Please."

"I'm not going with you."

"Teddy, I'm serious. Is she—was Robin her brother?"

"No. Her dad. They had her young."

Bill nods. "He was a bad dude, Teddy. Scary guy. For real. I didn't like messing with him. That night I took Angie home, she was trying to get away from him."

"It's Mickey," I say. "She's a kid. I'll sort it out."

I slam the door before I can hear any more of his objections, but when I go upstairs, I can see that Bill is still parked on the street. I close the blinds and head to the bedroom, to the drawer where Mickey keeps her stuff.

I find the plastic bag that she used to bring her things to Portland. The one where she kept her cigarettes that we smoked on the way back to the hotel, after Celeste's reading. The pack she bought at a gas station on the way up while I was pumping. Because she forgot her vape and she needed a fix.

It's half-empty, slightly crushed. I turn it over in my hand: Parliaments.

I think back to Gary, months ago now. To his saying that Angie's mystery boyfriend left Parliaments in her car. To the kids at the party who always insisted that Angie was picked up by her boyfriend. To Bill, who said he had to get Angie away from Robin that night he got in trouble with my dad. To Jake saying that he was with Angie on the night she died. Died, not vanished. To the childlike Polaroid that Jake sent me, with Angie wearing that shirt, that fucking green shirt. To Mickey saying she was trailer trash. To her insistence on finding Gary, on finding my brother, on finding the au pair. To her childhood interest in the case. To the way that Jake would pop up every time I told Mickey I was done. To Jake doxxing me. To Jake tormenting me. To the fucking tattoo on my leg. To Mickey in Mom's bathtub. To Mickey in bed with me.

There it is. I thought it was me, the last gossamer thread connecting Angie to the world, but it was Mickey.

I did it, Dad. I figured it all out. Are we happy now?

I call Mickey a dozen times or more. She's not at the apartment, I haven't seen her since Wolfie died, and now she isn't answering the phone. I rehearse what I will say, but it keeps changing. I can't seem to hold the words in my head. They burn up and turn to ash.

I text her: *Where are you?*

The dots appear on the phone and then disappear again.

I position myself so that I'm facing the door. I don't watch TV or listen to music or check my phone. I stare.

She doesn't come. I don't know how she knows that I know.

For three days, I barely leave the house, and Bill stays parked outside, save for short trips home, presumably to let Rocky and Red out. When he returns, he honks and I come to the window. That's our routine.

Even after he leaves, I don't go anywhere. It's easy enough to blame traffic—it's officially peak season now and the tourists are stealing all the good parking spots and clotting up the roads and the aisles at the grocery store.

I'm fairly certain that I'm not suicidally depressed in the same way that Dad was, and yet all I can think about is what would happen if I died. I get rid of my gun in its case—dropping it straight into the garbage bin on the curb, wrapped in old towels and plastic bags.

If I died suddenly in an accident—a car crash, a freak aneurism, a school shooting—I think that people would mourn me very loudly. My students, Rick, the parents—they'd forget all the shit they talked about me at the end. They'd leave out my firing and the gun and everything, and they'd only remember what a great teacher I was. How young, how beautiful, cut down in the prime of life, etc. I imagine a packed church, Mom crying, maybe Bill delivering a eulogy where he suggests ever-so-subtly that he thought I would be the mother of his children. I would be a lovely, tragic angel.

If I killed myself, on the other hand, I think Mom might kill herself, too, but not because she couldn't go on without me. I think she definitely could, and in the first scenario, she would. I just think she would see the poetry in cutting off the whole line, ending her suffering. If everyone else gets to, why shouldn't she?

If I disappeared, I think Bill would look for me for a bit. Mom wouldn't let herself commit suicide, because she'd want to be alive in case her daughters turned up one day. She would live a monastic life, get some dogs, wait it out till the end. She'd assume whatever she thinks happened to Angie happened to me. Maybe she'd convince herself I was bad, I did bad things.

I search for home tattoo removal tips and find suggestions for lightening the ink through salt rubs or lemon and aloe soaks. Lightening it is not enough. I need it off my body. I need it gone. I gather my supplies and keep them near. Turning on HGTV, I sit on the floor with my right leg folded under me, and I drink as much as I possibly can without passing out. By the end of the first episode my leg is fully asleep, so I wrap the exercise band around my lower calf, as tightly as possible, and I spread the towel underneath, and I pour the hydrogen peroxide on my skin.

I make even cuts in a grid pattern with a razor blade from the tool kit Bill gave me, the lines spaced so closely that they form a solid square. In my mind, I'm creating a waffle of scar tissue—a honeycomb of waxy pink lines that will distort the goofy Disney trademark beneath it. But fuck it hurts. Much more than getting the tattoo hurt. It is hard to keep going. It is hard to be the one to do this painful work. There is a lot of blood. There are a lot of veins near the ankles, I'm realizing now. They throb and glug out spurts of red blood that pool in the cracks on my heel. I tighten the tourniquet with both hands, and I finish up as quickly as I can. The last few lines are shallow and crooked, but it's okay. It's okay. I'm done. I press the towel down on the wound, and I feel myself growing lightheaded, weary, sleepy. I can't tell if it's from the booze or the blood loss, which makes me nervous. I'm not sure if I even have health insurance anymore.

I panic, imagining Mom finding me on the living room floor, having bled out from the foot, of all places. I imagine her coming into this freaky scene and finding me in a puddle of vomit and peroxide and blood. The disgrace.

The adrenaline sobers me enough that I can haul my body onto the couch and prop my leg up. The bleeding is getting lighter already, I can tell. I settle into relief. I can get a new rug. I can get a new couch. As long as I don't die, it will have been worth it. The pain and the mess will have been worth the scar tissue. I can't have her on my body anymore.

I find Mickey's dad with a few hours of research, when I finally work up the nerve to look. He's not dead. He lives an hour away, at an address registered to Frances Greeley.

My phone directs me straight inland, and the temperature rises the farther I get from the ocean. The AC in my car is shot, so I have to lean my head out the window like a dog in order to cool down. In the rearview mirror, I can see that my face has turned bright red.

I take the highway until the last stretch, where I get off and drive on some crumbling roads past rundown houses and shuttered schools. I'm finally instructed to stop when I reach a faded sign that reads *Garden Park: A Manufactured Home Community*. The lot is across the street from an overgrown cemetery, and the park houses at least fifty trailers of all different colors lining each side of a single road, like shipping containers dropped from the sky. The asphalt is cracked, and the yards are in bad shape, scarred by tire tracks and littered with broken bottles and roadside trash.

I park at the end of the street and take my time walking over to the right trailer. The trailer park in Hogshead, the one that used to be down by the tracks, is nicer than this one. I wonder what happened. I wonder if I ever ran into Mickey when we were both kids, at the fish market or the drug store. Strange to think that we could have stood feet apart from one another completely unaware of what we'd one day be.

I knock on the aluminum door, softly at first and then louder. A woman answers. She's clearly a relative—the resemblance to Mickey is strong. She's thin and tired-looking, with gray roots and stains on her shirt. Her feet are bare—small, dainty, and veinless. Her toenails peek out from beneath the hems of her sweatpants with a flash of hot pink polish. I know instantly, without asking, that Mickey painted them.

"Hi," I say. "I'm Mickey's friend."

Mickey's aunt's eyes narrow, almost imperceptibly.

"Is she home?"

The aunt looks past me to the street. "I think she's at work, or maybe she went back down to see her college friends today."

"Is her dad here?"

"You're Mickey's friend or Rob's?" I can see her examining me—my face, my clothes—trying to figure out my deal.

"I'm sorry," I say. "You're Franny, right? She talks so much about you."

For a second, the woman's mouth twitches up in the corners.

"Fran," she says. "Come on in."

She leads me through a narrow hallway into a tight living area, where three secondhand chairs are covered in plastic. She touches my shoulder and gestures to the recliner in the corner. I place the upholstery right away—the picture of Angie, the one that Jake first sent me.

"Wait here. I'll get Robbie."

I feel the adrenaline in my blood like an amphetamine. My knees bounce involuntarily. I breathe heavy. But the man she brings back is not the right man. He is not big and menacing with a knowing, charismatic edge that makes you feel naked. He isn't thuggish and wry, like the gangster demon I've imagined in my head. The man she brings back has one leg. The other has been amputated above the knee, and he uses an arm crutch to get around.

"I'll get you guys some Snapples."

Robin won't look me in the eye. He chooses the seat farthest from mine and folds his body into the arm of the couch in a C-shape. He grabs his sister by the elbow as she's walking away. "Who is this?" he asks in a low, nervous voice.

"Mickey's friend."

"Teddy," I say, not bothering with fake names.

He looks up at me slant, with his head down, only daring to steal glances. He reminds me of a small child left alone with a strange adult.

I must look as confused as I feel, because Fran beckons for me to come with her to the kitchenette.

She pulls two cold Snapples out of the fridge and hands me one. The other she pours into a short plastic cup and adds a straw.

"What exactly were you expecting?"

Now I'm the one who avoids eye contact. Fran is examining my face with such scrutiny under the bright fluorescent overhead light.

"I didn't know," I say. "What's wrong with him?"

"Heroin overdose," she says, staring straight at me. She doesn't bother to lower her voice so that he can't hear us. I can tell it's a point of personal pride for her not to shy away from the truth, not to cloak things in euphemism. She's the kind of woman who says people died, never that they passed away. "A long time ago now."

"Oh," I say. "I didn't know."

Fran gestures to the cracked tiles below my feet. I stand in the middle of a circular stain—the color of rust, nearly three feet in diameter, perfectly round.

"He passed out right there one day," she says. "Usually, when you sleep, you turn a lot. When you're on drugs, you don't do that. Your body is turned off." She looks at me and I nod, like I know where this is going. "All the blood pools on one side when that happens." She traces the outline of the circle with her foot, and suddenly I feel claustrophobic with the trailer's low ceilings and single point of egress. "His leg swelled up to twice its normal size before it split open," she says. "That's what the doctors said, anyway."

"God."

"You have no idea," she says, grinning at me with a manic look in her eye. "The smell. I thought I'd never get it out of here."

"Is he . . ."

"What? Retarded?"

"No, I mean. I was going to say—"

"Yeah, he's basically retarded. Too little oxygen to the brain," she says. "Why are you here, Teddy?"

I can't remember anymore. I needed to talk to him. I needed to tell him that I know he knows something about my sister.

"Franny!" Robin is calling out from the living room. "Franny!" His voice is thin and shrill, strained with alarm.

"His Snapple," she says, with a wink.

I want to leave. I want Mickey to come through the door and rescue me. I can feel my skin itching with every second I stay in this house, where things are obviously not right. Still, I find my feet trailing behind Fran, following her into the living room, where she holds the glass in front of her brother, positioning the straw in place for him to suck.

Robin is balding on top, and his hair is combed into a tidy sweep. He's wearing a tidy polo and dungarees. He still won't look me in the eye.

"I'm a friend of Mickey's," I say, slowly. "Your daughter."

Robin sips his Snapple and looks up at his sister to check how he should react. She smiles a genuine smile, a kindness that radiates to her eyes. She touches his hair to the side where it's fallen over his brow.

"Ma-kay," Robin says.

"Michaela's at work, Robbie. Her friend stopped by to see if she was here."

"I wanted to meet you, Robin," I say. "You knew my sister. A long time ago."

I bend down to Robin's level and find his eyes. He tries to escape me, but I follow his gaze.

"You knew her—Angie Angstrom—do you remember? Angelina? My sister?"

I get a little closer, put my hands on Robin's one remaining knee.

"Robin," I say. "Look at me. Do you remember my sister, Angie?"

Frances puts her hand on my shoulder, but I throw her off.

"You were with her, Robin. You were with her the night she went missing. What happened, Robin? What happened to Angie?"

Robin is rocking back and forth now and humming a single loud note to try to drown me out. Frances tugs at my shirt, but I push her away. She stumbles back into the other chair.

I keep my fingers dug into the meat on Robin's thighs while I look at her.

"Were you a part of this?" I ask her. "Did you help him?"

"Fuck off," Frances says.

"What happened, Rockin' Robin? Was she being a dicktease? Maybe you wanted to put her in her place a little bit?"

Robin starts crying, wailing, and it is a sound I've never heard before—a grown man weeping with the abandon of a child.

A door slams behind me, and I jump up. There, standing in the frame, is Mickey.

"Hi," I say. I stand between her and her dad. I see that she wants to reach out to him, to comfort him, but she can't get past me.

"What are you doing here?"

"I was worried about you," I say. "You weren't answering your phone."

Mickey looks to Fran.

"It's okay, Franny," she says. "I'll handle it."

Mickey turns and goes back outside. I follow her. The minute I step away from Robin, Fran jumps up to shut the door behind me.

I walk slowly behind Mickey in the thick humid air. She stops at my car. "Let's go," she says. "There's a diner up the street."

We don't speak on the drive. I watch the asphalt disappear under my tires and replay the surreal scene at Mickey's house. That man—that broken shell of a man—I try to imagine him at his worst, but my imagination stalls out. That woman—that ghost of a woman—the closest thing that Mickey has to family. The crushing weight of the hopelessness fills all the space in the car, presses down on my shoulders.

The diner is filthy and empty. Everything smells of ketchup and my shoes stick to the floor as I follow Mickey to a booth in the back.

I slide in across from her.

The waitress comes and drops two enormous spiral-bound menus on our table along with a pitcher of water and two plastic cups.

"Just coffee for me," I say. "Thank you."

"Same," Mickey says.

The waitress takes our menus back with a sigh.

Mickey leans forward onto her elbows. "What do you want to know?" She's softer now. Maybe even contrite.

"Everything."

Mickey nods over and over. "Right," she says. She downs half a glass of water in a single sip. She cocks her head and looks up at me, eyes heavy. "You came to me, Teddy. On Reddit. In the library. You came to me. I didn't hunt you down."

"Whatever," I say.

"I just think you should remember that."

"You're Jake," I say. "The picture. The message, with the beach—" I stop. "You doxxed me."

She glances down. "I shouldn't have doxxed you. I just needed to get your attention."

It worked. Right after I told Mickey I wasn't interested in the investigation, I had to go running back to her. Change of heart. "You didn't even know who would see that," I say.

"There's nothing scary on those boards, Teddy. You keep acting like there are murderers out there, but that's just not the case. You're paranoid."

"You have to tell me," I say. "You have to tell me what happened to Angie. If you know, you have to tell me."

Mickey sighs. "Where should I start?"

"Start at the beginning," I say. "Don't skip anything."

"My parents were addicts," Mickey says. "First my mom. Booze. That was always her problem. But then my dad, too—Oxy. He got it prescribed after a construction accident."

"When?"

"Around third grade," Mickey says. "They dropped me off at Fran's. Said we needed to be apart for a while. So that they could get better."

"Your aunt took you?"

"I think she thought it would be fun, like a movie. But—you know—kids are expensive."

"Right."

"My dad came back eventually. He couldn't get a straight job. The pain made him edgy."

"From the accident?"

"No," Mickey says. "What I remember most was he said he hurt all the time and there was no source for it anymore. It had been this one specific vertebra. But then it was just—everywhere. Like his blood hurt."

"From the painkillers?"

"Yeah." Mickey empties another sugar into her coffee and stirs it slowly with a spoon, not looking up to meet my gaze. "I tried it," she says, quietly.

"Oxy?"

"Made me so sick."

"When?"

"Fourth grade."

"Fourth grade?"

"I woke up vomiting. I spent the whole night in the bathroom. At one point, I remember lying with my face on the cold tile and wondering if I would actually die."

"Jesus."

"No one heard me." She empties another packet of sugar into the coffee. "I took a shower. That helped. But I still couldn't eat."

"Where was your mom?"

Mickey shrugs. "I don't know. She dropped by sometimes. I can't remember the last visit." She looks up at me. "I didn't know it was the last time, so I didn't think to remember it."

I imagine Mickey as a kid—small, thin, quiet. Wondering where her mom was and if she was thinking about Mickey. Worrying that maybe she wasn't.

"Where is she now?"

Mickey looks to the window, waves a hand in the air. "Out there," she says.

We sit in silence for a minute. Mickey cups her coffee with two hands. I sip slowly on mine, even though it's barely tepid. We listen to the sounds of the diner—the bell on the door, the sizzle of the grill, the chitchat of the waitresses behind the register.

"Anyway," Mickey says, finally. "My dad couldn't work construction anymore, so he started dealing."

"And that's when you met Angie."

"Yes," Mickey says. Her face turns wistful and soft. "She arrived like a sunbeam."

Not how most people would describe my sister.

"My dad's friends—or whatever they were—they sat around smoking weed and scratching their balls all day. They were like zombies. But Angie—she *fizzled*."

"What do you mean?"

"She was so smart. And she teased everyone relentlessly. But not me. She was really nice to me."

"How often was she there?"

Mickey frowns. "Not sure. Felt like a lot. She always had her hair different. She would braid mine."

It is hard for me to imagine the person that Mickey is describing. It is hard for me to picture Angie braiding a little girl's hair.

"She let me take pictures of her."

"That picture," I say. "Do you have it?"

"No," Mickey says. "It's all gone."

"What?"

"You scared me," Mickey says. "When I went home, I deleted everything."

I press my eyes closed to keep from exploding. *We'll come back to it*, I think. *She has it. She's lying. She wouldn't delete it.*

"Okay," I say. I do my best to sound sympathetic, to keep her talking. "I'm sorry."

Mickey sucks down what's left of her coffee in one big, sweet sip. She sets the empty mug on top of its saucer. "Angie came over in the middle of the night one night," she says. "Her and my dad were playing Super Smash Brothers. Drinking Mountain Dew. I remember because I wanted to play," Mickey says. "But Angie wouldn't let me. She had her hand on my dad's leg, and she smiled at me in this phony way and she said, 'It's late, kiddo.'"

"Okay."

"I took some Oxy," she says. "Crushed it between my teeth so that it would hit faster."

"One?"

"Maybe more."

"What happened?"

"I don't know," Mickey says. "I just remember hearing, 'drink this.' Angie had Powerade. It was blue flavor. Warm." Mickey closes her eyes. "She touched my hair, and she said something about her dad. And maybe you." She opens her eyes again. "I wish I could remember it better."

Suddenly, I remember Angie climbing up to my bunk while Mom and Dad fought downstairs. Telling me about her day, making small talk, despite my shushing her. Whispering loud enough—close enough—to my ears to drown out the conversation downstairs.

"She was like an older sister," Mickey says.

"It sounds like she was fucking your dad."

Mickey blushes, something I've never seen. She looks down at the floor. "She didn't usually stay the night."

"But sometimes?"

"Sometimes."

"What about the night she went missing?"

"I'm sorry," Mickey says. The pitch of her voice rises, grows thinner. "I don't know. She was there at some point. There were others, too. They were playing music and dancing. That was when I took that picture. Then, Angie needed her inhaler. She lay down on the couch. I went to bed."

"That's it?" For years, I remembered Angie in my bed early that morning. Now, the memory is like smoke. It swirls in and out.

"No," Mickey says. "I woke up to go to the bathroom—later, much later—and there was a girl, in the living room. Covered in a blanket. With dark hair."

"Angie?"

"It could have been someone else. I didn't see her face." She looks down at her nails. When she speaks again, it's quieter. "But she was fucked up."

"Fucked up how?"

"I barely remember. I just—"

"What?"

"I could only see her arm and her hair. Everything else was covered. Her arm was bent." Mickey tries to mimic the pose but gives up. "Bent in a strange way. Broken. Her hair was dripping. It smelled bad. Like puke."

"And you just went back to bed?"

"I guess. That's all I remember."

"Where was your dad?"

"I don't know," Mickey says. "But we had a bad stretch after that. When the news ran. He was really upset."

"Upset how?"

"He took a lot of pills," Mickey says. "And Fran kicked us out."

"Where did you go?"

"Just . . . drifted. For a while." Mickey catches my eye. "You know, even in other towns, Angie was famous."

"I know."

"I knew her, but I couldn't tell anyone I knew her," Mickey says. "I thought about her all the time."

I can see it—Mickey on internet boards, late at night. Cashing in on her connection to Angie, calling out the liars and the phonies, becoming increasingly possessed by Angie's case.

"What about the cam stuff?" I ask. "When did that start?"

"I had to make money," Mickey says. "It was part of the deal for Fran to take me back."

I'm horrified. "She told you to do that?"

Mickey says, "She thought I did something with eBay."

"I know my dad paid you," I say.

"That was way later," Mickey says, matter-of-fact. She doesn't seem embarrassed. She doesn't ask how I found out. "After we met in the library and I gave him my credentials so we could talk online about Angie. It used to be all one account."

"The cam stuff and the Angie stuff?"

Mickey nods. "He started bothering me about it, bringing it up at the library, telling me that I was too young to be 'throwing my life away.' I got a little freaked out, honestly, so I started avoiding him. But then he joined my chats and told everyone I was a teenager—not pretend—and that he was going to send their usernames to the FBI."

"He did?"

"I was so mad," she says. "It really fucked up my money. But he told me he'd pay me instead."

"He just gave you the money?"

"No," Mickey says. "I had to do things."

"Jesus," I say. My head shakes involuntarily. I feel an urge to actually cover my ears.

"Not like that," Mickey says. "He wanted me to read him things from Angie's LiveJournal, pretend to be her reading them."

I try to conceal my relief. It could be so much worse. "What's LiveJournal?"

"It's like a blog."

"Angie had a blog?"

"Your dad found it, got the credentials somehow. He must have deleted it right before he died. Or had the site delete it. I haven't been able to find it recently."

Immediately, I start thinking of everyone I know who is good with computers. Bill or the guys at work. Those pages must be archived somewhere. Nothing is ever really gone on the internet.

"What was on it?" I ask.

"Bad poetry. Whining about teachers. Nasty stuff about your

folks. Typical teenage bullshit. There wasn't a lot, actually. I think she gave up on it."

"Why did he want you to read that?"

"I never asked. I think maybe it was a kind of penance. Me as Angie, saying over and over again how much I hated him. Him saying sorry. Like some kind of role play."

"He paid you for this?"

Mickey nods. "That and the help online."

"Looking for her?"

"On and off. He liked coming by to talk to me. Sometimes we'd do a little digging online."

"What digging?"

"Aimless. Looking through the cam sites, sometimes."

"Why?"

"He got it into his head that Angie might be on one of them."

"Why?"

"I suggested it."

"Why?"

"I figured—maybe she thought like me."

I let that one hang in the air. I swallow the urge to refute it or at least to tell Mickey that she has no idea how Angie thought. Because if I don't know, then she can't know. No one can know.

The waitress drops the check as she moves past, not stopping to check on how we're doing. Mickey folds it into an origami nothing. She creases the paper with the nail of her thumb.

"He told me that at ten years he was going to give up, but I didn't know what that meant."

"He told you?"

"By that point, I was basically feeling like maybe I was Angie?"

"What?"

"Like Angie was a ghost who visited me when I was a kid, and it was my job to preserve her. For your dad, but also just for her."

"What are you talking about? With the tattoos? The outfits?"

"I know it sounds crazy."

"You knew about Gary," I say, the thought just occurring to me, popping into the fore of my brain. "You saw his MySpace before you met me. *Chinatown*."

Mickey offers nothing.

"And Jake was . . . your way of stringing me along?"

"No."

"I'm a real person," I say. "Gary. My dad. My brother. His kid. Real people. Not, fucking, ghosts."

"Jesus. I know." Mickey takes out her phone and presses the home button impatiently. She sees me staring at her. "What?"

Petulant, snide, edgy. She could be any one of my students. I can see it now. "You're a kid."

Mickey laughs. "That's rich coming from you. I've never met someone so stunted."

"What if I don't believe you."

"About what?"

"Any of it." I pull my phone out of my pocket, too. "What if I called the police?"

"Go for it," Mickey says.

"Tell them about your dad. Tell them about what happened."

"I don't even know what I saw," Mickey says. "It was all blurry."

"It was Angie!" I say. The waitress looks over at our table, and I lower my voice. "You can't protect your dad."

"It's too late for that," Mickey says. She covers my phone screen with her hand. "Listen. This is a bad idea." Her face hardens into something grotesque. She doesn't resemble one of my kids anymore. "Best case scenario, you subject Clare to whatever stories they could squeeze out of my relationship with your dad. That's it."

"I have to," I say.

Mickey takes my phone and puts it down on the booth bench beside her. She grips my hands over the table. "She is gone," she says. Her voice cracks a bit but she coughs through it. "I wish she weren't, but she is."

"You did all of this just to torture me."

"I'm sorry if you think that," Mickey says. She takes a breath and stands. "I liked being a part of your family."

"You liked getting paid."

"No," she says, holding firm.

"You're not her sister."

"Fine."

"You're some kid who happened to be around. You're no one."

"I said fine."

I put my head down and by the time I look back up, she's gone. Out of the diner, out of the parking lot.

I drive home, a failure. There's no returning to how it was. Things that are broken cannot be unbroken. Men who split in half cannot be patched together. Daughters who are lost can never be found. Guns drawn in front of children. Mothers predeceased by their daughters. Dogs betrayed in the woods. Veins filled with hot, toxic liquid. Women slammed into walls, crumpled against the floor. The violence of the world that was always there, lurking behind a thin scrim now brought into the stark gray light that passes for sunshine up here.

Angie is soaking wet, and she is standing in the hallway of Mom's house. I come out of the basement. I had been sleeping. The light switch is high on the wall and my sister is much taller than I am, which is how I realize I'm small again. Angie takes my hand, and we walk down the hall toward our room. She lifts a finger to her lips to keep me from talking.

I squeeze Angie's hand in quick bursts, demanding to know what's going on, but she keeps tugging me forward. Her hands are clammy, frigid, and slick, like her flesh is covered over with a thin layer of moss.

We stop outside of our room. The hallway is mostly dark, but Angie's room is illuminated by a table lamp next to her pillow. My dad is sitting on the side of her bed, reading something—a journal.

He looks to me and then to Angie and then he stands. He comes toward us and embraces her. With his head resting on her shoulder he looks at me—I'm back to my normal height, slightly taller than Angie—and somehow, without talking, he tells me not to tell her that he's dead. She doesn't know, and I shouldn't tell her. It would only make her upset.

Despite their embrace, Angie is still holding my hand, which she squeezes now, hard. I understand instantly, without words, that I shouldn't tell him she's dead. He doesn't know.

I know I'm dreaming, but I don't want to wake up. I want

to spend one more moment with both of them. I lean into their embrace, put my head on my dad's head, which is on Angie's shoulder. I try to breathe them in, but I can't inhale all the way. My lungs are heavy, petrified rock.

I wake hyperventilating. I can't find the rescue inhaler that Bill left behind. It's not in the nightstand. I can't find my glasses to look for it under the bed. I scramble to the bathroom, run the sink until it's steaming hot, and lean over the running water, throwing a towel over the back of my head to contain the vapor.

In through the nose, out through the mouth. In through the nose, out through the mouth.

The water condenses on my chin. I turn the faucet off and let the steam go cold on my face. All I can hear is the sound of my own breaths, deeper now, but still tight and labored. I worry that if I move, I might fall. The safest thing seems to be to stay perfectly still, propped on the counter with both hands. The safest thing seems to be to sleep on the floor in here, on the teal bath mat, under the bright lights of the vanity. I lie down, tuck my toes under the radiator, and close my eyes.

"Help me," I say. "Help me."

It feels like a prayer or a mantra, and it keeps the dream from bleeding back in.

Help me. Help me. Help me.

Mom makes me sit outside behind the house because she is sure that the sunshine will do me good. She drags her lounge chair next to mine and watches me nervously. She strokes my hair with a heavy hand, full of purpose, but she doesn't voice the question that is forming in her throat. She knows that something happened with Mickey. She knows it involves Angie. But she doesn't ask, because she doesn't want to know, and I don't tell her. Not being able to tell her is the worst part.

Instead, we complain about the mosquitos and the rising humidity. Everything is getting worse every year. That we agree on.

Most days now, Angie doesn't even seem real. My memories seem less sure—more like air, more like invention. When Mom and I talk about her, it feels untrustworthy. I don't have faith in our brains' ability to make sense of the world. Mom says things about Angie or Dad, and I think, is that true? She says, your dad had such a dry sense of humor, and I struggle to think of a single example to support it. She says, your sister was such a sensitive girl, and I think of all the times she called me a bitch. Maybe neither of us knew either of them, I want to say, but I don't want to upset her.

One day, Mom will die, and I will go on. And when that happens, the only memories I have of her and my dad and Angie will be my own. No corroboration and no dissent.

I've been trying to memorize everything about Mom when I'm with her. It's too late for me to get it right with Angie, but I can try to get it right with Mom. I've been spending whole days trying to catalog her smell in my brain, struggling to find the perfect adjectives. I've been spending hours studying the lines on her face. I've been listing memories from growing up in the Notes section on my phone.

- *Mom putting in her contacts without a mirror, sitting on the edge of her bed*
- *The inside of her pocketbook always smelled like mints*
- *Mom putting on her lipstick and blotting it by kissing a tissue*
- *When I'd crawl into bed with her and Dad after a night-mare, Dad would always leave, because we ran too hot. Mom and I together would soak the sheets in sweat*

Mom turns to me, blocking the sun from her eyes with her forearm. "You're looking a little—what do the Jews say?" She snaps, searching for the word.

"I have no idea what you're talking about," I say. "And don't say 'the Jews' like that."

"Why not? It's a good word," Mom says. She stops snapping as it comes to her. "Zaftig! Great word."

"Mom," I say. "Honestly, you can't tell people they look fat."

"I'm not telling *people*. I'm telling my daughter," Mom says. "And not fat. Zaftig."

"It's the same thing."

"Nay," Mom says. "It innit." She pops into the kitchen and comes back with snacks. Pretzels and watermelon slices.

"I'm not touching that now," I say.

"Suit yourself," Mom says.

I think about how Angie would have agreed with me,

that zaftig was fat and fat was bad. Then I think about Mickey. Mickey wouldn't have taken offense. She would have smiled and smacked her own butt. She would have let Mom explain the origins of the word, tracing it back to the German for "juicy."

I'm working up the nerve to say something very mean. Something like—*Have you ever considered that maybe he was right to kill himself?* Or—*Really though, what kind of woman lets a man leave his children for her?* Or—*Do you believe in karma, Mom?* But before I can sharpen my tongue, Mom speaks.

"I was thinking," Mom says, quietly, "how you never know your kids."

"You don't feel like you know me?"

Mom grabs my bad foot, and I pull away instinctively. "What do you think?"

I think of my nights with Bill, how horrified I would be if Mom could see me with him. I think of all the weird shit I do during the day. The way in which I act like an animal at home, in the bathroom, when no one's looking. I think of how I haven't told her the truth about Mickey, or shown her my ankle scar, or told her that I lost my job. I'm my best self in front of Mom, because I don't want to let her down with my real personality.

"You know me," I say.

Mom taps each of my toes, counting them, like when I was small. "You think you'll have kids?" she asks.

"It seems hard."

Mom shrugs. "I guess. It can be," she says. "They're so great though, kids. They shape your life into a recognizable form."

I can't believe that I shape Mom's life. At most, I tether her to reality, or at least to a reality that used to be. We exist almost in a vacuum, the two of us, ignorant to the rest of the wide world spinning round.

"You missing them?"

Mom stares intently at my big toe, unmoving.

"Me, too," I say.

A therapist I saw in college suggested at one of our appointments that my mom was fundamentally broken. She had been orphaned and widowed, and as a result, she couldn't be trusted to mother correctly. The woman didn't put it that way exactly, but that was the message.

As the doctor spoke, I thought of the old pit bulls I used to look at on the animal shelter websites. Half-blind three-legged freaks, scarred by years of abuse, abandonment, whatever. I pitied them, but I wasn't about to let them in my home. It seemed dangerous. They were not like Wolfie. Some animals can't be redeemed, not when they've suffered that much pain. It isn't their fault, but that doesn't change anything. Case in point—my mother had misplaced one of her own children. No idea where Angie had vanished.

That was the last time I saw that therapist. Not out of any excess of loyalty to Mom, but more because I knew that whatever she was, I was that, too.

"Mom," I say.

She looks at me, but I don't have anything else to say.

"I love you, Thea," she says, which is the exact right thing. How unusual it is that someone says the exact right thing. She pets my hair. "Sweet baby."

I start crying, and Mom grabs me fast, like she thinks I might fall off my lounge chair, like she was expecting it, like I seemed precarious.

"Mom," I say, along with some other stuff. First words. Help. Mama. Please. I cry in a snotty, wild way, so that my whole face is wet with tears but also sweat and mucus. She squeezes my ribs in tightly, clasps her hands behind my back, gives me something like the Heimlich.

"Stop it," she says, over and over as she compresses me. "Stop it."

It takes a long time, but eventually I fatigue. I cry myself out. I relax all my muscles and stop resisting. I lay my head against her crepey chest skin, slick with sunscreen and sweat, but she doesn't let up the pressure. It feels really good to be totally still and whimper. To not worry about being quiet.

If I could come over here every day and howl and drool and have Mom wrestle me into submission like I'm possessed by a Catholic devil, I could sleep like a baby at night. If I could feel her light fingers gripping the back of my neck and be assured that I'm still holdable, then I might be able to function in this world.

"Stop," Mom says, one last time, a whisper. She shushes me and scratches my back in wide, slow circles, and for a brief moment I worry about falling asleep on top of her—I'm so much bigger than she is—but then I stop resisting my eyelids and sink, unfettered, into her body.

The last thought I have before I fall asleep is something that another teacher said to me once, on the day she returned from maternity leave. When we're born, she told me, we can't tell ourselves from our mothers. She said that when her son looked at her, he thought he was looking at himself. That when she held him, there was no distinction between them. Total unification. Mother as home. You have to learn that you're alone. That comes later.

Back on the apps, but this time I keep the radius local. I have no intention of vetting my suitors first, like I usually would, in a public place. Dinner, drinks—fuck that. Everyone is coming to me.

The men are surprised when I open the door and I'm semi-attractive. No one recognizes me from the news or the internet. All those years of paranoia for naught.

"You look better than your picture," one guy says.

"Oh, thanks."

"I'm not sure you appreciate how rare that is," he says. "Usually I have to add twenty pounds in my brain."

I don't waste my booze on them, but sometimes I ask them to bring a bottle of something. We never open it. I add it to my collection for next time. I like to drink beforehand. When they're here, I don't offer them anything, and they don't ask for much. Some of them seem pleased to not be meeting in public, and I assume those ones are married.

We start on the couch, because if I took them straight to my bed, they'd be freaked out. I have the TV on to keep them from talking.

"You like this show?" I ask about whatever comes on first.

They all say they do. We watch twenty to thirty minutes of a procedural or medical drama or reality show before the men work up the nerve to touch me. Over the clothes first. We spend a lot of time kissing. I don't rush things. When we're done, they'll be gone—they never stay the night. I have to stretch it out on the front end.

I let them touch my nipples gingerly, even though I hate that. I let them bite my neck and shove their dirty, sharp fingernails inside me. I try not to offer too much direction. I let them approach the whole thing however they see fit. Some of them fuck me unapologetically, like they know they won't see me ever again, and they aren't afraid to let me know either. Some of them fuck me trepidatiously, like they're worried they'll come too quickly. It's been a long time since most of them have gotten laid.

"You don't need to," I say to this guy as he's rolling a condom on.

"Why wouldn't I?"

"Whatever," I say. I'm too drunk this time, and I know it, which is the worst feeling. "Who cares."

He looks suspicious, and I worry he'll go soft on me.

"Wear it or don't," I say. "Let's go."

The minute we're done, he's gone. I check the clock and it's only 9:30. I pour myself another drink. I go back on the apps. Slim pickings. Too much texting back and forth. I don't want to deal with the flirtation and the banter.

I text Steven, from school, the young douchey one who gave Bill a hard time. Bill would hate the idea of Steven seeing me naked. Hate the idea of me touching Steven's taut, small body.

Steven comes over at midnight, later than we agreed. He's twitchy. Coke or something.

"Sorry," he says. "My night ran long."

I don't even get off the couch to greet him for fear I'll fall down.

"S'okay," I mumble, and I pat the cushion next to me. "It's my birthday."

He doesn't try to make small talk, which I appreciate, and he doesn't worry about feigning ignorance as to why he's at my house now, for the first time, in the middle of the night. He gets right down to business.

It's as we're fucking that he ruins it when he gets close to my ear with his itchy, sticky breath and pants, "I always figured you for a slut."

And at that point, I give myself permission to stop fighting the whiskey in my blood and fall asleep. When I wake up to get water at three, he's gone.

I chug a glass of ice water in the kitchen, naked, and I return to the couch to sleep under the throw blanket. When the light comes through the blinds in the morning, I retreat to bed and draw the blackout curtains.

The emptiness of my bed is like a physical hurt these days. No Wolfie, no Bill. No one to wake with a start if I stop breathing in the night. I bought a weighted blanket online, and the box was so heavy, I had to check if I ordered the right size. It's hard to get on and impossible to get out from underneath, but it helps. I pull it up from where it's folded at the foot of my bed and heave it on top of me, and I sink down into the mattress. If I don't move at all, I can imagine that I'm being poured in concrete. My heart rate slows. It's a pleasant suffocation.

You have to wake up when you have a dog. Dogs make you keep schedule like a good citizen. It's the last thing to cross my mind before I drift back into oblivion.

I had always thought of my memory as something like a historical record. Evidence.

Now, I'm not so sure. Now, I have a new appreciation for the unreliable narrator. Now, I understand how a normal person could go mad. It takes one tug at one thread, and the whole illusion vanishes.

The thread, a memory: Angie in my bed, smelling fresh, like laundry. For years, I have revisited that memory, a fond spot in the recesses of my mind. The last moment I saw my sister. The last moment anyone saw my sister.

Now, when I think back, I wonder—did Angie ever smell clean? Now, when I try to locate her smell, I conjure the smell of sex—sweaty, animal, disgusting. She always smelled like she'd been out all night swallowing come and smoking pot. But then I turn that over and it feels like a fabrication, too, like something recently added.

When I try to work out the timeline of her disappearance, it unravels further. How could she have come home to see me in the early hours of the morning? When would that have happened?

When I think about that week and how we'd been fighting, how Mom and she had been fighting—why would Angie crawl into bed with me? Wouldn't I have thought it unusual? Unusual enough to wake up for?

Mom and Dad. For years in my mind they were put-upon,

grief-stricken parents. Innocents. Now, I remember fights. Lots of fights. Angie and them. My dad heavy-lidded at the dinner table or absent from the dinner table altogether. Mom angrily drinking her wine, withholding food, cancelling birthday parties over slight infractions. Sometimes now, when she calls, I let it go to voicemail, half-convinced the soft-spoken woman on the phone is a changeling, an evil spirit.

I don't trust the old version or the new version of anything. I can't pin them down, any of them. And if I can't trust my own brain, how can I go on?

Did I ever know you, Ange? I hope I did.

Am I accounting honestly for our relationship? Am I lying?

A woman comes on the local news to talk about education reform in advance of a town hall meeting. Five minutes in, she is making overt references to Satan worshippers corrupting Maine's youth. Something she read on Facebook. Celebrities are involved. There are secret messages in the speeches given by national political figures. Pull your heads out of the sand and pay attention!

She is not schizophrenic and she is not alone. There are lots of people who subscribe to this theory. The news anchor is wholly unprepared to unpack it. She shakes her head weakly, but the look of horror in her eyes is mixed with derision and amusement.

For my part, all I feel is a sinking kind of shame. I hope I never looked like that.

I spend a few more hours in front of the TV, but I change the channel to something mindless. A reality show that I don't need to follow. I watch the women on screen tease their hair and bicker, but I'm in my own head, touching every memory until they all collapse, until each one propagates, turns into three incompatible versions. I'm sure that I have scrambled myself, and I'm not sure that I can be unscrambled.

My dad's suicide note makes waves on the r/AngieAngstrom board. It is picked up by the other murder sites and a few other places—r/Interesting, r/Depression, r/TodayICried.

Clare,

I don't know how much longer I can go on like this, but I'm going to try. I'm going to try to make it a few more days, months, years. In case I should fail, in case my resolve should break (and I feel it breaking), I'm sorry.

I can't tell you how much it pains me to know that my last act will be one that brings you more pain. But nothing works. The therapy doesn't work. The journaling doesn't work. I used to get some relief from the pills, but now even chemistry fails.

Perhaps you sensed how I felt all these years—that you were never really mine, that we were managing borrowed time, the two of us. Still—your girls growing up—I loved every minute of it. Even the parts that hurt. They were a gift.

You will be okay. You are stronger than any person should have to be. You will have a whole, full life. Maybe we two will even have grandkids one day, and you will get a second chance at this whole thing. Maybe you will look down at their wrinkly faces, and it will be a rebirth. I can almost reach out and touch it, grab it, but it's slightly out of reach for me. I'm against the ropes now, and I don't think I have another round in me.

I was running on hope, Clare. Then fumes. And now—I don't know. I think she's gone. I think I can say that now. I know you've been telling me this for years, but I couldn't hear it before. Ten years. How did I manage to burn up ten years in a haze. The other day it occurred to me that if she came back to us now, she would be a grown woman, and she would be disgusted by me. She feared this for me the way I feared it for her. I'm not proud of what I've become.

I'm so sorry, Clare. When you should think of me, don't judge me too harshly. I always loved you more than I could say.

Yours,
Mark

Before I post it, I introduce myself. I verify myself by taking a selfie, holding my passport. Under the picture:

Teddy Angstrom here. Longtime lurker. This community has meant a lot to me, so I wanted to share this with you all. I know some of you aren't big fans of my Dad, but that's okay.

I wait for the comments to roll in.

- **hop_on_Pop:** Did not think I'd be crying over Mark Angstrom today. Hang in there Teddy!
- **brewerswife304:** Teddy, you've grown into such a beautiful woman. Thanks for joining us over here. Hope we can help you with whatever you're looking for.

- **CatDad0340:** i no i have a tendency to think of these ppl as reddit names and not irl people with lives and families. good reminder for me.
  - **milk-n-cookies:** Ditto.

Only one person calls me out, and I start to panic. By the time I'm halfway through creating a handwritten version, everyone else jumps on him and I don't have to bother:

- **Anon34567:** you copy-pasted his suicide note. yeaaa calling bs on that one.
  - **manny_manny:** People on this fucking sub sometimes . . . you won't be happy until she shows you a picture of his body. Damn.
  - **milk-n-cookies:** dude . . . this aint it.
  - **cyberbaby22:** people type suicide notes bro. this isn't law and order.

By the end of the night, I'm beginning to feel moved by the letter that I wrote. I'm beginning to forget my own bullshit.

I print it out and bring it upstairs to Mom.

"I found this on Dad's computer," I say.

She reads it. If she recognizes something strange, if she questions the voice or the timing—she doesn't say. She hugs me tightly and thanks me.

"He loved you," I say.

"He loved you, too," she says.

There is a version of the story that I like. It is a movie I play in my head when I can muster the strength to hope for something good.

They all begin the same: Angie is in my bed smelling clean, fresh. She's not high—I have always known she was not high, and she's not in this version—the right version. Angie is stroking my cheek as I drift to sleep. She is staring at her little sister and trying to memorize my soft features, trying to imagine what I will look like when I am grown. Right now, my adult face is taking shape, but it is still cushioned by puppy fat in places. Angie is sorry that she'll never get to know me as an adult, but this is necessary.

Angie kisses me on the head and slides herself out of bed. She doesn't say goodbye to Wolfie, because she can't afford to wake him. He's still in his loud, barky puppy stage, and she can't take him with her. She would, but she knows that I will need him.

She takes up the bag she packed last night. It's small and light. Only a couple changes of clothes and the money that she's earned the hard way over the last few weeks. She can't put into words the sense of displacement that she has here. Perhaps she has never felt at home. She feels bad, guilty even, because her parents are good people. Her mother, despite all of her morose gazing and dull poetry, is a sweet woman. But she is made from different stuff. The way Angie sees it, Mom and I are the same—buoyant, resilient, serious. Angie is something else—anger, heat. Everything in her body itches like she's allergic to her own blood.

She thinks that what she's doing will be best for us. Her step-father—my dad—has never been right around her—not even since she was a girl. He favors her to his own daughter, to me, and Angie is sure that it can't be a good thing. When he's in a room alone with Angie, he stares at her like he's keeping company with a ghost. She is not a child to him, she is the remainder of a person. She is not herself, she is a piece of a man she never knew.

It's time for her to let the three of us be a proper family. It's time for her to recede into a quiet, simple life somewhere.

She leaves the house and finds the bike that she's stashed in the woods. She peddles backroads for days. It's summer, and she can get by at night sleeping on park benches in different towns. By the time she starts to smell, they're conducting the local missing persons search, and she's near Canada. She rents a motel room and cuts her hair short in the sink. She crosses the border the next day.

Years pass. She gets by honestly, working three jobs to cover her expenses. Then two. Then finally just the one. Without her blue hair and the piercings, no one has ever recognized her. She is another invisible checkout girl. Skinnier now, her jaw has taken on a sharp quality that combines with her newfound dark circles to harden her features, age her, make her even more unmatchable.

Eventually, she meets an actual good man. He does something simple and decent—like raising trees on a farm that's been in his family for generations. Or maybe sheep. Sheep that he shears to make beautiful handwoven sweaters for their children.

Angie thinks about me from time to time. Her daughter has a way of smiling that reminds her uncannily of her little sister. She sleeps well, because she knows there is no way I am still thinking about her. She knows we're both right where we belong.

Sometimes, it's not so easy to play the movie that I want to see. Sometimes, the story I see is the one that gnaws its way through from the back of my head, from the deepest recesses of my mind. It lives on top of my brain stem, slowing my breathing, nesting its way into the very fiber of my being.

This one is a parasitic worm, consuming the healthy gray matter to survive. Over time, it starts to decay the other version of things, until I can't remember where in Canada Angie ended up, until I can't recall if she had one kid or two, boys or girls. And once it has lost its specificity, the other one—the good story—is useless, dead.

This version of the movie is grainy and silent. It plays on a handheld crank against the ragged and yellowing bone of my inner skull when I'm alone in a dark room.

Angie is on a couch—Mickey's aunt's couch. She's high. It's unclear what time it is.

In this version, I am never sure if Angie has already come back home and crawled into her bed. If this is before or after or if that never happened at all. If that was something I invented after the fact as a way of saying goodbye before I could admit that it was over.

Angie is on the couch. Her chest rises slowly, almost imperceptibly. Her eyes are not quite closed, but only the whites are visible.

There is a man there. He is about thirty, but he carries himself with the violent bravado and reckless swagger of someone younger. He is an animal, and he is dangerous. He pulls at the skin of his forearm and paces, stopping every so often to throw something onto the ground or squat down suddenly and slap both his thighs in nervous panic.

I see all of this through the crack in a door. The interior room is dark, and I look out into the brightly lit living room where all the action is happening. I am a girl, fifth grade. I am crying, but making sure to stay so silent that no one hears us.

In this version, the door closes. Mickey curls up in bed and covers her ears with her hands. The door always closes at this moment when I want to lunge forward and give Angie chest compressions, even though I can barely remember the CPR classes I took. Even though all I remember is pressing down on the child dummy and feeling sure that I would crack some ribs if I applied that kind of force to a living human being.

The movie picks back up in a car. I know it's a car because of the bumps. I can feel the bumps every time. Angie is lying on the backseat. She can see and she can hear, but she can't speak. Her heart doesn't feel right. She can't remember if she's ever felt her heart before—felt it the way you feel a stubbed toe or a stomach cramp. Something is wrong. There is pain and her saliva tastes of metal.

In this version, Angie dies in that car, alone despite the presence of a driver, whom I can never see. She dies while her brain is screaming for me.

At that moment, I dream Angie is in my bed with me. For years, I will think this happened. When in truth, we were separated by miles, and Angie was cold and covered in a thin film of her own dried vomit.

In this version, Angie's body is treated like something that might contaminate those who handle it. She is dragged across pavement and dirt and rolled through a wooded space until she rests face down. With her open mouth against the forest floor, her body waits. A hole is dug, but it is not deep enough. A decision is made instead to go a bit farther, to leave her in the river. She is dragged again, this time still face down by a man who is too high to realize what he is doing. Rogue sticks and rocks shred her face. She is unrecognizable by the time they get to the water. She is tossed in.

For weeks, the man looks over his shoulder, sure that eventually a body will turn up. All rivers lead somewhere, right? But he gets lucky—Angie's body is trapped between two big rocks somewhere along the path—her foot or arm or femur—trapped exactly so. The rivers take their toll, and whatever is left sinks, disintegrates, gets frozen for the next season. She is never discovered. Some bodies are never discovered.

In this version, Angie can feel everything. In this version, I am living my life, sleeping in my warm bed, daring to feel angry with my sister for vanishing, for throwing lives into disarray. In this version, Angie is always eighteen—still a girl—and always alone in the moment of her death.

I find an obituary in the back of the *Sunday Telegram*, where it is accompanied by a picture of a mousy teenage girl failing to make eye contact with the camera.

Georgette Nelson, a rising senior at Gorham High, died on Saturday night in a no-fault car accident. An online article with which I followed up indicated that she was a pedestrian and was struck by a passing car at an intersection that has been considered highly dangerous for years. The driver was an out-of-towner, and Georgette's death has sparked a wave of petitions about everything from traffic lights and crosswalk paint to limiting the number of Airbnb permits the town allows. What a legacy.

On the day of the wake, I text Mickey. It's been weeks since the last time, and today, miraculously, she answers.

I tell her to wear black and meet me at my house in an hour. I don't even know where she's staying these days, but she obliges, showing up in black jeans, a black tank top, and Doc Martens at my front door forty-five minutes later. A person I've never seen drops her off at the house and pulls out of the driveway before I open the door. I give her one of my sweaters to wear before we get in my car.

"Cover your shoulders."

"It's too hot," she says, but she puts it on.

For a while, Mickey doesn't speak, and neither do I.

"I'm surprised you came," I say.

"I was surprised you texted me."

"Fair enough."

"Why did you?"

I don't answer. I can't. I need her to tell me she's sorry so that I can forgive her. I badly want to forgive her. I want to tell her that I understand the mitigating circumstances—she was only a kid. I want to absolve her of everything that she did. *We can absolve one another*, I want to say. I want her to tell me that she loves me and misses me and she wants to find a way to get past everything that has happened. I want to be mad at her, but in a way that isn't terminal. I don't want her to be mad at me at all.

Mickey cranks the volume knob on the radio and takes out her phone and starts texting other people.

Parking at the funeral home is backed up half a mile. The entire street is lined with cars, and suburban nuclear families, huddled together, trudge through the street from their SUVs, looking like zombie packs. I have to honk to get past them.

Mickey follows closely behind me. She stops when I stop to examine the photo collage. She watches me watch the girls who are collecting outside the women's bathroom to take a group photo.

The room smells overwhelmingly of flowers and air freshener and dirty carpeting. The folding chairs, once in neat rows, have been rearranged by family members and are in a state of disarray.

At the front of the room, next to the casket, stand a man and a woman. I recognize Georgette's parents from the article I read online. My feet take me to them as though I'm sleepwalking.

"Hi," I say to the mom.

"Hi," she returns. She waits for me to continue, but I fail to speak. "Who are you?"

She looks like an older version of the girl in the photos— the same small features, pulled close together on her face, the same plain hair and slumped shoulders. The only things distinguishing her are her crow's feet and some red lipstick that looks like it was done with a shaky hand.

Mickey reaches out for a handshake. "I was classmates with Georgie," she says. "And this is my cousin Rachel. She substitute teaches sometimes."

"Oh," the mom says. "Nice to meet you. What's your last name? Maybe she mentioned—"

"We're so sorry for your loss, Mrs. Nelson," Mickey says. "We'd like to pay our respects now." She inserts a knuckle into the gap between two of my lower vertebrae and nudges me toward the casket in the front, leaving Mrs. Nelson behind, looking confused.

Mickey takes the kneeler and I follow suit.

"Closed casket," I whisper. I fold my hands so that it looks like I'm praying.

"Why do you sound disappointed?"

"I'm not." But I am. I wanted to see what they look like—teenage girls—after the lights have gone out. I wanted to be close to her body. I want to tell her parents a story that will allow them to think about her the way they want to. I lay my hand on the wood.

Mickey pries it away. "Stop that." She crosses herself and tries to stand.

I grab her wrist. "How did you know she was Georgie and not Georgette?"

Mickey pulls a prayer card out of her back pocket and hands it to me. *Georgie Nelson*, it says at the top. She walks away.

I'm aware of a line forming behind me, but I take my time at the casket, staring at my distorted reflection in the varnish. I try to imagine her body, brutalized from the crash, but no doubt reconstructed in some way with whatever means the mortician had. I picture the garish makeup that I know they've put on her, even though they aren't going to open up the lid. Her hair shiny and smooth. Someone washed her head after she died, cleaned the dried blood from her roots and maybe even gave her a blowout with a round brush and some sticky hairspray.

It's dizzying. When I stand, I must look like shit, because the woman who was waiting right behind me takes a look at my face and frowns, her lower lip trembling like in a cartoon.

She throws herself at me with a hug. "I'm so sorry," she says. She's speaking right into my eardrum in a loud whisper, but every time I try to pull away from her muggy breath, she squeezes me tighter.

"However you left things with her," she says, "she knows you loved her. She knows you were a good friend."

"Thank you," I say. "It's hard." I can't stop thinking about how mere feet away from us, concealed by a couple inches of expensive pine, a girl's dead body lies cold, but not cold enough to keep it from rotting. How if we all stayed here a week or two, the stink of it would be undeniable. We'd have to bury her in the ground and walk away, because there would be no other choice. But today, for these people, leaving their girl behind in the ground will be hard. It's too fresh.

"You did your best," she says.

"I did." I can feel my sinuses tingling, my brain getting ready to pour through my eyes and nostrils. "I did."

Mickey pulls me away before it goes any further. "Let's go," she says. "Now."

The lack of release, the feeling of having gotten almost to the finish—rage charges through my limbs on my march back to the car.

"I didn't like that," Mickey says, and she plugs an address into my GPS.

"I could give a shit."

"Keep your eye on the road. You're driving like a maniac."

"That's me. A maniac."

"Whatever."

When I arrive at Mickey's destination—a beautiful brick colonial that looks dark and empty—she opens the door before I've even put the car in park.

"Take care, Teddy," she says. "Take it easy on the drinking."

I have the urge to tell her to fuck off. I have the urge to tell her to reach out to me if anything happens. To tell her that I'm mad at her, but I would still serve as an underwriter, a job reference, a sounding board, a mentor.

"Wait," I say, before she can close the door. "I'm not sure I'll be around much longer."

I see her eyes flash with panic. "What does that mean?"

"No," I say. "Not that. I mean—I'm moving."

"Oh," Mickey says, relieved. "Where?"

"I'm not sure yet," I say.

"You're moving, but you don't know where?"

"California," I say. "Just don't know the exact town."

"Nice," Mickey says. She offers a weak smile. "I've always wanted to go to California."

"You should," I say. "Definitely. And you will."

"Is that an invitation?" Mickey laughs.

"Any time," I say.

"I was just kidding."

"No, I know. Me, too. I just meant—you'll figure it out."

"Good luck, T.," Mickey says. "Mean it."

"Thanks," I say. "I'm thinking golden retriever."

"Happy dogs."

"Yeah."

"Okay," Mickey says. She starts to close the door. "Bye, I guess."

"Mickey," I say.

"What?" She's an inch from clicking it shut.

"Thanks for coming today. I'm sorry. It wasn't—"

She cuts me off. "It's the least I could do, probably."

We look at each other and we both see Angie and my dad. I wonder if under her clothes, she still has that little Corduroy Bear expanding across her ribcage with each breath. I can't remember if hers is missing a button or if he's the Corduroy from the end of the book who has met his girl, found a home, and gotten himself repaired.

"You're going to be fine," I say.

"Will you?"

I try to answer honestly. "I think so. It's not so easy."

Mickey nods. "You should move," she says. "Fresh start."

"Or I could start fresh here," I say. "My mom's here. My house."

"Bill," Mickey offers.

I nod. "Lots of people."

"Harder here," Mickey says.

"Yes," I say. "It would be."

I want to ask her—*what if we could wipe the slate, you and I? Tabula rasa. Records expunged. We're young. All anyone ever really needs is time, and we've got great big bundles of it. We're rich in time.*

"Okay," Mickey says, after a moment of silence. "Good luck." She raps on the side of the car with her knuckles and closes the door as gently as possible.

I wave to her through the glass and she waves back before walking away from me. I try to will her, telekinetically, to turn and look at me one more time, but she doesn't. The back of her head disappears inside, and I head back to Hogshead alone.

WHEN I RETURN HOME, I return home to Bill's house. The first thing I do is tell him how I shot Wolfie in the woods. I need him to know everything bad about me.

Before I can explain to him how everything fell apart, before I get a chance to tell him that he was right and I was wrong, I'm on his lap, my mouth melting into his, like we are drawn together by two great magnets buried in our middles where organs slide against other organs.

When we have sex, I ask him to come without pulling out. I tell him I want to have his baby. He huffs and buries his head in my hair and obliges. After, we say nothing, but he holds me tightly. I stay awake and imagine all the tadpoles in the wetness—a million different lives and a million different deaths.

I love them all already—all my impossible babies. I grieve for the ones that will never make their way into the world. I hunger for the one that could—the feeling of her tiny feet pulsing under my ribs, my middle swelling and swelling, my ankles widening under the weight of additional personhood. I crave it.

I want to grow myself a new family, to carry everyone I love inside me. I want someone who can breathe underwater. I want a direct line—a ropey tether of gelatin and blood. I want to chew through it myself. And I want it to hurt in my body so that I know it is real.

ACKNOWLEDGMENTS

At the top, I need to address my core *Rabbit Hole* team, whose tireless efforts have shaped and refined this story. Hillary, Taz, Allegra, and Emma—thank you.

Hillary Jacobson, agent extraordinaire and granter of childhood dreams, I am in awe of your massive talent. Thank you for taking a chance on me, and I'm sorry I made you read such an inhumane number of drafts. Thank you to the rest of the team at CAA, including Sarah Harvey, Josie Freedman, and Randie Adler.

Thanks to everyone at Soho Press, including Bronwen Hruska, Juliet Grames, Rachel Kowal, Janine Agro, Lily DeTaeye, Emma Levy, Steven Tran, Rudy Martinez, and Paul Oliver. You all have made this experience an absolute blast. Most especially, thank you to my dedicated editor, Taz Urnov, whose passion for this story was what brought *Rabbit Hole* to life.

Immense thanks to my UK team at Bloomsbury, including my editor, Allegra Le Fanu, who was one of the first believers in *Rabbit Hole*. Thank you to Emma Finn at C&W, who has been the perfect shepherd of this strange text.

Thank you to David Ebenbach, who believed I was a writer before I did. That faith sustained me through many rejections. Thank you to Susan Minot, Norma Tilden, Dinaw Mengestu, Amy Hempel, and the entire NYU Creative Writing Program. Thank you to my second-grade teacher, Tali Axelrod, whose forward-thinking writing workshop set me on this course over two decades ago.

Thank you to my students, especially the Regians who were patient with me while I learned the ropes. I hope I was a better teacher than Teddy. I had the most fun.

Thank you to my early readers: Kris Lee, Lexia Schwartz Leary, Abby Carignan, Nicole Illuzzi, Steve McMullen, Joe Masco, Katharine Gorynski, Laura Taylor, and Margaret Chernin.

Thank you to Nick Thomas for your guidance in all things publishing. Your friendship over the last decade has been an unexpected gift.

Thank you to Jacquelyn Stolos, for your notes and camaraderie. It has been a joy to come up alongside you.

Thank you to Megan and Peter Chernin, whose generosity and encouragement allowed me to pursue a life in the arts.

Thank you to my sisters, Emma Azzi and Mary Brody, for their comprehensive support of this project, from soundboarding to babysitting. You two are why I am so obsessed with writing about sisters.

Thank you to my parents for filling my childhood with language and stories. Dad, sometimes I imagine you holding a book with my name on the cover. Wouldn't that have been something? Yours will always be the voice inside my head.

Thank you to my children, Brody and Henry Insana. I am tempted to say that I wrote this novel in spite of you and your constant demands for snacks, but that wouldn't be accurate. I never wrote with more focus than after you were born. I did it for you, because I hope that you will be proud to call me your mom. I'm sorry about all the sex stuff.

And finally, Chris Insana. We did it. I love you.